**Dirty money, cold-blooded murder,
and deadly secrets...**

Zane blinked to focus and never saw her hand coming as she delivered a stinging slap. He grabbed her wrist as she drew back for another blow. "Do that again, and I'll turn you over my knee."

Her eyes smoldered. "You'd love that, wouldn't you? Even way back then you wanted to push the envelope with sex. I'll bet you've learned a lot of new tricks since then."

He yanked her up against his body, holding her in an iron grip. "I don't remember you running away screaming."

"I might shoot you this time, lawman. Just because you piss me off."

They stared at each other for a long moment before he let her go.

She backed away, rubbing her wrists, her eyes stabbing at him like daggers. "Get the hell out of my house. And stay away. It'll take a lot more than your macho swagger to run me off."

"We aren't done, Jamie. Not by a long shot. Keep that in mind."

Cocked And Loaded

by

Desiree Holt

Cocked And Loaded

Contact Information: info@thewildrosepress.com

Cover Art by *Angela Anderson*

The Wild Rose Press
PO Box 708
Adams Basin, NY 14410-0708

Visit us at www.thewilderroses.com

Publishing History
First Scarlet Rose Edition, September 2009
Print ISBN 1-60154-712-9

Published in the United States of America

Dedication

To the Muses, who gave me the courage to try.

Chapter One

Zane Cameron stared at the figure walking out of the supermarket. He lifted his sunglasses just to be sure his eyes weren't playing tricks on him. When he heard she'd showed up two days ago, he was sure someone was pulling his leg. But no, there she was. Jamie Randall. Big as life. Not even a hint of shame or embarrassment for either her leave-taking or her current situation.

The last time Zane saw her she was a flowering eighteen-year-old who'd teased him with her body, then left town so fast her heels kicked up a cloud of dust. All she left behind was a drunk for a father and stinging words for Zane. And, of course, a bitterness and resentment that built up in him all these years.

Now here she was again and he smelled big trouble.

He watched her wheel her cart to her shiny dark blue SUV. A symbol of her ill-gotten success. The worn jeans and old Texas Tech T-shirt were little camouflage for what had become a lush, ripe body. Thick blue-black hair pulled back in a ponytail bounced as she moved. Huge sunglasses barely concealed the tight set of her face. And where he'd expected her walk to still be graceful and tempting, now it was purposeful and angry.

Five feet four inches of sexual dynamite that he hoped wouldn't blow up in his face.

No one could miss the fact that Jamie was mad at the world, both about being home and the circumstances that brought her here. Well, no madder than he was at the way she'd left, despite

1

everything between them. Or everything he'd *thought* was between them.

She loaded the groceries into the truck, climbed in, and slammed the door. He didn't need to follow her as she roared out onto the highway. He knew exactly where she was going. What he needed to do was get his anger under control, the rage that always bubbled up whenever he thought of her. A rage heavily colored with lust. In twelve years, that feeling had built itself to quite a level.

Get over it. She wasn't worth it then and she's not worth it now.

So why, after all these years, did his traitorous dick still get hard whenever he remembered her naked body? Why did his hands twitch, remembering the feel of her young breasts in them? His nose still remembered the scent of roses and honeysuckle in her hair. His mouth, the taste of her tempting juices. One would think by this time he'd have himself under control.

Except Jamie Randall was like a festering sore inside him, one he needed to lance and get rid of, once and for all.

All these years, he'd been able to deal with the way she'd just flat out left him because she'd been far away in a different life. But to see her every day now, to know the contempt she'd held him in, would be an impossible situation.

No way was she coming back to Amen, Texas and twitching her ass in front of his face. She left town once. He planned to make sure she did it again. Jamie Randall would have to leave whether she wanted to or not. Only this time it would be on his terms and not until he'd satisfied a twelve-year-old itch.

Easier said than done, cowboy.

He cranked the engine a little too hard, and pulled away from the curb, heading out on the dusty highway. She should be home by now. There was no time like the present to get on with business, but it wasn't business he was looking forward to.

All the way to the scrubby patch of land her father had left her, Zane talked to himself. *Face her. Get it over with. Move on.*

The caliche driveway leading to the old Randall house was potholed and bumpy, a sign of long neglect. The house itself was a reflection of the man who'd lived there, alone. Decaying, rotting away, making a pretense at something but not quite pulling it off.

He pulled the department's big Expedition in behind Jamie's smaller SUV and cut the ignition. As tiny as Amen was, he hadn't been in this house since Jamie left town. He didn't even want to go there now, but the whole mess from the past was like dry toast stuck in his throat.

Suck it up, man. Speak your piece and get it over with.

Taking his time, he climbed out of the car and walked up the cracked cement path. The inside door stood open and, through the screen door, he could see her moving around in the kitchen. Gritting his teeth, he raised his hand and knocked on the wood door frame.

"Go away." The words had a harsh bite to them. "No curiosity seekers allowed today."

Zane cleared his throat. "Jamie, it's Zane Cameron."

She froze in place, then turned in his direction. For a moment, he wasn't sure she'd even come to the door. Finally, she padded over the wood floor on bare feet, slowly, not rushing. He guessed she wasn't any more anxious for this meeting than he was.

"Well, well," she drawled. "Nice of you to drop by, Sheriff. Did you come to arrest me?"

"I came to talk to you. How about letting me in?"

She shook her head, the tight, angry look still on her face. "I don't think so. I'm in no mood to play Twenty Questions today."

"Damn it, Jamie. Open this door." He pulled, but the door was latched on the inside.

"Go away. I can't think of anything we have to say to each other."

"Oh, I have plenty to say. Open the damn door, or I'll break it down."

Nice going, asshole. Smooth.

She stared at him through the screen. Then he heard the snick of the latch being released and she stepped back to allow him to enter.

"Okay." She posed arrogantly in front of him, hands planted on her hips, mouth in a thin line. "Say what you came to say and get the fuck out of here."

It was obvious she'd been working. A few wisps of her hair had straggled loose from her ponytail, clinging to her cheeks like threads of fine silk. A smudge of dirt decorated her straight nose, and a thin scratch marred the smooth, tanned skin of her slim forearm. As unglamorous as a woman could look, yet somehow, she was more tempting than if she'd been wearing a slinky dress and high heels.

Zane had to resist the urge to stare at her breasts, outlined by the soft T-shirt material. Mature Jamie Randall's breasts were making his mouth water and his palms itch. But they also made his dick want to stand at attention again so he shut down his mind. All he needed was an erection right now. Then again, maybe that was exactly what he needed. "Nice language you've learned since you've been gone."

"That's not all I've learned." Her blue eyes, the color deepening to navy, flashed. The thick lashes framing them only enhanced the intensity of her fury. She was like a time bomb set to go off.

"Anyway, pardon my lack of social graces, but I'm not in a very good mood right now. I don't have the patience to take crap from anyone, so what is it you want?"

"I came to find out why you're here in this, let's see, what did you call it?" He frowned. "Oh, yeah. 'Godforsaken town you'd never spit on again.'" His pent-up anger, stored away all these years, wanted to rise up and overtake him.

"Well, we can't all make the choices we'd like to." Jamie's gaze swept over his face, studying him. "So. I'll ask you again. Why are you really here? You trying to run me out of town, Sheriff?" She spat out the last word as if it had a bad taste to it.

"Seems to me the last time you and I had a conversation, I distinctly remember you saying you wouldn't come back to Amen unless hell froze over." His eyes never wavered from hers. "Must be mighty cold down there right about now."

And that's how cold it would be before she threw her lot in with him, she'd told him. Twelve years ago he was just the half-breed son of a man always in trouble. She'd been willing to fuck him all right—fuck the half-breed with the legendary dick—but then it was adios.

He waited for her to comment, but she stood there, silent, vibrating with anger. Her nipples pushed stiffly against the thin fabric of her T-shirt, and a pulse beat heavily at her throat. Sex and anger. Two sides of the same coin. He had to suppress an urge to rip off her clothes and run his hands over that now-adult body. Time hadn't diminished one bit of the lust he felt for her. Damn it.

At last she shook her head and took a step back. "If you came for all the sordid details of my fall from grace, you wasted your time. Read the newspapers. They had plenty to say. So is that it? Are we done?"

"Not by half." He moved closer to her. "You're damn straight I want to know why you're here and when you're leaving. I can't believe this is some big homecoming for you."

Yes, when will you get out of my life again and leave me to my accustomed misery?

"Well." Her voice was bitter. "You don't mince any words, do you?"

More silence. He forced himself to outwait her.

"Why the hell do you think I'm here? I guess I'm lucky my drunk of a father got himself killed and left me this worthless piece of property. Which is a damn good thing since, at the moment, it seems I have no place else to go." She stuck out her chin in defiance. "Why? Are you planning to run me off?"

Yes, if I could. But first I'm going to fuck your brains out the way I've wanted to do all these years since you ran from me. This time you'll take more than a little taste of the half-breed Zane Cameron with you.

He shifted his weight. "Just trying to keep up with what's going on in my little corner of the world. I heard you were living in some fancy condo in Florida."

"Why, Sheriff," she drawled. "I didn't know you kept up with my activities."

Gritting his teeth, he barely held onto his temper. "We have a newspaper here in Amen, in case you forgot. And surprise, surprise. I have a computer and know how to use it."

"Oh. Well, then." She unclenched her fists and shoved her hands in her jeans pockets. "I'm sure you read all about my big scandal and just salivated over my fall from grace." Her voice had a spiteful quality to it.

"We don't get that much to talk about here in Amen," he retorted, determined to give it right back to her. "Local girl makes bad is a hot topic of conversation."

She stared at him again, then turned to walk toward the kitchen. "Coffee should be ready now. If you're going to grill me, you might as well have a cup."

He hated the fact that the movement of her hips still mesmerized him and his fingers curled with the remembrance of touch. Common sense told him to refuse the coffee and get the hell out of there. Forget about anything but staying away from her. But then, he'd had plenty of times when he and common sense didn't even shake hands.

He distracted himself while waiting by glancing at his surroundings. The inside of the house didn't look any better than the outside. Scarred wood floor. Walls covered in grimy paint without a picture or anything to relieve the depressing sight. Furniture worn down to the bare bones. Dust everywhere.

He spotted the cleaning supplies on the chipped Formica counter. She'd need a lot more than soap and disinfectant to make this place habitable. And no matter how much she scrubbed, she'd never get the stink of whiskey or the dark presence of her miserable father out of it.

"So," her voice broke into his train of thought. "Tell me." She was busy taking chipped mugs out of a cupboard and filling them. "How did someone like you end up sheriff of Diablo County? I thought for sure you'd be on the inside of the jail looking out."

Zane's gut clenched and bile rose in the back of his throat. "You mean, how did the good citizens manage to elect a half-breed to keep the peace? Maybe they figured I could run around with my tomahawk and scalp anyone who pissed me off."

"Damn it, Zane." She whirled, her eyes burning into him like wildfire. "That's not what I meant at all."

"Oh, no?" he challenged. "You made it very plain

when you left here that I had nothing to offer you. Me and my kind, you said. No mistaking your words. You couldn't get away from me and Amen fast enough."

"Is that what you thought? Well, you're wrong. The only one ever sensitive about your Comanche blood was you. That had nothing to do with my reasons for walking away from you."

"Yeah, right. Your alcohol-rotted father couldn't have made it any plainer. And you were right there with him when he made his little speech."

"One loser was the same as another to me. No matter what he said, I wasn't talking about just you but all the losers in this stinkhole. Your heritage had nothing to do with it, and you damn well should have known it." She poured the hot liquid into the mugs.

"Should I?" He accepted the mug she handed him. Their fingers brushed, and he had to work to control the shock at the electricity the brief contact generated. Oh, god, this was worse than he thought.

"Anyway, that wasn't the reason I asked the question. I just want to know how someone wilder than the wind ends up as a lawman."

His face hardened. "We all change, Jamie. You certainly did."

Her laugh was like ice falling on glass, not tinkling but chilling. "So this call is really all about my recent notoriety, right? Well, here's the long and short of it. I've joined a very elite group of reporters who got scammed and drummed out of the corps. Lawsuits and legal fees broke me, and the condo was the first thing to go. I'm back here because I have no other choice." Her mouth twisted in a caricature of a smile. "Does that give you the satisfaction you were looking for, lawman?"

"Listen, Jamie—"

"I'll bet you've read every story about my firing,

all about how I've been blackballed in the industry, and enjoyed the hell out of it. Right?" She took a healthy swallow of coffee, grimacing as she realized how hot it still was. "But that's okay, Zane. You can join a very big crowd." She watched him over the rim of her mug. "Listen, I've got stuff to do so say what you came to say and get out."

He leaned against the wall, trying to get a fix on her. He couldn't help the way his eyes swept over her body. He wondered if anyone could look as disheveled as she did and still exude raw sex. She was still lithe and toned, and the memory of those graceful legs wrapped around his waist, pulling him deeper into her, made him want to pull out his dick and take her on the hard floor right there.

He wondered, too, what she'd say if she knew how he really liked his sex. The things he really wanted from her. The kind of demands he wanted to make on her.

His jaw worked as he dug for his hard-won iron control, the control that seemed to be slipping with Jamie in front of him. He exhaled slowly.

"What happened to you, Jamie?" *Yeah, what happened to those pie-in-the-sky dreams that made you look at me and this place like dirt?* "God knows I hated your ass for the way you ran out of here, but you said you had a plan for your life, being a top investigative reporter. And it sure looked like you were well on your way to completing it. How could you pull a stunt like you did?"

She shrugged and stared at a point beyond his shoulder. "Not that it's any of your business, but I got sandbagged."

He raised an eyebrow. "Excuse me?"

"You heard me." She sipped at her coffee, still staring at nothing. "Don't believe everything you read in the papers, Zane. Or hear on television. I, of all people, know firsthand how the news can be manipulated."

Zane narrowed his eyes, waiting for her to go on.

She sighed, a heavy sound, as if the weight she carried was too much to bear. "Someone gave me a tip about a scandal in the Miami-Dade Police department. I met with two sources who gave me what I thought was proof of their authenticity. All the evidence they pointed me toward seemed to prove out their story."

"And?" he prompted.

"I broke the story, and included the mayor in it, smearing just about everyone I could. I thought for sure I'd win the Pulitzer for it. My boss was salivating."

"So what was the problem? Did you trip over yourself running down the yellow brick road? What I read said you'd made the whole thing up."

She made a sound of disgust. "That's not my style, and people should have known it. If I was anything, it was gullible and stupid. I had visions of the *New York Times* begging me to come to work for them. All the networks calling me for interviews."

Zane sipped at his coffee, waiting while she gathered her thoughts. He'd heard and read the stories. He wanted to hear her version from her own mouth. Get it settled, take what he came for, then tell her to leave.

"Well, it turned out the whole thing was an elaborate hoax, engineered by the mayor's opponent in the upcoming election. Every other news outlet got the real story and I got fired. And sued, right along with my newspaper." She ran her finger around the rim of her cup. "One day I'm the golden girl, the next no one will touch me with a ten-foot pole. End of story."

Zane put down his mug. "Well, I don't think it's a good idea for you to hang around Amen. Nothing here for you, and you know how people talk. Sell the property and get on with it."

Yes. Please get the hell out of my life again.

Jamie's face took on a hard look. "Do not presume to tell me what to do. I'll stay here as long as I damn well please. Maybe until this place falls down around my ears."

Zane moved closer to her so they were barely a breath apart. "Don't do this. You'll be happier if you're gone."

She raised her eyebrows? "I will? Or you, Zane Cameron? This is really all about getting even, isn't it?"

"Why, Jamie." He looked her up and down. "What would I have to get even about? I got over you and your lousy attitude a long time ago."

"Yeah, right," she snorted. "That's why you hightailed it over here to ride my ass."

Zane didn't even think about what he did next, just knew he had to get his taste of her before running her out of town. He took the mug from her hands, put it on the counter, gripped her head in his palms, and took her mouth.

God, it was just as hot and sweet as he'd remembered. Lips like spun silk, a taste like sugar. A thrill of satisfaction ran through him that her nipples, pressed against the cotton of his uniform shirt, were stiff and hard. And, that without thinking, her mouth opened and accepted his tongue. He pressed it against the roof of her mouth, devouring the soft wetness, and skimmed the insides of her cheeks and her lips. His hands held her head like a vise, as if he'd never let her go. If his cock was hard before, it was painful now, pushing into the softness of her belly.

She still smelled of strawberries, and the scent inflamed him. He wanted to fuse himself to her, suckle her nipples until they swelled to twice their size. Slide his fingers into that hot, tight pussy of hers and bring her to a breathless orgasm like he used to give her. Put his mouth on her cunt and drink of her sweet, sweet juices. Oh, yeah, he'd get his.

God, I'm losing my mind.

He finally lifted his mouth just a fraction. "In two seconds flat I could have you stripped naked and flat on your back, my cock buried deep inside you. And you'd love it. You know that, don't you?"

With sudden strength, she jerked her head away and pushed at him. Hard.

Zane blinked to focus and never saw her hand coming as she delivered a stinging slap. He grabbed her wrist as she drew back for another blow. "Do that again, and I'll turn you over my knee."

Her eyes smoldered. "You'd love that, wouldn't you? Even way back then you wanted to push the envelope with sex. I'll bet you've learned a lot of new tricks since then."

He yanked her up against his body, holding her in an iron grip. "I don't remember you running away screaming."

"I might shoot you this time, lawman. Just because you piss me off."

They stared at each other for a long moment before he let her go.

She backed away, rubbing her wrists, her eyes stabbing at him like daggers. "Get the hell out of my house. And stay away. It'll take a lot more than your macho swagger to run me off."

"We aren't done, Jamie. Not by a long shot. Keep that in mind."

He was at the door when she called his name, and he turned. "What?"

"Where's my father's old truck?"

"You mean the one he ran off the road in? It's totaled." He frowned. "Why? You sure can't do anything with that hunk of junk."

"I'd like to get it. I can at least sell the undamaged parts for scrap."

Zane raised an eyebrow. "Money that hard to come by now?"

"Yes. Not that it's any of your damn business. So where's it at?"

"Duke Warren's got it at the junkyard. That is, if he hasn't crushed it yet. You could maybe make some kind of deal with him."

"Fine. Oh, and Sheriff?"

"Yeah?"

"Thanks so much for stopping by. But don't bother doing it again. You aren't welcome."

The sarcasm in her voice was sharp enough to draw blood.

"Is that a fact? Listen to what I'm saying. There's no place for you in Amen. You need to take care of business and get out of here." His gaze raked every inch of her body. "But before that happens we're going to handle *our* unfinished business. Then I can get you out of my life for good."

He slammed the door to the Expedition and ground the engine, tearing out of the driveway. He sped down the highway until he reached a hidden turnoff where he could pull in, away from passing traffic. Turning off the ignition, he leaned his head back, closed his eyes, and twelve years disappeared as if they'd never happened.

****

Zane spread the quilt he'd carried from the truck onto the space beneath the oak trees. Thirty feet away the waters of Fallen Creek shushed over pebbles, moonlight reflecting off its surface and peeping through the trees. He stretched out full length and reached a hand up to Jamie, feeling the trembling in her fingers.

"It will be all right," he assured her, although his own insides were quaking.

All the heavy petting they'd done up until now, touching each other, crossing new boundaries, had them in such a fever pitch of excitement that waiting for tonight had almost been a hardship.

Shyly, Jamie lowered herself to her knees beside him, then folded her body against his, her head on his shoulder. Her soft breasts pressed against him, and he could feel her nipples poking against the thin fabric of her sundress.

No bra!

His cocked jumped behind the denim fly of his jeans.

Her skin was so soft as he caressed her arm, and her scent—ripe strawberries—filled his nostrils. He couldn't wait to taste her. Everywhere.

Shifting his body, he tilted her chin up so he could see her eyes. "Are you sure, Jamie? I don't want you to—"

She pressed a fingertip against his mouth. "I'm not a kid, Zane. I know what I want."

"Darlin', you're eighteen years old."

"Old enough to vote and drive," she told him.

"And I'm four years older than you."

"And we both know we've been working up to this for a long time."

"I want you to know this is very special to me." His voice was so thick with controlled lust he almost didn't recognize it.

"Me, too."

"What happens when you go away to school?"

"I won't be going anywhere unless I get that scholarship. Let's not worry about that now."

"Jamie, our lives are so different. Amen is my home. You want out of here. What can we possibly—"

She pushed herself up. "Are you saying you don't want me?"

"You know that's not true."

He wanted her more than she could possibly

know. But they had no future. All she'd talked about this past year was leaving Amen behind. And him, too, he was sure.

But he was through arguing. His body was telling him he'd done enough talking. He traced the outline of her mouth with the tip of his tongue, then the seam of her lips, sliding inside when she opened for him. Her mouth tasted like it always did, sweeter than heaven, setting fire to every nerve in his body.

One hand stole beneath her skirt, sliding the fabric up to her waist. He stilled when he encountered nothing but naked skin.

"No panties, Jamie?"

She gave him a shaky laugh. "I didn't want to waste more time than we had to."

"Then, darlin', get ready for a hot ride."

He rolled her to her back and spread her legs wide, saw her pussy outlined in the moonlight. Kneeling between her thighs, he pressed his thumbs on her labia and gently peeled them back, exposing that hot, honey opening to him. Like a starving man he lowered his head and traced her slit from end to end with his tongue. Her juices were already flowing and tasted like sweet cotton candy.

He licked every inch of the heated flesh, lapping up her feminine cream as fast as it flowed. Soft little moans floated from her throat as he flicked his tongue at her clit, then nibbled at it lightly with his teeth.

"Yes, yes, yes," she chanted, bending her knees and planting her feet on either side of him.

Sliding his hands beneath her hips, he lifted her to his mouth and feasted. His tongue probed every inch of her cunt, the tip searching out the sweet spots, his teeth taking little nips here and there then returning to her clit again. When he rimmed her vagina with his tongue, then swept it lower toward her anus, she gasped and pushed herself at his head.

15

He spread his fingers so the tips reached into the cleft of her ass, but he held himself back from probing any further. One virgin hole was enough for tonight.

When he thrust his tongue inside her again, the walls of her pussy quivered and her cream thickly coated his tongue. God, she was so hot. He wanted to wrap her up and run away with her, keep her all to himself.

He lowered her hips to the quilt, and she protested in a low voice. "Don't stop. Please don't stop."

"We've only just started, darlin'."

His hand trembling on her zipper, he managed to pull the rest of her dress over her head. His mouth watered at the sight of her tempting breasts, nipples pointing straight at him. He bent and took them in his mouth, one at a time, nibbling and sucking, pressing them against the roof of his mouth.

Jamie reached for him, her hands yanking away the leather thong he used to tie his hair back, then threading through the loosened strands.

He cupped her breasts, molding them in his palms, pressing the soft flesh with his fingers as he continued to suck at the tips.

When she reached down to tug at his T-shirt, he lifted his head. "Give me a minute."

He'd rapidly stripped off his clothing, the night air cool on his naked skin. He couldn't take his eyes from her, her body, so tempting, so sweet, so hot. If only he could keep her forever.

He fished a foil packet from his jeans pocket before dropping them to the ground again. In seconds, he had himself fully sheathed. He didn't want to have to stop again for anything.

Then he was over her again, kissing her breasts, the valley between them, her navel, swirling his tongue over the soft pubic curls, tormenting her clit.

His cock was so hard he was afraid it would break if he hit it against something. All the play and experimentation, all the nights of fucking her with his fingers, of her sucking him until he exploded in her mouth, couldn't hold a candle to what awaited him.

He lifted her legs over his shoulder to give himself better access and to make penetration easier for her. Testing her with his fingers to make sure she was still well lubricated, he pressed the head of his penis against the mouth of her vagina and pushed gently. He felt her tense beneath him and held still, giving her time to adjust to even that small intrusion. His own body was taut with lust and desire.

When her body relaxed again, he pushed a little further into her warm, wet channel and reached to tweak her nipples. Murmuring to her, soothing her, whispering erotic things he wanted to do to her, he pushed slowly until the head of his dick touched the thin barrier.

"Hold on, darlin'," he gasped. "One little pinch. That's all. I promise."

He flexed his hips and pushed, hard enough to break through. She cried out, and he stilled, giving her time again to adjust.

"Okay?" Sweat was pouring from his body, and his blood was boiling. "Do you want me to stop?"

"God, no," burst from her lips. "Don't stop."

"Okay. Okay."

He rolled his hips and set up a slow, steady pace, watching her through slitted eyes as her breathing changed and her blue eyes stared up at him. Slowly, in slight increments, her body accepted his cock completely, her moist heat so tight around him it stole his breath. Her cunt was like a wet fist gripping him, squeezing him.

Don't rush, don't rush, don't rush.

But in a moment, the tempo of her body changed,

her legs wrapping around his waist, heels digging into the small of his back.

"Do it," she panted. "Do it now."

He increased his pace, moving one hand to take her clit between thumb and forefinger, stroking it harder and harder. The arm he braced himself with shook with the effort. He gritted his teeth, waiting for the sign she was ready to climax. When the tremors began in her vaginal channel, he thrust harder, again and again, until her orgasm roared through her, taking him with it, and he emptied himself into the latex reservoir, his cock pulsing until he was afraid he would never stop.

When he collapsed on top of her, bracing himself on his forearms, his heart thundered and his pulse raced like a roller coaster. He dragged air into his lungs in huge gasps. Finally, he rolled to the side, his penis still inside her body as he pulled her against him. His hand caressed her arm and her back; his fingers sifted through her hair.

"Are you all right?" he asked, seeking the truth in her eyes.

She smiled at him. "More than all right. Maybe perfect."

"Did I hurt you, darlin'? I tried not to."

"Only for a second. And then...God, Zane. It was like nothing else I've ever felt." Her eyes glittered. "It was...like magic." She molded her body against his, her hand making little circles on his chest.

He brushed kisses on her cheeks and forehead, then took her mouth as if he'd never get enough of it again. Her heart beat as fast as his, her uneven breath mingling with his. There were so many things he wanted to do with her. To her. He wondered how far he could push her before she left him behind in the dust.

Pushing the hair back from her face, he gave her one light, last kiss. Then he slid reluctantly from her body and stood up, disposing of the condom in a handkerchief and stuffing it in his pocket. He pulled out another square of white cotton and knelt between her legs, tenderly wiping away the evidence of their coupling and planting a soft kiss on her pouty lips.

She had given him a gift tonight, and he would treat her with the proper respect. If only he didn't know deep inside that Jamie Randall thought staying in Amen was like a bird trapped in a cage. And he had no idea how to change her mind.

****

Zane opened his eyes and glanced quickly around him to make sure he was still hidden and alone. The memory of that night remained so vivid it might have happened yesterday. Despite their bitter parting, he'd never been able to completely kill his feelings for her. God knows he'd fucked enough women, trying to erase the imprint of her body from his memory. The feel of her like a wet glove around him. The unbelievable feeling of that first time.

He certainly had enough regrets. He'd tried to tell her things would be different between them, that he wanted more from her than just sex, and she might have believed him if he hadn't made a stupid mistake.

Two nights later, he was in the Roadkill Bar, drinking with his buddies, tying one on for no good reason at all. And Darlene Esquivel had come onto him full force. It was tragically unfortunate that he'd been all but fucking her against the side of his pickup when Jamie pulled into the parking lot of the Gas 'n Go right next door.

The sex they'd had after that was just that—sex. She was once again on her kick of blowing away the dust of Amen and him, too. Nothing he said could make a difference. Only her absence had allowed him to deal with it.

But now she was back.

Damn it.

His skin was burning and his body ached. One kiss and he wanted her more than ever before. He wanted her worse than a doper wanted his next fix. Zane knew, one way or another, he'd have her, and then he'd be even sorrier than he was now.

Jamming his foot down on the accelerator, he laid rubber pulling back onto the highway and tearing off down the asphalt.

Chapter Two

Jamie dumped the remains of her coffee in the sink and rinsed her cup. She wished she could rinse out her brain as easily.

Shit, shit, shit.

Her bad luck seemed to be holding.

The very last thing she needed was a confrontation with Zane Cameron. *Sheriff* Zane Cameron. The town must have been pretty damned desperate to elect that egotistical asshole sheriff. He'd been the wildest boy in town, drinking, brawling, fucking everything that had a pulse. All that crap he'd fed her about their relationship being special. As if she'd believed him. Especially after the scene she'd come across in the Roadkill parking lot.

At eighteen, she'd had no intention of spending one more minute in Amen than she had to. Certainly not with a man whose future and fidelity were both called into question. That, at least, she'd been smart enough to know.

Sex with Zane had been great. Outstanding. Off the charts. Especially to an eighteen-year-old virgin. She'd held that first night close to her like a hidden treasure all these years, afraid to take it out and look at it. Afraid to see what it really meant to her.

But no matter how good it had been, it was not nearly enough to derail her plans. Promises made in the heat of passion weren't worth a nickel. And she especially hadn't trusted hot-blooded Zane Cameron one inch. Rutting pigs never changed their skin. She should have known better. It had only strengthened her resolve to get out of town as fast as she could.

And never come back.

Besides, there'd been her father, a drunk since she was six years old. Since the day her mother disappeared, leaving behind a short note as the only evidence she'd even been there, life had gone downhill very fast after that.

She had no idea where her father even got the money to support them as poorly as he did, or to buy the whiskey he consumed by the gallon. Odd jobs, he'd told her. She never asked questions because she didn't want to know.

The scholarship to Texas Tech was her ticket out of nowhereland. She'd taken it and never looked back. Clawing her way up the journalistic ladder had toughened her while it honed her skills. The job at the *Herald* was a plum she'd plucked gratefully and eaten with relish.

Now it was all gone. She'd been set up like the greenest rookie, tempted into the promise of "writing the big one." Yeah, right. All she'd be writing now, if she got a job at all, was obit notices.

Shit.

And Zane Cameron was sure to come sniffing around again. She just knew it. She hadn't missed the signals he was sending out. He wanted her gone but not before he fucked her brains out and got her out of his system.

Great.

He still wore his midnight black hair—almost the same color as hers—long enough to need that familiar leather thong to tie it back from his face. His normally bronzed skin was tanned even deeper by constant exposure to the desert sun. High cheekbones gave his face a rough yet classical look, and thick lashes fringed eyes as black as obsidian.

His body had filled out magnificently, muscles rippling beneath the skin with every movement. The uniform he wore emphasized his broad shoulders and narrow hips.

And fine muscular ass.

Shut up, Jamie.

She needed some time to build her defenses before having to face him again. She feared—no, was unhappily certain—what her reaction to him would be. Not one day had passed since she left town that she didn't dream of him, long for him, wonder what would have happened if she'd believed his promises.

Impossible. She knew it. He had more than enough reason to hate her. What better way to take his revenge than to seduce her again and toss her in the garbage the way she had with him. She needed to pull up those hackles she'd come to be known for and drive him away before she did something really stupid.

She'd done her best to hide the fact that he'd knocked her off balance. All six-foot-four of him towering over her, his raven black hair still long, despite his position as sheriff, held back in a ponytail with a leather thong. How unfortunate for her that all that bronzed skin, those hot black eyes, and that sensuous mouth still made her body melt and liquid gush from her cunt.

Holding herself together in front of him had taken all her discipline, especially after that unexpected, scorching kiss. She'd need some rigid self-control not to reveal what he could do to her after twelve years. She wanted to see him again, yet at the same time, she was afraid. One slip and he'd know exactly how she still felt. And that would mean big trouble.

Jamie sighed and turned to the cleaning supplies. The house was a pigsty, but no less than she'd expected. Maybe she could scrub away the depressing memories while she got rid of the dirt.

She'd just gotten started on the downstairs bathroom when the phone rang. She frowned.

That better not be Cameron calling me.

"I was worried about you," were the first words she heard from Kit London's mouth. "What's with the no calls?"

Kit had been her first friend at Texas Tech, and the friendship had blossomed over the years. They worked in different cities, at totally different jobs— Kit was a financial researcher for an investment broker in New York—but they were bound together somehow, as if they were emotional Siamese twins. When the axe fell, Kit had taken vacation time and come to Florida to mop up the pieces.

"Oh, Kit." Jamie sighed. "I wonder if this was such a good idea after all."

Kit made a rude sound. "I told you to come to New York. You could lose yourself here instead of sticking out like a sore thumb."

"I haven't been here long enough to attract much attention. Although..."

"Aha!" Kit pounced. "Big Bad Zane Cameron been hanging around?"

During a long night of sharing secrets, Jamie had told Kit about her ill-fated relationship with the town bad boy, a fact she was sure she'd now regret. The last thing she wanted to discuss was the visit he'd just paid her.

"Come on," Kit prodded. "Give."

Jamie dropped down on the lumpy couch and stretched out her legs. "You won't believe this, but he's the sheriff now."

"Get out of town! The wolf of Diablo County?"

"One and the same. Go figure. They must have been desperate."

Kit chuckled. "So how was it?"

"It was nothing," Jamie insisted. "He practically tried to run me out of town." She let her eyes scan the walls while she was lying down, an activity that depressed her more than she already was.

"Oh, I doubt that."

Jamie could just picture her friend, kicked back in her funky arm chair, a wicked look on her face. For just a moment, but not the first since the unknown attorney called her with the news of her 'inheritance,' she was seized with the desire to chuck it all and head for Kit's welcoming presence.

"I'm going to pick up my dad's truck tomorrow at the junkyard," she said, changing the subject.

"And do what with it? You said he'd gone off the side of a hill in a rainstorm. How much of it can be left?"

"I can sell the undamaged parts."

Kit made her strange noise again. "Fuck that. Tell me how much money you need and where to send it."

"Uh uh. No way. I told you. But thanks anyway."

She eventually ended the call, with great reluctance but before she could tell Kit how truly awful her so-called homecoming had been.

She hadn't shed a tear when an unknown voice had called her early one morning to tell her Frank Randall had died in an accident. Drunk, as usual, she was sure. For a panicked moment, she thought the man was going to ask for money to bury him. She was shocked to learn her messenger was an attorney from Austin her father hired to draw up a will. Now she was in possession of all his earthly goods, such as they were.

But small as Diablo County was, the filing of the will at the courthouse had engendered a flurry of gossip. When Jamie finally arrived in town, she was met with hostile, knowing stares. No one was reaching out a hand to the daughter of the town drunk, least of all the now-holier-than-thou sheriff.

Well, fuck them all. She'd lost everything in the lawsuit except her car and her personal possessions. This was what she had left.

Suck it up, Jamie.

She went back to scrubbing the layers of grime from the downstairs bathroom, Zane's face still swimming in front of her eyes and the taste of him still strong on her lips.

She was surprised his anger had simmered all these years. The Zane she knew twelve years ago would have cursed for a while, blown it off, and gone on to the next female he could find. She was shocked he hadn't. As stunned as she was to discover he was the sheriff.

Funny that none of the town busybodies had seen fit to tell her that little fact while she'd gone about her business. Of course, today was the first time she'd left the house. She'd deliberately gassed up and laid in a small supply of groceries before she hit Amen, knowing she needed to fortify herself to make her grand entrance. But today she'd decided a full bore shopping trip was in order. She'd especially needed cleaning supplies.

Maybe I should just toss a match over my shoulder and walk out the door.

The house was even shabbier than she remembered it, the hundred acres that stretched out in back waist high in wild grasses and other growth. Once, long ago, the Randalls had run a small herd of cattle on the land. Just enough to bring in extra money, not too large they couldn't handle it themselves. But then her mother left, the remaining cattle were sold, and the life went out of everything.

There was an air of decay, as if, like the man who'd lived here, the building had rotted away through the years. She'd never brought anyone home when she was growing up, too ashamed of what they'd see. Although, of course, there wasn't a living soul in town who didn't know the truth of the situation. Some of her friends' parents took pity on her and invited her over now and then, but she couldn't say she ever had a close friend. Not until she met Kit.

After that night with Zane, she had almost, for one brief moment, thought about changing her mind and not leaving. But Zane's tomcat reputation clung to him like a second skin, his mother hovered like a full blown harpy, and she knew deep down he'd never settle down with the daughter of the town drunk. So she'd used her temper and her smart mouth to push him away, breaking away before he could. Protecting herself.

She cringed every time she remembered the nasty words she'd hurled at him, but they were her defense mechanism. And lord knew she'd needed one. He'd spit on the ground and cursed her, shouting angry words. Finally, her father, that soul of social graces, fired a shotgun at him, called him a stinking half-breed, and said he'd skin Zane alive if he saw his ugly face on the property again. She'd stood on the porch stone-faced, her eyes never leaving the rear of his truck as he drove away like hell was on his tail. That was when she realized life didn't exist for her anymore in Amen.

The next day, she'd packed up and left.

Closing her eyes, Jamie conjured up Zane's image as he'd looked standing in front of her. She thought again of how her body burned when it touched his. How her nipples peaked and her breasts ached. How betraying liquid trickled from her traitorous pussy. If he touched her there, slipped his fingers inside her hot sheath, he'd have known the truth of the matter and she'd have been dead meat.

She ground her teeth and picked up her cleaning rag again. She needed hard labor to work off the sexual heat she didn't want to acknowledge.

An hour later, she finished the bathroom at last, stood and stretched. Maybe if she went without sleep and worked twenty-four/seven for a month, she might make the place habitable. Right now, she'd settle for two bathrooms and her bedroom.

She peered at herself in the mirror over the sink and grimaced in distaste. Eyes with no life to them, rimmed by dark circles. Sallow skin stretched too tightly across the bones of her face. Hair with no shine pulled into a messy ponytail. A mouth that no longer knew how to smile. An overall look that was hard, edgy. A woman who had lost every bit of softness and peppered her conversation with curses.

What a mess. Why would anyone want to kiss her, least of all Zane Cameron, who'd always been able to get any female he wanted? Why would anyone want anything to do with her, bitter and angry as she was? She hardly wanted anything to do with herself.

She traced her lips where Zane's had touched them with bruising force and remembered other times and other kisses. Her entire senior year when she'd played with fire, tempting the bad boy. Hot kisses, groping hands, panting breath. And that night when she'd given it all to him and he'd taken it. Nothing she'd tried since then had been able to wash that night out of her mind.

Jamie turned away, unwilling to look at the harsh reality of herself any longer. She was considering a break and a beer when the telephone rang again. Startled, she stared at it. Who on earth would be calling her? She had no friends in town. Kit was her only link to the outside world. And she was sure if Zane wanted to talk to her, he'd show up in person.

On the fourth ring, she finally picked it up.

"Miss Randall? Jamie Randall?" The voice was unfamiliar.

"Yes. Who's this?"

"You don't know me, Miss Randall. I'm Grayson Ballou."

Jamie pulled the receiver away from her ear and stared at it as if it had grown horns. Who the hell was Grayson Ballou? "Who?"

"Grayson Ballou," he repeated, his voice friendly but matter-of-fact, as if he called strangers every day. Maybe he did. "My friends call me Gray."

"I wouldn't call us friends, Mr. Ballou." *Let's get that straight right up front. I am definitely not your friend.* "I don't even know who the hell you are." She swiped at a stray hair tickling her cheek. "Listen, I don't mean to be rude, but this isn't a number too many people call. What is it you want?"

"Ah. Get right down to business. I like that."

I don't give a damn what you like. I just want to know why you're calling. "I'm not much for socializing these days. Speak your piece."

"To get right down to it, I'd like to talk to you about buying your property."

Jamie nearly dropped the telephone. Buy the property? It couldn't be worth more than ten cents. Could it? "Excuse me?"

He cleared his throat. "I said I'd like to discuss making an offer to buy your property."

"Mr. Ballou." She stared at a spot on the counter where something had spilled months ago and been left to sit. "Why would you even think this place is for sale? And how do you know who I am?"

He gave a soft chuckle. "Not much goes on in Diablo County that I don't know about. I heard of your father's unfortunate passing and thought someone like you might be happy to have the place off your hands."

"Someone like me?" Jamie frowned. "Exactly what does that mean?"

"Please. I mean no offense. I just happen to be aware that Amen has not been your home for many years. I assumed you'd want to get back to your life as soon as possible."

Jamie wanted to laugh out loud, only it wasn't funny. "If you know so much about me then you know I currently have no life to get back to. And I can't even imagine what you'd want with this run-down piece of land. In any event, I have no intention of leaving, so the place is not for sale. Sorry you wasted your time."

"But—"

"Good-bye." She cut him off in mid-sentence, hanging up with a little more force than necessary.

Well, that was out of left field. Just who in the hell is this guy? I'm not here forty-eight hours, and he's on my tail. Why?

The only person she knew to call and ask about Grayson Ballou was Zane, and she'd burn the damn house down before she'd do that.

Not that she couldn't use the money. But then where would she go? No newspaper worth its print would hire her right now. She'd be lucky if the Podunk Press let her write photo captions. She didn't want to be here, but she didn't want to be anywhere else, either.

Truth be told, she had so many unresolved issues, she couldn't make a decision if her life depended on it. Not the least of those issues was Sheriff Zane Cameron. Only Kit knew how often she'd looked back all these years, wondering if she could have made a different choice. If there was a way she could have had both—a career and the man who made her body sing.

Or maybe she could have some kind of surgery and cut him out of her brain.

Chapter Three

The morning was damp with the threat of rain, and everything in Amen looked as if it had been painted from a gray palette. As Jamie drove down Main Street, she spotted the early risers, opening stores or hustling toward the Buckhorn Diner for breakfast. She wondered if Alice and Craig McDowell still owned it. Maybe she'd get up the nerve to put herself on display and check it out.

When she stopped for a red light, she was conscious of eyes watching her. She turned her head both ways and gave it right back. No way would these people make her hang her head. Sipping coffee from a travel mug she'd filled before leaving the house, she wondered why she was chilled when the temperature was already in the seventies.

Duke's Scrap Metal was clear on the other side of town, on the highway leading west out of Amen. She was probably running a fool's errand, but something inside her demanded to see the truck. Despite everything, she was still surprised that after all those years of driving with a load of alcohol in his body, her father had somehow rolled his truck on a curve he'd taken hundreds of times.

And she needed closure, much as she hated to admit it. A funeral had been the last thing she wanted, so she'd just told the attorney who called her to get it over with. She was more than a week getting here, anyway, and the body couldn't hang around all that time. Seeing the truck ought to be the final chapter in a part of her life she did her best to forget.

Jamie pulled through the chain-link gate into the yard and parked near the trailer Duke used as a combination office and living quarters. It sat on concrete blocks surrounded by the detritus of other people's lives—discarded and wrecked vehicles, old machines of every description, piles of anonymous junk. It always reminded her of a scene in a Stephen King movie.

After taking a last swallow of coffee, she climbed out of her vehicle, marched up to the trailer, and knocked on the door.

Duke yanked it open and stuck his head outside. He gave her a half-smile. "Zane called yesterday and said you'd probably be by this morning."

"Did he now?" She didn't smile back. "How thoughtful of him."

Duke pulled the door shut behind him and clumped down the little three-step flight. "He was just wanting to make sure I hadn't crunched it up yet. Don't know what you want with it, junked up as it is."

"I just want to take a look at it, okay? Technically, it now belongs to me."

"Suit yourself." He headed away from the trailer. "This way. Watch your step."

He led her around towering piles of this and that and rows of cars waiting for the crusher to get them, stopping at the end of one row. "Here it is, missy. Don't know what you want to see."

Jamie wasn't sure, either. But there it was indeed. An ancient Ford pickup with a powder blue amateur paint job that flaked and peeled over the years. It had accumulated a few more dents since the last time she'd seen it, and the windshield was smashed. Otherwise, it was the same piece of junk she'd learned to drive on. Rambled to town in. Made out in with Zane Cameron on more than one memorable night.

No. Don't go there.

She walked around it, eyeing it, not knowing what she was looking for. Maybe a blown tire or some other sign of what had caused Frank Randall to lose control. And wondering why she should even care. Dead is dead. Good riddance.

She'd covered enough automobile accidents in her life as a reporter to know what cars looked like after the fact. What happened to them when they hit a tree. Another car. Went off the side of as hill like her father had done. So what did she hope to see?

She kept circling the truck, kicking the tires, banging her fist on the destroyed metal. Duke stood to the side watching her.

"So, Jamie," he said at last. "You planning on sticking around here?"

She shrugged. "I guess. At least for a while." She twisted her mouth into a caricature of a smile. "Don't have any place else to go at the moment."

Duke gave her his half-smile again. "Sorry about all the trouble you've had. Don't hardly seem right to blame you for someone else's crookedness."

Jamie shoved her hands in the pockets of her jeans. "You'd think so. But the final responsibility rests with the reporter. I didn't dig deep enough to verify my sources and authenticate the documents. So, it's my head that rolls."

She walked around the truck once more, stopping by the tailgate. Or what was left of it. As she stood there just looking at it, something tickled at her brain. She walked over and ran her hand over the crumpled metal.

"Say, Duke?"

"Uh huh?"

"I was told the truck missed the curve and rolled over down the hill. Did it go side-over-side or front-over-back?"

Duke gave her a strange look and scratched his

neck. "I don't know for sure, Jamie. When Zane called me to come fetch it, the truck was lying on its side. But no telling which way it fell. Why?"

"Oh, nothing, I guess." She touched the tailgate again. "It just seems there's a lot of damage at the rear end if it bounced on its sides. These dents look fresh, the way the paint's scraped. Do you happen to know if my father was in some kind of accident recently?"

Duke kicked at a stray rock. "I'm sorry to say, unless it was a big deal, I wouldn't know about it. Your dad made it hard for people to talk to him or have any kind of relationship. So, if it wasn't anything major, it isn't likely I'd hear about it."

Jamie nibbled on a fingernail. "I know, I know. It's just...oh, well. Maybe it's my overactive imagination." She straightened her shoulders. "Listen, crazy as this sounds, I'd like to get this towed back to the house." She held up her hand when Duke opened his mouth to protest. "I know, I know. But I just want to do it. How much would you charge me? And I guess I'd owe you for the original tow, also?

"Uh, Jamie..."

"Just do it, Duke. Please?" She dug into her purse and pulled out her wallet, mentally counting her cash and trying to remember what was still in her checking account.

Duke shook his head. "Fine. If you want this piece of shit, I guess that's your right. And you don't owe me a thing. The county paid me enough for hauling it here to cover my gas out to your place." He looked at his watch. "How about late this afternoon. You be home then?"

She wanted to laugh. "Sure. Where else would I be?"

"Okay. See you around four." He led her back to where she'd parked. "Uh, Jamie?"

"Yeah?" She stopped, wondering what he had to say.

"I just wanted to tell you I'm real sorry about all the bad luck you've had lately."

One corner of her mouth turned up in a weak grin. "Thanks, Duke. You're probably the only one around here that doesn't think I deserved it."

He opened his mouth as if to say something more, then just turned away. "See you later."

The coffee in her mug was cold by now so she dumped it out the window. She wasn't hungry, but her empty stomach demanded she put something in it. She thought about stopping at the Buckhorn but wasn't ready yet to face the town's scrutiny.

There was, however, one stop she dreaded but needed to make. She wanted to get a copy of the report on her father's accident, and the only place to get it was Zane Cameron's office. He was bound to give her a hard time, but something about the pattern and shape of the dents on the tailgate bothered her.

Holding it together and not letting him get to her would be the biggest problem.

The parking lot at the sheriff's department was almost full with a combination of county and civilian vehicles. Just great. Well, she had to run the gauntlet sometime.

Two people filling out forms on a clipboard were the only ones sitting in the small lobby. Jamie walked up to the window in the administrative section and pulled out a smile for the woman sitting there. Her eyes widened when the woman looked up. Patsy Madigan, mother of one of her high school friends. Patsy's eyes opened even wider.

"Jamie? Jamie Randall?" She half rose from her chair.

"It's me, Mrs. Madigan. How are you?"

"I'm just fine. I, uh, heard you were back in

town. Planning to stay around for a while?"

"Maybe. Listen, I need to see the sheriff for a few minutes. Is he in?"

Instantly, Patsy's face took on a sympathetic expression. "Oh, my goodness. Are you having a problem?"

Problem? Hysteria threatened to bubble up. *My whole life is a problem right now.*

"No. Not at all. I just needed to ask him a couple of questions."

"Oh." The woman couldn't hide the naked curiosity on her face. "Well, then. Let me just check. I think he's still in his office."

Jamie stood in the tiny space and fidgeted until the door to the inner office opened and Patsy beckoned to her. "He says he can give you a minute or two."

Well. Isn't that just damn big of him?

"Thank you."

She followed Patsy through the big open bullpen where the deputies did their paperwork and the detectives had their desks. Most of the deputies were out on patrol. Diablo covered a vast area, and Jamie could remember L.C. Craddick, the previous sheriff, always complaining he never had enough men to cover everything. It looked like the manpower hadn't increased much since then.

Absolute silence surrounded her and eyes followed her with open curiosity as she let Patsy lead her to a corner office. Zane was leaning in the doorway, arms folded across his chest. His face was carefully expressionless. He uncrossed his arms and nodded to Patsy.

"Thanks. I'll take it from here." He stood back to let Jamie precede him into his office, then closed the door. "This is unexpected."

"For me, too."

He gestured toward a chair in front of the desk.

When she was seated, he leaned against the front of the desk and stared at her, waiting.

"Um, thank you for seeing me."

He dipped his head. "I'm the sheriff. I serve the entire county population."

"Thanks anyway." She shifted uncomfortably in the chair. Should she just blurt out what she wanted?

"Well?" he asked when she still said nothing. "I assume you had a specific reason for coming here. We don't get many big city visitors in this place. Oh, that's right." He snapped his fingers. "You're not from the city any more, are you?"

Jamie drew in a deep breath and let it out. Apparently, he wasn't about to cut her any slack. How was she to know he'd carry a grudge for twelve years? She'd love to know what happened to him in all that time.

No. No, she wouldn't.

"I'd like to see the report from my father's accident. Please."

Zane stood abruptly, a hard look on his face. All pretense of courtesy disappeared. "Exactly why would you want that, Jamie? Think us hicks can't handle a simple rollover properly?"

She gripped her hands together, determined to hold onto her temper. "I didn't say that. I just want to look at it."

He stood there, waiting for her to say something more.

"Please," she said again.

"I don't have to open the file for you if I don't want to."

So much for holding her temper. "Yes, you do. Haven't you heard of the Freedom of Information Act?"

He snorted. "Trust a reporter to know every word of that one."

She bit back the retort that bubbled up automatically. "I'm just saying...look, Zane. I don't want to make this difficult. Maybe I could just speak to the investigating officer."

"You're talking to him right now. What is it you want to know?"

She goggled. "You? Since when does the sheriff investigate simple highway accidents?"

"Since he doesn't have enough manpower and takes up the slack where he's needed. And I'm telling you, it was a drunken rollover. That's it. Or don't you think I know what I'm doing?"

"I'm not questioning you. Please don't think that." She rose from the chair. Sitting down while he towered over her gave her a distinct disadvantage. "I just want to look at it for myself. Is that a problem?"

"I can tell you anything you want to know. It was raining. The road was slick. Frank probably had a bigger load on than usual and missed that curve. End of story."

She planted her fists on her hips. So much for holding her temper. "Damn it. If it's that cut and dried, you shouldn't mind me looking at the report." She glared at him. "Right?"

They stared at each other across two feet of space. The buzz of the intercom broke the heavy silence.

Zane moved to the desk and pressed the button. "What?"

"Sorry to disturb you." Patsy's voice was tinny over the speaker. "You wanted me to remind you about the county commission meeting."

"Thanks." He turned back to Jamie. "I have to go. The commission meets in Copper Ridge, and that's a thirty minute drive." He opened the door and waited for her to move.

"The report?" she persisted.

"Damn it all, Jamie. Fine. I'll dig it out and

bring it by later this afternoon. I assume you'll be home?"

"I'll check my busy social schedule. You can call first."

She swept out in front of him, walking through the bullpen again with as much dignity as she could muster, sure that every ear had been tuned to the last part of their conversation.

She slammed the door to her SUV and jammed the key in the ignition. Insufferable ass. Egotistical jerk. Walking testosterone.

What did I ever see in him, anyway?

A rap on the window startled her. She turned her head to see Zane standing there and lowered the window. "What? I thought you were in such a big damn hurry."

"I sure don't remember you swearing this much before you left town."

"Yeah, well, I've had a real education. What it is?"

"I'll be by about four. Be sure you're home."

Before she could object or argue, he was gone, striding toward the big Expedition.

Now he was giving her orders? Well, didn't that just suck? If she hadn't wanted to see the report so badly, she'd make sure she was as far away as she could get.

She gunned the engine and headed out to the highway. Yes, it was sure going to be fun being back in Amen.

Chapter Four

The restaurant was one of the more exclusive in San Antonio, a muted environment where deals on cattle, oil, and other business were discussed on a daily basis. It was rumored that more money changed hands in The Stock Club than in any bank in the state. And, above all, it was a place where the most delicate discussions could be conducted in private.

Grayson Ballou sat back in his chair, pulled a cigar from the pocket of his pearl gray, custom-tailored, western cut suit, and lit it with his monogrammed gold lighter. As the thin spiral of smoke curled into the air, he looked across the table at his lunch companion. The man had the title of special assistant, but in reality, he did all Gray's dirty work. All the things he couldn't afford to leave his fingerprints on directly.

"Manny, you've got to stop being so nervous," he chided. "People will think you've got something to hide."

Manny Alvarado took a large swallow of his drink, the tremor in his hand barely visible but still obvious to his host. "It's all right for you to be so calm," he said. "I'm the one out on the line who'll catch all the trouble."

"You worry too much." Gray blew a perfect smoke ring, studying it as it disappeared in the air. "We have a minor problem, and we'll solve it."

"Minor? You call this minor?"

"Don't squeak." Gray frowned. "It's unbecoming for a man. I told you we'll take care of it, and we will."

"What if she won't sell the land to you? What then?"

"I'll cross that bridge when we come to it. Meanwhile, it's highly unlikely that she'll be wandering around those godforsaken acres in the middle of the night. We'll wait a few days just to track her habits. Then I think it can be business as usual."

Manny used his napkin to wipe the perspiration from his forehead. "I'm not so sure that's a good idea. Not until we have control of the area. I told you. I'll be out there exposed to the world."

Gray picked up his bourbon on the rocks and sipped at it, trying to control his irritation. True, he was annoyed that their profitable operation seemed to have hit a slight bump in the road, but this wasn't the first time. They'd weathered it before and they would now.

"Tell me. Have I ever let you down? Sent you out to take risks without protection?"

"No, but—"

"No buts. Just listen. A few days to get the lay of the land, so to speak." He chuckled at his own joke. "Then we'll regroup and start up again."

"That old man's turning out to be more trouble dead than he was alive."

Gray drew his brows together. "And whose fault is that? Of all the ways to handle him, you had to pick the worst." He sighed. "Sometimes, Manny, I wonder if you're up to this anymore."

Manny finished his beer in two quick swallows and signaled for the waiter, ignoring the look on Gray's face. "Who else could handle things the way I do? Practice makes perfect, *padrone*. So I misjudged the old man a little. But like you say, we'll get past this." He swallowed half of the fresh beer in three gulps.

"We won't get past anything if you're drunk." Ballou blew another perfect smoke ring. The exercise was excellent for maintaining an attitude of calm. Those who knew him best said when Gray Ballou blew smoke rings, he could be planning a multimillion dollar deal, a party at his ranch, or a plot to kill someone. It was impossible to tell.

Life had been good to him, but he always said it was because he knew the value of a deal. No one could actually say what he did.

"I conduct business," he told anyone who asked him.

And that was as much as they got.

He'd stumbled onto the value of an operation Manny had been running for a long time on his own and discovered the income was limited only by the man's imagination. He'd assessed the situation and simply told Manny he was taking it over and expanding it. So what if some of the people he dealt with weren't invited to the best houses in Texas society? He wasn't looking for people with refined social skills, only those who could put large amounts of dollars in his pockets.

And somehow, because he was providing a sought-after commodity, it had opened doors for him previously closed. Only his offshore bankers knew how much Grayson Ballou was worth.

The operation had provided an unexpected bonus or two, and he had to swallow a smile as he thought of them.

The waiter approached and discreetly placed the check next to Gray's plate. He signed it and waved the man away.

"Let's let the dust settle for a day or two," he told Manny. "Then we'll see which way the wind blows and if the dust kicks up again. Meanwhile, just keep your head down and don't call attention to yourself."

"Of course, *padrone*."

"And no more bodies."

If push came to shove, Gray would shut this down altogether, maybe find another place to start up again. But he'd refined this one over the years and was far from ready to let it go just yet. A disgraced journalist, nearly broke, was no match for him when he had his mind set on something. And he had an ace up his sleeve that he'd play if he had to. He'd done it before. He could do it again. One way or another, Jamie Randall would hand her land over to him.

****

Zane dropped his Stetson on the seat beside him and headed the Expedition back toward Amen. The meeting had lasted far longer than he expected. Then he had to have lunch with the commission chairman. And as long as he was in the area and nothing was shaking that needed his attention, he took a few minutes to say hello to his mother.

And a few minutes was all she had for him. When he was ten and his father was killed, Anita Cameron faced raising a child with few skills and little money. Her own people, the Comanche, wouldn't help her because she'd married outside her race, despite her father forbidding it. Out of nowhere, the office job with Diablo Ag Con had appeared, offering her a lifeline.

About the time Zane was elected sheriff the first time, she'd been promoted to assistant manager. It meant, however, she needed to move to Copper Ridge. Zane needed to stay in Amen where his headquarters were, so they'd sold the little house he'd grown up in, split the money, and each bought their own property.

Since the move, his mother had risen to manager of the entire operation with a schedule that kept her hopping. Today, as he came in, she was on her way out to a meeting. At least he'd had a chance to say hello. Not always an easy thing with his schedule.

He should have moved the sheriff's headquarters to Copper Ridge three years ago after the last election when the commission approached him about it. It would save this drive back and forth for meetings and certainly keep him removed from the problem that just dropped back into his life.

But he loved the house he'd bought, old but suited to him. He worked at restoring it in his spare time—whatever that was. At the time, he had no idea that he'd walk into his office one morning to the news that Jamie Randall was back in town. He rubbed his hand over his face, wishing he could wipe away his problems with one easy swipe.

Jamie.

He hadn't even started to figure out how he was going to handle her coming home when she'd walked into his office this morning. He should have used his brains instead of his dick, found her the report, and sent her on her way. But no, instead, he was doing the dumbass thing and walking right into the fire. Giving her a chance to spit on him again.

He wheeled into his parking lot of the sheriff's office and shut off the engine. He was an adult. He could do this. Make a copy of the report, drop it off to her, and get the hell out of her house.

Yeah. Right.

****

Jamie was edgy enough to jump out of her skin. Duke had hauled the truck up the driveway and left it at the side of the house, still fussing at her about what nonsense it was and seeing ghosts where there weren't any. And still refusing to take any of her money.

"I'm not a charity case," she told him angrily.

"Nope. That's a fact. But you need to be frugal

when money's tight. Don't let your pride lead you into a hole in the ground."

God, the man had more strange mixed metaphors than anyone she'd ever known.

Now, she was working in the kitchen, polishing the stained and crusted countertop, and keeping her eye on the stove clock. Zane had said four o'clock and it was already past that. She'd actually hoped he'd get here and be gone before Duke arrived and she had to answers questions about the truck.

No such luck. Not only wasn't he early, he was already late.

Maybe he wouldn't show. Maybe she could call him and tell him she'd just stop by tomorrow and pick up the report.

She couldn't think of him coming to the house without recalling yesterday's kiss. Her nerve endings still sizzled from it. And last night she'd made up her bed with the sheets she brought with her, lain down on their cool, smooth surface, and masturbated herself to climax with Zane's face burned into the underside of her eyelids.

In the anonymity of the darkness, she'd squeezed her thighs together, locking her fingers inside her cunt and hating herself for wishing it was Zane's cock inside her, fucking her as she remembered, taking her higher and higher until her body exploded into a million pieces.

God, I am so fucking pathetic.

The scene in his office earlier should have cured her. They were like two cats hissing and clawing at each other, neither of them giving an inch. Her antidote to her uncontrollable eagerness to see him again was to make herself as unattractive as possible. Ratty T-shirt, faded cutoffs, messy ponytail. Turn him off and maybe she could turn herself off.

She had just refilled the bucket with water and cleaner when she heard the crunch of tires on the driveway. Her stomach tightened at the sound of booted feet on the porch.

"Door's open," she called, keeping her back turned.

The sound of his footsteps drew nearer. She set her scrub brush aside and wiped her hands on a paper towel. When she turned to face him, he was only inches away. Right there next to her, big and looming and powerful.

She tried to swallow but her mouth was too dry. "Thank you for coming by." It came out like a croak.

"What's the truck doing in the driveway?"

She backed up a step. "You sure get right to the point, don't you?"

He moved a step forward, crowding her. "I asked you a question."

"What's it to you? I own it. I can do whatever I want with it."

He moved again until their bodies were almost touching. "You always were a pistol, you know that? I don't know what's in that head of yours, but I won't let you come into my county and make a problem where there isn't one."

"*Your* county?" She swatted his chest. "In case you haven't noticed, I live here so it's my county, too. Get off my case, Cameron. So. Did you bring the report?"

"You get right to the point, too, don't you?"

"No time to waste."

He closed the last little bit of distance between them, his eyes burning into hers like twin torches. Then his mouth was on hers, just like the day before, burning her, sucking the life out of her while infusing it back into her body. She wanted to hit him, push him away, but her traitorous arms wounds up around his neck and clung to him, holding his head to hers. Her panties were already soaked, and that old familiar quiver raced through the muscles of her cunt.

His tongue probed her mouth, taking, taking. There was nothing gentle about this kiss. And to her shame she gave as good as she got. She couldn't have moved away if her life was threatened, not even when his hands slid down to reach under her T-shirt and cup her breasts through the thin cotton of her bra. One touch of those rough-silken lips and those big hot hands and her brain simply melted away.

His tongue had a life of its own, probing into the recesses of her mouth, licking, tasting, teasing. His fingers pinched her nipples just hard enough to cause a shiver of pleasure-pain. She hung onto him for dear life, drowning in the sensations that assaulted her body.

The harder he tugged on her nipples, the more he plundered her mouth, the weaker her legs became until she wasn't sure she could stand at all if she took her arms from his neck.

When every bit of breath had left her lungs, he lifted his mouth just a fraction, tracing the edge of her lips with the tip of his tongue. "Jamie?"

"Mmm?" She forced her eyes open.

"You using your old bedroom?"

"What? My bedroom?"

He extricated himself from her grip and lifted her in his arms. "Your bedroom. I'm going to fuck the life out of you, and I don't want to do it on that ratty old couch."

She could barely focus enough to point toward the stairs. "Yes. Same room. Second door on the right."

Later, when her brain kicked into gear again and she could pluck one rational thought from it, she'd wonder why she hadn't just ordered Zane Cameron out of her house. He certainly wouldn't take her by force. That wasn't his style. No, even after all this time, he knew just which buttons to push and how to push them, and in an instant all her defenses were down. But at the moment, all she could think of was how good he felt next to her and the explosion his kisses had set off in her body.

He held her against his chest as he took the steps two at a time. Using his foot, he pushed the door to her room open and in seconds had her flat on her back on her clean white sheets, legs dangling over the edge of the bed. She opened her eyes again to see him staring at her with a look of intense hunger on his face, and instantly heat warmed her blood.

With hands that shook slightly, he pulled the T-shirt over her head, disposed of her bra, and stripped her shorts and panties from her, tossing everything to the floor. Then he bent her knees and spread her thighs wide, exposing her to his ravenous gaze.

He drew in a deep, ragged breath, and let it out slowly. "God, Jamie, you have the most gorgeous cunt in the world."

One long finger traced her slit from clitoris to vaginal opening and back, gathering the cream she knew was gushing from her. He lifted the finger to his mouth and sucked on it.

"Taste good, too. Just as I've remembered all these years." He took two steps back, his heated gaze burning into her sex. "Open yourself for me. Pull those cunt lips wide so I can see all that delicious pink flesh."

Jamie's skin was so hot she thought it would burst. The smart thing was to jump off the bed, smack Zane in the face, and kick him out of the house, but smart wasn't even in her vocabulary at the moment. She burned for his touch, for the feelings he aroused in her. Closing her eyes, she reached for herself, her breathing unsteady.

Zane's firm hand gripped her wrists. "No. Open your eyes. Look at me while you do this. Don't hide yourself from me. I want to see the desire I know is there."

She forced her lids open enough to see him as her hands touched her labia and slowly pulled them apart. His gaze never left her cunt as he unclipped his holster from his belt and set it on the night stand. Before stuffing his wallet back in his pocket, he removed a foil packet and set it next to his gun. He toed off his boots, then his shirt, trousers, and boxers joined her clothes in the heap on the floor.

Her mouth went dry at the sight of him, all hard muscle and bronze skin. Dark hair lightly dusted his chest, a genetic throwback to his white ancestors. Her eyes followed the line of it across his flat abdomen to the thick nest of dark curls surrounding the root of his cock.

And what a cock it was. She licked her lips in anticipation. Larger and thicker than she remembered. But he was a man, she reminded herself, with a man-size erection, one that would put to shame the few others she'd seen. The flared head was a dark purple, a swollen vein roped around the length of it, and a tiny pearlescent drop of liquid sat atop the slit.

As her cunt pulsed and her breasts ached for his touch, all she could think was *Ohmigod*.

In a second, his hands were on her knees again, separating them even wider.

"Touch your clit, Jamie. Wet your fingers with those juices I see flowing and rub that hard little button."

She moved her fingers back and forth, feeling tiny quivers vibrate the walls of her pussy. A tight coil started to unwind deep in her belly.

Zane eased one hand down her thigh and slowly slipped a finger into her tight vaginal sheath. Her muscles clamped around him, and she sped up the movement on her clit.

"God, your pussy still drives me wild. All this wonderful, wet flesh. How tight you are." He loomed over her, his finger probing her pussy. "Have you had many lovers, Jamie? You're still as tight as a virgin."

She couldn't answer him, couldn't form a coherent thought. She pushed against his finger, but it was his cock she really wanted inside her.

He laughed, a sultry sound. "You want me to fuck you, don't you? And I will. I plan to give you the ride of your life. But not until I've driven you wild with need. Keep fingering yourself. Don't stop until I tell you to."

When he backed away, an incredible sense of loss gripped her and she couldn't hold back a tiny moan. She heard the *thunk* as his knees hit the floor, saw his head dip, and in seconds his very educated tongue was flicking along her slit and probing into her needy channel. Like a smaller version of his cock, his tongue fucked her, scooping at her juices with its tip. And all the while her fingertip played over and over her throbbing clit.

She threw her head back, eyes closing automatically, the orgasm building inside her. When his tongue left her pussy and slipped down toward the entrance to her ass, she lost it. Her climax jolted her, roaring through her like a tidal wave, pounding at every one of her senses. Mercilessly, Zane held her pussy wide open, his broad shoulders keeping her thighs apart, denying her the ultimate satisfaction her body craved. Desperately, she tried to slide her fingers inside herself, but he nudged her hand out of the way.

"Uh uh, Jamie. I want to see those tight cunt muscles throb and shake. God, you have so much cream running from you it's like a lake. Keep going. That's it."

When the last quiver had subsided, leaving her

Cocked And Loaded

wanting more than ever, he licked her juices from
her labia and the crevice of her ass where they'd
dripped. She heard the crinkle of foil being ripped
open and, through barely open eyes, saw him roll the
condom onto his enormous, thick erection.

Then he was over her again, his big hands
moving her up on the bed, his lips rubbing against
hers. She could taste herself on him, a salty/sweet
flavor, arousing her even more.

He wrapped his fingers around her wrists and
held them down on either side of her head. Lowering
his head, he took one of her nipples into his mouth,
nipping at it then soothing it with his tongue.
Rolling it around inside his mouth and pulling on it.
When it was hard and heated from the blood rushing
to it, he moved to the other one, paying it equal
attention.

"Mmm." The sound rolled from her mouth in a
long sigh and she pushed her hips against his body.

That same sultry laugh rumbled from his throat.
"You want my cock in you? Is that it? Oh, you'll get it
soon enough, but not until I'm good and ready. I've
been saving up for this for a long time."

"Please." She couldn't stop the word from
bubbling out of her mouth.

"Please what?" Golden flecks danced in his hot
dark eyes and deep lines grooved his face. "Please
suck you again? Please stick my tongue in your
cunt? Or is it my cock you want so badly? God, I'd
love to slap my handcuffs on you, lock you to this
bed, and pound you until you scream." He ran the tip
of his tongue over her open lips. "Maybe I will,
Jamie. Would you like that?"

Yes!

She swallowed the word so she wouldn't shout
it. Do it, she wanted to tell him. Do anything you
want. In a few short minutes, he had her as
mindless as the night he'd taken her virginity. And

51

all the nights after that. How pathetic was that?

"Well?" he prodded. "Tell me you want that." He bent his head so his mouth was at her ear. "Would you like me to fuck you in the ass?" He shuddered. "Just the thought of my dick inside you there almost makes me come. I'll bet you're so tight there you could squeeze the head of my dick right off."

"Oh." The word came out on a breath of air. She hooked her legs over his thighs and tried to pull him closer.

"You like that, do you? Let's just take a look."

Before she realized it, he flipped her over and knelt between her thighs. When she tried to push herself up, he held her hands palms down on the pillow. "Be a good girl and keep your hands like this, or I'll have to get out the cuffs before we're ready for them."

Jamie took a deep breath to steady herself and kept her hands where he'd placed them. The wild orgasm had hardly taken the edge off her aroused state, but the image of Zane kneeling behind her heated her even more. She closed her eyes and waited to see what he'd do next.

"Beautiful," he breathed, running his hands down her back and over the curved globes of her ass. "You've turned into quite a woman, Jamie. You make my mouth water."

His warm lips touched her everywhere, trailing over her buttocks, feathering kisses over her shivering skin. Her fingers clawed the pillow as he nipped gently then soothed with soft licks of his tongue. But when he put his hands on the cheeks of her ass, separating them, and ran his tongue along the cleft from top to bottom, the muscles in her pussy convulsed again.

"Tasty." His voice with husky and thick with lust. "Do you feel as good as you taste, I wonder?"

He slipped one finger into her liquid cunt and

gathered her cream, spread it around the puckered rosette of her anus, then pushed the finger inside her dark heat.

"Oh, god." She hadn't expected the surge of desire that raced through her. She'd had lovers since Zane, but that was always forbidden territory. Yet, with him it seemed as natural as breathing. Her heart tripped as she thought of him fucking her there.

Bending over her, finger still inside, he brushed a kiss against the nape of her neck. "Soon, Jamie. Soon I'll have my cock in your mouth, in your ass, every place I want to put it. And you'll take it and love it. But not tonight." He moved his hand away and flipped her onto her back again. "Tonight I have to feel your pussy around me before I go crazy."

He pressed her knees back to give him greater access, took his swollen cock in his hand, and pressed the purple head of it against her opening. Jamie rocked her pelvis, urging him to thrust it all the way inside her.

"Here it comes, Jamie. All the way to the balls."

One roll of his hips and he was fully seated, his testicles slapping against her buttocks. Every muscle in her body clenched. Her cunt felt so very full, stretched beyond its normal limits. The head of his cock bumped the mouth of her womb. They froze, immobile, adjusting to each other before he moved in slow strokes. She gripped him with her arms and legs as if she could pull all of him inside.

Then Zane's hips rose and fell as his cock filled every inch of her. The dance accelerated, retreat and thrust, faster and faster. The only sounds in the room were their panting breaths, the slap of flesh on flesh and the rustle of the sheet beneath their bodies. Jamie's body throbbed everywhere as the hot spot low in her belly burned with need and her nerves stretched to send that final jolt to her muscles. As tight as Zane's cock fit in her pussy, still she could feel the walls fluttering with the need to clamp, shudder, spasm. She tried desperately for that ever elusive pinnacle, but Zane knew just how to time his movements, how hard and how fast to make them, to hold it just beyond her reach.

But then she felt the muscles in his buttocks tense, his back tighten, and his breathing rasp. One final, hard stroke and she burst into flames, her climax shaking her so hard she thought her bones would break. His cock pulsed inside her as he emptied himself of his seed.

She clung to him tightly, anchoring herself. The world spun as her body convulsed again and again, and her blood, like liquid heat, burned her body from the inside out.

And then it was over. Her heart rate slowed, her pulse steadied, and she drew gasps of air into her lungs. Zane's sweat-slickened body lay over her, pressing her into the mattress.

Her brain spun with the reality of what had just happened. The tension was still in the air, but the tenor of it had changed and it scared her to death. A chill raced over her, and she pushed hard at him to lift him away from her.

"Move," she told him. "I have to get up."

Chapter Five

Zane rolled to his side, away from Jamie, his arm over his eyes. "Damn it. I knew this would happen. Fuck, fuck, fuck. Why the hell did you have to come back here anyway?"

Jamie got to her feet and glared at him. God, he was just as infuriating as he'd ever been. And just as self-centered. "Gee, thanks for the kind words, Zane. I didn't notice being in that bed by myself."

"You always did bewitch me." He moved his arm and looked at her. "You left here with your tail on fire. Why can't you stay the hell out of my life now?"

She didn't know what to do with the anger that consumed her. "Get out of here, Zane. I didn't ask for this, and you can be damn sure it won't happen again. This is the last time you'll catch me off balance. Excuse me, I need to shower."

"Still the same smart mouth on you."

Smarter than my brain. How the hell did I let this happen?

"If you didn't want this, all you had to do was say so," he called after her. "Why didn't you?"

She ignored him and kept on walking.

"Hey! I asked you a question."

"Well, you're not getting an answer." *Because I don't have one.*

Jamie stomped into the bathroom and slammed the door. She turned the shower on full blast, the drumming of the water against the bottom of the tub vying with the drumming of her heart. Well, wasn't that just the stupidest thing she'd ever done? She'd better get tighter control of her hormones if she was going to survive this blip in her life.

She'd walked away from Zane Cameron the last time before he could bury her in this godforsaken place. She didn't intent to let him suck her in now. She might be down but she wasn't out. As soon as she got her act and some money together, she'd be out of here.

Screw Zane Cameron.

No, wait. That was what she'd just done. So first she needed to find her brains again.

She had just finished soaping her body and started to rinse it off when she heard the bathroom door open. Damn. She'd forgotten to lock it. Another stupid mistake.

A large hand pulled the shower curtain aside, and Zane stepped under the spray with her.

"Do you mind?" She backed up two steps. "This is my shower."

"I'm just borrowing it." His eyes had a wicked gleam. "Jamie, we have to talk."

"We have nothing to talk about. Take your shower and get out." She ducked under his arm and stepped out onto the bath mat. "I'll leave a towel for you. Don't slam the door on your way out."

She pulled on another T-shirt and shorts, equally as unattractive as the one's she'd been wearing, brushed her wet hair away from her face, and tugged it into its usual pony tail.

Stomping angrily down the stairs, she got out the coffee can and filter and set a pot to brewing. What she really wanted was a beer. Or better yet a shot of really good bourbon. How had she let herself be seduced like that?

No. Not seduced. Taken. Zane had given her no choice. Not that she'd protested at all. And that made her even more furious. She had business to take care, business that was sure to get under his skin, and sex would only cloud the issue. No matter how mind-blowing it was.

She'd just taken two mugs out of the cupboard when she heard Zane's footsteps behind her. She turned to face him, determined to get this straightened out once and for all.

Freshly showered, his straight dark hair combed back and tied with the leather thong, his bonze skin glowing, the image of him nearly killed Jamie's resolve. Especially when he was so close, he stole her breath away.

"I told you we need to talk and we're going to."

She drew in a breath to steady herself and let it out. "Talk. Okay. Sure. What happened was a mistake. It won't happen again. Good-bye."

"That's not talking," he objected. "That's just you spouting words." He gripped her arms. "When I heard you were back, I wanted to run you out of town so bad you're lucky I didn't throw a hitch on that fancy SUV of yours and tow it."

"Try it," she spat at it.

"Oh, I think we're past that, darlin'."

"I'm not your darlin'," she corrected, a little louder than necessary. "I'm not your anything."

"Is that a fact?" He started to lean his head down toward her. "You sure could have fooled me."

She held out both hands and tried to back up, but the counter was right behind her. "This is not good. Not good at all."

Zane cocked an eyebrow. "Oh? I thought it was pretty damn good myself. And I for sure wasn't the only one enjoying it."

"This was a mistake, like you said. It can't happen again."

His slow smile made her knees buckle. Damn him.

"Tell me you didn't enjoy it, and I'll call you a liar. You were so hot for me your cunt was extra juicy. I'll bet you haven't had an orgasm like that in years."

"That's beside the point. We did it and it's over."
Liar! "That's the end of it."

His face tightened. "Still running away from me,
Jamie? Afraid my mixed blood isn't good enough for
you?"

"Damn it, Zane. You know that's not it at all."
She turned back to pour the coffee.

"You could have fooled me. I didn't see you
objecting or contradicting when your drunk-as-a-
skunk old man threatened to blow my head off and
called me every dirty name he could think of."

She gritted her teeth. "That was a long time ago.
Life's happened in the meantime. And I have no
intention of getting sucked into something here in
lousy little Amen that will wreck what's left of my
life."

"You nearly got your wish, darlin'. All I had in
mind was to take what should have been mine all
these years and then run your ass out of town.
Pronto."

She glared at him. "Go ahead. You got what you
wanted."

Zane moved until they were belly to belly and
thigh to thigh. "Not by half. It seems the joke's on
me, because you're in my blood thicker than ever."

"Zane, don't—"

"You listen to me, Jamie. I didn't come after you
when you left, although I damn well wanted to. But
at that time I had nothing to offer you. Only my
word, which wasn't worth a whole hell of a lot then
and you knew it. That's one of the reasons you ran. I
don't blame you. But times have changed. I let you
do this to me once before, but not this time.
Whatever's between us is hotter than ever. We're not
once and done the way I planned, damn it. Either
pack up and head back out of town, or you can count
on me taking what's mine. Consider this fair

warning."

She wrenched herself free. "What's yours? I am not yours, Zane Cameron."

His eyes were like hot coals. "Maybe not yet, but you will be."

"I might have something to say about that." *That is, if I can find the courage to say it. Don't touch me, Zane. It makes my body melt and my brain turn to mush.*

"We'll see. Oh, yes. We'll just see."

Jamie's knees wobbled and liquid seeped from her cunt. *No, damn it!*

Zane backed away and poured himself some coffee in the mug she'd taken down. His hard eyes studied her over the rim as he sipped it.

"So." She moved away from him. "One more time. Did you bring the report?"

His face darkened. "Jamie—"

"Well?"

"Fine. Whatever." He slammed his mug down hard enough that some of the coffee sloshed over onto the counter and his hand. He swore, shaking the liquid off over the sink. "Give me a towel."

"I'll get it." Jamie tore a sheet off a roll of paper towel. "You just get me that piece of paper."

He unbuttoned his uniform shirt pocket, pulled something out, and handed it to her. "Here, but I don't know what you think you're looking for."

Jamie took it from him and studied it carefully. She'd read enough accident reports in her life to know this one was pretty thoroughly filled out. Yet there were some details missing she was curious about.

"Did the truck just roll over and tumble sideways?" she asked. "It doesn't say here."

"Yes. It did." Zane gritted his teeth. "I didn't think I needed to add the details. The condition of the truck spoke for itself."

She frowned, her teeth dragging on her lower lip. "I just can't imagine him letting that happen. He's taken that curve in rotten weather when he was so drunk he couldn't stand up."

A muscle ticked in Zane's cheek. "Are you saying you don't think I investigated the accident properly? That I'm just a dumb hick cop who doesn't know anything?"

She looked up at him. "I'm not saying anything, except there are some things that bother me. Come outside a minute." She led him to the side drive where Duke had dropped the truck. "See? Those dents in the tailgate? They look fresh. If he rolled on the side, how did those dents get there?"

"Damn it, Jamie. How the hell can you even tell when those dents were made, as old and beat up as this piece of crap is?"

She glared at him. "If you look at it, *Sheriff,* you'll see the paint under the scrape marks hasn't had time to weather. These are fresh. Like someone bumped him from behind and tried to push him over the edge of that hill."

Zane ran his hand over the metal, anger rolling off him in waves. "That could have happened any time." He stood up, glowering at her. "What the hell's going on here? Everyone knows what a drunk Frank Randall was and getting worse every year. It's a wonder he hadn't killed himself before this."

Jamie scowled right back. Let him get mad. She wasn't about to be put off. "And where was he coming from?" She looked at the report she was holding. "This says the accident happened at four in the morning. The Last Call Saloon was long closed by then. He'd been somewhere."

Zane shook his head. "You're making something out of nothing here. Frank wandered all over the place. Anyway, why are you making such a stink? I don't think you ever said one word to him after you lit out of here like a cat with its tail on fire."

She went back to chewing her bottom lip. "So what? That doesn't mean I don't want to know what really happened. Or nail the person who did it if someone's at fault."

One lean finger tilted her chin up, forcing her to look at him. "There's nothing here to find, darlin'. Diablo County has little crime to speak of, so there's no reason why anyone would want to pitch old Frank over the side of the hill. You've been living in the city too long. You're seeing trouble where there isn't any."

Jamie jerked her head away. "I said I'm not your darlin'. Or your anything. I can see how much help you'll be to me here, so why don't you get on your way, *Sheriff*." Each time she said the word, she spat it as if it were an epithet.

"Fine." His voice was thick with anger. He dropped his hand and moved away. "Do whatever you want. Knock yourself out. I'll be waiting for your apology any time you're ready to give it to me."

"Don't hold your breath," she called as he stormed away from her.

He didn't answer her, just climbed into the Expedition, turned in a flurry of gravel, and roared out onto the highway.

Well, damn it all.

She hated to admit he'd been right about one thing. Why was she so hung up on this, anyway? Was she really seeing monsters where there weren't any? Not that Frank hadn't been a prime monster himself. She still wondered how she'd come out of all those nightmarish years without permanent problems. Or maybe she had them and just didn't realize it.

And now there was this *thing* with Zane to face. She was sure both of them had thought one roll in the sack would get it all out of their systems, but that wasn't what happened. No, damn it, not at all. She just wasn't sure how to handle it.

Sighing she trudged back into the house, realizing, in the heat of the moment, she'd forgotten to ask Zane if he knew who Grayson Ballou was.

****

"Gray, she's had the damned truck towed to her house." Manny's hand on the cell phone was slick with sweat. He hated giving unpleasant information to his boss.

"Let's not panic, okay?" Gray's voice was calm and even. "That piece of junk is so banged up you can't tell one dent from the other."

"Then why did she bother? What does she suspect?"

"Nothing, you idiot." A note of impatience crept in. "There's nothing *to* suspect, right? She's just wasting time."

Manny's stomach knotted. This tone of voice always made him nervous. Things were about to go to hell in a handbasket. He could feel it. And all because of one old drunk. "If you say so. But she had the sheriff out there again today."

Gray chuckled. "Zane Cameron's been sniffing around her ass since she was in high school. He's just looking to get him a piece if he can."

"She must have turned him down, then, because he didn't look any too happy when he passed me a while ago."

"Just don't get caught playing I Spy. Cover yourself. She won't find anything."

"And if she does?"

"Then we'll just take care of that little problem, too. Only this time, Manny, we have to make the body disappear. Too many in Diablo and even the half-breed sheriff will get suspicious."

"I hear you. I'll figure out a way to keep an eye on her without getting spotted."

"Good, good." Gray's tone of voice turned jovial. "I knew I could count on you. Be sure to keep in touch."

Manny clicked off the call and mopped his face with a handkerchief. He'd better find a way to derail whatever Jamie Randall was doing. If this lucrative little business of theirs blew up in their faces, Gray Ballou would be sure to blame him.

****

Zane had the air conditioner blowing on him full blast. It wasn't just the heat raising his temperature. How had he let things get out of hand this way? Only twenty-four hours since he'd seen her again and already Jamie Randall was leading him around by his cock just as she always had.

Damn!

He never should have fucked her. That put him in a vulnerable position, letting her see how he felt. But his body was already telling him he couldn't stay away from her. All that delicious wet heat, those soft but firm breasts, nipples like chocolate candy against her tanned skin. He wanted to sink himself inside her and stay forever.

He'd have her again. There was no mistaking that. But on his terms. All he had to do was get her hot like he did today and she was his for the taking. Getting close enough might be a problem, but he could work on that.

Only what was all this business about the truck and his accident report? He couldn't think of a living soul who'd want to kill Frank Randall. Not that there weren't a lot of people who wished the old scumbag dead, himself included. But it just didn't seem worth the effort to anyone. They all expected him to drink himself to death one day, anyway.

Zane wished his feelings for Jamie weren't quite so confused. He'd been a real fuckaround when she was in high school, and that had put her off when he came sniffing around her. Still, something had connected between them. He knew it, just as he was sure it had never gone away. Not for him, not for her.

She didn't trust him then, and she had big ideas of her own. He'd hated her all these years for leaving. She said there was nothing for her here. That included him.

He sighed as the station came into sight. He'd have to figure out how to handle this. The thing that terrified him was the stark realization that this was about more than the best sex he'd ever had in his life. And just as Jamie hadn't trusted him all those years ago, he didn't trust her now.

Chapter Six

Jamie dumped out the rest of the coffee and took a cold can of soda from the fridge. Carrying it with her, she went out to the back patio and dropped into an old metal folding chair. She couldn't even care that it was filthy dirty and probably about to fall apart, just like everything else in the house.

Tears stung her eyes. It just wasn't fair. She worked hard to educate herself and build a new life away from here. Someone's political agenda had destroyed it all, and now she was back where she started—broke, no prospects, in a house about to fall down around her ears. She'd never get it back in shape to live in, even if she decided to stay here. And what a depressing thought that was. If she was smart, she take whatever Grayson Ballou offered and try to put her life back together.

That little tango in the sheets with Zane wasn't helping, either. She'd come back to Amen, determined that very thing wasn't going to happen, yet here she was, her body still aching for his even after two mind-crushing orgasms. She could just imagine him walking around with his chest all puffed up, sure he had her right where he wanted her.

With the back of her hand, she brushed away a lone tear that trickled down her cheek. Damn it, she would not cry. She was tougher than that. And she'd find out what happened to her father, no matter how much of a waste case he was. Or what Zane Cameron said to deter her. Something didn't add up and she'd find out what.

The phone rang, but she ignored it. Maybe it was Zane calling to chew her out again, and she didn't need that aggravation. Eventually the ringing stopped, but then her cell phone, which she'd stuck in the pocket of her shorts, vibrated. She flipped it open to see Kit's number. At least one person was safe to talk to.

"So have you seen the hot sheriff again?" were Kit's first words.

"Give it a rest," Jamie told her friend. The last thing she wanted to discuss at the moment was Zane Cameron.

"Not on your life." Kit laughed, a silvery sound. "Honey, you've been like a nun for so long I'm not sure you'd know what sex is all about any more. You need to get laid. Bad."

Oh, Kit. If you only knew. "Sex never solves anything. Especially with the wrong person."

"Oh, yeah? And what makes you think he's the wrong person? You haven't stopped talking about him since the first minute we met."

Jamie shifted in her chair, swinging her legs over the side. "Complaining is more like it."

"Honey, a woman doesn't complain about a man for twelve years. So what's shaking?"

Jamie swallowed a sigh and angrily brushed away another tear. "Nothing's shaking. I'm just trying to figure out what to do with the rest of my life."

There was a long silence at the other end of the connection. "Jamie, you don't sound so good. What's going on?"

"I'm fine, Kit. Really." If only her voice didn't quiver so much.

"Oh, you lie so bad. Shame on you. This is Kit you're fibbing to. Remember?"

Oh, yes. Kit who could spot a lie a mile away.

"I'm doing all right, considering. I just have to

get some things straightened out."

"Like the big bad sheriff?" Her tone was light, but Jamie heard the concern underneath.

"You can stop worrying about me. Honestly. I'm getting it together." Jamie held the cold can of soda against her forehead, rolling it back and forth. A bitch of a headache was growing behind her eyes.

"Pardon me if I don't quite believe you. Listen, where is this place you are, anyway? How far out in the middle of nowhere?"

Jamie sat up quickly, banging her arm on the chair. "Kit, do not even think of coming out here."

"Cool down, okay? I just want to know where to go and claim the body when you do away with yourself."

"Ha ha. Very funny. Listen, I have things to do. It's nice to hear your cheerful voice, but I have to get going."

Before I do something stupid like break down and bawl on the phone.

"If you say so. But since you won't pick up the phone and give me a ring to let me know you're still breathing, I'm calling you again tomorrow, you hear?"

"Absolutely." Jamie actually felt her mouth turn up in a tiny smile. "I live for the sound of your voice."

She hated the sarcasm she knew came across in her conversation. Kit was her lifeline, the one person who was always there for her. But she didn't need her friend's mothering right now or her insistent habit of giving orders if she thought Jamie was headed in the wrong direction. She'd wisely held her tongue when the story of the hoax came out. She'd been the only one to tell Jamie it sounded too good to be true.

A faint breeze stirred the leaves of the ancient oaks in the back yard, sweeping away some of the day's heat that still clung to the air. Summer in

Texas was often only a step away from the fires of hell. Jamie finished the soda and pushed herself out of the chair. She realized she hadn't eaten all day, a good probable cause of the headache. Food had no appeal for her, but common sense told her to put something in her stomach.

She'd only bought a meager supply of groceries on her way into town, but she sure didn't feel like going out. A survey of her supplies and she settled for a peanut butter sandwich and milk. Her old standby.

She was standing at the counter eating when the phone rang. Without thinking, she lifted the receiver.

"Hello?"

"Miss Randall."

Oh, God. Gray Ballou. She was hardly in the mood to talk to him tonight. "Listen, Mr. Ballou. I'm really very busy right now."

"I just wanted to see if you'd taken a minute to think over my offer. I can make it a very attractive one."

Jamie resisted the urge to slam the phone down. Better to just get rid him of altogether. "I told you earlier. I'm not interested in selling, so you can stop calling here."

"I think you're making a big mistake." His voice had turned hard, even while it never lost its smoothness.

"Then it's my mistake to make. Good-bye, Mr. Ballou."

Jamie washed down the last bite of her sandwich with milk, irritated because she knew she was about to make another error in judgment. But she had no one else to call in Amen except Zane and she really wanted to find out who this jerk was.

She pulled the ragged telephone book from a drawer and looked up the number, dialing it with great reservation.

"I'm sorry, Sheriff Cameron is gone for the day," the deputy who answered told her. "You might could catch him at home, unless he's outside working."

"Thank you."

Call him at home? Wonderful. She leafed through the phone book again until she found the listing for Z. Cameron. The phone ran four times, and she was just about to hang up when he answered.

"Cameron."

"Hello, Zane. It's Jamie."

Silence.

When he spoke, his voice was tight. "What can I do for you? It must be pretty damn important for you to call me at home."

"Listen, this was a bad idea. I'm sorry I bothered you."

"No, don't hang up." The words were sharp enough to keep her on the line. "I'm sure it wasn't easy for you to call me. After today, that is."

She didn't want to ask him exactly which part of today he was referring to. "I just had a question, and I didn't know who else to ask."

"Go ahead."

"Do you know a man named Grayson Ballou?"

"Gray? Sure." Another strained silence. "What do you have to do with Gray Ballou?"

"First tell me who he is," she insisted.

"He's a businessman. Owns a number of businesses, as a matter of fact. One of them is Diablo Ag Con where my mother works."

Great. Just great. His mother, the bitch, whose most familiar expression was a sneer. Who the hell did she think she was, anyway, looking down on other people? And she had to work for this Ballou guy, whoever he was.

"Does he live around here?"

"Jamie, why are you asking all these questions about a man you've never met?"

She could visualize Zane gripping the telephone and scowling. "Well, does he? Answer me and I'll tell you."

"He lives in San Antonio, but he has a house in Copper Ridge. Now, tell me what this is all about?"

She drew circles with her finger in a tiny puddle of milk on the counter. "He called me today and said he wanted to buy this place."

"But that's absurd!"

She could hear the surprised skepticism. "I thought so, too."

"Jamie, at the risk of pissing you off again, that place isn't worth more than a pile of dog shit. Why would a sharp businessman like Gray want to buy it?"

Her sandwich and milk were beginning to roll in her stomach. "I don't know. I thought you might know something I don't."

More silence. "Are you sure you heard him right?"

"For god's sake, Zane. He called me twice."

"Something's screwy here. Why don't I give him a call tomorrow? See what gives."

"No." She hadn't meant to shout. "No, please." Her voice was lower. "I told him not to call again so he probably won't."

"Maybe."

She could almost hear his brain working. "Zane…"

"This is just so out of character for him. Gray's a sharp businessman. People say he could cut himself without a knife. I can't imagine any reason why he'd want a worthless piece of property like you've got sitting out there."

"Me either. Listen, please don't call him. All right?"

He took a long time answering her. "Okay. But if he calls you again, I want you to let me know."

"All right."

"Jamie?" His voice was low and deep now.

"Yes?"

"Today wasn't the end of it. Not by a long shot. I won't let you run away from me again."

She gave a hollow laugh. "Where would I run to? Listen, Zane, I'm the last woman on earth you want to have anything to do with right now. I'm used up. Discarded. And my outlook on life would depress Pollyanna. Do us both a favor and stay away."

"Now, darlin', you know I can't do that." His voice was like a heated caress, like warm syrup sliding over her skin.

Her stomach clenched again, but this time for a different reason. If she closed her eyes, she could feel his tongue again lapping at her pussy, his cock plunging into her to the hilt.

"Zane..."

"I'll be by to see you tomorrow, Jamie. Just to see you're doing okay. You hear me? Oh, and by the way, if you're through looking at that stupid accident report, put it away somewhere. And get Duke to give you what he can for the parts and haul that wreck back out of your yard."

Anger surged through her again. "Damn you."

He chuckled. "Night, darlin'."

Shit!

She slammed the receiver down. The man was infuriating. She had been right. Calling him was a mistake. So why did hearing his voice make her pulse race and her mouth turn dry?

Could she possibly be any more messed up?

She looked around the house. The task of cleaning the living room seemed more daunting than she wanted to think about at the moment. She had a passable bedroom and bath for herself; the tiny downstairs half bath was usable. The kitchen could take as much as a week to do, as bad a shape as it was in. Maybe it was time to dig through the stuff in her father's bedroom.

She'd studiously avoided it since she first walked into the house, unwilling to touch anything that had been a personal possession of his. But maybe if she went through everything, tossed out most of the junk, it would be like exorcising a demon. Maybe the house would seem more like hers.

She stretched and forced herself to walk down the hall to the closed door. She hadn't set foot in this room since she was a child. Most of the time, she'd hidden in hers, coming out to forage for food when he wasn't around. She'd learned at a very young age how to wash her own clothes and braid her hair.

Was it any wonder she'd run away from here as fast as she could? Some days she felt twice as old as her thirty years.

When she opened the door, a wave of musty air hit her. She wrinkled her nose and hurried to raise one of the windows. Even hot air was better than no air.

Standing by the window, she let her eyes roam around the room. The bed was unmade, as expected, the sheets a dingy grey. Dirty clothes were piled on a chair and tossed on the floor. A thick layer of dust covered everything.

Swell. Just what she needed.

Fetching a garbage bag from the kitchen, she began tossing things into it—old clothes, magazines, newspapers, scraps of things. When she'd filled up one bag, she got another. She worked like a woman possessed, as if discarding everything of her father's would free her from some kind of emotional prison. And maybe it would. Maybe this was what she needed to break down the emotional wall she'd lived behind all these years.

An hour later she'd filled five garbage bags, emptied the dresser and nightstand, and picked up everything from the floor. She stripped the bedding from the mattress and threw it on the pile. Tomorrow she'd call Duke and ask him who she could get to haul away the mattress and all the furniture in the room. Then she'd clean the walls and the floor with the strongest disinfectant she could buy. But she could never sleep in this room. Nothing would wash away the memories of the miserable old drunk who'd lived here.

Finally, standing in the middle of the room and looking around, she drew in a deep breath and wiped the sweat from her forehead with her arm. All that was left to go through was the closet. Maybe she could finish tomorrow.

But something pushed at her to get at it tonight. Get it done and over with. Snagging another soda from the fridge, she threw open the closet door and almost gagged at the stench that greeted her. Frank Randall must have stored his really dirty laundry in here.

As before she just pulled things out and stuffed them in garbage bags. She wished she'd thought to get herself a pair of gloves before starting this project. God only knew what kind of diseases were hiding out in the ragged, filthy garments.

By the time she'd emptied the hangers and pulled everything up off the floor she was sure she was ready to vomit. How could anyone live like this? But then she remembered all those years growing up here and her revulsion at the condition of the man who was her father.

She had to pull a straight chair over to reach the things on the shelf. Even then she had to scrabble to pull some of the things forward. A gym bag in the corner was stuck, and she had to tug on it to free it. When it finally came loose, it nearly hit her on the head, and she, and the bag, tumbled to the floor.

I'll have a hell of a bruise on my ass.

She scooted back against the wall and hauled the bag next to her. The zipper had a lock on it, but the fabric was so old and rotted that she was able to pull it apart with her hands. Opening it wide, she peered inside and thought for a moment she was seeing things. Her heart did a little stutter step and cold sweat broke out on her face.

Holy shit!

Inside the bag were bundles of money, some held together with rubber bands, some just stuffed inside in handfuls. The denominations were all fifties and hundreds.

Jamie just stared at it, stunned. Where would Frank Randall get this much money? What could an old drunk possibly do that someone would pay him like this? And, obviously, over a long period of time, judging by the aging process. All this time, just sitting in his closet.

She got up to retrieve her drink, then sat down again and hauled the heavy bag into her lap. Whatever her father had been doing, he'd been into for some years, which answered the question of how he put food on their table, kept a roof over their heads, and bought the necessities of life. She'd never questioned the fact that when she needed money, he always gave her cash. Even a child would not have expected him to have either checks or a credit card.

But where had it all come from? And how much was there?

She finished her drink, got up again and took the gym bag over to the bed to dump its contents onto the soiled mattress. With shaking hands, she began counting the money, putting it in stacks of a thousand. When those stacks multiplied fast, she made piles of ten thousand.

By the time she finished, both her back and her

head ached fiercely. Laid out before her was more than one hundred thousand dollars. Her mind boggled at how much more there had been over the years that her father used for his living expenses and to pay off the mortgage on the property.

Why hadn't the bank thought something amiss here? After all, everyone knew his reputation. Plus, there couldn't be too many people who made mortgage payments in cash. Why didn't that raise a red flag?

Questions tumbled around in her mind like stones in a pail, exacerbating her headache. Now her stomach really did roil. Her father had been doing something illegally all these years. Just remembering him the way he was, a drunk who couldn't be bothered raising his daughter, was bad enough. But the thought of him involved in criminal activities made her physically ill.

She had no idea what to do about this. Asking someone's advice would be the intelligent thing, but the only person she had to ask was Zane. She'd be damned if she'd open up this can of worms with him. That's all she needed.

Finally, she put all the cash back in the bag and hauled it upstairs to her bedroom. Hesitating only a moment, she took ten thousand out. She hated the thought of using tainted money, but she was teetering on the edge of totally broke, so she stifled her conscience and stuffed the cash in her purse. There was a loose board in the back of her closet where she hid things as a child. She pulled it free, stuck the bag behind it and nailed the board back in place. Unless someone took a magnifying glass to it, there wouldn't seem to be anything out of place.

By the time Jamie got into bed, she was exhausted, but sleep was a long time coming for her. She dreamed of a faceless man chasing her, yelling, "Give me back that money."

Chapter Seven

In the morning, Jamie was just as tired as when she'd gone to bed. Getting up took every bit of energy she could find. A shower helped, and by the time she'd put away half a pot of coffee, she was feeling at least functional.

Okay. She had some things to do. Number one was getting an Internet connection. She had some research to do about Diablo County and Amen, Texas. And while she was at it, Grayson Ballou. Not that she connected him with whatever happened to her father, but his sudden appearance needed answers.

Dialup was too frustrating, and she was sure most broadband was unavailable in Amen. But she knew about the Rural Telecommunications Act and she'd seen a dish on the roof of the sheriff's office, so she was pretty sure she could get satellite.

She found the number for Wild Blue in the phone book and had just finished setting the appointment for installation when she heard a car pull up in the driveway. Now who?

"Open up, Jamie." Zane was banging on the screen.

Jamie walked up to the open door. "What do you want?"

His smile disappeared. "What does it look like? I want to come in. Are we going to play this game every time I show up here?"

"I don't know. How often do you plan to show up?"

"I thought we settled things yesterday."

"*You* settled things. I didn't agree to anything. And I won't let you run me out of town because of it."

"Open the damn door, or I'll break it down." He grabbed the outside handle and jerked the frame back and forth.

"All right, all right." She slipped open the lock and headed back to the kitchen. "I guess you'll want a cup of coffee. Sorry I don't have any doughnuts. Isn't that what cops usually go for?"

He grabbed her arm and whirled her around, his fingers like hot bands of steel on her skin. "Where'd you get such a smart mouth? You were always sassy, but now you're hard." His gaze raked over her. "What happened to you, Jamie?"

She shrugged. "Life happened. If you let go of me, I'll pour your coffee."

"Forget the damn coffee. I want to talk to you."

"Sorry." She yanked her arm away and picked up her mug from the counter. "I'm all out of conversation."

Zane moved her so fast the coffee sloshed onto the floor. Before she could protest, she was seated at the old kitchen table with Zane across from her.

"Now, sit there, or I'll handcuff you to the chair."

Indignation burned through her. "Yes, sir, *Sheriff.* Whatever you say, *Sheriff.*"

"And you can park that backtalk somewhere, too." He took off his hat and placed it on the table, running his fingers through his hair. His eyes were like embers of coals, and anger stained his cheeks a dark red. His big hands clenched and unclenched as he fixed his hawk-like stare on her.

"Well? I breathlessly await your pleasure."

He leaned forward. "Oh, that you will. I promise you. But first we have some things to get straight."

"This is your party," she told him. "Let 'er rip."

"Grayson Ballou."

Her eyebrows shot up. "What about him?"

77

"That's what I'd like to know. I can't think of any reason for him to contact you. Or even know you at all. It doesn't make sense, and I don't like things that don't make sense."

"I'm so sorry to hear that." She couldn't keep the sarcasm from her voice. Why did he set her on edge this way? What was it about him that instantly put her on the defensive?

"Can you just can it for a while? Is that too much to ask?" He blew out a breath. "I want you to tell me everything he said to you."

"Please."

Zane frowned. "What?"

"Say please."

"Jesus, Jamie. You are some piece of work. All right. Please."

"See how easy that was?" She sat back in the chair and related every detail of both conversations she could remember.

"He called you twice?"

She nodded. "Yesterday, right after I got back from Duke's and then not too long after you left."

Zane searched her face, as if she were holding some answer back from him. "Like I say, it just doesn't make sense. Jamie, I don't mean to insult you, but we both know this place isn't worth the matches to burn it down."

"I agree. I'm afraid if I clean the house too much, it'll fall down around my ears with all the dirt holding it together. And the land itself would require a significant investment to make it usable even to grow hay."

"Gray doesn't do things without a reason. That's what has me puzzled."

"Do you think we might have a little exchange of information here?"

He raised an eyebrow. "Like what?"

"How about telling me a little more about this

man who's so hot to buy my property?"

Zane leaned back and stretched out his legs. "I'd say the man's in his seventies, although he looks twenty years younger. My mother went to work for one of his companies when my dad was killed."

"Murdered," she interjected. "That's one thing we might find we have in common."

"We'll get back to your conjecture later. But okay, murdered. Shot driving his truck out on the highway."

"Getting killed on the highway seems to be an ordinary event around here," she pointed out.

"I said we'll get back to that. I believe I'll take that coffee after all."

She brought him his coffee and set it on the table, glad of the chance to do something besides sit. "Go on."

"Okay. You can bet my father didn't have any life insurance, and we weren't exactly rolling in dough. But my mother had good skills, and someone told her they needed help in Diablo Ag Con's Amen office."

The name was familiar to Jamie. In Amen almost everything was familiar to everybody. "Agricultural services, right?"

He nodded. "It was just a two person office, serving the ranches around here. The main office is in Copper Ridge."

"So she went to work there."

"Uh huh. Must have been a decent salary because we always made out all right. Maybe better than all right."

"And Ballou? Did he come around at all?"

Zane drew his brows together. "I met him once when my mother took me to the office with her on a Saturday. Said he was just stopping by to check on things and did she need anything."

Jamie drummed her fingers on the table. "So

then what?"

Zane sipped at the hot liquid he was holding. "Damn, Jamie, you make good coffee. You wouldn't like to come by the station and take charge of it, would you?"

"I don't want to come by the station for anything." She swiped at a stray hair impatiently. "Forget the coffee, Zane. Gray Ballou."

"Yeah." He scratched his head. "All I know is Ag Con must make out all right because they've got fancy offices in Copper Ridge. My mother got promoted to manager there a few years ago. Ballou has a fancy estate home on the north side of San Antonio and drives the most expensive SUV I've ever seen." He paused, frowning again.

"And?"

"And I've never heard of him wanting to buy land around here. He shows up in Copper Ridge about once a week, but he has better fish to fry. I want you to let me know the minute you hear from him again, if you do. I've got a funny itch about this that needs scratchin' real bad."

"Maybe he's just looking for cheap land."

Zane shook his head. "If anything was going on with land around here, I'd have heard about it. And if Gray was involved, my mother would know. The thing is..."

"What would he want with this piece of junk, right?" she finished for him.

"Darlin', I don't mean to insult you, but..."

"I'm not your darlin', *Sheriff.* I told you that."

"Yeah, about that." He reached over and took one of her hands in his. His face was taut and golden flecks danced in his dark, dark eyes. It was obvious the subject of Grayson Ballou was off the table for the moment. "Let's talk about yesterday."

She tried to snatch her hand back without success. "There's nothing to talk about. What happened was a mistake. It won't happen again."

He lifted her palm to his mouth and ran his tongue lightly over the center. Lightning shot straight to her cunt, and juice flooded her panties. Damn! This was an impossible situation.

"Look at you, Jamie. Face flushed. Eyes bright with fire. I'll bet your pussy's soaked, too."

Her face heated even more, and she tried once again to pull away. Zane closed his big hand around hers and held firm.

"Yesterday was fantastic and you know it. I didn't want it to happen any more than you did. I'm still mad about the way you left here. But guess what, darlin'. The fire hasn't died at all in twelve years." He leaned across the table, his face serious. "Why do you fight it so much, this thing between us? If I can put the past behind us, why can't you?"

"Let me go." She tugged on her hand with no success. "This isn't what I want."

"Oh, yes, it is," he drawled. "Darlin', it surely is. That's what makes you so mad. But this time, Jamie, I'm going to make you want me as bad as I want you, so there won't be any question about what's going on. Running your ass out of town isn't an option for me any longer. Keeping it here is."

"You planning to hold me here at the point of a gun?"

He chuckled. "Depends on which one you're talking about. I'm always cocked and loaded for you, little hellcat."

Before she realized what was happening, he stood up and lifted her in his arms, just like the day before. The heat of his body burned through her thin shirt, and the hard muscles of his chest were like a wall around her. She was lost and she knew it, even though her pride demanded at least token resistance.

She'd run as fast and as far as she could to keep

this from happening, to keep from being tied to Amen, Texas and this man. Now she was falling into the very trap she'd worked so hard to escape.

Damn it. How could he keep doing this to her? No, how did she keep doing this to herself?

"This time, I know the way to the bedroom." His voice thick with desire, he bent his head and pressed the rough silk of his lips to hers again.

She tried to protest, but when she opened her mouth, there was his tongue again and reason fled. As he climbed the stairs, he kissed her until her senses melted and she forgot about kicking and squirming.

"Today it will be even better," he promised, opening the door to her room with the toe of his boot. "Your body isn't a stranger to me. I know what makes it tick."

In what seemed like seconds, she was stripped naked and laid out on her soft coverlet. When she tried to push herself off the bed, he grinned. "Still feisty are you? Remember what I said about the handcuffs?"

He pulled the set he carried from his belt, deftly threaded them through the headboard and locked them around her wrists. She was stretched out before him, helpless and exposed.

"I could scream, you know," she warned him.

"Why don't you?" A wicked grin played over his lips. "Go ahead. No one will hear you way out here anyway. And I love the sexy sound of your screams."

Truth to tell, she was shocked at how turned on she was by this. The helplessness of her situation only increased the rising desire taking over her body. "Damn you."

He grinned. "Many say I already am." He removed his holster and unbuttoned his shirt. "Bend your knees and spread your legs, darlin'. I want to see that pretty pink cunt."

"Go to hell." But there was little venom in her voice, only a slight tremor that betrayed how turned on she was.

Zane chuckled. "Okay, but other things first." His eyes burned into every inch of her as he finished undressing.

Jamie couldn't hold back a tiny gasp as his hair-roughened chest was exposed and his proud erection sprang free from his groin. Below it, his heavy testicles rested against his thighs. He gripped his cock lightly in one hand and stroked it once from the root to the dark purple tip.

"You want this, don't you, darlin'. Oh, yes, that little cunt of yours loves being filled with my dick, doesn't it? Go ahead, try and deny it. But your body gives you away."

He gripped her ankles and pulled her legs apart, bending them up as he'd ordered her to do. One forearm kept her that way while his fingers lightly traced a path the length of her slit, rubbing the juice she spilled onto her labia and lightly rasping the inner lips.

Suddenly, he stopped and leaned over her. His face was dead serious. "Am I making a mistake, reading the signs wrong? Tell me to stop, Jamie, and we're done here. I give you my word."

She opened her mouth to speak, but nothing came out except a soft, unintelligible pleading sound.

He ran his tongue over her lips. "Last chance, Jamie. Tell me for sure you don't want this and we're finished. I won't force you, darlin'. That's not my style."

Her body was shivering with need, her nipples so hard she thought they would burst, and the muscles in her vaginal sheath flexing with involuntary contractions.

"Don't," she croaked, cursing her traitorous body.

"Don't what, Jamie? Don't do this?"

"Don't...stop."

The heat in his eyes flared even hotter. "I thought so. All right then. Here we go."

His hand was at her pussy again, stroking the outer lips, teasing at her clit, then sliding along the sensitive skin between her vagina and her anus. A streak of electricity shot through her when he pressed the pad of one finger against that tight spot, the lure of the forbidden tempting her. What would it be like to feel him there, that thick cock of his filling every inch of her?

"Ah, Jamie, I knew you'd like this. You're so wet you're dripping." He scooped some of her cream with two fingers and rubbed them lightly against her anus.

When one finger probed gently inside, she couldn't hold back the purr of pleasure. "Oh, God. Yes, do it."

But he removed the finger and slapped her lightly on one cheek of her ass. "In a little while, darlin'. I promise you'll be begging for it."

He knelt between her legs, bent his head, and captured a nipple in his mouth. When he bit down gently, Jamie arched up to him in a convulsive movement. The streak of sensation raced all the way to her womb. Zane suckled and teased, nibbling, pulling with his lips, swirling his tongue around the distended nub.

Jolts of pleasure speared from her nipples to her womb and down to the sensitive walls of her cunt. They set up the familiar fluttering pattern, demanding something to fill that hot, liquid space. Something so big it stretched her to the fullest. Something that would drive the pleasure spikes into her harder and faster. Pushing her toward that release she craved yet holding back until she was ready to scream.

When he'd paid thorough attention to one nipple, he moved to the other, giving it the same treatment. Jamie felt as if a tidal wave was sweeping over her, lifting her body and tossing it about. Every touch of his mouth, every lick of his tongue, lifted her higher and higher on the crest of the wave. She tried to lock her ankles around his shoulders, but they were far too broad. All she succeeded in doing was spreading her legs further apart.

He moved away from her breasts, trailing light kisses down to her navel and stopping momentarily to tease her there with his tongue. Holding her hips firmly in place, he slid lower until his mouth hovered over her aching slit. When he pulled at her clit with his lips, she was sure fire would consume her.

He was merciless, teasing her with tongue and teeth, tormenting her already sensitized nub. She thrashed on the sheets, tossing her heads back and forth, straining again at the handcuffs. Zane's raspy chuckle vibrated through the pulsating walls of her pussy.

When he looked up at her, his lips and chin were wet with her juices. "You taste like sweet candy, darlin'. I could eat you up all day and all night."

"Please," she begged, thrusting her hips at him.

"Oh, I intend to please you." His eyes held a wicked gleam. "When I get through with you, there won't be a puddle left." His voice dropped. "And next time you won't put up so much of a fight."

With that, he bent to his task again, probing her vagina with his tongue, lapping at her tight channel, sucking at the quivering flesh. His tongue was like the flame of a candle, scorching her wherever it touched, heating her blood and driving her to a higher plane of pleasure.

Her manacled hands clenched into fists, nails digging into her palms. She was sure she couldn't stand it one more moment if he didn't give her release. But when it came, it still didn't give her the satisfaction she sought.

As she finally reached the crest and tumbled over it, Zane spread her labia wide, holding her wide open to his gaze, denying her even the feel of his finger inside her greedy, hungry vagina. She bucked and screamed and pleaded as her liquid poured forth and her body shuddered with spasm after spasm.

At last the aftershocks subsided, but her body was far from satisfied. "Fuck me," she begged, willing to do anything just to have that thick cock inside her. "Oh, please, Zane. I want you inside me."

He kissed her opening and lapped the fluid with his tongue, sending shivers through her. "Soon, darlin'. Very soon." He moved to straddle her, holding as much of his weight on his legs as he could. "But turnabout's fair play, don't you think?"

Her heart still bumping erratically, Jamie eyed the hot erection bobbing before her eyes.

"Think you can take this, darlin'? I don't want to hurt you."

Jamie licked her lips. "I-I can take it. I want it, Zane."

His breath hissed through his teeth. "God, you don't know how much I want those sweet lips wrapped around my dick. We'll go real slow. You wiggle your eyebrows any time you need me to stop, okay?"

She nodded her head and opened her mouth, saliva already pooled inside as she imagined his taste.

He took his cock in one hand and inched it slowly passed her lips and her teeth, sliding it over her tongue into the welcoming cavern of her mouth. Her cheeks hollowed as she sucked on it, pulling it deeper and deeper. He was thick and hard, and the veins just beneath the skin pulsed against her tongue.

When the broad head hit the roof of her mouth, her gag reflex kicked in and she bit down involuntarily.

Zane jumped as her teeth sank into him. "Easy, Jamie. Breathe through your nose. It'll ease up in just a minute."

She did as he told her, forcing her throat to relax. Sure enough, in a moment, he was sliding in even further. She had never had a cock this big in her mouth, and her lips were stretched almost beyond their capacity. But it wasn't an unpleasant feeling, and the thing that stood out was how good he tasted.

Fully seated, he held himself at the root and began to move his hips back and forth, working himself in and out with steady strokes. "That's it," he rasped when she caught the rhythm. "Just like that."

Impossibly, his cock swelled even more until Jamie thought it would explode in her mouth. His body tensed in her grip as his climax began to build. His testicles, resting on her chin, drew up and tightened. Then, without warning, he pulled out and moved back.

"What—"

"Next time I'll come in your mouth, darlin'. And in your ass. And maybe all over your body." He struggled for control. "But right now, we're a little short on time, and I can't wait to feel your tight little cunt wrapped around my dick."

His large warm hands settled on the backs of her thighs and pressed them until her knees touched her chest. If she'd felt exposed before, now she was as open to him as she could be, giving him greater access to her body. And greater pleasure. She nearly came when his cock filled every inch of her vaginal sheath, but she held her breath, wanting to ride the rollercoaster with him.

And then he began to move, hands on her knees to keep them far apart, balls slapping against her buttocks. Up the slope he took her, her body already inflamed from his earlier touching and nibbling and licking. She felt like one big fist ready to clench.

And then they exploded together, his thick cock pumping his seed into her, her cunt clutching at him, milking him, her name a hoarse shout in her ears. Her body shattered, splintering into a million pieces, vivid colors swirling against a black void behind her closed eyes.

She thought it would never end—the spasms, the spinning and whirling. Every bit of energy drained from her body, leaving her limp and exhausted. Zane collapsed on top of her, his heart thudding as hard as hers, his breathing rough and irregular.

"See how ready I am for you, little hellcat?"

She nodded, unable to make her mouth form words.

"Now tell me you don't want me," he whispered in an uneven voice. "You were mine then, Jamie, and you're mine now. Think about it, darlin'. The rest is just details."

God, how she hated to admit he was right. What did she do now? This couldn't possibly be love or anything close to it. She was confusing really great sex that tied her in knots with an emotional attraction. And so, she was sure, was he.

Just what she needed, with so much else unresolved between them. There was the money she still hadn't told Zane about. And, of course, the question of how her father really died.

No, this was a lot more than just details, no matter what Zane Cameron thought. They had a lot of barriers to crash through while everything played out. Then maybe she could sort out her emotions and see what she planned to do with the rest of her life. Falling in lust and falling in love were two very different things in her book.

"I can smell that brain burning," he joked, shifting to ease the weight of his big body off hers.

She opened her mouth to answer him when the front door crashed open and a familiar voice yelled up the stairs.

"Hello? Anyone alive in here? Jamie? What the hell is the sheriff's car doing in your driveway?"

Jamie looked at Zane with startled eyes. "Oh, my god, it's Kit."

Chapter Eight

Zane lifted his head and stared at Jamie. "Who the hell is Kit?"

"My best friend. My *only* friend. Get these damn handcuffs off me. Now."

"Okay, okay." Zane rolled off the bed, found the handcuff key, and unlocked her.

She scrambled to her feet and began pulling on her clothes. "My god, I need a shower. So do you. Shit, shit, shit." Frantically, she found her scrunchee and yanked her hair into a messy pony tail. "I'm coming," she yelled and turned to hiss at Zane, "Get dressed. Now. How am I going to fix this? Shit!"

Barefoot, still cursing under her breath, Jamie raced down the stairs. Kit was standing at the foot of them in the hallway, arms folded across her chest, a knowing grin on her face.

They were opposite sides of the same coin. Where Jamie was dark, Kit was light, a sunshine blonde. Jamie's eyes were electric blue, Kit's a flashing emerald green. Where Jamie was lush, full-breasted and wide-hipped, Kit was all angles and planes. But they complemented each other well, and their personalities blended, which was all that mattered.

"Don't say a word," Jamie warned. "Not one word."

Kit made a zipping motion across her lips. "Wouldn't dream of it." She looked over Jamie's shoulder. "Where's the hunk?"

"Jesus, Kit, who said he was a hunk?"

"He'd better be if you're doing the horizontal

tango with him this early in the day."

"What are you doing here, anyway?" Jamie smoothed stray hairs back from her face.

"What a great welcome. 'Hi, Kit. God, I'm glad to see you. You can't believe how happy I am that you took time off work and flew out here to Bumfuck, Egypt to see me through this trying time.'"

Jamie couldn't help herself. She burst out laughing. "I should scold you for using vacation time and wasting your money to come out here, but damn, I'm glad to see you." She linked her arm through Kit's. "Come on in the kitchen. I'll make some fresh coffee. What are you doing here, anyway?"

Kit dropped into a kitchen chair, crossing one slim leg over the other. She pushed her hair behind one ear, a gesture Jamie recognized as the prelude to an interrogation.

"We're not playing Twenty Questions," she told her friend. Then, realizing how harsh it sounded, she hugged Kit and kissed her cheek. "I'm sorry. I'm just all on edge with everything. I am really, really, really glad you're here."

"Wow. Three reallys. You must be in worse shape than I thought." She held Jamie at arm's length and checked her over with a very critical eye. "You look like shit. Oh, wait. You have an unfamiliar glow. Like shit that's just gotten laid. Is that what the sheriff's SUV in the driveway is all about?"

"God, Kit. You think that's the only reason he's here?"

"I surely do hope so." Kit's eyes took on a mischievous twinkle. "Lord knows you need it." Then she eyed Jamie again. "Bad news everywhere else in Amen?"

Jamie shrugged. "No worse than I expected. I wouldn't even be here in this hellhole if it weren't for..." Her voice trailed off. She busied herself, rinsing the carafe and making a fresh pot of coffee.

"That's what I figured." Kit's voice was warm and soothing. "Mama Bear is here to make it all better. Or at least tolerable. You sounded so down on the telephone I just had to come and see if I could cheer you up. Or help you in some way."

I will not cry. I will not cry.

Jamie turned, squeezing back the tears that threatened, so grateful for her friend that, for a moment, she couldn't speak. How had she gotten so lucky to have Kit in her life, the only constant in what seemed like forever?

"You are the best," she said. "You know that?"

"Hey, what are friends for? So, what's going on here that's got you so spooked? What did—"

"Jamie?"

Zane's voice. Both heads turned in his direction as he strode into the kitchen. He looked as well put together as he had when he'd first walked in the front door that morning. His face was set in firm lines, his eyes dead serious. Only the slightly dusky flush at his cheekbones betrayed anything, and Jamie was sure no one would have a clue as to what caused it.

Except, of course, Kit.

She held her breath.

"I checked all the rooms upstairs and the windows. I'd say you're tight as a drum. But you do need better locks on the front and back doors."

Jamie swallowed a hysterical giggle. "Thank you, Sheriff. I appreciate you coming all the way out here to check for me."

Kit snorted. "Just how dumb do the two of you think I am?" She stood up and held out her hand. "Hi, Zane. I'm Kit London. You can't imagine how nice it is to finally meet you."

Zane took her hand, a startled look on his face.

"Don't mind her." Jamie didn't know whether to laugh or cry. "Kit's my self-appointed watch dog and know-it-all."

Kit dropped gracefully back into her chair. "I just wanted the good sheriff here to know you both don't have to hide anything from me." She grinned. "Especially with that guilty look you're both wearing. If you think I believe this man is here to check locks, you really must think I'm dimwitted."

Zane recovered smoothly. "In that case, maybe you can convince your hard-headed friend that she needs to quit running away from things."

"Enough." Jamie banged mugs on the counter. "Zane, don't you have someone to arrest or something?"

When she turned, he was barely a breath away from her, apparently deciding that Kit needed to actually see them come out of the closet. Maybe help him plead his case.

He put his lips close to her ear. "You can't hide your feelings from me, Jamie, so you might as well quit hiding them from yourself. This isn't the end. Not this time. It's just the beginning." He pulled her into his arms and kissed her senseless.

"I give it a ten," Kit chuckled.

Breathless, Jamie pushed at him. "We'll talk later," she hissed.

"You bet we will." He stepped back, picked up his hat from the counter where he'd left it and slapped it on his head. "I want to know the minute you hear another word from Grayson Ballou. Or anyone. Oh, and Jamie?"

"Yes?" She frowned at the sudden change in his voice.

"Forget about that damn truck and report. You're chasing ghosts. You've got better things to do with your time." He nodded at Kit, then he was gone, the screen door slamming behind him.

"Well!" Kit wore a big grin. "Come on, I want all the details. You didn't mention exactly how hunky he was."

"You must have gotten up at the crack of dawn to get here. How *did* you do it, anyway?"

"Flew into San Antonio at an indecent hour, rented a car, and drove here with my trusty MapQuest directions."

"I told you not to worry about me," Jamie reminded her.

"Oh, yeah, like that's gonna happen. Get real. And don't change the subject."

"Ah, yes, the subject."

"And by the way, what was all that other stuff about? Who's this guy Ballou?"

"Nobody worth discussing." Jamie sat down with the filled coffee mugs. "And as far as Zane is concerned..."

Kit leaned forward and touched Jamie's arm. "Honey, you keep all this stuff bottled up inside you, you'll self-destruct. I know you feel like the world's closing in, but maybe you can take one good thing out of it."

"You mean Zane?" Jamie sipped at her coffee and shook her head. "That's complicated."

Kit raised her eyebrows. "How complicated can it be? I don't need a diagram to tell me what you were doing when I got here. And I know I didn't misunderstand the look on your face, or his. So what's wrong?"

Jamie yanked off the scrunchee, smoothed her hair away from her face, and pulled it into a neater pony tail. The glow from the incredible sex was fading, and all the doubts and resentments were welling up again.

She sighed. "Zane used to be known for nailing anything with a pulse. Maybe he still is. And I was the town drunk's daughter who wouldn't do the only thing she was good for—put out."

Kit nodded. "No less than I'd expect of you."

"Anyway. He was four years older than me, working in the feed store and getting into every kind of trouble he could. Then, for some reason, Zane Cameron decided to make me his target. I had a king-sized crush on him, and eventually he wore me down." One corner of her mouth turned up. "Funny thing about that, though. It turned into more than either of us ever expected. I'm not sure which of us was more shocked."

"That happens." Kit stirred sweetener into her coffee, her eyes never leaving Jamie's face. "So what's the story?"

"He wanted me to stay here. Get married, if you can believe that. Even promised to settle down." She snorted. "Like I could trust one thing that tomcat said. I'd be stuck in this place just waiting for him to come home when he felt like it."

"People change," Kit pointed out. "He certainly seems to have filled his part of the bargain. You can't be sheriff if you're still the town hell-raiser."

Jamie fiddled with the bottom of her T-shirt. "Kit, you can't imagine how badly I wanted out of this place. Away from my father. From everything. I was determined Zane wasn't going to tie me down and keep me here."

"So you spit in his face and set off to see the world."

"Yup. That about says it."

Kit was silent for a long moment, studying her friend. "So answer a question for me? Did you love him then and do you love him now?"

"That's two questions, you fink." Jamie shook her head. "Then? What does an eighteen-year-old know about love? I hardly knew how to talk to anyone. You remember."

"And now?" Kit pursued. "I know you. Casual sex isn't a big part of your life, although you suck at choosing relationships."

"Oh, thank you very much." Jamie rubbed her hands over her face, wondering if she had any signs of whisker burn. Despite the fact she was sure he shaved every morning, Zane's beard grew in fast. Although Native Americans usually didn't have much chest or facial hair, Zane had many of the genetic traits of his Irish father.

"Well, it's the truth, you know. But that's not the point. You wouldn't be doing what you're doing with him unless you had some really strong feelings for him."

"How about a really strong need for sex?"

Kit shook her head. "Not you. You'd get new batteries for your personal toy before you'd hop into bed with someone you have that kind of history with unless there was something deep involved."

"He hates me, you know." Jamie's voice was small.

Kit laughed, a full-throated sound. "Oh, yeah? I'd like to get someone to hate *me* that way."

Jamie sighed again, something she seemed to be doing a lot of. "I don't know. I guess I just don't trust him."

"Maybe it's yourself you don't trust." Kit got up and refilled her mug. "And maybe, Jamie Randall, there's a reason why life took the turn it did and you ended up back here in Amen. Think about that."

"I don't know. Right now thinking about it is the last thing I want to do."

"It won't go away, you know," Kit pointed out.

"No, but it'll keep." She stood up and hugged her friend. "Anyway, I am truly glad you're here. You're the one I can always depend on." She stepped back. "Let me make a quick phone call. Then I want to talk to you about something. While you're here, we can put that mega-brain of yours to work."

She took a few minutes to find the number for Wild Blue again and got them to promise installation of high speed satellite Internet the next day. Then she turned back to Kit.

"Now, how would you like to help me solve a puzzle or two?"

Kit cocked her head. "That wouldn't have anything to do with the things our good sheriff was cautioning you about, would it?"

Jamie stuffed her feet into running shoes with no laces and headed for the door. "It has everything to do with it. But now that you're here, I have another pair of eyes and ears."

Kit trailed after her to the driveway. "I have no idea what you're talking about."

So Jamie told her about the visit to the scrap yard, the dents in the old truck that didn't make sense, the incomplete accident report. Grayson Ballou. Everything. Well, not quite everything.

Kit stared at the truck, a puzzled look on her face. "Honey, I have to say, Zane may be right about this. How can you tell one dent from another?"

Jamie pointed out the things that had caught her attention. "And I'll show you the accident report when we go inside."

Kit shoved her hands in the pockets of her perfectly tailored slacks. "If you were asking me about stock performance or a startup company, I'm your expert. But all I know about cars and trucks is you buy them and trade them in. Oh, and I have a really good mechanic."

"Well, *I* know what I'm looking at." She couldn't keep a belligerent tone from creeping into her voice.

"So you think...what? The sheriff deliberately wrote an incomplete accident report?"

Jamie huffed in frustration. "No. Not that. I just think he looked at it the same way everyone else did. The town drunk finally did himself in. Zane said it was raining that night and the curve was especially bad. But Kit, my father took that curve every day of his life, most of them drunk out of his skull. And I've seen enough deliberate accidents to recognize what I'm looking at. Someone wanted to get rid of him. I just can't figure out why."

Kit walked around the truck, frowning. "I don't know, kiddo. This truck looks older than Methuselah and has more dents than a bumper car."

"I'm not letting it go, Kit. I felt like I used to feel when I had a story creeping up on me."

"Just make sure it isn't like the last one," she warned, then, obviously contrite, added, "I'm so sorry, honey. I didn't mean anything by that. Just me and my big mouth."

"It's okay." Jamie chewed on her thumbnail. "You warned me about that story from the beginning. I should have listened to you."

"Tell me about this Grayson Ballou." A change of subject was definitely indicated. "What does he have to do with this, if anything?"

"I have no idea. Maybe nothing. But out of the clear blue sky, when I'd hardly been back here three days, he called and wanted to buy my property."

Kit stared at her, mouth open. "Are you kidding me? I mean, I don't want to insult you, but—"

"It's okay. Zane said exactly those words. And you're both right. This place isn't worth shit. Hell, the house is liable to fall down around our ears, and the land isn't even good for growing hay."

She told Kit everything Zane had told her about Ballou, and when she added that there hadn't been any other big land purchases or the hint of a development in the offing, Kit was even more mystified.

"This just doesn't make sense."

"I know," Jamie agreed. She gave the truck a kick. "All right, let's get out of here. Just give me a few minutes to change. I know you've been riding since you got up, but I want to take you to Copper

Ridge for lunch. Then we'll shop at the big H.E.B. grocery over there. I only have the bare necessities in the house, and I at least want to feed you properly."

With my ill-gotten gains.

Chapter Nine

Amen might not have changed much, but Jamie couldn't say the same for Copper Ridge. A hundred years earlier, the founding fathers of Diablo County had made Amen the county seat. But it was thirty miles from the Interstate and physically unattractive as far as installing technology went.

Then the owner of a huge tract of land died with no heirs, and about five thousand acres of ranchland came on the market. A group of men led by the local banker had enticed some developers to scoop it up, got the court to set the price low enough so they could steal it from the estate, and Copper Ridge was born. Housing developments had sprung up everywhere, the quaint downtown was now a bustling shopping area with stone and glass office buildings, and two decent-sized strip malls had opened on either end of town. The old H.E.B. had moved to one of these malls since Jamie had left.

"We'll find a place to eat here," Jamie said as she drove the length of the mall.

"How about that?" Kit pointed to a fanciful sign that said Heidi's Café.

Jamie frowned. "I don't know if I want to eat in some place owned by someone named Heidi."

"Oh, come on. Be adventurous. This will be new for both of us."

The inside of the restaurant was as cute as its name. Wicker chairs painted blue and yellow were pulled up to yellow tables, and whimsical scenes right out of Old West tales were painted on the wall. Large cactus plants bloomed in terra cotta pots. And the place was jammed.

"You'd never have found a place like this in Diablo County when I lived here," Jamie griped.

"It must be good. There isn't a seat available anywhere." Kit scanned the room.

"Come on. Let's go somewhere else." Jamie grabbed Kit's hand and tried to tug her toward the door.

"Uh uh." Kit pulled back. "I want to eat here. I have to find out what the big draw is. Look. There's a table opening up right now"

Before Jamie could protest, Kit had corralled the hostess and they were seated in a corner, partially shielded by one of the big cacti.

"Now. Isn't this nice?" Kit opened the oversized menu and pretended to study it.

Jamie was about to open hers when she sensed someone standing beside her. Looking up, she wished she could disappear into the planter.

"Hello, Jamie." Anita Cameron's voice could have chilled iced tea by itself. "I heard you were back."

"Yes. I am." She couldn't make any other words come out of her mouth.

Anita's eyes flicked toward Kit momentarily, then dismissed her as apparently of no consequence. "Are you planning on staying long?"

Jamie took a moment to look the woman over carefully. Cool as always, light bronze complexion smooth and free and impeccably made up, dark hair showing only a little grey swept back in a French braid. She was meticulously dressed in what Jamie knew was a very expensive silk pantsuit, with discreet diamond studs in her ears and a diamond and turquoise bracelet set in delicate gold. Working for Gray Ballou obviously paid very well.

"I don't mean to be rude, Anita, but I really think that's my business, not yours."

Anita seemed to consider her words. "Stay away from my son."

Jamie opened her mouth to respond, but Anita had already turned away. Both women eyeballed her as she moved gracefully across the room to a table where two men waited for her.

Kit finally broke the stunned silence. "Well. Wasn't that special?"

Jamie picked up her water glass and drained it. Her throat was suddenly dryer than the desert. "She's never been the president of my fan club."

Kit quirked an eyebrow. "I take it she wasn't happy when you and Zane had your little fling that time."

"Hah!" Jamie waved for the waitress to refill her glass. "That's an understatement. As far as she was concerned, drunken Frank Randall's daughter wasn't fit to walk on then same street as her wildass son. And she made no bones about it."

"Oh, Jamie, honey. I am so sorry."

Jamie tucked her hair behind her ears. "No. Do not feel sorry for me. On a scale of one to ten, Anita Cameron only rated a three among the people who made me feel like trash. Now she's got a fancy job, making a ton of money, and as far as I'm concerned she still wouldn't wipe her feet on me. I'll bet she celebrated when my big scandal broke."

Kit was still watching the table against the far wall. "Doesn't this seem like a strange place for men to eat? I don't see too many of them in here?"

Jamie shrugged. "I'm sure they have their reasons."

"Jamie." She reached across and tapped her friend's forehead. "Hello. Are you in there?"

Jamie blinked. "What?"

"The other Jamie Randall would glom onto that fact and her brain would start whirling. Suspicious. Fishy. Something going on."

"Oh, yeah? Well, that Jamie's learned her lesson. Two men having lunch with a woman. A business lunch. Maybe she works out here, and that's why they picked this place." She opened her menu again. "Anyway, I want to stay as far away from Anita Cameron as I can."

"Would it pique your interest to know one of those men is doing his best to avoid looking at you?"

"No." She nearly shouted the word, then swallowed and lowered her voice. "No, it would not interest me in the least. I have my own projects to work on, which will take all my attention. Especially since you don't seem too terribly inclined to help."

"Fine." Kit rattled her menu. "I think you're crazy. For not being curious and for fixating on that stupid accident. But I'll help you, all right?" She looked around for the waitress. "Let's order. I'm starved."

****

Manny Alvarado had to force himself not to keep glancing across the restaurant. Of all the damned luck for that female to be having lunch here. And for Anita Cameron to approach her. Ballou would be furious.

"Keep a low profile," he'd said, very emphatically. "Don't make her suspicious of anything."

Why didn't the damn woman just sell the lousy piece of land and get her ass out of town? Life would be so much simpler for everyone. If this thing fell apart, Gray stood to lose an enormous chunk of his income, and that would make him very unhappy. And when Gray was unhappy, Manny was the one who suffered.

He rose as Anita reached their table and pulled out her chair.

"Thank you, Manny. Always the gentleman, I see." Her voice was as chilly as her personality, no matter how pleasant she tried to make it. Manny never liked being around her, but then, she was Gray's problem, not his.

"It is easy for such a beautiful lady," he murmured.

"Cut out the crap." She opened her menu. "We're past the point of unnecessary compliments, don't you think?"

Certainly for you, bitch.

"I saw you in conversation with Jamie Randall," he said.

Anita flicked her fingertips in the air. "Hardly conversation with that one. Jamie Randall is a piece of trash I thought we were rid of. Too bad she had to show up right now."

"What did she have to say?" Manny persisted.

"Not much. Before she left town years ago, my son had a fling with her." She grimaced. "Shows you what poor taste he had then. I just wanted to make sure she doesn't think she can start something up again. In addition to Gray's agenda, I have plans for Zane."

Manny's eyebrows rose. "Other than being sheriff?"

She gave him a wintry smile. "Much more than that, Manny. I'm going to introduce him to the world of politics far beyond this county. And Gray's going to help me."

So. Grayson Ballou had more than one reason to chase Jamie Randall out of town.

"Surely she doesn't plan to stay around here," Manny went on after the waitress had taken their orders.

Anita lifted her shoulders in a delicate shrug. "I know she's involved in some scandal with her so-called career, so she probably has no place else to go at the moment. Which presents quite a problem." She gave both men a wintry smile. "But not one I can't handle, I assure you. All I need is a little more time."

"Which we may not have," the other man pointed out to her.

"No one knows that better than I," she snapped. "But I'd rather do it my way than yours."

Manny shook his head. "If she'd just sell, she'd have money and could go anywhere she wanted to."

Anita's eyes narrowed. "If Gray wants her to sell, he'll have to come up with a plausible story. The last thing we need is for that little snoop to go nosing around."

****

"Looks like they're in heavy conversation," Kit commented.

"If it's about me, you can bet it's nothing good." Jamie stabbed at a piece of avocado. "Like her precious son is the prize of the earth, anyway."

Kit put her fork down. "Jamie. Honey. It's time to put down some of that baggage you keep carrying around with you. Zane Cameron being the biggest suitcase of all. You've got to face your feelings about him once and for all."

"My feelings. Well." Jamie picked up her glass of wine and took a sip. "Well, I *feel* like an idiot because I keep letting him pull me into bed. I *feel* stupid because I have no common sense where he's concerned. And I *feel* as if I'm caught in a spin cycle that won't ever stop. How's that for my feelings?"

"Pretty explicit and full of shit. This is me. Mama Bear. Remember?" She broke off a piece of roll and nibbled thoughtfully. "Tell me you're not in love with him, Jamie. That you haven't been for the past twelve years. Maybe longer. Go ahead. Your lie-o-meter will start flashing."

Jamie made a face. "I don't have the luxury of falling in love with him. I hate this damn town, and his life is here. His mother detests me. And I want out of here as fast as I can. I want to push for more details on my father's accident, and he's following up on it is all. So where's the happy ending?"

"Come on. Is this the same woman who looked her boss in the eye when he fired her and told him to go fuck himself? The same woman who sat in a van with no air-conditioning in South Florida all night to follow a tip on a story?" She picked up her fork again and speared a tomato. "We make our own happy endings, cookie. First you just have to admit you want one."

Jamie sighed. "Maybe I just figure I don't deserve one."

Kit smacked her hand playfully. "Enough of that. Let's eat, finish our shopping, and go home. I'll help you finish cleaning that junk pile you're living in. If you do it yourself, you won't have to worry about your future. You'll be spending it with a scrub bucket."

"I just wish I had some idea what those idiots at that table are discussing. That itch on my back tells me it's about me, for sure."

Kit chewed slowly, a pensive expression on her face. "Well, you can't ask the hunky sheriff about his mother, and we have no idea who the other men are." Her face brightened. "Want to follow them when they leave here?"

Jamie gave an emphatic shake of her head. "No, no, and no. I'm going to close my eyes and hope they go away."

"Yeah, right. Like that's going to work. All right. Let's finish up here. When we get home, we can brainstorm while we're shoveling grime."

Chapter Ten

But when they got home, an unpleasant surprise waited for them. Someone had been in the house and destroyed what was left of the worn, tattered furniture. No room had been left untouched. Furniture was over turned, cushions ripped apart, and the stuffing scattered like crazy dust bunnies. Lamps were broken. Even her dishes and coffee pot were smashed on the kitchen floor. The whole place looked as if King Kong had a raging fit in it.

Jamie stood there, shaking, as much from shock as from anger. Her heart beat against her ribs like a jackhammer, and her throat closed up like a trap door. She'd seen devastation like this but always as part of a story. Never when it was so personal. So close to her. There wasn't even a chair left to sit on. She wanted to sit down on the floor and bawl like a baby. How much more could she take?

The money.

While Kit stood in the middle of the living room staring at the mess, Jamie grabbed a screwdriver from the kitchen junk drawer and raced upstairs. Her clothes had been tossed out of her closet, but the board behind which the money was hidden was untouched. Untouched. Not even scratch marks.

If whoever it was had looked here, they hadn't seen anything to make them look further. Just to be on the safe side, however, she used the screwdriver to pry the board loose and there it was. The greasy, grimy gym bag. Still as she'd left it yesterday. She pulled it out and opened it, completely forgetting Kit until she heard the gasp behind her.

"Jesus, Jamie. I thought you were broke. Where'd you get all that cash?"

Jamie couldn't make her mouth work. She just sat on the floor holding the money and staring up at Kit.

"Come on, girl." Kit dropped to her knees. "My god, what a lot of bucks. Did you rob a bank?"

Jamie finally found her voice. "You can't tell anyone about this, Kit. Swear it to me, okay?"

Kit held out her hands, palms up. "Who would I tell? The sheriff?"

"Oh, lord, no. Please, Kit. Swear to me." She hugged the dirty bag to her chest.

"Okay, okay. My lips are sealed. Now give."

Jamie told her the story of cleaning her father's bedroom and finding the money in the closet, then hiding it in her own room.

"A good thing," Kit told her. "Otherwise it would be gone for sure." She frowned. "Where do you think he got all this money, anyway?"

"I have no idea." She waved a hand around. "Look at the way he lived. And this is after I've been cleaning for two days."

Kit nibbled on her lower lip. "There's really something funny about all this."

Jamie snorted. "No kidding. Tell me something I don't know."

"Maybe you're not so far off about your father's death, either. Whatever he was getting paid for, you can bet it wasn't legal. He might have done something to piss someone off."

"Not surprising." Jamie stuffed the bag back in the hidey hole. "He could do that even when he was minding his own business."

Kit reached out and put a hand on Jamie's arm before she pushed the board back in place. "Wait. Before you do that."

"What? I need to keep this hidden."

"Look at this place. You can't stay here now. Not with all this damage. We need to go to a motel, and you're going to need some money."

Jamie's face heated, and she knew her skin was flushed an embarrassing red. "I, um, already took some out of here."

"You did? How much?"

Jamie dropped her voice. "Ten thousand."

"Holy shit! Well, all right. But if we're leaving here, you can't just leave the money."

Jamie shook her head. She could almost hear the wheels in Kit's brain turning. "We're not going anywhere. Period."

"For god's sake. Be reasonable." Kit jumped to her feet and began pacing. "You don't even have a bed to sleep in. For either of us."

Jamie's jaw set in a stubborn line. "I'm not leaving. Someone wants me out of here, and they aren't getting their wish. And besides, Wild Blue is coming to install my Internet connection tomorrow."

Kit stared at her, speechless, then burst out laughing so hard she had to sit down on the floor, holding her sides while tears rolled down her cheeks. "You are the end of it all, Baby Bear. Your house is a shambles, you don't have a single stick of furniture left, and you're worried about your Internet connection."

Laughter bubble up inside her at the silliness of the situation. It was the first good laugh she'd had in months. "I know, I know. But I'm staying and that's that."

"Speaking of your computer, I'm guessing they didn't get it if you're so worried about Internet service."

"No. It's in my car. Oh, my god." She jumped up. "I almost forgot. The groceries. We left them in the car."

"I'll get the groceries. You call the sexy sheriff.

No, don't argue. You're a citizen of his county, and you've had a vicious break-in. If you don't call him, I will."

While Kit stashed food in the cupboards and the fridge, Jamie reluctantly made the call to Zane. She waited for him, still in a state of shock, fighting the tears that threatened to burst forth. Fifteen minutes later, he skidded into the driveway so fast gravel spewed everywhere. He was almost running when he hit the porch and slammed open the door. His eyes took in the scene, and a look of rage spread across his face.

"The asshole who did this better hope someone restrains me when I get hold of him." He clenched and unclenched his fists. "Jesus, Jamie. It's a good thing you weren't here."

"I can't even make coffee." She tried to keep her voice even and controlled, but inside she was still shaking. "They even broke the coffee pot."

Zane walked slowly through the house, making careful notes in a small notebook as he did. Jamie let him go upstairs by himself. She didn't think she could look at the destruction in her bedroom one more time. When he came downstairs, he went out to his car, returned with a digital camera, and did his tour all over again.

She sat on the bottom step, drinking a cold soda and trying to hold herself together. All she could think about was Zane in her bed that morning and the seemingly unbreakable sexual thread that held them together.

At the moment he was striding through her destroyed house, and she felt as if he were walking through the ruins of her life. She looked at Kit, who was doing her own visual survey of the house. Kit, who jumped on a plane without a second thought because she was sure Jamie was finally coming unglued. One look and she'd be damn sure of it.

The hits just kept on coming. When would her luck ever start to turn? Hadn't she paid enough for her stupidity? She'd lost nearly every dime she had as well as her condo in the law suit. Selling her furniture to give herself some cash, she'd left town with her clothes, her car, and her laptop. Now even her clothes were tainted. She was mortified that Zane and Kit should see her in this broken down condition, sure she'd have a tug of war to keep control over things.

When Zane finished, he crouched beside her and took one of her small hands in his larger one. "This wasn't just kids making mischief," he told her, concern in his eyes. "Someone was looking for something specific. And they wanted to send you a message while they did it." The look in his eyes hardened. "I don't suppose you'd have any idea what that is, would you?"

Jamie turned her head away, sure the guilt would show on her face, or her *liar* sign would light up and flash. "No, I don't."

"Are you sure?" he probed.

"Are you calling me a liar?' she challenged. "Gee, thanks a lot, asshole."

"Jamie—"

"Just do what you have to and let me be, okay?"

He gripped her chin in his other hand, forcing her to look at him. "I understand your hostility. I'd feel the same way. But I'm just doing my job here. I'll make out a report on this and start asking around. And I'm telling you as I stand here, you can't stay here. It isn't safe."

"I told her the same thing." Kit tapped her foot. "I'm trying to get her to go to a motel with me, but she won't budge."

"I'm not leaving my house." Jamie wanted to smack someone. Tears burned at the back of her throat. "Everything else is gone. This is all I have left."

Zane forced her to look at him. "Darlin', someone wants to do you some serious damage. Don't put yourself in harm's way."

"I'm not leaving," she repeated stubbornly and stood up. "I'll sleep on the floor if I have to. And I'm not your darlin', damn you."

His face tightened and irritation flashed in his eyes, but he didn't bite back at her. He and Kit did their best to argue with her, but Jamie refused to listen. This was the last place she had on earth and she might hate it, but no one was chasing her out of it.

"Fine." Zane threw up his hands. "I can see it's no use arguing with you."

"If you plan on staying, we need to get this mess cleaned up." Kit looked around at the devastation. "I think it will take backs stronger than ours."

"I can get that handled," Zane said, punching a number into his phone.

"And we need furniture," Kit said. "Is there any place in this dust bowl to buy any?"

"Palmer's on Main Street," Jamie told her. "But..."

"Palmer's on Main Street. It sounds like a line from a bad comedy routine. Will they deliver?"

Zane snapped his phone shut. "If they won't, I can get my truck and someone to help me. You don't need to fill up the house."

"I don't intend to. It's not like I'm putting down roots or anything."

Zane grinned at her. "Of course not. You have a number of other places to go, right?"

"Damn it." She curled her hands into fists. "I don't even know what's going to happen tomorrow anymore. Right now, the first thing I need is a table to eat at and a bed to sleep in."

"Whatever you say, darlin'." His face sobered.

"Have you got that kind of money right now?"

She stuck out her jaw. "You mean, since I'm not gainfully employed?"

"I only meant—"

"I'm not a charity case yet, *Sheriff.*" *Why did she let him get to her like that?*

Zane took off his hat, raked his fingers through his hair, and put the hat back on. "God, I hate it when you do that."

"Do what?" She had to hang on to her anger, or she'd fall apart completely.

"Children, children," Kit broke in. "Play nice. Jamie, I've got it covered. I'm not hurting for cash and I have a credit card with an ungodly spending limit. You can pay me back when you're able to."

"Kit, I can't—"

"Shut up. It's settled. Like you said, you don't need to fill up the house today."

"I...thank you." She rubbed her face with the heels of her hands.

Zane cleared his throat. "Just a word of warning. You can probably expect the whole town to be gossiping about this shopping expedition. No one expected you to come back here and actually live."

Jamie grunted. "Like I give a shit what anyone thinks. And who says I'm living here? So screw them."

She saw a muscle jump in his cheek.

"You better clean up your language, little girl, or I'll have to wash your mouth out with soap," he told her. "Life in the big city didn't do you much good, did it?"

"I just need a place to regroup," she insisted. "That's all."

"Regroup, huh? Is that what you're calling it?" His strong hand cupped her chin, forcing her to meet his gaze. "I'd say you and I are doing a lot more than that, Jamie." He dropped his hand. "Think about it."

"Ahem." Kit stepped between them. "About cleaning up this mess and hauling away the trash?"

Zane just shook his head. "Duke's coming with his big truck, and he's bringing the two high school kids who help him sort trash. They'll haul all this stuff out of here pretty fast." He looked over at Jamie. "Is there anything you'd like to keep?"

"No." She shook her head vehemently. She wished he'd move back a little. His presence was overwhelming her, and she needed space. This whole thing with Zane was getting too complicated. "Nothing. I don't even want my clothes since someone's grubby hands have touched them."

"Jamie," Kit began.

"No." She stood up and glared at both of them. "I'll figure something out. I couldn't stand to put anything on my body that some grubby stranger had pawed through. Forget it."

Kit looked at Zane and just shrugged.

Zane waited with them until Duke and the two boys arrived, making terse phone calls in the meantime and barking orders. As soon as they walked in, he gave them a rough picture of what was going on and led them upstairs.

Kit drew Jamie aside while Zane was out of the room. "You know you can't start throwing that money around, idiot," she warned. "If that's what they were looking for, they'll come after you. Besides, it would only make Zane suspicious."

Jamie swallowed against the tightness in her throat. "I know, I know. I just hate for you to have to do this."

"No problem. I've got it all figured out." She grinned. "You can just give the cash to me. No one will ever know."

Jamie gave a hiccupping laugh. "Okay. I'll slip it to you in the dark where no one can see us. Maybe we'll wear disguises."

Kit's laugh rolled out with the same boisterous sound as before. "I have to hand it to you, Baby Bear. You are the queen of absurdity. Someone's practically destroyed your house and maybe even wants you dead, and instead of heading for the hills, we're going out to buy furniture." She kissed Jamie's cheek. "You are definitely one of a kind."

Jamie dug out a faint smile. "I'm glad I can provide so much amusement."

Zane was back beside her, this time barely a whisker away, his big warm hands on her shoulders. His face was etched with worry lines. "One more time, darlin'. I don't think you should stay here. It isn't safe."

"I already told you—"

"I know, I know." He brushed her cheek with his knuckles, seemingly oblivious to Kit's presence.

Jamie jerked her head away. "Zane—"

"In that case, I'll be staying here, too."

Her jaw dropped. "What? You can't! I refuse to let you."

"Too bad." He quirked an eyebrow. "Just watch me."

"My god." She waved her hands at him in frustration. "That's all we need. What will people think? You can't stay here with the town pariah. You're the sheriff."

He chuckled. "Worried about my reputation?"

"Your reputation? That's bad enough. What about mine? And your mother. She'll have a fit."

He captured her head between his palms and placed a very gentle kiss on her lips. "I can weather the storm. Don't worry. And my mother doesn't make decisions for me. It's been a long time since I turned twenty-one."

"But Kit—"

"Is ignoring everything," her friend broke in.

"I'll take care of the locks, too." Zane started

toward the door, then called over his shoulder, "By the way, make sure the bed you buy is nice and big. I take up a lot of room."

Jamie stamped her foot. "Damn you, Zane Cameron."

But she knew—and he did, too—that her reaction was nothing more than habit. They'd crossed some kind of a bridge and the going would be unsteady, but it was laid and there was no going back. How had she let this happen?

"I told you to watch that language." He grinned, then his face sobered. "And don't try to get your friend involved in any of your crazy theories about Frank's accident. Let Duke haul that piece of crap truck back to his yard and pay you for the parts."

She balled her hands into fists and planted them on her hips. "You may want to discount the whole thing but don't expect me to. My father may have been drunk out of his mind, but so what? He was like that every single night of his life and still made that curve. And those dents didn't come from tumbling sideways." She was infuriated. "Some damn sheriff you are if you don't see a connection between that and what happened here today."

He was in front of her before she could draw her next breath, his anger as hot as hers. "I'm telling you. Don't start imagining things. Leave it alone. Right now you've got enough trouble without conjuring up more."

"*You* leave *me* alone, then," she spat and turned away from him.

"Not much chance of that." She heard his booted feet as he moved away. "See you tonight."

She picked up a plastic cup and threw it at him. "You go to hell."

"Probably will," he called back.

Duke, who had just come downstairs, was doing his best to swallow a grin. The teenagers behind him

116

would have gawked all day if he hadn't told them to get moving. "I'll just let the tail down on the truck, and we'll get at it," he told Jamie.

She leaned her elbows on the counter and dropped her head into her hands. "I'm going to kill him."

"No, you're not." Kit squeezed her arm. "You're going to learn to appreciate him."

"In a pig's eye." But even she knew they were just words, and so did Kit.

"Jamie, the man cares about you. It's as plain as the headline on a newspaper. And aside from everything else, he's the investigating officer on your break-in and seems to be going out of his way to help you here. Cut him some slack."

Jamie blew out a breath. "I don't know. Maybe. I'll see. But he's sure not sleeping in my bed tonight."

"Uh huh." Kit urged her toward the door. "Come on. Pity party's over. Let's go shopping."

Chapter Eleven

Manny Alvarado took out a handkerchief, wiped the sweat from his forehead, and settled his cell phone more comfortably against his ear. This whole thing was turning out to be a major clusterfuck. He'd made himself as inconspicuous as possible, watching Jamie and her friend do their thing at Palmer's then trundle off to Barbara's Boutique.

At the moment, hidden across the road and using his binoculars, he watched Duke and two teenagers carrying the last of the trash out of the house and dump it into the big scrap truck.

"Mess things up a little, that's all they were supposed to do." Gray's voice was sharper than a kitchen knife. "Now you tell me they wrecked the house, and she's out buying new furniture. How the hell is that supposed to get her out of town?"

Manny patted his face with the damp square of white linen. "I guess they got a little carried away."

"Understatement, Manny. Big understatement. What they did was make her dig in her heels. If she's buying new furniture, she won't be leaving town any time soon."

"I'm sorry, *padrone*. I'll make sure they understand what a huge mistake this was."

There was silence for a moment. "I'm guessing they didn't find any money, either."

"*Nada*. And like I said, they really took the place apart."

"So. No money and they definitely put the Randall woman on notice." Ballou grunted. "Just what I need. All right." His sigh was loudly audible.

118

"Get rid of them."

A sour taste filled Manny's throat. "Excuse me?"

"You heard me. We have a deadline coming up, and you know what that means. Miss it and the whole thing falls apart. I don't intend to lose that kind of cash pipeline. We can't afford to have anyone around to screw things up. Dealing with the Randall woman is bad enough."

"But—"

"I don't care how you do it. Just do it. And don't leave anything around for someone to find. Do you understand me?"

"Of course, *padrone.*"

This thing was getting out of hand. Damn that stupid old drunk, anyway. If not for him, none of this would be happening.

Manny sat with his eyes closed for a moment. When Grayson Ballou's voice took on that tone, there was no choice except to do as he asked. No, demanded. But Manny didn't have the stomach for the killing himself. That meant another call to the only person he ever trusted in situations like this.

Manny punched a number into his cell phone, then loosened his tie and collar. He had the distinct feeling a noose was tightening around his neck.

****

The shopping trip had proved to be an exhausting experience. Sally Palmer had come out to handle things herself, apparently unwilling to believe what her salespeople ran into the back to tell her. Jamie Randall wanting to buy a load of furniture in her store. For that rat trap of a house her father left her.

By the time Kit and Jamie had finished making their selections, it looked like everyone in Amen who wasn't working was window shopping at Palmer's.

"Bloodthirsty ghouls," Kit commented as they sipped cokes in Jamie's car in the parking lot of the

Gas 'n Go.

Jamie scowled. "I'm sure they wondered where I even got enough cash to pay for this. And watching you hand over your credit card, they're sure of it. I might as well have a sign on my back that says *Charity Case*."

Kit sucked on her straw noisily. "Since when did the opinion of people like that matter to you?"

Since I grew up here with people not even wanting to spit on me.

"Anyway," Kit went on, "you're probably the most exciting thing that's happened in this town in years."

Jamie shrugged.

Kit stared at her. "Wait a minute. You're actually thinking about staying here, aren't you?"

"Where the fuck else would I go?" Jamie sucked up the rest of her drink, crushed the cup, and stuffed into the car's litter bag. "It's not like I have a big choice."

"Honey, sooner or later, this mess will get cleared up and you can have your life back."

Jamie made a face. "Like I'd even spit in the faces of those assholes who kicked me to the curb."

"Oh, wait." Kit snapped her fingers. "I get it. The sexy sheriff. He's what's keeping you here."

"Puhleeze."

"At least I know why you won't sell. Won't go stay at a motel. Why you're buying all this new furniture. You did the deed with him, sweetie. You can't get away from it."

"I told you." Jamie shredded the napkin she was holding. "This is where I live now. A bunch of shitheads saw to that."

"And the sexy sheriff is going to paddle your ass if you don't clean up your newly-acquired potty mouth." Her eyes danced with mischief. "Or maybe that's what you're angling for."

Jamie tossed the napkin shreds in the litter bag. "Let's get out of here."

"I'm just telling you," Kit said. "You can't fool old Kit. I see what this is about."

Jamie burned rubber as she pulled out of the lot. "What I'm doing is taking a stand. Putting people on notice that they can't push me around. I'm not about to cave in to their tactics, whoever 'they' are. They can turn up their noses at me all they want. Jamie Randall isn't going anywhere, sheriff or no sheriff."

"Good attitude. Let them see you doing it well dressed, too. Come on. We're not done shopping."

She tromped on the accelerator, and they flew down the street, narrowly missing a van pulling out of a parking space.

They managed to take care of business at Barbara's Boutique, despite the arrival of the rubberneckers who seemed determined to follow them all over town. Jamie picked out enough clothing to carry her over until she and Kit could find someplace anonymous and out of sight to shop. And where she could use some of her cash.

By late afternoon they were in Jamie's kitchen, waiting for the truck from Palmer's and admiring their handiwork. With all the debris removed, they'd scrubbed the floor in the living and dining rooms. Kit cleaned the woodwork while Jamie washed the windows.

"Not too bad," Kit commented. "I wish we had time to slap a coat of paint on the walls, but that can come later."

"Forget it." She glared at Kit. "I'll take care of it. You have a life to get back to."

Kit laughed. "I'm on vacation, didn't you hear me? And no way am I going home and leaving you in the middle of this mess. Someone wants something, and they don't care what they have to do to get it."

Jamie leaned against the counter and brushed

stray hair off her forehead. "I just wish Zane would take me more seriously. He still doesn't see anything wrong with my father's death. Just another rollover by another old drunk."

"But you don't believe that."

Jamie shook her head. "Not for a minute. I covered enough accidents to know what a vehicle looks like in that kind of situation. And I don't care how many dents there are in that old truck. The right ones aren't there."

Kit shrugged. "Maybe Zane just thinks you're in denial."

"About what? I have no illusions about my father. I'd be the first one to say that's what happened if I didn't see signs that told me otherwise."

Kit pulled a cold soda from the fridge and popped the top. "What if you got someone else to take a look?"

Jamie frowned. "Like who? I can't exactly call in another cop, can I?"

"No, but I know someone we *can* ask a favor of. Remember that insurance investigator I used to date?"

Jamie burst out laughing. "Mickey the Moustache?"

"You are too unkind," Kit chided. "So what if he thought more of his moustache than he did of me. At least he was good for a night out now and then."

"All right, all right. What about him?"

"His big thing is investigating auto accidents. Have you still got your digital camera?"

"Yes, I do. Why?"

"Because we're going to take pictures of that decrepit old truck, and tomorrow, when you get your Internet set up, we'll send them to Mickey and get his opinion." She dug in her purse and pulled out her cell phone. "In fact, I'm calling him this minute to set it up." She grinned. "But if it costs me another date with him, you'll have to come to New York and go with me."

The heat of the day was finally starting to fade by the time the furniture was delivered and put in place. Jamie and Kit were sitting on two new patio chairs in back, sharing the bottle of wine they'd bought, when they heard the crunch of tires in the driveway.

"That'll be the sheriff," Jamie said. "Come to do his good deeds."

"Honey, he can do any kind of deeds he wants to with me," Kit teased.

A door slammed, then booted footsteps echoed through the house and the back door creaked on its hinges.

"God damn it, Jamie." Zane's voice was harsh and angry.

"And good evening to you, too, Sheriff," Jamie said sweetly. "Care for a glass of wine?"

"You left the front door unlocked and wide open." His voice was impatient and accusing. "Whoever tossed your house could just walk right back in."

Jamie glared at him. "I'd say they did about all the damage they could, wouldn't you? I don't think they're in the business of looking for new furniture to destroy. They've already done what they came to do."

He clamped his hands on her arms and lifted her from her chair so abruptly wine sloshed over the rim of her glass. "If you aren't concerned for your safety, at least I am. What if they didn't find what they were looking for and decide to come back?"

She refused to let him see that his words frightened her. "Protecting your piece of ass, Sheriff?"

For a moment, she thought he might shake her

like a doll, the anger in his eyes burned like a living flame. Instead, he captured her mouth in a kiss so hot it burned straight through to the soles of her feet. When he lifted his head and set her down on her feet, she could hardly breathe. And the anger had been replaced by something a lot different.

"You might have been right about that a couple of days ago, darlin', but let's get this straight. You are far more than a piece of ass to me now. And yes, I'm protecting what's mine, even if you don't acknowledge our situation yet."

For once, Jamie couldn't think of a smart remark. The kiss hadn't been about sex; there was too much emotion in it. She wasn't sure she knew how to handle it, but Zane was right. Despite the barriers she kept trying to throw up, somewhere along the way they'd crossed a line. It scared her to think she'd reached a point where there was no going back. She was nowhere near ready for this.

Zane turned his glare on Kit. "Jamie's too stubborn and pissed off to take good advice, but I had you figured for someone with more sense."

Kit had the good grace to blush. "You're right and I apologize. It won't happen again."

"Did you just drop by to chew me out?" Jamie asked.

"Actually, smart mouth, I brought dinner for us. Barbecue from The Branding Iron."

Jamie couldn't help the smile that spread over her face. The food at The Branding Iron was one of her few pleasant memories of Amen. "Well. Maybe I'll have to be nice to you after all," she teased, suddenly relaxing.

Zane bent his head and put his lips to her ear. "You'll be amazed at how nice you're going to be to me a little later on."

"I heard that," Kit laughed. "I'll be sure to wear my earplugs to bed tonight."

They were only partially finished with their meal when the cell phone on Zane's belt rang. As he listened to the voice on the other end his face hardened.

"All right. Give me about thirty minutes to get there. String tape around the scene and call in a couple of off duty guys to keep folks away if you have to." He snapped the phone shut. "I have to go. I'm sorry."

"Sheriff business?" Jamie asked.

"I'd say so. Two dead bodies on the other side of Red Canyon Ranch." He shoved back his chair. "Jamie, have you got an extra key to this place?"

She was confused by the sudden change in her feelings for him. Her willingness to give him open access to her house, knowing why he wanted it. The sudden tumbling of her heart when she looked at him. Was it really possible they could bury the past and move forward?

"Well?" he prompted.

Jamie nodded. "In the drawer next to the sink. It opens the deadbolt, too."

"We need to change that tomorrow." Zane fished the key out and stuck it in his pocket. "Lock every door, ladies, and don't open them for anyone. No matter what. I'll let myself in when I get back."

He leaned down and placed a hard kiss on Jamie's mouth, and then he was gone.

She stared after him, stunned.

"I'd say there's been a major shift in things with the hot sheriff," Kit commented. "And personally speaking, and you can thumb your nose if you want to," Kit rose from her chair, "but I'm taking the sheriff's advice."

Jamie sat frozen in place. Two dead bodies? No way could they be connected to what was happening to her, yet Diablo County didn't have a high murder rate. The barbecue she'd eaten suddenly congealed in her stomach.

"Thanks." She finally made herself get up from the table. "I'll clean up and put this stuff away. Maybe Zane will want something to eat when he gets back."

"Yeah, maybe," Kit grinned. "But I don't think barbecue will be on his mind."

Jamie was about to toss a comeback at her when the phone rang. Startling them both.

"Don't answer it," Kit told her.

"Don't be ridiculous. What if it's Zane?"

"Jamie, he just left here."

But she shook her head and picked up on the third ring.

"Miss Randall?"

She had become familiar enough with Gray Ballou's voice to recognize it. Kit was right. She should have let the damn thing ring.

"I'd appreciate it if you'd stop calling me. We really have nothing to discuss."

"I understand you've had a little misfortune befall you. I wanted to let you know I'm still prepared to make you a good offer for your property. You might want to reconsider."

Anger shot through her. "Did you have something to do with what went on here today?"

"Please. I'm a business man, not a thug. Just letting you know you have an opportunity here."

"Like I said, don't call here again." She slammed the phone down, her stomach churning.

"Ballou, right?" Kit guessed. "Tell him next time he calls you'll meet him and gut him with a hunting knife."

Jamie laughed, a release from the tension of the phone call. "What a bloodthirsty person you are."

"I just wish we could figure out why he's so hot to buy this property."

"One thing I haven't done is look at any part of

this place except the house. I don't really have any way to get around because the weeds and prairie grass are so high."

"Let's talk to Zane about it," Kit suggested. "Maybe he'll have some ideas."

Jamie snorted. "Zane Cameron already has too big a grip on my life. Let's see if we can figure this out ourselves."

Kit shrugged. "Suit yourself, but if it were me..."

"It's not you," Jamie snapped.

Kit threw up her hands. "Okay, okay. In that case, when he shows up here later, you can tell him to crawl into my bed instead of yours."

Jamie finished putting away the leftovers, ignoring her friend. When the counters were wiped, she tossed the sponge into the sink and pushed her hair off her face.

"Let's sit out back for a while. It's cooler at night, and I get a nice breeze from all those oak trees."

"Okay. How about finishing that wine we opened earlier??"

"Sounds good to me. "

Neither woman was much in the mood for conversation. The events of the day were finally overwhelming Jamie, raising her stress factor higher than it already was. And Kit seemed to be lost in her own thoughts. Finally, when the bottle was empty, Jamie pulled herself out of the lounge chair and stretched.

"I'm going to take a shower. I don't know if Zane was serious about coming back here—"

"Oh, trust me," Kit interrupted. "He was dead serious."

"If he's hungry, I'll get up and fix him something. Otherwise, I'm getting into bed."

"Have fun," Kit winked.

"You coming?"

"No. I think I'll just sit here for a while before I try out that brand new bed in your guest room."

"There's not much here to entertain yourself with. I'm sorry. I should have thought about buying a television set today."

"Not to worry. If I get bored, I have a book to read. I'm just grateful your air conditioning works."

Everything in the bedroom smelled brand new, a fact Jamie was grateful for. She hadn't wanted to move into her father's old room, but it was the biggest and Kit finally convinced her she was stupid not to take it for herself. They'd made the bathroom shine and decked it out with new accessories. Maybe they'd washed away the memories of the miserable old man, too.

The hot water felt good on her tired body. She poured a liberal amount of lavender body wash into her palm and began smoothing it onto her skin, eyes closed, mind wandering. She almost screamed when the shower curtain was jerked aside and Zane grinned at her through the steam.

"You almost gave me a heart attack," she told him.

"I plan on giving you something else in a minute. Don't get too far ahead of me."

He let the curtain drop back into place, and Jamie heard the *thunk* of his boots coming off, his gun placed on the vanity, the rustle of his clothing. Common sense told her she was heading down a path of self-destruction. No good could come of this. Even if she wanted a relationship, Zane didn't. In her heart she knew he just wanted to take what he thought was his, fuck her brains out, then leave her in the dust as she'd done to him.

But the sexual heat that pulled them together was stronger than ever, no matter what she thought. She was already shaking at his nearness and the images of what he had in mind.

Then he was inside the enclosure with her, the steam surrounding them both, his body a huge presence. His hands cupped her cheeks in a newly-familiar gesture, and he kissed her with incredible fierceness.

"I need to get rid of the stench of death," he said when he lifted his head. "Don't push me away, Jamie. I need *you*. I need your body to make me clean."

Whatever he'd found on the highway tonight had obviously upset him. No matter what resentments she might harbor against him, no matter how confused her thinking where he was concerned, she could help him forget. At least for a little while.

He took one of her hands and placed it on his cock. "Feel what happens to me just by looking at you." His voice was as hot as the water.

Jamie looked down and sucked in her breath. His cock was so swollen she could hardly get her fingers around it. The head was a deep plum color, and the slit at the top winked at her like a hungry eye. Water was already streaming over his bronzed skin, dripping onto his dusky nipples and his navel.

"Suck me, Jamie." His voice was so thick and husky she almost didn't recognize it. "I've been thinking about your mouth on me all day long. Suck me, darlin', and I'll give you a shower you'll never forget."

He didn't have to bribe her. She could hardly wait to wrap her lips around that huge shaft. Kneeling in the tub, she took him in both hands and slid her lips slowly over the head, swirling her tongue over the velvet skin, probing the slit with the tip of her tongue. He tensed and braced himself against the tiled wall.

She worked him into her mouth slowly, a little at a time, her lips stretched wide and her teeth

129

grazing the skin covering that hard steel. The solid shaft jumped in her mouth, pressing against her tongue. Sliding her hands up and down the soft covering, she worked it in a millimeter at a time, sucking deeply at each forward thrust, then releasing the pressure.

She found a rhythm that allowed her to move her mouth and hands in the same cadence, each time taking in just a little more of his cock. When the soft head hit the roof of her mouth, she tilted her head backwards, out of the stream of the shower, to take him deeper. One of his hands came up to cup the side of her head and help her adjust the angle of penetration.

When she'd finally taken as much of him as she could, she slipped one hand beneath his thighs and cupped the heavy sac of his balls, lightly drawing her fingernails over the wrinkled skin, then reaching to scrape the tender skin leading to his anus. His groan vibrated through his body so she did it again, a slow, teasing move. His thigh muscles tightened, and his hips jerked forward.

Her hands worked in a steady, coordinated rhythm, one sliding up and down the rigid shaft, the other squeezing and tormenting his balls, while her mouth continued to pull on him, drawing him ever deeper.

She couldn't miss the signs when his orgasm began to rise. His body tensed, his balls tightened, his cock grew heavier in her mouth. Then it grabbed him, ripping through his body as spurt after spurt of thick semen hit her tongue and the back of her throat. She swallowed as fast as she could, determined not to lose a drop.

Zane braced himself against the tile wall with one hand while the other gripped her head and held it tight to his groin.

"Jesus, Jesus, Jesus," he chanted as spasm after

spasm rocked him.

At last she'd sucked him dry. Easing him from her mouth, she held him in her hand as the shower spray washed his cock, and he stood there trying to steady his breathing. She rose when the water began to run cold and turned it off, shoving the shower curtain aside, and grabbing two towels from the stack on the vanity. Brand new large fluffy towels she'd bought during the day's shopping spree.

Handing one to Zane, she stepped out of the tub and began to dry off.

She jerked when his big hands gripped her shoulders and turned her to face him.

"I didn't get to take care of you like I promised." His warm breath fanned her face. "But I'm going to now."

Tossing the towels aside, he bent to retrieve something from his jeans, then lifted her in his arms and strode into the bedroom with her, laying her down on the bed crosswise, her buttocks on the edge of the mattress. Just like the other day, he knelt between her outspread thighs, lifted her legs over his shoulders, and bent his head to devour her.

She hadn't known there were so many nerves in her pussy, so many places his tongue could touch and ignite. Her juices were running, and already tiny flutters rippled through the walls of her vagina.

He was taking his time, slowly licking every surface, sucking at her clit and nibbling it with short nips, then thrusting his tongue deep inside her. The puckered ring of her anus tingled as she remembered when he'd slipped his fingers in there the other day. What would he think if she asked him to do it again?

But she could barely get enough thoughts together to form words as his assault on her cunt took her higher and higher. Every time he brought her to the edge, ready to tumble over, he backed off and left her panting until she didn't even know her own name.

He never said a word, just worked at her and worked at her until she didn't know if she could stand it anymore. She dug her heels into his neck, signaling her need, panting as she fought for her climax, but he was the devil himself, holding her off again and again.

"Please," she cried. "God, Zane, please let me come."

"You want to come, Jamie?" His voice was heavy and hoarse.

She nodded, unable to say more.

"All right, darlin'. I'm going to give you the orgasm of your life."

Without warning, he flipped her over and pulled her to her knees, spreading them wide. His tongue blazed a trail over every inch of her buttocks while one hand reached beneath her to squeeze and rub her clit. His fingers plundered her vagina, gathering her cream then painting it on the tight ring of her anus.

She heard the rip of foil and knew he was sheathing himself. Her stomach muscles clenched in a mixture of anticipation and dread. He was so damned big she didn't think she could take him, but the darkness of the thrill beckoned to her.

He leaned over her and feathered a line of kisses the length of her spine, even as his large hands spread the cheeks of her ass.

"I need this, Jamie. I won't hurt you, I promise. But tonight, I need this."

She wet her lips with the tip of her tongue and managed to say, "It's all right, Zane. It's okay. I want you to."

He licked the top part of the cleft of her buttocks, then she felt the sheathed head of his cock pressing against that tight hole. One thought flashed through her mind. In none of her relationships since Zane had she ever allowed her partners anal sex. Somehow it hadn't appealed to her with them. But with Zane, her body craved every pleasure he could give her. That would make twice she'd given her virginity to him.

Then she couldn't think at all, as he pressed, pressed, pressed, crooning to her all the time, as that broad, flat head finally breached the virgin hole and he was inside that hot, dark tunnel.

"I'll go slow," he panted. "I swear to you, if it hurts, you can tell me to stop."

"Don't stop," she ground out. "Don't. Stop."

But he did for the briefest of moments. "You've never done this before, have you." It was a statement, not a question. "Jesus god, Jamie. Christ, darlin'." She heard the rasping sound of his breath as he struggled to slow himself down. "Okay, listen to me. Breathe, Jamie. It makes it easier. Do what I tell you. Breathe in and let it out slowly."

Don't go slowly. Do it hard and fast.

Where had that come from? She'd never enjoyed this kind of sex. At least, she hadn't thought so. Or maybe it just took Zane to wake something inside her that she'd been hiding for a long time.

But she knew tonight was no time to do anything but comply. Be pliant. And maybe that was what she wanted, too. So she did as he told her, drawing in the deepest breath she could then letting it out. As she did, he pushed in a little further.

"Keep doing it, darlin'." His voice was so tight with control she hardly recognized it. "Again. Breathe in, then out."

With his hands holding her hips and guiding her, she took one deep breath after another. As she exhaled each one, that fat, thick cock invaded her just a little further, until, wonder of wonders, he was completed seated inside her. She was so full, so stretched, she didn't know if she could breathe again.

He stopped moving, giving her time to adjust to him. One hand stole around to her pussy and found her clit, stroking it even as he pulled her up against him. Spears of pleasure drove through her, heating her blood and making her nipples harden and ache. Reflexively she pushed back, and the head of his cock hit the hot spot in her rectum.

Zane's hands stilled her. "Jesus, Jamie. Don't do that. Not yet. God, I'll lose it."

He was working her clit, rubbing and tweaking it and cream poured from her as the muscles in her vagina pulsed and throbbed. Her blood was racing in her veins, and her body was so full of Zane she couldn't think.

His hands tightened on her hips. "Okay, Jamie?"

She nodded, the high state of arousal in her body preventing her from uttering a word.

"Good. Here we go, darlin'."

Rolling and thrusting his hips, he began a steady in and out stroke, hard and deep. Jamie grabbed a handful of coverlet and jammed it into her mouth, stifling her cries. As he increased the pace, he moved his hand faster on her clit. She could feel the tension in his body, the pulsing of his cock and knew his climax was near. Pushing back, she took him deeper, feeling her own orgasm rushing through her, her body nearing its peak.

"Now, Jamie." The words burst from him. "Damn it, now."

"Yes," she cried, and then it caught her, like the riptide in the ocean, tossing her and turning her as spasm after spasm ripped through her. She shook like a leaf in the wind, still thrusting back at Zane, still riding his cock, her cunt flexing and quivering. Inside her rectum, his cock pulsed and pulsed as he emptied himself into the latex.

It seemed to go on forever, yet eventually the shudders were reduced to shivers, the spasms to ripples. Zane's fingers on her hips were like branding irons, searing her body with heat.

When she fell forward, Zane's big body on top of hers, she could barely draw air into her lungs and the pounding of her heart echoed in her ears. Her entire body felt torn apart and barely reassembled. Zane kissed her shoulder, then slowly withdrew from her.

She heard him in the bathroom, disposing of the condom and running water. Then he was back, gently lifting her into place on the bed, soothing her anus and vagina with a warm washcloth.

"So good," he kept murmuring. "So damn good. Jesus, Jamie. So good." He traced her ear with his tongue, his breath still uneven as it fanned lightly against her skin. "You okay?"

All she could manage was a soft, "Mmmhmm."

He tossed the washcloth into the little glass dish on the night stand, then pulled the covers over both of them and wrapped his arms around her. "Sleep, darlin'." One hand cupped a full breast. "And Jamie?"

"Mmmhmm?"

"Thank you."

The strangest thought popped into her head as she drifted off. He didn't seem to be angry with her anymore. Tonight hadn't been about taking what he thought was his but about being together. Now what was *that* all about?

Chapter Twelve

"Jamie? Darlin', I hate to say this, but I need to get going."

The deep voice rumbled in her ear, and she fought her way up from the fuzziness of sleep. "Zane?"

A soft chuckle. "It better not be anyone else."

She roused and turned herself to face him, squinting over his shoulder at the window. "It's not even light out yet."

"I know. But I really have to get to the office. They'll have finished up everything from the crime scene last night, and I'll need to call a meeting. And I'd like to get out of here before Kit wakes up with one of her smart remarks." He kissed her nose. "I don't know if she gets it from you or the other way around."

"Was it really bad last night?" She searched his eyes for some kind of clue. "I thought the devil was after you."

An angry look slashed across his face. "Two Hispanics, killed and mutilated. It wasn't pretty."

"Oh, Zane." She snuggled against him. "I don't know how you handle it."

His arms tightened around her. "Sometimes it's harder than others."

"Let me get up. I'll fix you breakfast. Coffee at least."

"That's okay. I'll get coffee at the office, and someone's sure to bring donuts. But I'll take a rain check."

She dropped her gaze, focusing on his chest.

"Zane, what's happening here? With us?"

He took so long answering her she nearly told him to forget it.

"More than I expected, Jamie." His voice was slow and thoughtful, as if he couldn't quite get his mind around the situation. "Much more. I always thought..."

"That if I came back, you'd have your chance to get back at me," she finished.

He nodded, watching her with thoughtful blue eyes. "Get my piece of ass and run you out of town." One corner of his mouth hitched up. "At least it started out that way."

"And now?" She knew she shouldn't push him, especially since her own feelings were so unsettled, but the words just kept flying out of her mouth.

"And now it's different. How about you?"

"I don't know." She kissed the hollow of his throat, tasting his unique flavor. "It's all turning into...something else, isn't it."

And was it because she'd allow him the most intimate entry into her body possible? Because once again she'd given him access to a virgin part of her? Somehow as he'd pounded into her ass, as he'd awakened and then fulfilled a dark need she didn't even know she had, the tenor of things had changed.

Zane raked his fingers through his sleep-mussed hair. "Yes. You're right. It is."

"I get the feeling you aren't so mad at me anymore. So...so ready to punish me for the past."

He tilted her chin up and placed a tender kiss on her lips. "You're right. Something's changed. I don't know how or what." He put her gently away from him and rolled out of bed. "And damn it, I can't stay and talk about it right now, much as I'd like to. I need to get home, shower, and dress. This isn't the time for us to sit down and figure out what's happening with us."

"If anything," she pointed out.

His gaze lingered on her. "Oh, trust me. It's something. I just don't know what. And I don't think you do, either."

Jamie sat up in bed, admiring the taut lines of his naked ass as he walked toward the bathroom. "Zane? I wanted to let you know that I'm emailing the photos of Dad's truck to an insurance investigator Kit knows. I don't want you to get an attitude about it."

He stopped and turned toward her. There was frustration on his face, and still traces of anger, but he was holding it in well. "Darlin', if it will make you feel better, go right ahead. I'm confident the investigation was proper, but you do what you have to do. It's all right."

She tossed the covers back and hurried to where he was standing, throwing her arms around him, naked body pressed to naked body. "Thank you. I mean that."

"Okay, but if you don't get away from me, I won't make it into the shower." He took a moment for one quick but incendiary kiss. "I'll call you later."

She waited until he was gone to splash water on her face and pull on a pair of her new shorts and T-shirt. She was in the kitchen pouring her first cup of coffee when Kit came in, eyes full of mischief.

"I expected to see the hunk here." Her voice carried the hint of a chuckle. "I heard him come in last night."

Jamie pretended to study the coffee pot. She needed time to straighten out her feelings for Zane before opening them up to Kit's razor-sharp mind. "He had to leave early. Something about the bodies they found last night."

"But he'll be back tonight, right?"

Jamie shrugged. "We'll see." She wasn't yet ready to discuss the riptide her feelings for Zane had fallen into. Especially since the intensity of them frightened her. She couldn't afford to lose herself in him and end up nowhere again, with a man who had very different views about relationships than she did.

She looked at the clock, determined to change the subject. "The people from Wild Blue should be here by nine to hook up the satellite so we can have an Internet connection. I'm going to take a quick shower."

"Coward," Kit teased. "You have to talk about him sooner or later."

But not right now.

The metamorphosis her feelings for Zane were undergoing was too extreme, too new. She could hardly understand them herself, let alone discuss them with someone else. She'd run away from him twelve years ago because she wanted him but didn't trust him. And she'd wanted something for herself. More than Amen had to offer.

Well, that certainly worked out well, didn't it?

She'd come back here full of hate and resentment, stunned by the fact that Zane had harbored his bitterness all these years. Resentful of the fact that he seemed so determined to have all the sex he felt she cheated him out of. So what had happened last night to make it different? Was this just another way for him to torment her? And what was she supposed to do about it?

****

Zane stood in the shower, letting the water beat down on him and trying not to think about the one he'd taken just the night before. But the memory of it clung like tentacles and his cock hardened just thinking about Jamie's sweet mouth wrapped around it. God, that had been heaven. Pure, unadulterated bliss.

And what happened to all the anger he'd been

139

holding onto for so long? He'd gone from trying to chase her out of town to deciding he wanted all the sex he'd been thinking about since that night before she'd left Amen to...what?

He wasn't a man given to emotions. That was probably one good reason why Jamie had left. He'd known good and well that, while he'd had very special feelings for her, he'd been far from ready to settle down. Still was, he tried to make himself believe. And Jamie Randall wasn't a woman who allowed tomcatting.

Well, he'd certainly lived up to her expectations of him. Since she'd left, he had plenty of time to screw anything that breathed, always discreetly and never, ever in Amen or even Copper Ridge. Not where people could be aware of it and certainly not under the cold eyes of his mother.

His mother! Jesus. That was a confrontation he wasn't looking forward to but one he knew for damn sure was coming. Enough tongues in Amen would be wagging about his visits to the Randall house, not to mention his spending the night. His mother would be front and center on that little piece of business.

She'd worked hard raising him and done well for herself, but he was a big boy now. He wasn't going to let her interfere with what was happening between him and Jamie. Just as soon as he figured out exactly what that was.

As he soaped his groin he thought again of the night before and his lathered hands gripped his penis. Every muscle in his body was tense with passion. No, lust. Just pure lust. That's all he wanted it to be. All it *could* be. But if he didn't get some relief at the moment, he wouldn't be able to get his uniform pants on.

Closing his eyes and leaning against the shower wall, he stroked himself in a steady motion, trying to imagine that it was Jamie's small fingers wrapped around his shaft. What he really wanted was her mouth, those soft velvet lips that stretched unbelievingly to take his thickness. He had no idea what her sex life had been for the past twelve years; her technique was a combination of sophistication and inexperience.

Stop! Don't think about anyone else she might have been with. Not that he'd expected her to live like a nun. But imagining her with someone else made his gut twist and bile wash up into his throat. He forced himself to concentrate on what he was doing, feeling himself swell enormously as he'd done when she took him into the hot well of her mouth.

He could still feel her small tongue as it twirled itself around him, licking the head of his dick and probing the slit until he thought he'd lose his mind. His hand picked up speed as hers had done, coaxing alive every nerve. Her fingers on his balls had about driven him crazy. When her small finger probed his asshole, electricity had driven through him in sharp spikes. He'd wanted her to do it again, but he hadn't wanted to push her. Not yet. Fucking her in the ass had stolen his breath but only whetted his appetite for more. More things. More acts. More, more, more.

How far could he push her? He wouldn't say the sex he liked was rough, but it was...okay, rough. He wanted to handcuff her to the bed and lick her pussy until she came so many times she didn't even know who she was. He wanted to spread her legs, plunge a dildo into that hot, greedy cunt and suck her clit while the vibrator took her from one climax to another. He wanted to spank her until the delectable ass was hot pink, then plunge his cock into her ass while the vibrator in her cunt buzzed away. He wanted to suck her nipples until they stood out, then pinch them with nipple clamps that would show her how much pleasure pain could be. He wanted to feel her fingers inside his ass while she sucked his cock

Would she be willing or would it turn her off? Would she embrace it or be afraid of him? Jesus, he wanted those things with her so much he could hardly breathe.

All those images were driving him forward. He felt the familiar tingle in his spine and the tightening of his balls. His hand moved faster and faster until the thickness of his semen spilled over his fingers. He gripped his shaft hard, feeling it pulse in his hand until at last he was drained.

He could hardly move. His heart thundered against his ribs, and his breath seemed stuck halfway in his throat. He couldn't remember the last time he'd been driven by the need to jack off. It gave him the relief he sought, but not the satisfaction. Only Jamie could give him that.

Jamie! Her naked body danced behind his closed lids. He wanted to brand her as his. And he wanted to bind her to him forever.

Forever? Where the hell had that come from?

Forever with Jamie Randall?

His gut told him he was buying himself trouble. As soon as her problems got resolved, she'd be off down the road again, Amen not even a blip on her radar. He'd lasted this long without recognizing his real feelings about her, he could just keep on doing it. Get everything from her she had to give.

You aren't a user, Cameron. Not really. But he wanted it all from Jamie. And not to punish her, or to feed his anger. So what did that mean? Was he storing up memories for when she blew him off again?

Admit what it is, you fool. And figure out what to do about it.

The damn woman still had the ability to tie him up in knots. He wanted to bang his head against the shower wall, see if he could knock some sense into it.

142

At last he turned off the shower, thoroughly drained, and tried to pull himself together. He had two horrendous murders waiting for him, and a bunch of other muck. Not to mention figuring out why someone wanted Jamie Randall off that moth-eaten piece of land.

****

Roy Galvan, his chief deputy, had the crime scene photos laid out for him on the conference room table along with a typed set of the Criminal Scene Unit notes and a diagram of the scene. Two other deputies also sat waiting for him.

"Coroner said he'll have his report in by tomorrow," Roy said. "This one was a bitch to do."

"I can believe it." Zane took a sip of the strong black coffee, for once grateful for its bitterness.

"Who the hell would do something like that?" one of the other men asked.

"Someone with a very sick mind," Zane told him. "He also didn't want us to have an easy time identifying the bodies."

The fingers of both men had been amputated and their teeth ripped out, apparently with pliers. And just for good measure, acid had been dumped on their faces.

"So where do we start?" Roy wanted to know.

He pointed to one of the photos. "This one had a tattoo that the killer either didn't know about or forgot. Send it out to every database and all the police departments in Texas. See if anyone recognizes it. They're probably illegals, but someone might recognize this. It's about all we've got right now." He looked at the other two deputies. "And the two of you hit every place up and down that stretch of road for ten miles. See if anyone, anyone at all, saw or heard anything last night. You can bet they weren't killed there, but maybe we'll get lucky and someone saw them being dumped."

"Wouldn't they have come forward?" the younger deputy asked. He'd been on Zane's force less than a year.

"Around here?" He grunted. "You may be a new deputy, Chuck, but you've lived around here all your life. When was the last time anyone volunteered anything to the law?"

"Got it. Ask lots of questions."

"I don't think we'll find out where they were killed," Zane continued, "but I'm curious as to why they were dumped where we'd find them so easily."

"A message?" Roy suggested.

"But to who?" He stood up. "All right. Let's get out there and see if we can find answers to these questions. Everyone back here at noon unless you're hot after something. Then call in."

Patsy Madigan, who served as his receptionist/secretary, caught him as he stopped in the tiny kitchenette to refill his mug.

"You've got company," she told him in a low voice.

He raised an eyebrow. "Oh?"

"Yeah. Thought I'd give you a heads up. Your mother's waiting for you."

Shit. Just what I need today.

Anita Cameron, in a summer business suit and impeccably groomed as always, rose from the chair she'd been sitting in and presented her cheek for his kiss.

"Well, Mother." Zane settled himself behind his desk. "This is a surprise. What brings you to the sheriff's office this early in the morning? Trouble at Diablo Con Ag?"

"Can't I just stop by to see my son?" She arranged her face in a pout when she saw that Zane's smile had little humor in it. "Is it so strange that I just wanted to say hello?"

"On a workday? Yeah. You don't drop in unless

something's on your mind, so give."

Anita closed the door, then arranged herself in the chair across from him. "I thought we might have a little chat about something that's bothering me."

"Bothering you?" He swallowed some of his coffee, watching her over the rim of the mug. "I can't imagine what that would be."

She brushed an imaginary piece of lint from her skirt. "People have seen you frequenting Jamie Randall's house in the past few days."

Zane set his mug down carefully. "Frequenting? Are you suggesting something here?"

"And you were there all night last night."

Zane reminded himself to stay calm. He seldom won an argument with his mother. "I wasn't aware you were having me followed."

"People talk, Zane. And Jamie is certainly a topic of conversation. I don't want you included in it."

He counted to ten before answering her. "Don't you think I'm old enough to control my own social life?"

She sniffed. "Sex life is more like it. You need to go back to Austin or San Antonio to do your whoring, where people won't see you."

I won't lose my temper. I won't kill her. "Nice talk from my mother. And Jamie Randall is not a whore."

"She's a piece of trash and you know it." Anita's hands tightened into fists. "I don't want you associating with her."

He didn't know whether to laugh or explode. "I'm thirty-four years old, in case you haven't been counting. A little old for you to be giving me orders."

Her black eyes turned even darker. "I have plans for you, Zane. You're going to be somebody. You won't get anywhere with a tramp like that clinging to your arm."

145

Now his anger was threatening to overtake him. He made himself take a long breath and slowly let it out. "We've had this conversation before. I'm not interested in politics, not now, not ever. And in case you haven't notice, I'm already somebody. The sheriff of Diablo County. A job, I might add, that I'm very happy with."

"Nonsense. You can be so much more."

"Forget it. And forget about bringing it up again."

"Gray could help you—"

He slammed his hand down on his desk. "And I don't want one thing from Grayson Ballou. Nothing. That alone would make me say no." He paused, forcing himself to settle down, slow down his breathing. Get control. "You don't happen to know why he's so hot to buy Jamie's place, do you? It can't be worth half of what he's offering."

"Probably to get her out of town." She brushed at her skirt again. "Zane, you're really being stubborn about this."

He pushed back his chair and stood up. "Call it whatever you want, but the subject is closed. You can also stay away from her as a topic of discussion. Whatever's between us is my business. And tell Gray to stay the hell away from her, too. Whatever game he's playing, she's off limits."

Anita's eyes widened and her mouth tightened. "Zane, I can't believe I'm hearing you right."

"Believe it." He knew he'd done it now, but for a long time his mother had been getting on his nerves. He wasn't a kid any more, and she was no longer pulling the strings. He could tell she was pissed off, but that was certainly the least of his worries. "And now, if you'll excuse me, I have a double murder to solve."

"Oh?" She raised an eyebrow. "I hadn't heard anything about it."

"Turn on the radio or television. The media vultures must have psychic powers. They're already gathering to pick over the bones. Good-bye, Mother."

"We're not done with this," she told him, opening the door.

"Yes. We are."

She turned at the doorway. "One more thing. Cut your hair. My own people didn't want you, so you don't need to wear that part of your heritage like a badge. And it won't help you get elected."

"It already did," he muttered.

He barely restrained himself from slamming the door after her. Sitting down again, he pulled his cell phone from his pocket and perversely punched in a number he'd already programmed to speed dial. His tension began to ease when the soft voice answered.

"Hi. Just checking to make sure everything's okay."

"Yes. Why wouldn't it be? Do you know something I don't?" He heard the surprise in Jamie's voice.

"Nope. Just checking." He paused, searching for just the right tone. "I'm not expecting another double murder tonight. Okay if I come by when I'm done here and bring pizza?"

Now it was her turn to let the silence hum between them. "Well, sure," she said at last. Again, she sounded surprised, probably that he asked rather than commanded. "Kit's here, you know."

His mouth turned up in a grin. "She's welcome to join us in anything except our bed."

"*Our* bed?"

"Damn straight." He lowered his voice. "And I'm looking forward to using it again. Don't you forget it for one minute, Jamie Randall. Not even for a second." He exhaled, not realizing he'd been holding his breath. "See you later."

He hung up, wondering why the call had made

him feel so much better. And how this thing between him and Jamie had turned so upside down. He absolutely had to get a handle on it before things got more out of control than they already were.

****

Manny Alvarado mopped his forehead and wished Gray would turn up the air conditioning in the car. He didn't know why the man insisted on meeting on this hidden side road that it took forever to get to. He grumbled as much to his *jefe.*

"Use your head," Gray snapped. "I don't want to talk about this in a place where we could be overheard."

"And this couldn't be handled over the telephone?" He'd had a bad night and he could foresee an even worse day.

"I wanted to look at your face when I asked you how you could possibly have fucked up a simple task so badly."

"You wanted the men taken care of. I had it done."

"No, you idiot." Gray breathed heavily through his nose, fighting for control. "I wanted *you* to do it. They were your problem. You hired them. You didn't see they did their task properly. *You* needed to be the one to get rid of them."

"But *padrone,* I—"

"Save it. We're in a pile of horse shit now. Zane Cameron will be like a bulldog. He won't give up until he finds out who those men were and who killed them. And now you have yet another problem. *Another* fuckup to get rid of. We can't have any loose ends dangling." Gray pulled out one of the thin cigars he favored, bit off the end, and spit it out the open window. "And we still haven't found the money."

I hate those stinking things.

"Grayson, I am not a killer," he insisted. "That's

148

why I hire people."

"Well, you make very poor choices in the hiring department. Damn it." He smacked his hand on the steering wheel. "All I wanted to do was get rid of that bitch. If she'd just sold me the fucking house, none of this would have been necessary. We still don't know where that old drunk stashed the money. Now we've got a nuclear meltdown here and horny Zane Cameron is riding to the rescue."

Manny frowned. "I don't understand."

Gray narrowed his eyes. "Why the hell have I been thinking you were so fucking smart? The sheriff is fucking the Randall bitch. He's taking a personal interest in this."

"Shall I delay the next scheduled appointment?"

"Damn. I forgot about that. Manny, you couldn't possibly have made a bigger mess if you'd deliberately set out to. Yes. Get hold of our contact and have him push everything back a week. One week from tomorrow. I'll have things taken care of by then. And I'll get the damn money, too."

"How? How will you do this?"

"That's my business. Meanwhile go clean up your mess. And find a way into that house again. If she stumbles over that cash, she'll be asking more questions than we want to answer."

"*Si, padrone.* I will fix this."

"I'd hate to think I can't depend on you any longer. We've got a sweet thing going here. Too bad to see it fall apart."

Manny mopped his face again. "I said I will handle it."

"Make sure you do so. Go on. Get out of here."

Manny climbed out of the car and waited until Grayson Ballou had headed back out to the highway before he bent over and vomited. He really, really didn't have the stomach for this.

Chapter Thirteen

"How long will it take until we get an answer back?" Jamie asked.

They had just emailed the photos of Frank Randall's truck to Kit's friend. Jamie looked at her half-filled coffee mug, made a face, and poured the liquid down the drain.

"Give him a couple of hours, and I'll call him," Kit told her. "Meanwhile, your pantry is severely understocked. Don't tell me you live on Pop-Tarts and yogurt."

"They have all the essential nutrients," Jamie said, grinning. "But I owe you a breakfast for helping with this. Let's go flaunt ourselves in the Armadillo Cafe. I'd take you to the big city, but I want to wait for answers on the accident."

"No problem. I'd love to stick it to the locals."

"One good thing. Anita Cameron doesn't grace the place with her presence. Thinks it's beneath her."

"Did you happen to tell the sheriff his mother told you to leave her baby alone?" Kit asked when they were in the car heading to town.

"No." Jamie sighed. "To tell you the truth, I'm still trying to figure out what's going on with us. I don't know if we've crossed into new territory—or back into old territory. Or if he's just leading up to the big finale when I get kicked in the teeth so he can extract his revenge."

"Then you have blinders on, girl. Maybe he had a grudge to satisfy at first, but I see the way he looks at you. That man's fighting a big battle with himself."

Jamie snorted. "Yeah. When I first got here, he couldn't decide whether to toss me on the trash heap or run me out of town on a rail."

"Then you haven't paid careful attention." Kit smacked the dashboard. "I can't believe how stupid you are. Maybe you should look at it from his point of view. You know, you ran away from this piece of no place once before. He's probably thinking you'll do it again and making sure he doesn't come out on the short end of the stick a second time."

Jamie turned into the parking lot of the Armadillo, parked, and turned to look at Kit. "First of all, I have no place to go. Second of all, I can't believe that a man who couldn't stay faithful for more than five minutes has changed his stripes. I'm sure I'm just another toy to him, like the last time." *Please don't let that be true.* "Meanwhile, he's getting all the sex he can."

"I don't see you putting up any objections," Kit pointed out.

"But—"

"I also don't see him hopping into anyone else's bed, this man you said has the morals of a mink." Her voice softened. "Honey, you have to decide what you want, then figure out if Zane's part of it. The rest will fall into place." She opened the car door. "Meanwhile, I'm starving. Let's eat."

****

Zane took the back roads until he was sure he could safely enter the Interstate without anyone spotting him. He was sure Copper Ridge would have what he wanted, but he wasn't about to do his shopping there. Not when he was one of the most recognizable people in Diablo County. And certainly not under the glare of his mother. So here he was, sneaking out of town, on his way to San Antonio.

But it would be worth it. Oh, yes. Besides, he

had a place to go in the city where he could slip in and out without any fanfare.

As he drove, he actually found himself whistling, despite the garbage going on in his life. His mother was about to drive him out of his mind, he had two mutilated corpses on his hands, and he had a bad feeling that trouble was dogging Jamie. And that last was something he planned to do something about, starting with that asshole, Gray Ballou. He'd have to be careful about that because of his mother's job, but he figured to get to the bottom of this whole mess one way or another.

This thing with Jamie had caught him totally by surprise. He'd been completely prepared to fuck the life out of her. Get her out of his system once and for all and then make it too unpleasant for her to stay around. Only it hadn't quite turned out that way. Payback sex had turned into some of the hottest sex he'd ever had, and somehow the woman who'd left him in the dust had found the crack in his heart that had never completely closed.

Dangerous. Very dangerous.

Of course, he had to admit he hadn't done much to help the situation back then. Fidelity hadn't been one of his strong suits, and he'd all but flaunted it in her face. It was her father's half-breed insults that had nailed the coffin shut and festered all these years.

Now he couldn't get her out of his mind. Images of her naked beneath him. In the shower. Spread out before him like a sexual banquet, that hot little cunt soaking wet, the tissues soft and waiting for him. Gripping his cock like a tight, wet fist, milking him, surrounding him with her liquid heat.

He'd certainly done his share of fucking. That little fact was one of the reasons Jamie had been so reluctant to trust their relationship before. The ages of his partners had changed over the years, along with their degree of sophistication, but none of them had driven him to an orgasm as explosive as Jamie had. And none of them had reached his core the way she did. Just thinking about her made his groin tighten and his dick press hard against the fly of his pants.

Jesus. He knew he was getting in deep, but sex with Jamie was turning into an addictive drug. That was it. A drug. He just needed enough to get it out of his system. Once again he wondered how she'd react if he showed her what kind of sex he *really* liked now. How he *really* wanted to fuck her. How rough he liked it. And how rough he'd like it with her.

Well, only one way to find out. This would either kick what they had up another notch or kill it altogether.

By the time he'd finished chasing thoughts around in his head, he was pulling off the Interstate in San Antonio and turning into a familiar strip center. Parking at the rear of his destination store, he shucked his Stetson and his uniform shirt and pulled on a T-shirt before ringing the bell at the back door.

"Why, Sheriff." Annabelle Gold's mouth turned up in a knowing grin and mischief flashed in her eyes. "Did you come to arrest me for purveying indecent items?"

Zane leaned down and kissed her cheek. "Not today, sweetheart. I'm doing a little shopping."

"Oh?" Her voice was filled with curiosity. "I didn't know you were involved with someone new."

"Someone I need some very special gifts for." He pulled a folded sheet of paper from his pocket. "Think you can rustle up some of these things?"

Annabelle's eyes widened as she looked at the list, but she just grinned at him. "Come have a seat in my office, and I'll get the goodies for you to look at."

Zane's arrangement with Annabelle, even though he always came to the store in civvies, was he got to do his shopping away from the prying eyes of her customers.

"This must be some woman," Annabelle teased as she placed yet another array of nipple clamps and rings on the desk for him to see.

"You have no idea," Zane muttered, wondering once again if he'd completely lost what passed for his mind.

While Annabelle worked from his list, he set aside a selection that included three different kinds of vibrators, two butt plugs, and two dildos. He almost closed his eyes as he sat there, wanting to visualize Jamie spread out on the bed, knees bent, both openings filled with the toys as he stimulated her clit and her cream seeped around the edges of the dildo. He gritted his teeth to keep the images at bay, or he was sure he'd embarrass himself right there at Annabelle's desk.

With each of his choices, Annabelle's grin widened. She chuckled when he was finished at last and handed over a chunk of his cash.

"I hope the poor girl is resting up," she commented as she wrapped his purchases.

When he left The Playroom with a bag filled with expensive sexual toys, images of how he and Jamie would use them had his cock about to burst through the heavy twill of his trousers. He hoped Jamie wouldn't be turned off by any of this, that she would accept the way he liked his sex. He could hardly wait for tonight. Too bad he had work to take care of first.

Slipping back into his uniform shirt, he pulled out of the parking lot and headed back toward Amen.

****

Anita Cameron fought to keep her anger under

control. The rage had been building since she left her son's office. Things were getting way out of hand, and Gray was not providing the help she expected. After all she'd done for him, it was his turn to pay up.

"I'll never get him on the political track if that tramp is still around," she told him, a vicious edge to her voice.

They were having coffee in his office in Copper Ridge, not an unusual thing for the manager of Diablo Con Ag to do. She often met with him there, so no one ever gave their meetings a second thought. Besides, he'd taken the precaution of having his office soundproofed, and someone swept it every day. Most of his business was not the kind that he could afford to expose to eavesdroppers. Especially with Anita.

"You'll have to be patient a little longer," he said. "I've run into some...difficulties."

Anita set the delicate china cup in its saucer and placed them carefully on the table next to her chair. "I don't know why you can't just arrange a convenient accident. You seem to be quite good at it."

"I have other things happening," he pointed out. "As you well know. I have better reasons than your son's political career for getting rid of Jamie Randall, and so do you. But we can't do it in a way that will endanger any other plans."

"That little bitch is nothing but trouble." Anita's voice was edged with venom. "She showed up here at exactly the wrong time."

"Agreed. But we need to be careful how we proceed here. If something happens to her, you can bet your ass your son will be all over it like green on grass."

"You're right, damn it." She picked up her coffee again. "So what do we do? Time's getting shorter."

"I told you I'd take care of it and I will. Even if it

means some things have to be temporarily postponed. Or juggled around."

"Yes. Well. I hear you. You're the man with the connections. Mr. Fixit. So fix this before everything blows up in our faces."

****

Jamie and Kit carried the groceries into the house, putting the frozen foods away at once.

During her furniture shopping spree, she'd also bought a desk and two chairs. She might be unemployed, but that didn't mean she couldn't do some work. Only this time it would be private and personal. Creating a simple work station, she set her laptop up on the desk and booted it up in eager expectation.

"We'll get to the rest in a minute," Jamie said, opening her inbox. "I want to see if your friend got back to us yet on the accident photos we sent. Hey, Kit," she yelled. "Your friend already sent something. Come here and take a look."

Kit pulled up the other chair and sat next to her. "Open it up and let's see."

Jamie clicked on the email to open it.

"Hi, Kit," she read. "I see you haven't stopped sticking your nose in other people's business."

Kit snorted. "He is *such* an ass."

"Hush. Let's read the rest."

"Anyway," the email continued, "at least you send me interesting stuff. I had another investigator look at the photos, too, just to confirm what I thought. The only way the dents on the bumper and the tail gate could have come from rolling down the hillside would be if the truck rolled end-over-end. In that case, we wouldn't see the damage to the doors."

Jamie smacked her hand on the desk. "I knew it."

Kit pointed to the next paragraph. "He says the dents on the rear of the truck are more consistent with being bumped by another vehicle. The other investigator agrees with him that the truck was probably pushed over the edge and tumbled sideways to the bottom of the hill."

The rest of the email was a personal message to Kit. Jamie stood up so Kit could take her chair and went into the kitchen to get a cold drink. She rolled the can against her forehead, trying to ward off the niggling headache that had suddenly popped up.

She had a feeling Zane would not be too happy with what she'd found out. Unlike when she'd first confronted him, it was important now for her to make him believe she wasn't questioning his attention to the accident. Or his professionalism. Her father was a well-known drunk who finally had one accident too many. She'd have looked at it the same way.

"I'm going to have to call Zane," she told Kit, her stomach knotting in anticipation. "Maybe I can fax this over to him or email it."

Kit frowned. "You sure you don't want to wait until you see him?"

Jamie shook her head. "No. I told him we were doing this, and I want to be upfront all the way."

Besides, things between us are already getting too complicated. I need to be as controlled and objective about this as I can. Kit will never understand.

God, I'm not sure I understand.

"Yeah?" Kit raised an eyebrow. "Then how come you haven't told him about the money?" When Jamie didn't answer, she said, "Uh huh. So we're only being partially open and honest here, right?"

The knot in her stomach tightened.

"What exactly am I supposed to tell him? I don't know where the money even came from. What if he doesn't believe me when I tell him I just found it? It's obvious my father was involved in something damned illegal. That's the only way he could ever get this kind of cash."

"The longer you wait to tell Zane, the less likely he is to believe you didn't know anything about it." Kit shook her head. "Then you and he will be right back where you were when you crawled home to Amen."

"Damn it, anyway." Jamie kicked at a chair. "Damn that rotten old man."

"You want to call Zane? Go ahead and do it. But ask him to come over here. Let him look you in the eye. He'll know you're telling the truth. And he'll have a better chance to help you if you aren't keeping anything from him."

But the dispatcher told her the sheriff was out of the area. She'd give him the message when he called in.

"Well, that's all I can do for now," she told Kit. "Let's put the rest of the groceries away."

****

Zane was a half hour from Amen when he called his office and got Jamie's message. Twenty minutes later he was knocking on her front door. When she opened it, he could see Kit doing something in the kitchen, doing a poor job of ignoring him. He reminded himself he was technically on duty. But Jamie looked somehow so fragile. What the hell. Telling himself—lying to himself—he was just comforting another human being, he hauled her into his arms and pulled her tightly against his chest.

She wound her arms around his neck, pressing her soft body against his. His hormones smacked his brain with a baseball bat, and he kissed her with all the desire that had been building since his visit to Annabelle's. Her taste exploded through him like a heady flavor, her lips soft as velvet, her tongue a wet bolt of lightning.

Only the sound of Kit clearing her throat

brought him back to reality. He sucked in a deep breath and looked down at the woman in his arms, wishing he could strip off every stitch of her clothing right now and try out the new toys. "You call for the sheriff?"

She stood on tiptoe and placed another quick kiss on his lips. He felt the anxiety humming through her body as she took his hand. "Yes. Come into the bedroom with me."

"Uh, Jamie? Not that I'm not up for it, if you'll pardon the pun, but don't you want to give Kit a dollar and send her to the movies or something?" He gave a soft chuckle, trying to lighten the situation. "I didn't realize this was your urgent message."

But he couldn't coax a smile from her. "Maybe later. This is serious business. Come on."

He followed her up the stairs, her small hand clasping his tightly. Almost nervously. Nervously? What was happening here? When she tugged him into her bedroom and pushed him down to the bed, he raised an eyebrow. "What the hell is going on?"

She wet her lips with the tip of her tongue, a movement that made his cock stand at attention again. "Zane."

"Jamie?"

"I know years ago when I left here, we were on bad terms, and when I came back, we didn't start off too well."

He was beginning to get a bad feeling about this. "Is this some kind of kiss-off?" he demanded. "Because it could have waited, don't you think? Or are we replaying that old scene all over again."

She shook her head, jamming her hands into her pockets. "Nothing like that. The opposite, as a matter of fact." She blew out a long breath. "At first I wasn't sure I could trust you. Even when we had sex, you seemed so...so...angry. Still. But now..."

"But now?" he prompted.

"But now things have changed. I know we have...feelings for each other." She looked at him anxiously. "Right?"

"Yes. Right." He flipped a hand impatiently. "Can we get to the point, please?"

"And I don't want to hide anything from you."

"Jamie."

"Okay, okay. Just promise you won't be made at me."

She was so edgy he held out a hand to her and reluctantly she took it. The connection between them sizzled at the contact. No, he wouldn't be angry with her. Whatever it was, he'd help her. No matter what it was. "I won't be mad. I promise. *Now* can we get to it?"

"Okay." She dropped his hand and opened her closet door. Picking up a hammer lying on the floor, she poked at a board that, at first glance, didn't even look loose. It came away with a slight groaning sound, and she dropped the hammer and pulled out a grungy-looking gym bag. Dropping it on the bed next to him, she unzipped it and opened it wide.

Shock and anger battled inside Zane. He'd promised Jamie he wouldn't be mad, but Jesus! He clenched his jaw as he fought to keep himself under control. The bag was stuffed with bundles of money, fifties and hundreds. Mentally tabulating from practice, he'd say there was close to a hundred thousand there. His mind was whirling with possibilities, but one thing he was sure of. Jamie had been as shocked at finding the money as he was to see it now.

"Let's check the issue dates on the bills," he told her. "Maybe this cash has been here forever."

"Maybe." She bit her bottom lip. "But maybe not. This could just be the latest payoff he got." She snorted. "We certainly didn't have any relatives to leave us any money. Unless they're in jail, I don't even know where any of them are."

"I agree. I don't think this came to him through legal activities."

"My father kept a roof over our heads and food on the table after my mother died. And he never had what you could call a steady job. Do you think whatever this is, he was mixed up in it way back then?"

"I hate to say you're right, but it's possible, darlin'. Frank Randall wasn't a candidate for citizen of the year. After all, he supported the two of you somehow all those years. I'm guessing anything he had before he already spent."

Zane was already thumbing through the stacks, spot checking the information. He tossed one pack on the bed. "You're right. These dates are all from the last two years."

"Maybe my house wasn't torn up just to run me out of town," she suggested, her voice shaky. "Maybe they were looking for the money. And need to get me out of here to do it."

"If—and I only say if—your father was murdered, whoever did it wants the money back before anyone finds it."

"In case it can be traced back to them?"

Zane shook his head. "Traceable or not, it would start us asking a lot more questions and digging into a lot more places."

His heart was galloping as he realized exactly how much danger she was in. People killed for a lot less than this, and if it was dirty money, which was more than likely, whoever it belonged to would want it back. Badly. No way was he letting her stay in this house without him now.

"When did you find this?" he demanded, trying to keep his voice even.

"A-a couple of days ago." She twisted her hands nervously.

Zane blew out his breath. "Have you counted it?"

She nodded. "Almost a hundred grand."

"That's what I figured, too."

"Zane, I swear I wasn't keeping anything from you." Her body was a study in anxiety. "I found the money, and at first, I was afraid to tell you and then—"

He held up a hand. He had a choice to make here, and he knew it better be the right one or it was all over between them. "Come here."

"Zane..."

"Come on, darlin'. Come over here."

The last thing he needed right now was intimate contact with her, but again, his brain took a vacation. She moved closer, and he pulled her against his body, her legs between his thighs, his arms banded around her.

She looked down at him, anxiety flashing in her eyes. "What?"

"Now. Listen to me. I'm not mad. Not even pissed off, okay? Just...maybe a little irritated. But it's my own fault you didn't think you could tell me about this. So why don't you tell me everything from the beginning."

She perched on one thigh and told him the whole story, from the moment she'd made the discovery right through everything that had happened since then.

"I would have told you before, but—"

"Shh. It's okay. You're telling me now. But this puts a whole different face on what's happening."

"You mean the break-in and everything?"

He nodded. "I'll bet my ass this is what they were looking for."

"I have something else to tell you, too." She picked at a fingernail. "I went ahead and sent the photos of the accident scene to a friend of Kit's who investigates these things for a living."

Zane tensed. "What did he find out?"

"That it definitely was no accident." She told him what was in the email, watching his face for his reaction.

"Then the money definitely has to come into it."

"But we don't have any idea where my father got it. And it still doesn't tell us why Grayson Ballou wants this scrub land so badly."

"No, it doesn't."

Zane pulled out his handkerchief and used it to lift the bag by the frayed handles. "Can you get me a large garbage bag? Your fingerprints and Frank's are all over this, but we can check the money to see what else we come up with. You'll have to be printed for comparison."

"Okay. When do you want to do it?"

"Let me get to the office, and I'll call you. Did you take any money out of here?" he asked.

They walked out of the room, Jamie about three steps ahead of him. "Ten thousand," she answered in a small voice, her eyes focused on where she was walking.

Christ. Well, nothing I can do about it now. And getting mad at her won't help, although I'd like to wring her sexy little neck.

"All right. We'll just ignore that for the moment. Where have you got it?"

"In my purse." She turned to look at him, desperation and humiliation in her eyes. "Zane, I'm about broke. I had to sell everything I owned and use most of the cash I'd saved up to settle the law suit. I only took enough to give myself some breathing room."

"And the big furniture spree?"

"Kit's credit card. I owe her. I figured—"

"To pay her back when you discovered where the money came from?"

She nodded.

"We'll work it out. Meanwhile, I need to get back to work and take this with me."

Jamie pulled a garbage sack out of the cupboard and opened it so he could drop the gym bag in.

"Let's hope that doesn't occur to whoever these idiots are." He tied the sack and pulled a little notebook out of his pants pocket. After writing on a blank page, he tore it out and handed it to Jamie. "Here's a receipt. Lock it away somewhere. When this all gets cleared up, I'll try to get it back to you."

Kit came in from the living room. "Thank god. I'll be damned glad to get that out of here." She handed Jamie a sheet of paper. "Here. I printed this out so you could show it to Zane." She looked up at the man. "This is an analysis of the photos from the accident."

Zane studied it carefully, his gut twisting. He'd definitely misread this whole thing, but then he hadn't been looking for anything out of the ordinary. He'd have to get Duke to tow it to the impound yard and have the tech go to work on it. "Shit. I guess my stupidity is showing. I owe you a huge apology. If I hadn't been so pompous and pig-headed..."

"Don't beat yourself up. Please." Jamie was looking up at him. "I'm not sure anyone would have handled it differently. If I wasn't so pissed off when I came back here, I might not have forced the issue, either. But I looked at that truck and just...just...Maybe there was no love lost between us, but I wasn't about to let someone get away with his murder, either."

He pulled her into his arms again, hugging her tightly, an action he was allowing himself all too frequently. He was just afraid to show her just how scared for her he was. Something really bad was going on. He hoped Gray Ballou wasn't involved because that meant another clash with his mother. It also meant whatever this was, someone with brains was behind it and that upped the danger factor.

"All right." He had to get out of here and get to work. Thank god he had urgent things to take care of, or he might have carried her into the bedroom and lost what was left of his mind. He needed to put some emotional distance between them.

"Here's the deal," he told her. "I'm having Frank's truck brought in so we can go over it in detail, and I'll get the money fingerprinted." He thought for a minute. "I may call the state lab for that. I'm not sure I trust my own office not to leak. In fact, I think I'll bring the portable kit tonight and take your prints myself. We don't need to stir up gossip. Meanwhile, you don't go anywhere without checking in with me on a regular basis. Got it?"

"Zane," she began.

"No room for argument, so don't even try. And tonight when I come back, I'm bringing a suitcase with me. I'll be here for the duration."

And maybe longer. Just as long as I make sure we both know the ground rules.

She looked for a moment as if she was getting ready to argue with him, her face reflecting the battle she was fighting with desire, the need for independence, and the remnants of hoarded anger.

He was glad when Kit spoke up to break the impasse.

"For once, Jamie, use your head," she said in her 'you'd better listen to me' voice. "I have no desire to die in my bed, and I don't think you do, either."

"Okay, okay." She threw up her hands. "Whatever."

Zane took the garbage sack in one hand and Jamie's hand in the other, tugging her out to the driveway with him. He should have just said good-bye and walked out the door, but instead, after tossing the sack in the SUV, he pulled her into a tight embrace.

"I will not let anything happen to you," he promised. "No matter what happens between us— and I don't think either of us has a handle on that yet—I will find out what the hell is going on in my county and put a stop to it."

"*You* be careful, too," she told him.

He put his mouth next to her ear. "I have some presents for tonight, too, darlin'. Something to spice things up a little. If you're willing, that is."

The look she gave him was so heated he wasn't sure he'd last until evening. He hoped that look would still be there when he opened the shopping bag.

"You just bring it on." She rose on her toes to give him a kiss that had every hormone in his body on full alert.

He broke the kiss with great reluctance. "Later. And you be damn careful, okay?"

"I will."

She stood watching him as he backed out of the driveway. When he pulled out onto the road, he forcibly tucked her in a corner of his mind to concentrate on business. As he headed toward his office, he wondered if his two mutilated bodies could possibly be part of this, too.

The shit just kept piling higher and deeper.

****

Jamie popped the cap on one of the bottles of Lone Star she'd bought at the market and dropped into a kitchen chair. "This calls for more than coffee or soda," she told Kit.

"No kidding. I'll take one of those, too."

They sat at the table staring at each other. Finally Kit said, "Things are getting heavy with the sheriff."

Jamie took a long swallow of her beer before she answered. "Yeah. And I'll be damned if I can figure out just when it all took such a big turn."

Kit laughed. "Jamie, admit it. You've been in love with him all your life, and I'd say the same goes for him. But you both had a lot of growing up to do. Coming back to Amen may have been a last resort for you, but it looks as if this is what you were meant to do."

Jamie rolled the cold bottle against her forehead. "I just don't know if he sees this as long term. Or if I could spend the rest of my life here in this chicken shit place."

Kit shrugged. "Maybe Zane wants to spread his wings a little. Try someplace else."

"There's still a lot of prejudice in the Southwest. It wouldn't be so bad if he was full-blooded Comanche, believe it or not. But mixed race can put you right behind the eight ball. People aren't quite so...forward-thinking."

"Then it's something you and he will have to work out. If you want to. Meanwhile, figuring out what your dear old pappy was doing to bring in that kind of money should be high on your list."

"I know Grayson Ballou has something to do with it. It's the reason he wants to buy this land. But damned if I can get a handle on it." Jamie stood up and tossed her empty bottle in the trash. "Meanwhile, I'm too edgy to sit around here. Let's go for a ride. I'll show you the rest of Diablo County."

Chapter Fourteen

"Are you sure you want to do this?"

Jamie licked her lips nervously as Kit stuffed a few items in an overnight bag.

"Absolutely. I sure don't want to hang around and listen to you and the hunk have sweaty sex." She zipped the bag closed and straightened. "Think what a fortunate coincidence it is that I tried to call Carol Andrews only to find out she's in San Antonio for a conference."

"But won't she be busy?" Jamie asked. "What will you do with yourself?"

Kit laughed. "Honey, she'll be through for the day by the time I get there. We're going to have dinner at a fabulously expensive restaurant, then hang out in the hotel bar." She winked. "Who knows? I might get lucky myself."

"You watch yourself," Jamie warned. "You and I know what kind of men you'll be running into."

Kit kissed her on the cheek. "Not to worry. Old Kit can take good care of herself. And Carol's a dragon with the barflies. We're just going to have some fun."

"I don't like the idea of you driving all that way by yourself, either." Jamie rubbed her arms as if chasing away the cold, even though it was hot as a furnace. "What if—"

"What if nothing. I'm leaving in daylight, and I'll be fine." She patted her purse and grinned. "Besides, I've got your pappy's six shooter just in case."

Jamie had insisted Kit take the gun she'd found, cleaned, and loaded. God knew who could be waiting out there on the highway, and she refused to let Kit drive away without it.

"Okay." Jamie hugged her. "It's only a couple of miles to the Interstate. If you see anyone following you, call Zane right away."

"Yes, Mom." Kit hugged her back. "I'll be back first thing in the morning."

Jamie walked out to the driveway to watch as Kit backed out into the road. She waved at her, then at the young deputy sitting on the gravel shoulder in his county SUV. When she'd called Zane to tell him Kit was going into San Antonio, he'd told her he was sending someone to keep an eye on things and he didn't want an argument.

And truthfully, with the situation the way it was and as isolated as her house was, she wasn't any too anxious to be by herself.

Zane had sounded harassed when she talked to him, but in a low voice he told her he was looking forward to tonight more than she could imagine. Her pussy muscles clenched at the sensual purr in his voice.

Just sex, Jamie. Keep telling yourself. Just sex.

"I'm going to swing by my house and grab some things and then pick up a pizza. You still like the same kind?"

"Some things never change," she told him.

"And some things do," he said in the same low voice. "Good thing, too. I'll see you around six."

That gave her an hour to get ready.

This is not a date, this is not a date, this is not a date.

She repeated it to herself as she moved about the kitchen. It was important not to read something into this that wasn't there. Keeping a lock on her feelings for Zane was necessary for her sanity. She had no idea what would happen to them when this was all over, but she didn't see herself settling down in Amen or Zane following her to the city.

If she even wanted to go back.

Another thorny issue to wrestle with.

It wasn't as if she had such an itch to get back, but she wanted vindication more than she'd ever wanted anything. All her life she'd been on someone's shit list—her father's, the kids at school, Zane's. She'd invested all of herself in building a new life and a career, only to see it flushed down the toilet. If she didn't get it back, she wasn't sure she'd even know who she was anymore.

So. Tight lid on the emotions. Tight.

She set the table with place mats, candles, and wine glasses. Just because they were having pizza didn't mean they couldn't eat in style. Then she changed the sheets on her bed, fluffed up the pillows, and set out fat, scented candles in the holders she'd picked up while she and Kit were doing their county tour. Zane said he had big plans for the evening. She'd do her part to make it so.

This is not a date, she kept repeating as she ran hot water in the tub and dumped in half a bottle of bath salts, immersing herself in it with a glass of wine. But she definitely planned to have great sex. That didn't require emotional commitment. Zane Cameron of all people should know that.

She had just finished rubbing lavender lotion into every inch and crevice of her body and was pulling on a short satin robe that somehow had escaped destruction when she heard booted feet in the hallway.

For a moment, her heart stopped, then she heard Zane's voice. "Glad you took my advice about locking the door."

He carried a large duffel bag in one hand and looked so weary her heart ached for him. Again, she was startled at how quickly the tenor of their relationship had changed.

"Bad day?"

"You could say." Then one corner of his mouth turned up. "But I think it's about to get better. Right?"

"I put myself in your custody, sheriff," she teased.

"I have to say I'm glad Kit's not here." He winked and dropped his duffel in a corner. "Let me shower first. I stink of rotten humanity."

Planting a quick kiss on her lips, he stripped off his clothes and headed for the bathroom. "By the way, you look good enough to eat. And that's first on the menu, before the pizza."

She almost said the same to him. The taut muscles of his buttocks and thighs flexed as he walked across the room, the last of the sunlight filtering in through her window enhancing the bronze of his skin. But what really captured her attention was the erection rising proudly from the nest of pubic hair, stiff enough to hammer nails. Her mouth watered and her pussy dripped at the sight of it.

"No peeking." He laughed over his shoulder as he closed the bathroom door.

She was shaking with anticipation while she stuck the pizza in a low oven to keep it warm, opened the Chianti Zane had brought, and poured two glasses. By the time she had the candles in the bedroom lit and their scent drifting into the air, the bathroom door opened.

And all the liquid in her mouth dried up.

He'd shaved as well as showered, obviously washed his hair and let it loose on his shoulders in a sleek fall, and he wore only a towel knotted low on his hips. There was no mistaking the tent in the fabric or the heat in his eyes.

He took the glass of wine Jamie handed him and touched it to hers. "To new beginnings."

171

"New beginnings." Her hand shook slightly as she lifted the glass to her lips and took a sip of the rich red liquid. The fingers of warmth that stretched through her body calmed the jitters she'd been fighting all day, torn between hot anticipation and the lifetime fear of letting go of her emotions. Last night had shown her she wanted this man more than she'd ever believed possible, but the fear of risking her heart still clung to her.

We'll see. We'll wait and see.

Zane set his glass down on her nightstand and reached out both hands. She put down her own drink and came forward to him. His hands were work-roughened but warm, and his touch was tender.

"Tonight I'm going to make love to you in so many ways you won't even know your own name," he said, his voice coarse with passion.

"I thought you already did," she whispered.

He pulled her close, one hand stroking her hair, his eyes fixed on a point somewhere beyond her. "I've had a lot of women these past years, Jamie. Both before you left and afterward. I'm not necessarily proud of the fact, but what's done is done." He dropped his gaze to capture hers. "But I did learn a lot about what pleases me sexually. And how to please my partner."

Jamie swallowed hard, surprised by his confession. Unable to tear her eyes from his, she wondered what was coming next.

"I want to do all these things with you. I don't want there to be any boundaries between us, but I also don't want to do anything to turn you off."

Her pussy clenched as erotic images danced through her head. She may not have done everything, but she certainly had read enough. The thought of doing those things with Zane made arousal sweep through her body.

"I'm not a child," she told him. "I may not be as

experienced as you, but just because I haven't done certain things doesn't mean I don't know about them. Or that I'm not willing to try them with you." She bit at her lower lip. "Last night is the first time I...that is, that I ever...I mean..."

"Let someone fuck you in the ass?"

She nodded.

"I'm glad. I'm glad I was the first. And if things...work out...I'm damn sure going to be the last. But there are other things. Things that..."

"What exactly are you saying, Zane? That you like your sex rough? That you like a lot of...variety?" She was quaking inside but determined not to show it. She wasn't sure she could handle things if they got out of control. But she was hot all over, the blood pounding in her veins.

"Yes. Rough...and hard. And wild. Can you take it, Jamie? Can you do this?"

She nibbled at her lower lip. "You won't...you know, hurt me?" For one crazy moment she wondered if he'd found a new way to pay her back, take out all the anger he'd been storing up. Her pulse kicked into overdrive.

No. This is Zane. He's a lot of things but physically cruel isn't one of them.

One corner of his mouth kicked up in a grin. "The only pain I have in mind for you is the kind that causes real pleasure."

She had to admit, she was more than a little enticed by the idea of exploring new sexual boundaries with this man. Things she'd read about but never been tempted to try with anyone else. Would she enjoy it? The sudden fullness of her breasts and the liquid dripping from her fluttering cunt were a good indication that the idea of this kind of sex with Zane aroused her.

She realized he was looking at her, waiting for her to say something else. "And you'll...stop any time I ask you to?"

He brushed his thumbs across her cheekbones. "This isn't a punishment, darlin'. If you don't like something, we won't do it. But Jamie, I hope you like it all. Because I want to do everything with you."

She was so afraid that once she said yes she'd be bound to this man forever, and there were so many obstacles to even reaching that point. Her own murky future. What he really wanted from her once they climbed out of bed. But she wasn't going to let him think she wasn't his equal. Whatever he promised, she wanted to try it. And give back as good as she got. It was a new sexual frontier for her, and if she moved in that direction with anyone, it would surely be Zane.

"I don't care what it is." She thrust out her chin. "Whatever you want, Zane, just bring it on."

Oh, god, I hope I'm not making a mistake here. Where's my brain when I need it? Lodged right between my legs, that's where.

He cupped her chin and tilted her face up to him. His face was dark with need and the fires of lust burned in his obsidian black eyes. "All right, darlin'. Here we go. Just remember. You can stop any time you want."

He picked her up in his arms, brushing his lips against hers with a feather light touch. His tongue traced the closed seam of her mouth, and his teeth nibbled at her lower lip. He traced the outline of her mouth, licking at it like a piece of delicious candy. Shimmers of heat cascaded through her body, and she opened for his tongue, sucking it inside.

The contact of his tongue against hers was like an electrical connection, shooting sparks throughout the warm well of her mouth. She tightened her arms around his neck, the silken fall of his hair tickling her skin. She could feel wetness seep from her aching pussy, soaking through her robe to his arm holding her.

His chuckle against her mouth was low and sensual. "Ready for me so soon, darlin'?"

I'm always ready for you, it seems, she wanted to say, but she didn't want to take her lips away from his. Somehow, without her being aware of it, he removed her robe and placed her nude body on the cool sheets of her bed. The ceiling fan turned lazily overhead, stirring the air just enough to spread the scent of the candles throughout the room but not enough to cool her heated flesh.

Zane stretched his long body out beside her, kissing the underside of her jaw, the spot behind her ear, the column of her neck. When he reached the sensitive place where neck and shoulder joined, he nipped the skin lightly and once again sparks of heat danced through her.

His large, warm hand plumped one breast, lifting it to his mouth. He swiped his tongue over the already beaded nipple. Sensations shot straight to her womb, and the inner muscles of her cunt fluttered. Zane suckled the hardened tip, pulling it first with his lips, then with his teeth until she thought it would burst from pleasure.

"Jamie, Jamie, Jamie. You can't begin to know how many nights I lay in my bed, so hard I thought my dick would break, dreaming about loving you like this."

Her legs shifted restlessly and she rubbed her thighs together. "Did you? I shouldn't admit it, but I've had my own fantasies."

"Tell me what they are and I'll fulfill every one of them." Zane lifted his head from her breast. "Spread your legs wide for me, darlin'. Move your hand down and touch yourself. I know you're wet. Rub your fingers through it, then let me see you lick them."

A thread of dark need began to uncurl inside

Jamie. She'd tried a lot of things in previous relationships, but somehow she knew Zane was going to take her past all her boundaries, push her to places she'd never been before. To heights of pleasure she'd never attained. She moved her legs apart, touching her wet pussy with her fingers until they were covered with her liquid, then lifted them to her lips.

Zane was nibbling on her nipple again and turned his head to watch her. When she sucked her fingers into her mouth, his thick cock jerked against her thigh and his breathing hitched.

"Wet your fingers again and rub your juice on your other nipple," he told her.

Touching herself sent tiny shivers through her, frissons of excitement, and when she rubbed her own cream on her nipple, it hardened almost painfully.

At once Zane shifted his mouth to that nipple, licking the cream glistening on it and raking it with his teeth.

"Touch me," she begged.

"You want my fingers inside your cunt?" he asked, flicking her nipple with his tongue. "Is that what you want, darlin'?"

"Yes, yes. Please."

Again that dark, sensuous laugh. "All in good time. I have more plans for these gorgeous sweet nipples first."

Her nipples were already so inflamed, so ultra sensitive, she didn't know what else he could do to them.

He rolled lithely off the bed and went to the duffel he had brought. Unzipping it, he took out a small box that he carried back to the bed. Kneeling beside her, he opened the box and showed her what looked like tiny gold bars with clusters of jewels.

She'd seen pictures of nipple clamps before but not the real thing. In her fantasies, she'd wondered what it would be like to feel the cold metal pinching her, her nipples swelling between them.

Jamie stared, fascinated, anticipation flooding her, as Zane removed them one at a time from the box and placed one of them on the bed next to her. With thumb and forefinger, he plumped one nipple, pinching it just hard enough to make her gasp. Pain mingled with delight. Holding the bud with one hand, he tugged it between two thin gold bars, then tightened the tiny screws on each side.

At first the pain seemed intolerable, but then it morphed into a new level of pleasure and more juice dripped from her cunt. When he took his hand away, the tiny pearls dangling from the clamp brushed the sensitized skin of her breast.

Zane's eyes were hot, dark, and a flush of sensuality stained his bronze cheekbones. He looked almost dangerous, and the edge of danger aroused her even more. He attached the second clamp to the other nipple, then moved off the bed to admire his handiwork.

"They look gorgeous on you." His voice was thick and heavy. "I knew they would. I bought them just for you."

He pinched each swollen nipple once more, then stepped to his duffle again. This time he had a small paper tote bag in his hand. Jamie fixated on it as he placed it on the night stand.

"Do you like to play with toys, Jamie? Use a vibrator on yourself?"

Yes, she did, but she actually felt herself blush.

Zane leaned down and kissed each protruding nipple. "Ah, good. I love to use toys on women. But I've never wanted to see anyone do it as much as you, darlin'. I like my sex innovative. Maybe a little rough." He lifted his gaze to hers. "We still okay here?"

She swallowed hard and nodded.

"All right, then. Close your eyes for me. Real tight. When you can't see, all the other senses are sharper."

Jamie lowered her eyelids, the edge of the unknown exciting her. The next thing she knew, a soft cloth covered her eyes and Zane's hands lifted her head as he tied the ends behind her. Warm fingers circled her wrists, lifting her arms up and over her head, replaced in a moment by metal. A quiet snick, and when she tried to lower her hands, she realized she was cuffed to the headboard.

"I don't want this to be unpleasant for you, Jamie. Not for one minute. Any time we go too far, just tell me to stop and that's it. It's only good if we both enjoy it. Okay?"

She nodded, her mouth so dry she didn't think she could make a sound.

The pinch on her nipples again sent bolts of pleasure to her womb. Then the mattress dipped as Zane knelt between her legs, bending them so her feet were flat, pushing them wide apart. Waiting for his next move, his next touch, was more arousing than she could have believed.

His hands stroked her entire sex, then one finger trailed the length of her slit, from clit to anus.

"Such a beautiful cunt," he murmured. "I could fuck you all night every night and never get enough of you. You're in my blood." His voice dropped. "In my soul."

Her heart stuttered at his words, and she drew in a deep breath to steady herself.

His fingers separated the pussy lips, opening them wide. His thumbs pressed into her heated flesh on either side of her slit, massaging the flesh, coaxing the little bundle of nerves from its protective hood. His tongue flicked lightly over the exposed tip, and she nearly jolted off the bed at the contact.

"You are so wet. So deliciously soaked. You taste

like the best peaches, not too tart, not too sweet. I could go to sleep every night with my tongue in your pussy."

Fresh cream gushed at his touch and his words, and her hips jerked up at him.

"Your little clit is so red, darlin'. It's just begging to be tormented." His thumbs continued to massage the flesh beside it. "What a dilemma. Shall I suck it? Bite it? Rub my thumb over it until you scream for release?"

A warm stream of breath blew over her clit, and she quaked with need.

"Would you like something in this gorgeous cunt, Jamie? Something to fill you? Stretch you?"

"Y-yes." Her voice was a whisper. "Please."

"Let's make it even better, shall we?"

She had no idea what he was talking about until he bent her legs back, her knees touching her chest. His forearm held them in place, easing the strain on her muscles. Her entire sex was exposed to his vision, nothing hidden or concealed. He could see it all. One hand smoothed lovingly over her buttocks.

"Do you know what I want to do? What I've been thinking all day about doing?"

"What?" She barely got the word out.

"Seeing this absolutely gorgeous ass turning bright red. Have you ever been spanked by one of your lovers, Jamie?"

She shook her head, her pulse racing as she realized what his intention was.

"Good." His voice was low and soft but still smug with satisfaction. "And no one else ever will. I want to watch you squirming with pleasure every time my hand touches you." His hand continued to stroke the curve of her buttocks, brushing softly against the tender skin.

He ran a nail lightly over her perineum, back and forth, and she could almost feel his eyes on her.

Her pussy muscles clenched, and she tried to squeeze her thighs together to clamp down on the feeling rocketing through her.

"I want to take you higher than you've ever been," Zane crooned, fondling her ass again. "All day I've thought about this, about watching you helpless, writhing with need, struggling for the orgasm that I hold just out of reach. Can you picture that, Jamie? Know how that would feel?"

He was toying with her clit now, rasping it with the pad of his thumb. She heard the sound of her own rough breathing in the air, felt her blood race through her veins as her body responded to him.

"I want to watch you come apart and know it's only for me. Just for me."

Although she was expecting it, her body jerked when the first slap landed on her ass. The heat from it spread over the surface of her skin. She couldn't swallow the moan that rolled up from her throat.

"You like that, don't you?" Zane's voice was husky and slightly unsteady. "The sting of my hand feels good to you, right?"

She nodded, heard a whimpering sound cutting through the air, and realized it was her. Strangely, after the first minute or two, she found it actually aroused her, if it were possible for her to be any hotter than she was. When the next stinging slap landed, she couldn't hold back, pushing herself into the flat of his hand. She wanted to shout, "More! Harder!"

Her pussy was dripping and her nipples throbbed with a heavy pulse. God, what was happening to her? Where was she letting him take her? No, not letting. Craving. She *craved* whatever he had in mind. She wanted him to fulfill every dark, depraved fantasy she'd ever had and never stop.

His hand came down again and again as he held

her helpless to his movements. She tried to anticipate each touch, but the rhythm was uneven, as if he wanted to keep her off balance. Fire streaked from her ass to her thighs and cunt, and when one slap landed on her clit, she nearly came just from that contact.

Abruptly the spanking stopped, leaving her shockingly unfulfilled. What was he doing? Didn't he know she wanted more? When a finger pressed on her anus another wave of heat washed over her, blistering her skin. Another moan broke from her lips. The pounding of her blood roared in her ears.

"Know what I'm going to do, darlin'? I'm going to fill this little hole back here. It won't feel as good as it did last night with my cock in it, but this way I get to see it being stretched and taking a new toy I bought just for you."

His voice was hypnotic, mesmerizing her, and she realized no matter what he wanted, she would let him do anything to her. She sensed movement on his part, then something thick and cool touched the tiny ring of her anus.

"Just some lubricant, sweetheart, to ease the way for you."

His fingers worked it into her rectum, massaging her inner tissues, pushing the thick substance deep into the channel. Then he was pushing something at that tight opening, pressing, forcing the muscles to open.

"Breathe through your mouth, Jamie. Just like last night. This is a brand new butt plug I bought with this particular butt in mind. I promise you'll love it when it's all the way in."

Zane was right about being blindfolded and restrained enhancing every other sense. With her eyes blindfolded and her hands cuffed, her entire being was focused on what he was doing. Slowly, he inserted the plug into her rectum, pausing frequently to let her adjust to its thickness. She had never realized the sensitive nerve centers in that dark tunnel, but now they seemed to explode like incendiary devices, spreading their fireworks everywhere in her body and making her cunt clench in need.

"It's in, Jamie. And god, it's just the most beautiful sight." There was a slight tremor in his voice. "Seeing your ass filled like that...Jesus. I can hardly keep from coming right now."

Jamie wanted to come herself. All she could think about was how Zane's cock had felt in her ass the night before and the intense pleasure it gave her.

"All right, darlin'." His breathing was nearly as ragged as hers. "I've got another little present here for you." His mouth closed over her clit again, pulling on it, while two fingers slid easily into her vagina. "Oh, yeah. Nice and juicy. When you come, sweetheart, you'll lose your mind."

Something cool touched the opening of her pussy. A dildo. A rather large one. She worried whether she could take it with the butt plug so firmly inserted inside her, already filling her.

As if he could read her mind, Zane said, "It'll be fine, I promise you. Don't fight it. Just think about both of your channels filled to the max, not an inch of room to spare, and the need to come as it builds in your body. Your little muscles clamping down so tightly, squeezing, convulsing, spasming." She heard him suck in a breath. "If I don't shut up, I'll come just from listening to myself."

Just as he'd done with the plug, he eased the dildo in slowly. By the time he'd inserted the entire length, she was so full she was sure she was stretched to the limit. Her nipples ached, her ass burned, and she had the sensation of two giant cocks inserted in both of her channels. She'd never experienced anything like it. Tremors raced over her body.

"Here we go, darlin'." Zane's voice was low and rough.

He pressed against the bottom of the dildo, and when it began to buzz, Jamie realized it was a vibrator. The sensations radiated from her pussy throughout her body and through the thin membrane into the butt plug. Everything in her body seemed to be shaking.

And then Zane took her nipples between thumb and forefinger and placed his mouth over her clit, sucking hard.

It was too much, the intensity of it frightening her. She tugged at the handcuffs and thrashed her head back and forth, her hips twisting. Every part of her body was being stimulated, driving her to a plane she'd never before reached. The climax was roaring down on her, and she tried to pull away.

Suddenly, everything stopped. The vibrator was still and Zane's mouth and hands left her body.

"No," she cried. As much as the place he was taking her terrified her, she wanted it. Wanted that wrenching climax that her body demanded.

When Zane pressed the vibrator's button, this time he upped the level and her body shook as if tossed by a gale force wind. She reached for the peak of ecstasy, but just as the wind was ready to toss her over the edge, everything stopped again.

Again and again he took her way up, only to pull her back at the last moment, until she was mindless with need.

"Please," she begged. "Please, Zane." She was nearly sobbing by now.

"All right, darlin'." He placed a kiss on each cheek of her buttocks, then turned up the vibrator and went to work on her aching clit and nipples.

The orgasm built in the pit of her stomach and

roared through her like an inferno. She wanted it. She was afraid of it. She couldn't handle it. Even as she fought it, the spasms built in intensity.

"Go with it, Jamie," Zane crooned to her. "Let it take you. Don't be afraid. Ride it out."

"I can't," she cried, trying to pull back. "Please, Zane. It's too much."

She fought it as the grip of something more powerful than she'd ever known clutched at her, but Zane was relentless. And then it took her, a tidal wave of sensation that shook her and tossed her. Her stomach muscles clenched, her pussy clenched, her rectum tightened on the plug, and her entire body shuddered. It went on and on until she was sure it would never stop. She couldn't catch her breath, couldn't stop quaking.

At last, the force of it began to subside. Zane turned off the vibrator and began to caress her, bringing her down slowly. He eased the plug and vibrator from her body, then gently trailed kisses from her ankles up the insides of her thighs, across her stomach and up to her breasts. When he released the clamps, pain surged through her nipples with the rush of blood, and he soothed each one with his mouth.

Finally, he unlocked the handcuffs, removed the blindfold, and lay next to her, pulling her into his arms. Her body was covered with a fine sheen of perspiration, and she couldn't stop trembling. Her heart was thudding so hard she was sure it would leap from her chest, and all the air from her lungs seemed trapped in her throat.

She burrowed into his body as if it were the only thing that could stabilize her, the aroma of the candles and Zane's rich male scent, a clean, earthy scent, filling her nostrils like a tranquilizer. Aftershocks still raced through her body, and her thighs were sticky with the release of her juices. And still she couldn't stop trembling.

Zane murmured to her in his low, rich voice, his hands stroking her, easing her. His kisses were like feathers on her eyelids, her cheeks, and the line of her jaw. At last, she heaved a sigh into his chest and relaxed against him. Her bones felt like jelly, her skin like wet tissue paper. She wasn't sure she'd ever be able to stand another orgasm like that one.

Then she realized that, like last night, Zane had seen to her pleasure first. His penis was hard as a spike pressing against her, yet he only concentrated on her well-being.

Cocked and loaded, but he hadn't pulled the trigger.

Once again he seemed to know what she was thinking. "If you think I didn't get pleasure from this, you're very much mistaken," he told her.

"But you didn't...I mean, last night, too, you..."

"Hush." He silenced her with a soft kiss on her lips. "The best is yet to come."

Chapter Fifteen

Zane drew a hot bath, dumping the rest of her bath salts in the water. While the tub was filling, he took a small bottle of oil from his bag and rubbed it into Jamie's aching nipples.

"The nipple clamps looked beautiful on you," he said, massaging gently. "I picked them out especially for you."

She wrinkled her forehead. "When did you do all this shopping, if you're supposed to be solving two murders, checking into my father's accident, and trying to find out who broke into my house?"

He grinned. "I'm the boss. I get to take some personal time when I need it. Come on." He lifted her in his arms. "The tub's almost full. I've been dreaming about taking a bath with you."

Jamie wound her arms around his neck. "You have? Was that before or after you thought about running me out of town?" She wanted the words back as soon as they left her mouth.

Zane stopped just inside the bathroom door, every muscle in his body tense. "I thought we were past all that shit. Otherwise what was last night and tonight all about?"

She reached her hand up to his cheek and forced him to look at her. "I'm sorry, Zane. My mouth works without my brain attached. That was a rotten thing to say, but I haven't yet figured out how not to be on the defensive."

He shifted his gaze away from her, just standing there, holding her, her legs draped over his arm. Suddenly, he seemed a million miles away from her.

"Zane? Please forgive me. I *want* to be with you. To make love with you. Any way you want. It just seems I've been fighting the world for so long..."

Tears gathered in her eyes.

Shit. I'm going to ruin everything.

She pressed her face to his chest and kissed the hard muscles, tugging at his nipples with her teeth and licking them the way he had with hers. Her tears plopped onto his skin.

Zane drew in a deep breath and let it out slowly, and she felt the tension seep from his body. His gaze drifted back to hers, and she flinched at the pain still lurking there. Then he forced a grin. "Maybe I'll have to spank you again for that."

She hugged him. "You can put me over your lap any time, Sheriff. Spank me as hard as you want."

His mouth crushed hers, the kiss stealing her breath and fogging her senses. "Don't ever bring that up again," he said when he lifted his head. "We were both wrong, and it's over and done with. We're moving forward, Jamie. If you want to."

She pressed her cheek against his skin. "I wouldn't be here with you, like this, if I didn't want to."

"Okay." One corner of his mouth hitched up. "Just watch that smart mouth of yours, darlin'. And I *do* owe you a spanking. Keep that in mind."

He stepped into the tub, still holding her, and lowered them both into the steaming, richly scented water. He cradled her between his thighs, his legs bent because the tub was too short to accommodate his length. His hands slid under her arms to palm her breasts again, his thumbs barely whispering over her sore, swollen nipples.

She nestled back against his broad chest, sighing, until the thick hardness of his cock pressed against the cleft of her ass. She leaned her head back against his shoulder, a grin teasing at her lips.

"Feels like someone wants attention."

"And we're going to take care of him. In a minute." He kissed the top of her head. "Just lie back against me and close your eyes. Let me soothe your body, ease those sore muscles, so I can pleasure you again."

"Much more pleasure and I won't be able to walk for a week," she teased, but she leaned her head back against his broad chest obediently, closed her eyes, and let his fingers work their magic on her. She drifted, cocooned in his arms, the scented water lapping at her, her body rising and falling with every breath Zane took.

He bathed her as if she were a child, soaping the washcloth and trailing it over her. He washed her arms, her hands, even each individual finger. When he soaped her shoulders, he massaged the muscles until her head was simply lolling on her neck. With her breasts and nipples, his touch was like a whisper of wind, barely there. She gave herself to the lethargy that stole over her.

Her eyes popped open when Zane's strong hands lifted and urged her forward onto her hands and knees, her chin touching the surface of the water.

"What—"

"Shh," he soothed, his deep voice like warm honey. "Easy. Let me take care of you."

He washed every inch of her cunt, working the soap into her with one lean finger, her inner muscles clenching as her nerve endings woke up again. He barely touched the tip of her clit, yet when he did, the tight coil low in her belly began unwinding again. Surely she couldn't be ready for him again so soon?

Next came the insides of her thighs, his hands working the lather into her skin. And finally, he separated the cheeks of her ass and inserted a soapy finger into that hot tunnel. He rubbed the lather into her tissues, then squeezed water inside with the wash cloth to rinse it away.

By now Jamie was panting, the calming effect of the bath replaced by growing heat.

"Spread your thighs." Zane's voice was hoarse, his hands firm on her hips as he adjusted her position.

Water sloshed over the tub as he reached for something, she heard the tearing of foil, felt the movement of his hands as he sheathed his cock. He lifted her, his thighs between hers, spreading her wide, positioning her over his cock. The head of it nudged her open vagina, pressing firmly against her. When he was partway inside, Zane pulled her up and back so she was sitting on him, the heavy shaft sliding home until the tip of it bumped her womb.

"Tighten your cunt around me," he murmured in her ear.

Jamie clenched her vaginal muscles, milking him, pulling a groan from him that rumbled through his chest. Bracing her hands on the tub she began to ride him, a slow up and down rhythm at first, then faster.

"That's it, darlin'," he moaned. "Move on me, just like that. Jesus, Jamie, slow down. Slow down. I want this to last."

His hands gripped her hips again, guiding her, setting the pace he wanted. As tender as her flesh was, it still softened to accept him and then tightened around him, long pulls at his thick rod as he moved her up and down. Her heart thudded heavily against her breastbone and her blood roared in her ears as passion exploded within her. She was aware of nothing except the two of them, connected, him inside her, and the steady ride up the rails of the roller coaster.

Zane's fingers tightened on her and pulled her harder onto his shaft with each movement.

"Reach down and touch my balls," he whispered. "I've got you."

Sliding her hand beneath the water Jamie felt between her thighs and reached backward until she cupped the heavy sac. Gently, she kneaded and massaged it, rubbing her fingers over the pleated surface. When she pinched the skin gently, his body jerked. With his hands firmly on her waist, he surged upward from the water, carrying her with him, still impaled on his cock.

"What—"

"I need to be in a bed for this." His voice was raspy, hoarse. "I can't fuck your brains out in the bathtub."

He lifted her from his penis, then swept her up and carried her to the bed, grabbing towels from the vanity counter on his way. Zane tossed the towels onto the sheets and laid her out on her back. Warm fingers grabbed her ankles to spread her legs wide and, without preamble, plunged back into her.

Spikes of pleasure drove through her, radiating sensation to every part of her body. He rolled his hips and set a steady pace, driving into her harder with each thrust. In and out, in and out, and in and out, stretching her already swollen tissues. The tiny edge of pain burst into an explosion of sensual delight that consumed her. She was so stimulated, so electrified, she never wanted him to stop.

Harder, she wanted to shout, shocking herself. Locking her ankles around his neck she pulled herself to him as tightly as she could, trying to move her body more, but he had her nearly immobilized. She couldn't do anything except grab the sheets in her fists and hold on tight.

The air in the room was filled with the heavy sounds of their tortured breathing and redolent with the rich scent of sex. Through half-opened lids Jamie saw Zane's taut face, heat blazing from his eyes as they feasted on her body, hips rocketing as he slammed into her over and over. In the muted light of the room, he looked like a bronze god. *Her* god.

Without warning, she climaxed, her vaginal muscles clutching at him as spasms rocked her. Her liquid heat bathed his sheathed cock as her pussy clenched around him. He rode her through it, never lessening his pace, sweat dripping from his body, her legs still held wide in his hands.

The contractions subsided, leaving her struggling for breath, but Zane never changed his rhythm, stroke after stroke slamming into her body. Just as she was dragging air into her oxygen-starved lungs she was suddenly caught by yet another climax, slower but no less intense, her cunt tugging hard at the cock pounding into it. It was too much, more than she was used to, terrifying in its length and intensity, and she struggled to pull away.

Zane slid his hands from her legs to the cheeks of her ass, bending low over her as he pulled her even more tightly against him.

"Don't fight me, darlin'," he gasped. "Go with it. Let it take you."

"I...can't." She barely got the words out. "Please."

"Ride it, Jamie. Right now."

His hands gripped her buttocks, his rhythm increased, and with a final roll of his hips, he plunged them both into a black void. She was whirling, tumbling, rudderless as hard spasms shook her. She didn't think she had anything left in her, but her body obviously thought otherwise. As Zane's latex-covered shaft pulsed inside the tight walls of her vagina, her orgasm went on and on, seemingly without end.

She had no idea how long it lasted, only that when it was over, she lay back limply, unable to move, just praying she could get her next breath.

Zane's head dropped to her shoulder, his own breathing rough, his heart thundering against her breasts.

Finally, he pulled himself up and slowly pulled his cock from her unresisting, spent body. She was too weary even to open her eyes, but she heard him move away, probably to the bathroom to dispose of the condom. Then he was back, bathing her between her legs with a warm cloth, then drying her with a soft towel.

Sweeping all the towels off the bed into a pile on the floor, he lay down and pulled Jamie up against him, spooning her into his body. He brushed her hair behind her ears and kissed her cheek and her neck, light kisses meant to soothe rather than arouse.

"You belong to me now," he murmured in a low voice. "Don't forget it."

She roused herself enough to ask, "Belong to you? What do you mean?"

"You're mine now, Jamie. Just the way you should have been before. Only this time, I'm not letting you go."

Jamie swallowed the panic that suddenly surged through her. She'd thought about this, but was she really ready for it? Sex was one thing, but did she trust Zane enough to accept that kind of commitment? What the hell did she do now?

As she drifted off to sleep, she could have sworn she heard him whisper, "I love you."

****

Jamie stretched lazily in bed, eyes still closed to hang onto the memories floating around in her mind. Early that morning Zane had made slow, lazy love to her one last time before he had to get up.

"Do you remember what I said last night?" he asked as his cock slipped into her from behind. He had one leg pulled over his thigh and his fingers were busy at her tender clit, gentle but insistent.

192

"You said a lot," she answered breathlessly. "Which particular thing?"

"That you belong to me." He emphasized his statement with a hard thrust into her pussy. "That you're mine now."

"You...said something else, too," she reminded him, drifting in a haze of sexual pleasure, wondering if he'd admit to what she heard.

He was silent for so long, concentrating only on bringing her to the edge of climax, she was sure he was going to either ignore it or deny it. Then he put his mouth close to her ear. "I meant it, too."

Her heart stuttered and a warm feeling flushed through her body. She'd never thought to hear Zane Cameron admit he loved her. Ever. It had always just been about sex, and she'd thought it was now, too.

"I..." She set her lips, pulling the words from deep inside herself. "I...love you, too. But Zane—"

His arm tightened around her and he groaned softly.

"No buts. We have a lot of strikes against us, Jamie. A lot to work through."

"But—"

"I said no buts. We started out here for all the wrong reasons. We were both angry, both felt betrayed, both wanted some kind of payback. But I'd like to think we're past that. That we can figure it out as long as we're together."

Then there was no more talking. Her orgasm, when it erupted, had none of the explosiveness of the night before. Instead, it was a series of warm spasms that moved through her like slow waves. Zane held her clit between thumb and forefinger, rubbing it to prolong her pleasure while his cock pumped his fluid into the latex covering it.

His kisses had been deep and languorous before he reluctantly pulled himself from her body and rolled off the bed.

"Sex with you is so incredible, darlin'," he told her as he bent over her. "There's so much more I want to do with you. Tell me I don't frighten you or turn you off."

"Never." She smiled and pulled his head down for a quick kiss. "And I don't know who's more amazed, you or me."

"Treat yourself to another bath this morning. One where some horny man isn't bothering you. It'll do you a world of good." His voice deepened. "Relax and think of tonight. Think of how you can reward me for all my hard work today."

She chuckled. "I'll put my mind to work on it."

"I hope to have something to tell you about the truck tonight. And remember. Don't go anywhere alone and without calling me."

"Kit will be back before long. We'll be together all day."

"Good." He kissed her one last time and was gone.

After he left, she dozed off again, but now she was wrapping the memories around her like a familiar quilt. One hand stole naughtily between her legs, touching her well-used pussy. Zane took her to unbelievable heights. She couldn't wait to see what else he had in store for her.

Smiling she rolled over on her stomach and pulled the pillow over her head, savoring the feelings for a few minutes more. She heard the front door open and close and waited for the click of Kit's heels on the floor, the call of her voice. Instead, she heard heavy footsteps, and suddenly a heavy body was pinning her face down to the bed, a rough hand covering her mouth.

"You bitch." The voice was a whisper, disguising whoever it was.

She struggled against the person, trying to

throw him off, but he punched her in the side of the head, so hard that pain exploded behind her eyes and rocketed to her ears. While she was trying to recover, her attacker yanked her hands behind her back and tied them with rough-feeling rope. Then he blindfolded her with material that felt like burlap and scratched her eyelids.

"Now," he said. "Let's get down to business. First, where's the money?"

"I don't have it," she cried. "Please don't do this. Please."

"Bitch," he spat again and smacked her head again. "I can do this all day so give it up while you still can."

"I told you I don't have the money." The second blow made her sick to her stomach, and she struggled not to vomit. She heaved up against him, but he was too heavy to dislodge.

"Maybe I should try a little different approach." His whisper was guttural. His hands came around to her front and strong fingers squeezed her tender breasts so brutally she screamed at the pleasure/pain. "Ah, that got your attention. Thought so."

One tear escaped, trailing down her cheek. Jamie bit her lip, the pain in her head so bad she could barely stand it. How had this man gotten into her house? Where was Kit? What would happen to her when she walked in on this?

"You need to do yourself two favors, you rotten little cunt. Sell this house and get the fuck out of this town. Get as far away from Amen as the world allows. And don't ever come back."

He squeezed her breasts again, pinching the nipples hard enough to draw another scream from her. Then she felt the cold blade of a knife against her breast and the pain as it sliced into flesh. Cold fear stole over her.

He's going to kill me. Or make me wish he had.

Jamie had never been much for praying, but she was praying hard now.

"You hear me, you tramp? And give back the fucking money. It isn't yours. Your old man's dead so he's got no use for it. That sheriff isn't going to save you. We've got his number. He'll wash his hands of you in a hot minute." The knife made another small slice into the sensitive skin.

This time she couldn't swallow the scream.

"Pain makes people think twice, you know." His mouth was so close to her face, and his breath had a fetid quality to it. "Hey. Maybe I can get myself a little piece of ass while I'm here," the man laughed. "Seeing as how you're already naked and all. Then you can find out what pain's really all about. You'll never screw with the wrong people again."

He yanked the covers back, exposing her body, and shoved her legs apart. He knelt on her calves to immobilize her and one hand touched her pussy. The knife caressed the insides of her thighs, the edge of it sharp against her skin. She whimpered.

The front door slammed, and the man jerked, the knife twitching in his hand so that it skittered down to her knee, leaving a stinging trail.

"Jamie? You out of bed yet? I see the hunk has already left."

Oh, Jesus. Kit!

She heard the heels tapping on the hardwood floor, and Kit's voice getting louder as she neared the bedroom.

Go away, Kit. Save yourself.

Then she remembered. Kit had her father's old wheel gun. She'd said she knew how to use it, but did she really?

"Hey, girl. Answer me, will you? We don't allow people to lie in bed all day, you know. Did you...oh, shit."

Jamie's attacker lifted himself from her slightly. "Who the hell are you?" he growled.

"I can ask you the same thing." Kit's voice held a combination of fear and anger. "Get off of her. Now."

"Put the damn gun down," the man ordered, shifting his knife to press it against Jamie's throat, "or I'll slice your friend open like a ripe tomato."

There was a thud as something dropped to the floor and then a shot whizzed past Jamie so close she felt the breeze. The weight on her was suddenly gone as the man rolled off the bed, the knife scraping her skin as he went.

"Hey, watch that gun," he shouted.

Kit's answer was another shot, followed by a loud groan.

"God damn it. You shot me, you cunt."

Another shot and Kit screaming, "Get out of here."

Then the thud of heavy feet running down the hall.

One more shot echoed, but Jamie heard the front door slam. Whoever her attacker was, he was gone. She heard the gun fall to the floor, then Kit was beside her, trying to work the rope loose.

"Oh, shit, Jamie. Oh, sweet Jesus. Oh, god. Shit, shit, shit."

She finally got the rope off and yanked away the blindfold. Jamie's head was ready to explode, and her breasts were so sore she wanted to cry. She forced her eyes open to see Kit looking at her with horror in her eyes.

"Oh, my god. Shit, you're bleeding. Don't move. Wait. Stay there." She pulled the covers over Jamie.

"Aspirin," Jamie managed to get out.

"Did he hit your head?" Her fingers pressed against Jamie's temple, finding a tender spot.

Jamie winced, tears leaking from her eyes.

"Oh, honey, you've got a huge lump here. And

another one over here. I'm not giving you anything until a doctor sees you."

"Call...Zane," she managed before blackness rolled over her.

****

Jamie fought her way up from the bottom of the ocean, water choking her, suffocating her.

"I'd like to keep her overnight," she heard a strange man say. "She's got a concussion and some very nasty cuts and bruises. Apparently, he scraped the skin on her throat with the edge of the knife, too."

"Was she raped?" Zane's voice, filled with rage. Was he mad at *her*?

"No, but not for lack of trying from what I gather. It looks as if he meant to mutilate her with a knife."

She heard colorful cursing, long and low. Where was she anyway? She forced her eyes open.

The room was unfamiliar, a cubicle of some kind, and she was lying on what could only be called a piece of hospital furniture. No other bed was this uncomfortable.

"If I hadn't walked in, who knows what would have happened?" Kit, as angry as Zane but also holding back fear. "Thank god she insisted I take Frank's old gun with me."

"Jesus, Kit, when I saw all that blood..."

"Surface cuts bleed a lot, especially in that area," the strange male voice said. "I promise you, it looks worse than it is."

"Don't...talk...so loud," she managed to get out.

Immediately, Zane was kneeling beside the bed, holding her hand. He kissed her fingers, pressing them against his mouth.

"How do you feel, darlin'? Like hell, I'll bet."

"Got...that right." She hurt everywhere, and her mouth felt as if someone had stuffed cotton in it.

His kiss on her lips was so soft it could have been a fairy's touch. When she managed to look at him, she saw two Zane's and quickly closed her eyes again. "Hurts," she whimpered. "Head."

"Doc?" Zane's word was as much a question as a command.

"I can't give her anything until we're sure there's not brain damage." From the other side of the bed, a warm hand lightly touched her arm. "Miss Randall? I'm Dr. Laforza. You're at Diablo General's Emergency Room. You've taken some nasty blows to the head."

Jamie tried to focus on the man standing beside her, but like Zane, she saw two of him.

"Two...doctors," she told him.

"I was afraid of that," she heard him tell Zane in a low voice. "Double vision. Jamie, I'm just going to look into your eyes. The light will be bright, but I'll be very quick about it."

He was right. The light stabbed at her eyes painfully. She flinched as Dr. Laforza lifted first one lid then another.

"Well?" Zane's voice was impatient.

"Before we do anything else, I want to get a CAT scan of her head. Maybe an EEG. We've applied antibiotic cream to her cuts and given her a tetanus shot just in case. She'll hurt but she'll heal. It's the head that worries me."

"Do what you have to," Zane told him. "But wherever you take her, I'm going with her."

"Zane—"

"Not up for discussion. Deal with it."

Jamie closed her eyes and drifted off, trying to hide from the terrible pain in her head. When she roused again, she was in a darkened room surrounded by machinery, Zane was standing on one side of her, Kit on the other, and they were talking in low tones.

"I told my techs to go over every inch of that house," Zane was saying. "I want every fingerprint they can find."

"Jamie went through the place like Mr. Clean, so anything they find will be new."

"I'll need your fingerprints and hers for elimination," Zane told her.

"How on earth did he get in?" Kit asked.

"Either it's someone who had contact with Frank before and had a key or he picked the lock. Damn it to hell anyway. When I find out who this is and who's behind it, there won't be enough left of them to fill a tea cup."

"Don't forget," Kit warned. "You're the sheriff. You have rules to follow."

"Not where she's concerned. Those bastards will wish they'd never heard of anyone named Randall."

"Pretty damned brazen of him to do this in broad daylight."

"My guess is whoever's running this show saw you leave yesterday but then saw me show up last night. Otherwise they would have done it then. They waited until they saw my SUV leave this morning. And that damned house is so isolated no one can see or hear what's going on."

"And I wonder if that's the lure." Kit's voice was thoughtful.

"What do you mean?"

"That someone wants that house *because* of its location. They've got something going on that needs that kind of privacy. Not to disparage my good friend here, but why else would anyone want that piece of shit?"

A woman's voice sounding warm and soothing broke into the conversation. "Sheriff, we're ready now. You and the lady will have to step outside."

"Not on your life." Zane's voice had that 'don't mess with me' sound. Jamie would have smiled if her head hadn't hurt so badly.

"Dr. Laforza said you might be a problem. All right, then. But you'll have to stand where I tell you. And no talking, please."

Someone rolled the gurney, then hands lifted her to a cold, hard surface. Someone was telling her to take deep breaths and not to worry. Someone else asked Zane if she was claustrophobic. She had no idea what was going on and mercifully she passed out again.

****

Gray Ballou had insisted Manny drive all the way to San Antonio to meet with him, and Manny was less than thrilled.

"What's wrong with Amen?" he grumbled. "Or Copper Ridge? It's not like people don't know we do business together."

"I don't want to take the chance there are any stray ears in Diablo County," Ballou said, putting his china coffee cup down in its saucer. They were in one of his favorite high class, low key restaurants, where even the sound of china and crystal was muted.

"What's going on?" Manny popped an antacid tablet in his mouth, chewed it, and washed it down with water. "What's the big deal all of a sudden? I already know we're up against a deadline."

Gray stared thoughtfully at the man across the table from him, eyes searching for something. Manny didn't know what, but it made him nervous.

"What?" he asked again. "I haven't had time or the opportunity to finish our...project. You know that. The Randall place has been busier than the airport, people coming and going and the sheriff all but living there."

"So I can safely say you had nothing to do with this morning's fiasco?"

Manny's hand trembled as he picked up his

water glass again. "What fiasco? What's going on?"

"Someone got into the Randall house this morning when the girl was alone and threatened her with a knife. Did some damage. Hit her in the head hard enough to give her a concussion."

Manny stared at him. "How did you find out? *I* haven't even heard about it yet."

Gray idly stirred more sugar into his coffee. "I pay a lot of people to keep me informed of what's going on. How the hell else would I operate?"

Manny nearly spilled his water. "Is she okay?"

"No thanks to whoever pulled this stunt. Zane Cameron's got her in the hospital, and he's madder than a bear with a bullet in his paw. You know what that means. He'll be digging into everything...*everything*, Manny...to find out how this happened." He took a slow sip of his drink. "You didn't happen to have a hand in this disaster, did you?"

Manny shook his head so hard he nearly pulled a muscle in his neck. "No, no, no. You said to get the money. Even *I* know enough to wait until the girl's not there and look for it again."

"You'd better be telling me the truth because this is going to make a bigger mess than you and I want to see. The chance of getting that money just shrank, and I don't dare make another offer for the house and land on the heels of this. And we have another shipment coming through. This is going to be nothing but one big clusterfuck."

"I thought you were going to change the date for the shipment?"

"I did, but only by a couple of days. Otherwise we'll lose out altogether." He tossed his napkin on the table. "If this operation tanks because of what happened, some people are going to wish they'd never been born." He signaled for the waiter. "I need to get on this. Watch your step, Manny, and don't do anything else stupid."

****

When she woke again and could force her painfully sore eyelids open, Jamie realized she was still in the hospital, only now she was in an actual room and someone was holding her hand. She listened for sounds of another patient, but the room seemed to be a private one. Shifting her gaze to the right, she saw Zane's big body sprawled in a chair next to the bed, his eyes closed, her small hand swallowed up in his big one. The thumping in her head was only marginally better.

She vaguely remembered throwing up a time or two and fervently hoped Zane hadn't witnessed the humiliating process, although the chances of that were probably slim and none. Every time she'd managed to surface from the blessed fog, he'd been right beside her, holding her hand, giving orders, brushing soft kisses on her cheek.

She tried to wet her lips with her tongue, but her mouth was so dry it was a feeble effort.

"Hey." She sounded like a frog croaking.

Zane was instantly alert and leaning forward. "Hey, darlin'. How's the head?"

"Like something left over from the Mad Drummer's Party." She tried licking her lips again. "Water?"

"Right here."

He held a cup with a bent straw, putting the straw to her lips so she could sip through it.

A few swallows were all she could take at the moment. Her throat hurt inside and out. She leaned her head back against the pillow and closed her eyes. "Thanks. Now can you make this marching band in my head go away?"

"Let me ask the nurse for more acetaminophen. That's all they'll give someone with a concussion. But now that you're awake you can have an ice pack on your head, too."

"Anything," she moaned. "Anything at all."

She heard the sound of his booted feet as he left the room and again when he returned. A soft hand slipped behind her head and raised it a little.

"I've got some pills here for you, Miss Randall," a soft female voice said. "Can you open your eyes and take them?"

Zane held the water for her again, then helped the nurse adjust the cold pack, wrapped in a soft cloth, on her head where the lumps were.

"This should help a little," the nurse told her. "And I'm sure the sheriff will let us know if you need anything else." The last was said with just a touch of ironic humor.

Then Zane was right there, holding her hand again, feeding her his strength.

The ice helped more than she expected, and in a few minutes, the pain medicine began to work. She forced her eyes open, and this time it didn't hurt quite so badly. Especially when she focused on Zane's face.

"Bad morning," she tried to joke.

He lifted her hand to his mouth and kissed her fingers again, squeezing them slightly as if to assure himself they still moved. That *she* still moved. "You scared the crap out of me."

"Me...too," she croaked. She waited a moment, then asked, "Did he...I mean..." She shifted her legs and stared up at him. "I don't think so, but—"

"No. The son of a bitch didn't get a chance, thanks to Kit. But he would have." He held her hand up to his cheek, and she was startled to feel wetness. "Jesus, Jamie. When I saw you, I thought my heart would stop. It's bad enough what he did to your breasts. Thank god he didn't get to do anything worse."

"Thank Kit." Her smile was weak.

"You bet. Can you talk enough yet to tell me what happened? All I got from Kit was she walked into your bedroom, found some guy in a ski mask trying to slice you up, and shot him in the shoulder."

"Knew...that gun would come in handy." Her mouth felt stuffed full of sand, and she motioned for the water again. "Did she...kill him?"

"No, damn it. She winged him pretty good, though, judging by the trail of blood he left." He rubbed his thumb over her knuckles. "Tell me what you can."

Haltingly she explained as much as she remembered. The anger in Zane's eyes grew fiercer, and a muscle jumped in his cheek as she finished.

"They've gone way too far," he said, his barely controlled rage evident in his voice. "I'll get them if I have to call in the National Guard for help."

Something was running around in her head and with great effort she plucked it out. "He seemed...more interested in getting rid of me...than anything else. Why?"

"I don't know, but something isn't tracking here. Listen, I've got to get to the office. I have—"

She held up her other hand. "Don't...apologize. Go. Catch these bastards."

He leaned down and pressed a warm kiss to her lips. "I'll be back later. Kit's right outside, and she's going to stay with you. I've also got a guard posted on the door."

Her eyes widened. "Guard?"

"I don't trust them not to make a try for you here. You just be a good girl and do what they tell you. If all goes well, I can take you home tomorrow. But this time, I'm taking you to my house."

She raised an eyebrow.

"No back talk, darlin'. For one thing, I want to leave your place vacant and see what happens. For another, you're too isolated out there. So it's done.

That's it."

"Kit?"

He sighed then grinned. "There's room for Kit, too. I'll just tell people I'm collecting a harem."

She tried to laugh, but it made her head hurt.

Zane kissed her one last time, then he was gone, replaced at her bedside by Kit.

"You sure do know how to show a girl a good time," Kit joked. "And here I thought New York had all the excitement."

****

Jamie slept most of the day. The nurses fed her pain meds, changed the dressings on her cuts, and replaced the cold pack whenever it got too warm. When she was awake, Kit entertained her with details of her visit with her friend in San Antonio. She also agreed with Zane that they needed to use the house as bait, but not with either of them in it.

"This little episode scared the shit out of both of us," she pointed out.

"That's...why Zane wants us at his house, I guess," Jamie said.

"I'll try not to cramp your style." Kit winked at her. "Although, I don't know just how much playtime you'll be up for. The doctor said he'd be in late this afternoon to check you over again. Meanwhile, rest. That's an order."

"My...insurance card. The newspaper gave me an extension on my coverage. Can you get it?"

"It's the least the bastards could do," Kit spat out. "And yes, I found it in your purse."

Jamie looked around the room. "It...doesn't cover a private room." She struggled to sit up. "I can't—"

Kit was there at once, easing her back on the pillows. "The hunky sheriff took care of everything. And I don't think he's in a mood for you to argue with him. I'd just go with the flow if I were you."

Jamie closed her eyes. "You know, don't you?"

206

"That you're in love with him? Hard to miss, kiddo. And you couldn't have picked a better one." She paused. "But that might mean staying in Amen."

Jamie sighed. "I guess. We'll see." And then she was asleep again.

Chapter Sixteen

"The other bitch shot me."

Alone in his car, cell phone to his ear, Danny Christopher popped four more ibuprofen and washed them down with straight vodka. The bullet had been a through-and-through, thank god, but he'd bled like a stuck pig. Traces of his DNA had probably dripped all over Jamie Randall's bedroom and hallway.

Shit, shit, shit.

"I gave you specific instructions." The voice came through distorted by a synthesizer, making whoever was calling the shots impossible to recognize.

The instructions were always left in his car, as was his payment. Always taped under the driver's seat, and then the car was locked. Twice he'd tried to watch to see who delivered the payment, but then he'd gotten a call.

"Stop spying or you won't get paid."

So he still had no idea who it was, only that they paid well for every job he did. And there sure was a variety of them. But even the riskiest ones he'd gotten away clean.

"You said she'd be alone," Danny complained. "Just wait for the sheriff to leave."

"My contact in San Antonio failed to give me enough notice when her friend left. And you didn't answer your cell phone."

"I felt it vibrate, but I was little damn fucking busy, you know."

"Well, there's no help for it now. You'll have to get out of town. And stay gone, for a long time."

Danny took another long swallow of the vodka. "Just where the hell am I supposed to go? And who's gonna pay for my little vacation?"

"Tonight I'll leave money in your car. Go wherever you want, as long as it's not in the state of Texas. If they ever catch you, you'll wish I'd killed you instead."

The phone clicked off.

Danny swore and threw it on the bed. In the bathroom, he pulled off the stained bandage he'd improvised and gritted his teeth while he cleaned the wound again with peroxide. Clumsily, he smeared on antibiotic ointment and wrapped a fresh gauze bandage around it.

Two more slugs of vodka and he felt okay enough to throw his stuff into two large canvas bags. He didn't have much so there wasn't that much to pack. Renting one room didn't allow you to put down too many roots. For a situation like this, though, it was a benefit.

He flopped onto the ratty sleeper sofa and knocked back another drink of vodka. Nothing to do now but wait for dark.

Jesus, but his shoulder hurt like a son of a bitch. Too bad he couldn't stay around and show that cunt it didn't pay to hurt Danny Christopher.

Well after ten, he staggered down the stairs to his car. It took him two tries to unlock it, even with the remote lock, but finally he was inside, the package retrieved from its usual place. Draining the last of the vodka, he tossed the empty bottle to the floor and backed out of his parking space.

Gunning the engine, he roared down the street heading for the highway leading west. He'd always wanted to see Arizona. This was probably as good a time as any. If only his eyes didn't blur so much. Had to be the goddamn ibuprofen. Or maybe the pain itself. Wrestling with the steering wheel was no picnic.

Lucky for him there wasn't a lot of traffic on the road. Headlights coming toward him blinded him, and he had to keep jerking the wheel to the side, sending more pain shooting all the way down his arms.

He made it nearly to the county line when something big came over the rise at him. He couldn't seem to react fast enough. He felt as if everything was moving under water. When he managed to pull to the right to get out of the way, his vision was off, and he didn't even see the huge tree or the gully next to it until it was too late to avoid the crash.

****

Jamie was dreaming, a restless sleep, conjuring up images in her mind. She couldn't seem to get away from the pain in her head or her breasts.

Zane was there, walking toward her through a cloud of fog.

"Hush, darlin'," he soothed. "I'll make you feel better."

"Where are we?" She was confused. Nothing looked familiar.

"It doesn't matter. All that matters is I can make you feel good."

As he emerged more fully from the fog she saw that he was completely naked. His muscles rippled beneath his already bronze skin, kissed a darker shade by hours in the sun, his raven black hair like a fall of silk on his shoulders. His ebony eyes were like onyx fire.

Jamie's entire body quivered in anticipation, her pussy dripping with juices that coated her naked thighs.

Naked? Was she undressed, too? She didn't remember taking her clothes off.

She was floating, anchorless, and there was Zane between her thighs, his big hands sliding beneath her buttocks and lifting her up to him.

"When I get you out of here," he told her in a guttural voice," I'm going to fuck you until you don't even know your own name. Handcuff your wrists and tie your ankles to the bedposts, so I can eat that cunt until I've had my fill of your sweet juices. Until I've licked every inch inside that pussy. Until I've sucked that little clit so much it will stand up just like a little dick."

Jamie moaned, as much from the first swipe of his tongue across her slit as from his words.

"Then I'm going to untie your ankles, flip this sweet little body over and take you to your knees. Oh, yeah. With that gorgeous ass waving in the air. But first I owe you a spanking for being a bad girl, remember? So when those pink globes are fiery red and the heat streaks all the way into your cunt, I'm going to slide the butt plug into the hot little dark hole, fill your cunt with my cock, and fuck you blind. You'll never want another man again, Jamie. And I'll never want another woman. Ever."

Guttural sounds floated on the air, and Jamie was startled to realize they came from her. Zane was holding her up to his mouth, one pinky finger breaching her anus, the tip just inside her hole. His tongue was everywhere, inside her, outside, lapping at her labia then flicking at her clit.

"I don't want anyone else," she gasped as he took her right to the edge then pulled her back. "I just want you."

"Damn right." His voice was muffled as he pressed his mouth against her pussy. "This is mine. You're mine."

She thrust her hips at him, but she had nothing to brace herself on, only his hands. "Please," she begged, her body crying out for release.

"Do you want to come, Jamie? Pour all that sweet cream into my mouth?"

"Yes, yes, yes," she chanted.

"All right, darlin'."

He pressed his finger more deeply into her ass and grabbed her clit with his lips, pulling and tugging on it. Like a wave crashing on the shore her climax hit her, sharp and intense and fierce. She squeezed her thighs around his head as the last violent spasm shook her.

She reached for his shoulders, struggling to grab him when a shadowy figure morphed out of the fog, nothing but darkness. Its arm moved, a sharp crack split the air, and Zane slumped forward over her.

"Zane!" she shrieked. *"Zane! Get up, you're bleeding. Someone help me."*

"Jamie. Jamie, wake up."

Hands were shaking her, and she tried to shrug them off. "Zane!" she screamed again.

"Wake up, Miss Randall." An unfamiliar voice. "You're having a nightmare."

The fog dissipated and she forced her eyes open. She was sitting straight up in bed, still in her hospital room, Kit on one side, the nurse on the other, holding onto her. She looked at Kit's face and saw the lines of worry and the concern in her eyes.

She tried to wet her lips with her tongue, but she had no saliva in her mouth.

"Here." Kit held the cup and straw in front of her so she could drink.

She was so parched she took it all, then flopped back on the pillow. "What happened?"

"You had the mother of all nightmares. Scared the shit out of me." She looked at the nurse. "Pardon my language."

The nurse smiled. "That's okay. I felt the same way. I paged the doctor. If he thinks she's doing okay, he can order something stronger for her."

"Zane." Jamie was suddenly frantic. "Where's Zane?"

"He was here earlier, but you were sleeping so deeply he didn't want to wake you. Said he'd be back later."

"Later? How much later?"

"I don't know, honey. He's busy trying to find out who did this to you and what the hell else is going on. Come on. Lie back. The doctor will be here in a minute."

"I was...we were..." No, better leave the personal details out of it. "What time is it?"

"Almost ten o'clock. You've slept most of the day away." Kit fussed with her covers. "You can bet your body needed it."

She pushed Kit's hands away and sat up again. "Call Zane. Right now. This minute. I have to make sure he's okay."

"Honey, I'm sure he's fine." Kit tried to settle her down again.

Jamie's heart was beating erratically and fear chilled her blood. "Call. Him. Now. Damn it, Kit, I mean it. Just do it."

"Okay, okay." Kit fished her cell phone and the card Zane had given her with his number on it out of her purse.

Jamie waited while her friend punched in the numbers, frantic with impatience. "Did he answer?"

Kit nodded and held up a finger. "Zane? Sorry to bother you, but your girlfriend seems to think you're in some kind of danger. Hold on a minute." She handed the phone to Jamie.

"Are you okay? Tell me you're all right."

"I'm fine, darlin'. As fine as I can be with all the crap that's going on. What's the matter?"

She let out a slow breath. "You have to be very careful. I saw him shoot you."

"Shoot me? Who?"

"I don't know. Don't laugh at me, but I saw it in a dream, and Zane? It was too real. Please, please,

please be very, very careful."

He didn't laugh at her as she'd expected. "I promise. I believe in premonitions. I'm half Comanche, remember?"

She heard voices in the background and someone calling for him. "I'll let you go, but will you keep in touch until you can get back here?"

"Count on it. No matter how busy I am."

"Zane?"

"What is it, darlin'?"

She drew in a deep breath and let it out slowly, clutching the phone. In or out, she thought. "I l-love you."

There. She'd done it. What she'd sworn never to do, especially with Zane Cameron. Put herself out there with her defenses down. If he was going to hurt her, this would be the time. She didn't know if the silence on the other end was good or bad. He was, after all, surrounded by other people.

"You don't have to say it back," she added hastily. "I just wanted to tell you."

"I love you, too, Jamie." His voice had dropped to almost a whisper, but it was very firm. "Keep holding onto that. I'll be there when I can."

His words were the best medicine she could have had. He'd put it out there, too, and now she knew this was real. If she'd been in better shape, she would have danced around the room. She disconnected the call and handed the phone back to Kit, a foolish grin on her face.

"All better?" her friend asked.

"For the moment."

Kit stuck the phone back in her purse. "It's about time you admitted how you feel. I'm guessing he did the same."

Jamie nodded, her fear receding to the background, replaced by a warm feeling of security. But then a shiver skittered over her spine. She'd be happy when she could see Zane with her own eyes.

****

"It's a mess, sheriff." Deputy Roy Galvan stood on the shoulder of the road looking at the mess of twisted metal and broken glass in the gully. "This guy's been an accident waiting to happen for a long time. Probably just one more drunk making paperwork for us, but when I checked to see if he was alive or dead, I saw the bandage under his shirt. He's got a bullet wound in his shoulder."

Zane's face tightened. "Bullet wound?"

"Yeah. And after what happened with Miss Randall this morning, I thought you'd want to check this out yourself."

"You thought right."

"I also found this on the seat next to him." Wearing the latex gloves he'd pulled on as soon as he got to the scene, he handed Zane a torn, blood-spattered envelope with a thick wad of cash in it.

Zane stared at it. "Okay. Drop it in an evidence bag, mark the time and date, and initial it. I'll count it when we get back to the office." He looked at it again. "I'd say, though, there's close to fifty thousand."

"So here's an interesting question for you, Sheriff. Who'd pay a jerk-off like Danny Christopher this kind of money?"

"And what does it have to do with this morning's attack on Jamie Randall?" The rage in his voice was difficult to conceal. He knew his growing relationship with Jamie was no longer secret. Certainly not after the way he'd behaved at her house and the hospital. He no longer cared. This time what they had was real and he didn't intend to let go of it. The hate and anger were gone, replaced by a deeper emotion than he'd ever thought to feel. So whatever anyone thought, fuck 'em.

"Crime Scene Unit's been here for half an hour,"

Galvan told him. "They weren't far away so they got here real quick."

"Oh? What were they doing?" Zane hadn't heard a crime called in from anywhere in the immediate vicinity.

"Another illegal body. A kid, just like the other one we found. Brutalized and strangled."

"Shit." One more problem he couldn't get a handle on. "Okay, what did they say?"

"At first, I wondered if someone had run him off the road, but there were no other tire tracks. Only the skid marks from this junker, and it looked as if he just lost control. From the empty vodka bottle on the floor I can figure out why."

"That's not saying someone else didn't give him a nudge," Zane muttered. "Have the techs set up all the portable lights and do a thorough check of the roadway. Keep this one lane blocked off until they're through."

"You'll have some pissed off drivers," Ray grunted.

"Not at this time of night. Most of them will be on the Interstate. Which brings up another question. Why wasn't Danny on the I-10? Most people hardly use this road now."

"Haven't got a clue. I'll see if I can backtrack his movements."

Zane took off his Stetson, wiped his forehead on his arm, and clapped his hat back in place. "I'd heard Danny could be hired for some nasty jobs, but we never had any evidence. The few times I talked to him, he was a surly son of a bitch. Get a big shovel and start digging. Something has to turn up."

"Okay, boss. But with the two new bodies we found and what's going on with Miss Randall, our shifts will be stretched pretty thin."

Zane fisted his hands, then forced himself to ease up. "Call in the part-timers. I'll sign off on any overtime. And have one of the patrols check the Randall house on a regular basis. See if anything hinky's going on."

"Got it."

"Okay, Ray." Zane heaved a tired sigh. "You'll be lead on all of this."

"Where will you be?"

"I'm going to make a quick stop at the hospital, try to catch a little sleep, and head into San Antonio in the morning."

Galvan raised an eyebrow. "Business or pleasure?"

"Definitely business," Zane told him, his voice cold and uninflected. "I'm going to check in with a friend of mine with Immigration and Customs Enforcement. I want to know what they've got going and if any of it spills over into Diablo County."

Ray took a long look at him. "You think this might have to do with traffic in illegals."

Zane nodded. "I've had suspicions for a long time, but nothing I could put my finger on. Lately, though, too many things have been happening. I think this is a bigger operation than we've ever imagined around here, with very big bucks involved. But I have to step lightly because of the people I think are involved. I'll need a federal judge to sign warrants for me, and for that, I need to get ICE involved."

"Good luck. I'll take care of things here."

Zane climbed wearily into his SUV and headed back toward Amen. He had a sinking feeling in the pit of his stomach he wasn't going to like any of the answers he found.

****

Kit was curled up in the recliner reading when Zane walked into the room, the floor lamp behind her the only light. She put a finger to her lips. "She fell asleep again about an hour ago. I finally got her to eat some soup and gelatin, and she drank some more water."

"And she kept it down? Good. That's good." He kept his voice low. Standing beside the bed, he lightly touched Jamie's hand lying on the covers. "How's her head?"

"Much better since they gave her something stronger than acetaminophen." Kit smiled at the obvious emotion in Zane's gesture, stuck a bookmark in her book, and came to stand on the other side of the bed. "Her cuts look a lot worse than they are, and her bruises are already starting the fade."

"Thank god you walked in when you did." Zane's voice was raw with pain and anger. "I'd like to skin the little fucker alive."

"The doctor was in and said if nothing changes, she can go home tomorrow."

And won't I be forever grateful that I walked in when I did.

"I have to go into San Antonio in the morning, and I probably won't be back until noon." He glanced up at Kit. "I don't want her leaving here before then."

"Don't worry," Kit assured him. "I'll handle it. Are you still planning to take her to your place?"

"Both of you," Zane told her.

"Listen," she began, "I'm not sure—"

"I am. There's no way I'm leaving you alone in that house, and I don't think it would be good for Jamie if you left right now."

Kit grinned. "The two of you won't have much privacy."

Zane looked over at her, everything he felt showing in his eyes. "I haven't said much about it to her yet, but Jamie and I will have a lot of years for privacy. We can handle a few days."

Kit cleared her throat. "You're pretty sure of yourself. Are you positive about this?"

Cocked And Loaded

He nodded. "More than positive. We fucked up once. Both of us. It won't happen again. Even if it means I leave Amen. There are law enforcement jobs everywhere." He lifted Jamie's hand and kissed the knuckles. "But we've got a lot of business to attend to before we can even discuss that."

"How are things going? You look exhausted."

He told her about Danny Christopher and the accident at the county line. "I think something really nasty is going on right under my nose, and I have a feeling it's been happening for a long time. Tomorrow, I'm going to take some steps that hopefully give me some information and we'll go from there."

"Get some sleep," Kit urged. "I'd hate for you to fall asleep at the wheel."

"Me, too." He gave her a rueful grin. "I'll call you from the road, but I should be able to get here by noon to pick you up."

"I'll need to go back to the house and pack some things. For both of us."

"I'll have a deputy take you, then follow you back to my place so you'll have your car." He placed Jamie's hand carefully on the bed covers. "Tell her...tell her...just say I'll see her tomorrow."

Kit swallowed another grin as she watched Zane walk out the door. The sheriff was sure having a hard time verbalizing his feelings. But she'd figure out how to give him a helping hand.

****

Manny Alvarado opened the sack from the electronics store and took out four disposable cell phones, following the instructions to activate one of them. Wearily, he punched in Gray Ballou's cell number, recited the number on his phone, and disconnected. In less than a minute the phone trilled.

"What's this all about?" he asked Gray.

219

"Disposable cells? What's wrong with the ones we've got?"

"Things are getting out of hand, you idiot," Ballou snapped. "Throwaways are not traceable. They can't pull the log from them. And if we keep our calls short, they can't triangulate on them."

"What's going on, Gray? Has something else happened?"

"That jack-off Danny Christopher ran off the highway and killed himself."

Manny grunted. "Pardon me if I don't shed any tears, but what does that have to do with us?"

"He had fifty thousand in cash with him." The anger in Ballou's voice was barely controlled. "Someone paid him to go after the Randall woman, and now Zane Cameron will bring the hounds of hell down on everyone. And we've got a deal going down in two days."

"Three," Manny said. "I got us an extension. But only the one day."

"Let me know if it looks like anyone's around."

"Hey." Manny mopped the beads of sweat from his forehead. "I know what to do. This was my operation to begin with, remember?"

"And a penny ante one at that until I stepped in. *You* remember, okay?"

Manny was silent. Grayson Ballou could puff all he wanted to about how he'd expanded things and added things, but it was Manny's sweat that had provided the basis for what they had. One of these days he'd find a way to make sure the man knew it. Good.

He needed, also, to make sure his little sideline wasn't interrupted. A man had few enough bonuses in life as it was. He wasn't about to give this one up.

"Drive by the house tomorrow and see what's going on," Ballou continued. "See if she and that friend of hers are back from the hospital. Find out who set Christopher on her. Then call me. At this number. After that, throw this phone away and use the next one."

The line went dead. Manny wanted to throw the phone into the trash. And Grayson Ballou along with it.

****

Jamie stood in the hallway of Zane's house and looked around with frank curiosity while he reset the alarm. Somehow she had pictured him in something totally different. Something more austere. Colder. Harsher. This was a welcoming house, a place for people to feel comfortable.

The house was larger than she'd expected, with a wide entrance hall opening into a great room with a sweeping fireplace and floor-to-ceiling windows. She could see an entrance on the left side of the room that led to a kitchen and an open door on the right that gave her a glimpse of what was obviously a den.

Sunlight swept in from the windows and reflected on the polished wood floors, bathing everything in amber light. A large Native American woven rug was a splash of color on the wood floor, and throw pillows that could have been made by the same person gave life to a dark leather couch.

A graceful stairway curved to the second floor, the banister and the treads also highly polished wood.

"The woodwork is mine," Zane told her, catching her glance. "I found it was a good way to work off excess energy. Or frustration. Whatever."

"It's just beautiful," she told him, still somewhat awestruck.

"When my mother moved to Copper Ridge, I wanted to stay here. I could have moved the main sheriff's office, but I chose not to. And I wanted a house, a place I could immerse myself in when I wasn't working." He put his arm under her elbow. "Come on. Let's get you upstairs."

"I'm not an invalid, you know," she tried to joke.

"You lie like a trooper." He, too, was trying to keep it light. "I'll bet your head still feels like it ran into a bull at the rodeo."

Her lips curved in a tiny smile. "Maybe a very small bull. But I am a lot better."

"And I intend to keep you that way."

As they talked, he'd been gradually urging her up the stairs that led to a wide hallway. There was a door on either side and double doors at the end of the hallway.

"Guest rooms?" she asked.

A strange look flashed through his eyes. "I did a lot of remodeling when I bought this place. Like I said, it's a good way to sweat things out. While I was at it, I figured I'd do a little planning for the future, too."

Jamie's stomach did a flip flop that had nothing to do with her concussion or her attack. The future. Until this week, she'd never thought of Zane and the future in the same breath. Of course, until recently she hadn't thought of him as anything but an asshole who knew how to fuck, so her mind and emotions were going through a lot of changes.

Kit came chugging up the stairs right behind them. When they got to the door on the right, Zane opened it and gestured inside. "Kit, I think you'll be comfortable in here. If you need anything, let me know."

Kit's eyes widened as they took in the spacious bedroom with its quilt spread and Western prints on the wall. "Wow!"

"The bathroom's over there, and there's a big walk-in closet. I'll get your bags in a minute."

"I'm good," she told him. "Take care of the walking wounded."

When Zane opened the double doors at the end of the hallway and led Jamie into his bedroom, again she could only stare. The room was huge, with the biggest bed she'd ever seen in her life. The furniture was all hand-rubbed oak, and copies of Frederick Russell paintings hung on the walls. Over the bed was a framed Lone Star flag, the symbol of Texas.

"Somehow I never thought of you as a diehard Texan," she told him.

One corner of his mouth hitched. "My people were here long before yours," he reminded her.

"Have you...did you..." *Jesus, Jamie, quit stammering, and either ask him or shut up.* "I know it's none of my business and you don't have to say anything, but have you brought other women here?" *Dummy. Stop acting like a teenager.*

Zane stared at her for a long moment. "As a matter of fact, I haven't. This is my private space. I'm picky about who I share it with."

Jamie couldn't help the burst of joy his answer brought. She was still amazed at how her relationship with Zane had done a one-eighty in such a little amount of time. If only her bad luck didn't pop up again and disrupt it all.

"Come on." He urged her toward the bed. "You need to lie down. I want to check those cuts for myself, then Kit's going to fix lunch. I've got to get going, much as I hate to."

Ignoring her protests, Zane closed the door, pulled back the spread, then carefully removed her clothing. When she was naked, he placed her on the cool cotton of the sheets. As he catalogued the damage done to her body, a murderous rage flared in his gut.

I wish I'd been the one to walk in on that bastard. I'd have gutted him like a wild boar.

"When did they change your bandages last?" he finally got out, forcing a calm he didn't feel.

"This morning. Early. Why?"

"I checked with the nurse when I signed you out, and she gave me a schedule of sorts. I think they need changing again. Just to be on the safe side. Hold on one second," he said, heading for the bathroom.

He found a first aid kit and quickly returned to set it on the nightstand. Then he carefully removed the bandages covering the cuts on her breasts and the inside of one thigh. "Too bad the son of a bitch is dead. I'd like to kill him myself. Okay. The nurse told me what to do."

He cleaned each place with an antiseptic wipe, then applied antibiotic ointment and a self-stick bandage. When he pressed it in place, his hand brushed against her pubic curls and she shifted under his touch.

"Those tight little curls are rubbing against your thigh," he pointed out. "We'll fix that when I get home. If you're up to it."

Jamie raised an eyebrow. "Oh? Exactly what did you have in mind?"

He couldn't contain his wolfish grin. "I think you'd be a lot more comfortable if we got rid of them. Purely for medical reasons, of course."

"Of course." She tried to hide her grin. "Medical."

Unable to resist, Zane moved the tips of two fingers lightly the length of her slit, up and down, a feathery caress. Her juices seeped out around his touch, revealing her arousal.

"You're supposed to be an invalid," he reminded her.

She snorted. "Fat chance. Besides, that jerk didn't do all that much damage." A wicked light flared in her eyes. "But I do think I'll need some special attention to wipe it all out of my mind."

He placed a soft kiss on each injured spot, took a

careful swipe through her slit with his tongue, and pressed his mouth to hers, sharing her taste with her. They were both breathing hard when he broke the kiss.

"I'll be sure to take care of it the minute I get home." He looked at his watch. "Which might be late, depending on how long it takes me to put things in motion and what other crazy stuff comes along today."

"How was your meeting this morning?"

"Good. Skip Conway was very happy to bring ICE into this whole business. They've heard lots of rumors of a well-organized traffic in illegals around here for a long time, years, even, but haven't been able to get a handle on anything." His eyes darkened. "He also said they've heard all the young girls brought across are sold to wealthy buyers who use them, then kill them and dispose of their bodies. I told him about the two we found in recent months."

"Bodies of little girls?" Jamie was horrified. She couldn't even imagine something so vile and terrible.

"Yeah." Zane rubbed his jaw. "What mystifies me, though, is why someone would pay top dollar for this, then kill the child before they even get her out of the area."

Jamie's stomach turned over. "Maybe she was too much trouble? Or something happened?"

Zane shrugged. "I don't know. I get a weird feeling something else is going on we don't know about. Skip agreed with me."

"Does he have any idea who's behind all this?"

"Oh, yeah. So do I, much as I tried to avoid it."

Jamie looked at the expression on his face and chills prickled her skin. "Grayson Ballou."

Zane nodded. "He's the only one around with enough clout to run the kind of operation Skip's talking about."

"So what will you do?"

"Skip's getting me the federal warrants I need and driving them here himself along with two other agents. But he may not be able to get them until tomorrow. Then we'll go from there. Meanwhile, I'm going to see what we can dig up about Danny Christopher and also pull up anything on your father for the past twenty years."

"My father? You think he was involved?"

He shrugged. "I don't know, Jamie. If the property was used, he had to know about it. Besides, he kept it together for you without much visible means of support. And that money you found had to come from somewhere."

She shook her head. "I don't see what help a drunk like him could have been to anyone. Unless he was doing something that stuck in his craw so badly he drank to forget about it. Do you think that's possible?"

"Maybe. It could have something to do with why Grayson Ballou wants your property so badly. It's possible they were using your place for the 'exchange,' but we don't have any evidence of it yet."

"You'd think he'd worry about making me suspicious with his out-of-the-blue offers."

"Not necessarily." Zane shifted uncomfortably. "I'm not bringing this up for any reason except to suggest why he thought you'd jump at his offer. You didn't leave here on the best of terms with Amen. When you returned—"

"I know. It was under a black cloud, which, by the way, is still hovering over me. And no one exactly welcomed me with open arms."

He stroked her arms, emotions dancing in his eyes. "But at least one of us has come around." A smile played across his lips. "Come being the operative word?"

"It's a good one," she agreed, then frowned. "Something bothers me, though. I can't see a man like Ballou getting his hands dirty with something like this. He has so many other things going."

"Maybe. But that's usually the kind of person that sees the dollars in this kind of thing and figures out how to take ownership of it. And maybe he thought you wouldn't entertain an offer from someone without his so-called position."

"I guess."

"We can talk ourselves to death on this, but what I really need to do is dig into it more and find some answers." He picked up one of her hands and held it gently in his. "Jamie, we have so much to talk about, and this damn situation just keeps getting in the way. I need to make sure you know how I feel about you. What I want for us. To know if you feel the same—"

She reached up with her other hand and touched her fingers to his mouth. "We don't need the words right now, Zane. It's there, for both of us to see. I feel the same way you do. So let's get this taken care of and get on with our lives." She let out a soft breath. "Together?"

"No other way, darlin'." Relief washed over his face, as if he'd worried she might not feel the same way he did. He stood up and kissed her once more. "I picked up a robe for you in the city this morning. It's in the closet. I think you'll find it more comfortable against your skin than clothes. It won't bother your cuts and bruises as much."

She pushed herself out of bed and went to the closet, tears pricking her eyelids when she felt the soft, light cotton material. That he would think of something like this in the middle of all that was going on...

Zane cleared his throat, obviously fighting his own emotions. "Come on. Get back in bed. I'll tell Kit you're ready for lunch."

He made her memorize the alarm code and

repeat it back to him three times. "Don't turn it off unless you know who's on the other side of the door. That would be me or one of my deputies. No one else. I'll be home tonight as soon as I can. And I'll bring take out."

Chapter Seventeen

After he left her with Kit, Zane drove to Jamie's house and went through it again himself, inch by inch. Not that the techs hadn't done a good job. He just wanted to satisfy himself that nothing had been missed. But between the clean up job Jamie and Kit had done, the painting, and the crime scene unit, every space had been examined. They'd even taken out the board in Jamie's hiding place and scoured the space for anything else.

Finally, frustrated, he went back to the office to find Roy Galvan waiting for him, two folders in his hands.

"First of all, Dave's gone over Frank Randall's truck a hell of a lot better than he did the last time." Roy shook his head. "This is a good lesson to all of us not to jump to conclusions."

Zane grunted. "Me, especially. He found something?"

"For one thing, Jamie was right about the scrapes. The paint underneath hasn't weathered like the rest of it."

"Shit. She tried to tell me that, and I blew it off."

"Not only are the dents in the back made by another vehicle, there are some paint chips that stuck to the truck's tailgate. Dave sent them to the state lab to see if their mass spectrometer could pinpoint what kind they are. They can run the manufacturer through their database."

Zane sighed. "I'll have to eat plenty of crow when I tell Jamie about this. Tell Dave I want a full report as soon as he's got it."

"Will do." He handed over one of folders. "Here's everything we've got so far on the highway wreck. The car's downstairs still being taken apart, and the lab is testing all the various fluids and materials we found." He rubbed his jaw. "Jesus, what a slob the guy was. He had junk in there so old it was almost fossilized."

Zane dropped his hat on top of a file cabinet and lowered himself into his desk chair. He opened the folder and began flipping through the sheets of paper. "Anything I should look at first?"

Roy nodded. "Page three. Contents. We found a knife with blood on it in one pocket of his pants." He paused for effect. "We have to wait for final DNA, of course, but the lab says it's a match for Jamie Randall's."

Zane's stomach clenched, and a sour taste filled his mouth. Again, he imagined all too vividly what could have happened if Kit hadn't returned exactly when she did.

"What about the money? Any prints?"

Roy shook his head. "Looks like whoever put it together used latex gloves. So far only Danny's and what will probably turn out to be the bank teller who put it together. But I told the lab to go over every single bill anyway and test it."

"This money didn't come from any one bank. Fifty thousand is too big a withdrawal not to cause attention. Besides, it would leave a record. More likely, this came from someone's private stash."

"Who keeps that kind of money around the house?" Ray frowned. "And why?"

"I have some ideas, but I need more information." He closed the folder. "Tomorrow an ICE agent, Skip Conway, and two other agents will be showing up here with some federal warrants. Be prepared for whatever we have to do, but don't let it get around the office. We need to keep as tight a lid on this as possible."

"Why are they coming?"

"Because I asked them to. Keep yourself available. Meanwhile, keep backtracking Danny Christopher's movements for the last couple of days. Where he was. Who saw him. What he was doing."

"Finding out who hired him may not be too easy," Roy warned.

"Someone paid him," Zane reminded him. "And it's probably not the first time. Also, I want hourly patrols past the Randall house. During the night, too."

"You got it."

****

"There's nothing left in the house for us to find," Manny spoke into another disposable phone. "Zane Cameron and his crew have gone over every inch of it twice. If they discovered anything, we'd know about it."

"Fuck." Grayson Ballou usually kept his cursing under control, but he was rapidly approaching peak meltdown. "Where the hell is that money?"

"Maybe the Randall woman is just hanging onto it," Manny suggested.

"As close as she and that half-breed sheriff have gotten, I'd think she'd tell him about it if she had it."

"You'd know if she had, wouldn't you?"

"Maybe. But that line of communication isn't as open as I'd like it to be."

"We're still on for tomorrow night," Manny reminded him. "That was all the extension I could get. Some of the clients are getting a little, shall we say, testy?"

"They can't get too testy," Ballou snapped. "They'd have to find a new source and that's easier said than done. At least for what they want."

"I'm going to plant myself somewhere hidden and check what's happening at the house tonight.

Patrols have been going by all day, even though no one's there."

"It's empty? Is that little whore still in the hospital?"

Manny had to swallow his pleasure in knowing something the great Grayson Ballou hadn't yet found out. "The sheriff took her home with him. Her friend, too."

There was a long silence, then a soft chuckle. "Anita will have a heart attack over that. She has big political plans for her son that don't include white trash. If she plans to capitalize on what she calls his 'mixed heritage,' she'll want someone with a lot more class standing next to him."

Manny gritted his teeth. Ballou constantly made unnecessary ethnic references that irritated him. Manny was sensitive about his own diverse background and wanted to point out to the man that a good portion of Texans had more than one kind of blood running through their veins.

"Manny?" Ballou's voice was irritated. "You still there, *amigo?*"

Amigo? Like hell. Ballou thinks he can throw in a Hispanic word now and then and that makes him one of the crowd. Asshole.

"I'm here. I have to get moving. I have things to do."

"What you have to do is make sure we're set for tomorrow night and that no one is showing unusual interest in the Randall place. And make sure that Randall female stays put." There was a brief silence. "Damn it all, anyway. I'll kill whoever set Danny Christopher on her. That's liable to stir up a hornet's nest we can't control. Did you find out yet where he got the money?"

Manny was sweating again, even though he was sitting in an air-conditioned environment. "Not yet. It's not exactly as if I can come right out and question people, you know."

"Damn it. Squeeze your snitches. I want to know who's playing in our sandbox."

"I'll get on it right away."

Manny tossed the cell phone down and let out a long breath. Things were getting far too dicey for him.

****

Jamie dozed off and on during the day. The hospital had given her a prescription for pain pills, which Kit had filled at the hospital pharmacy, but Jamie insisted on sticking with acetaminophen if she could stand it.

"My head's a lot better," she insisted. "And I might want to have a glass of wine with Zane tonight."

"Up to you. I called the hospital to see if you could take a bath—I thought it might help with those bruises and sore muscles—and they said yes if you cover the bandages with plastic." She grinned as she held up a box of plastic wrap. "So come on. Let's make a present out of you."

The heat from the bathwater made the plastic stick to her like a second skin, but she couldn't deny how good it was to sit in the hot, scented water and let it caress her skin. She soaked in it until she pruned, then let Kit help her dry off and peel away the plastic. A lot of the soreness went down the drain with the bathwater.

Kit changed her bandages again, and Jamie smoothed scented lotion everywhere on her body that she wasn't injured in some way. At least she felt halfway to human. The robe Zane had bought for her was light as a feather against her skin. Again, she was touched by his consideration.

They were watching television in the great room when Zane walked in at seven o'clock, bringing the promised pizza, beer, and diet soda.

"No alcohol for you," he teased Jamie. "At least until tomorrow."

"Phooey," she grumbled, taking the can of soda he handed her. "I avoided the heavy meds so I could have a glass of wine." She fluttered her lashes at him. "Pretty please?"

"Not until tomorrow," he repeated. "Just in case."

While they ate, he brought them up to date on what little he'd been able to find out.

"I feel as if I stuck my hand in a bowl of spaghetti and all the limp strands are falling every which way." He finished the last of his beer. "My gut tells me there's more than one person pulling strings here and more than one agenda, but damned if I can figure out what."

"Maybe when your friend from ICE gets here tomorrow, you'll be able to get a better handle on things," Jamie said.

"I will if he brings the warrants I asked for."

He was about to add something when the doorbell rang. The three people at the table exchanged glances.

"Don't look at me." Kit got up and began clearing the table. "I don't even know anyone in this town."

"I do," Jamie put in, "but not anyone who'd care to see me."

Zane pushed his chair back. "It could be one of my deputies, but they'd most likely call first."

He strode into the foyer and opened the door. As soon as Jamie spied Anita Cameron, she nudged Kit into the kitchen.

"I'm sure she's here to give Zane grief about me," she whispered.

"He's a grown man," Kit pointed out. "Besides, this is his house."

The voices were low enough that they couldn't

make out what the two were saying.

Then Anita's strident voice rose. "I won't have it, Zane. I simply forbid it."

"I'm a little old for you to be giving me orders." His voice had the timbre of cold steel. "I make my own decisions. If that's all you came for, I think it's time for you to leave."

"We're not done here," she retorted. "Close the door."

"Yes. We are. And I think it's time for you to go."

Jamie and Kit heard the door close with a hard snap, but it was almost five minutes before Zane came into the kitchen.

"Kit, would you mind cleaning up the rest of this?" he asked. "I need to speak to Jamie privately."

"No problem," she assured him. "Then I'm going to put on my iPod at full volume and get back to my book. I won't be able to hear anything." She grinned. "Not a thing."

"I can help," Jamie protested and started to gather up the debris.

"Not tonight." Zane picked her up in his arms and carried her up to their room.

"Zane, put me down." She struggled against him. "Listen to me. I think it would be better if Kit and I go back to my house. I knew us being here would cause a problem, and I was right."

He set her on her feet and threaded his hands through her hair. "The only one with a problem is my mother, and I can handle her. She wants to run my life, and I don't want the agenda she's selling. I never have, but I can't seem to make her understand that."

"But—"

"But nothing. You're mine now, Jamie. That's what I was trying to say earlier. We can finally admit how we feel about each other, and we belong together. Permanently. Nobody, not even my mother, is going to take that away from us."

"I don't want to be responsible for a rift between the two of you," she insisted.

God, that's the last thing I need to cause.

His face hardened briefly. "There's a lot more between my mother and me than this. Years of history she refuses to acknowledge. Not to mention the fact that she wants to plan the rest of my life for me, and our agendas are miles apart."

Jamie looked up at him. "In what way?"

"Politics." He grimaced. "Haven't you heard? It's fashionable to have Native American blood these days."

"And a white trash girl friend won't make it on the political scene," Jamie guessed.

"You're not white trash, but it doesn't matter. Politics is the last thing on my list of career aspirations. Can we not talk about this right now?" He kissed her lightly. "How are you feeling?"

"A lot better than I did yesterday, that's for sure."

He smoothed her hair back. "I had plans for us tonight, but I think we'd better hold off until I'm sure you're healed. The last thing I want is to bring back that headache or do anything to aggravate your wounds."

She wanted to stamp her foot. "I am *not* an invalid, Zane Cameron. My head is great, and my *cuts,* not *wounds,* are healing just fine. I'm not some china doll to be wrapped up in silk, you know."

His mouth quirked in a reluctant hint of a grin. "Apparently not. But—"

"But nothing. I'm certainly not ready to do cartwheels, but I don't think anything else is going to put me back in the hospital."

"I think we should have a quiet night," he insisted, his jaw set at a stubborn angle.

Her lips turned up in an impish grin. "Then I'll

just have to be very quiet."

"Jamie, you're not being reasonable."

"That's the last thing I want to be. What I want is to feel alive. To wipe away the feeling of that creep touching me." She looked up at him. "Please don't make me beg."

"Okay," Zane gave in. "Then we have some personal business to attend to."

"Business?" Her heart began to trip-hammer.

"Uh huh." He untied the robe and slowly slid it down her arms, leaving her naked in front of him. "Very. Important. Business."

He bent his head and kissed each nipple, careful to avoid the bandages. Because of the cuts, she wasn't wearing a bra, and his lips made the plump buds harden at once. When he looked at the new bandages Kit had placed there earlier, anger burned in his eyes.

"I'll be happy when I can treat this tasty body properly. I'd like to pull Danny Christopher's body out of the morgue and kill him all over again."

She laid one hand against his face. "It's all right. They really don't hurt so much anymore. I didn't even need stitches."

"That's not the point. I don't want anyone harming you in any way."

A feeling of warmth crept over her. She couldn't ever remember a time in her life when someone had spoken about her with such caring possessiveness. More and more Zane Cameron was owning her heart.

"You sure your head feels okay?" he asked in a soft voice.

"Almost normal." The words strangled in her throat as he went back to kissing the undamaged areas of her breasts. His hands dropped to her waist, caressing the curves of her hips, and sliding down the outside of her thighs.

Jamie shivered at his touch.

Zane's hands stopped. "Am I hurting you?"

"Only if you stop what you're doing."

"I had more exciting things planned for the first night you spent in this house, but under the circumstances, I think we'll dial it way down. But I have to touch you, Jamie. Taste you. Hold you. I'll be very gentle, I promise."

She opened her mouth to say she was just fine with whatever he wanted to do, but his lips captured hers just as his hand moved between her thighs to cup her sex and every thought flew out of her head. His tongue tasted everywhere in her mouth, licking at the roof and trailing over the line of her gums. He drank from the well of her mouth like a parched man in the desert, as if he'd never get enough. While the kiss drugged her senses, his fingers were driving her crazy, teasing her slit and lightly pinching her clit.

When he lifted his head, they were both gasping for air.

"I'd better take care of that business I mentioned before I'm too far gone. For this one, you just get to lay back and enjoy it."

"I like the sound of that." She stood quietly as he finished undressing her and carried her to the bed.

He placed her sideways with her legs hanging over the edge, plumping pillows under her head. "I'll be right back. Don't move."

As he headed for the bathroom, he shed his own clothes, tossing them onto a leather chair. Jamie couldn't take her eyes off the flex of the muscles in his buttocks as he moved. He had the finest ass she's ever seen.

"Thanks," he called over his shoulder. "I could return the compliment."

Jamie's face warmed as she realized she spoken her thoughts out loud. Heat still suffused her when

Zane returned carrying towels, a bowl, and a razor.

"That's okay," he grinned. "You can admire my ass any time."

Setting everything down on the nightstand, he pulled over the footstool from the chair, draped a towel over it, and sat down. He placed his hands under Jamie's buttocks and scooted her back on the bed just enough so he could bend her knees and place her feet flat on the mattress. Very carefully, avoiding the bruised areas, he slipped a towel under her hips. Then he folded a small one and placed it across the thigh with the cut on it as protection.

"I feel weird doing this with Kit downstairs," she told him.

"As long as she's not in the room with us, it's okay," he chuckled. "And we'll be very quiet." He swirled the razor in the bowl. "Now, remember. This is strictly medicinal. We don't want anything scratching against that cut on your thigh."

The cut on her thigh was barely an inch long and hardly deep at all, but she knew Zane felt better using it as an excuse for what he wanted to do. Despite her aches and pains, all afternoon she'd been thinking about this, cream coating her thighs every time images crossed her mind. From the state of his erection, she was sure Zane had, too.

"Medicinal," he nodded solemnly, then ran a finger over her labia and circled the entrance to her vagina. "Gorgeous," he hissed, "but it will look even better totally bare." He looked up at her, mischief and passion mingled in his eyes. "Don't move, now. I'd hate to slip."

"Better not," she warned him, took in a deep breath, and let it out in a slow stream.

Using a warm cloth, he thoroughly wet her curls, then sprayed them with shaving cream. With careful strokes, he began to remove her pubic curls, one patch at a time. His fingers moved very carefully, tugging at her skin to pull it taut when he needed to, pressing her thighs wider to get the little curls that drifted into the seam of flesh. His touch was incendiary, and Jamie had to clench her fists to keep from reacting. Every time a knuckle brushed her clit, her pussy quivered in response.

"So sensitive," Zane murmured, rinsing the razor and wiping her with the cloth in slow strokes. "You're so wet. All I have to do is touch you and more cream trickles out. Your beautiful pink pussy turns a deep rose color as it warms with arousal. And such a sweet little clit, hiding in its little hood."

He pressed it between the knuckles of two fingers and rubbed.

Jamie jerked at the touch, the pulse in her womb setting up a throbbing beat. His erotic murmurings were arousing her as much as his touch. She closed her eyes tightly and dug her nails into the palms of her hands to maintain control.

He continued with his slow, careful strokes, avoiding the cut on the inside of her thigh. Instead, he pressed her knee outward to give him exposure to the edge of her curls at the seam of hip and thigh.

Her pussy felt strange as the hair disappeared, cool, ultra-sensitive to the warm cloth he was using to clean her after every area was barbered. The ache in her head and the soreness in her breasts had receded in the face of the erotic act. Shaving her sex was the most personal thing Zane could do to or for her, and her reaction to it overpowered everything else.

Using one hand, he separated the cheeks of her buttocks so he could reach the fine hair hidden back there. He continued to talk to her in a low, deep voice as he paid careful attention to every area.

"And your asshole. Jesus, Jamie. I could come just from looking at it. I can't wait to shove my cock in it again, see that tight, tight muscle close around it as I work my way into that hot, dark tunnel. You have no idea how hard it is to control myself. I could go off the minute I'm all the way inside you."

A soft moan floated from her lips.

"Ah, you like that. Good, because I plan to do it as often as I can once you're back in fighting shape."

"Okay...now," she protested in a breathless voice.

"Not exactly," he contradicted her. "But think how hot we'll be just thinking about it. Waiting for it."

She moaned again, forcing herself not to push her hips at him.

"There." His voice had a thick quality to it. "Finished. Want to see."

Oh, yeah. You bet.

"Yes. I do."

"Hold on."

He pushed back the footstool and carried all the shaving equipment into the bathroom. When he came back, he was holding a mirror. Sitting down, he positioned the mirror directly in front of her cunt.

"Go ahead. Look," he urged, his tone heavy with lust.

Carefully Jamie raised herself on her elbows and stared into the mirror. It wasn't as if she hadn't examined herself before. Sometimes she'd even propped her large hand mirror when she was masturbating so she could watch herself climax.

But this was completely different. All that naked flesh stared back at her, and her clit and vagina stood out in stark relief. Fascinated, she followed the path of a trickle of fluid seeping from her opening and wiggling down towards the crack of her ass.

"Touch yourself," Zane whispered, leaning toward her. "See how it feels. Come on, Jamie. See how soft your skin is without all those curls."

Desiree Holt

Tentatively she slid one hand across her tummy and down to her freshly nude pussy. He was right. Her skin was like a baby's, silky smooth, and the touch of her fingers on it sent sparks through her.

"Rub yourself," he coaxed, watching her with heavy-lidded eyes. "Move your hand all over the bare skin. Tell me how it feels to you."

"It feels...weird. Like it belongs to someone else."

"Didn't you ever shave yourself before?" he asked curiously. "Or wax?"

She couldn't stop running her hand over the smoothness. "Maybe a little trim, but that's all."

"Touch your clit." His eyes flared with heat. "Watch yourself rub it."

She couldn't take her eyes away from the mirror. She brushed her thumb over her clitoris where it peeped out from its protective hood. At once it swelled and tingled, darkening with arousal. She did it again, then pinched it between her thumb and forefinger.

"That's it," he said in a guttural tone. "More. Like that."

Jamie brushed her fingers back and forth over the hardening bundle of nerves, alternately pulling it and abrading it. With every touch, she saw more fluid trickle from her cunt.

Zane dropped the mirror for a moment, closing his fingers around her ankles and spreading her legs wider before picking it up again. "There. That's better."

It was true she could see more now. The flesh of her inner and outer lips was turning a rosy color, and the opening of her pussy stared at her like a miniature circle. It was like having an out of body experience, watching her hand move over the different parts of her sex as if she wasn't even the one doing it. She forgot about her headache, forgot about the tiny knife slices that stung if she moved

242

the wrong way. Everything was centered on what she saw in the mirror.

She tore her eyes away for quick glance at Zane and saw the deep flush on his cheeks, the fire burning in his eyes. Saw the pulse beating hard at the hollow of his throat. He wasn't even touching her, yet she felt him all over her. It could have been his hands gliding so smoothly over her newly bared flesh. His fingers probing and teasing.

But he was watching. Watching her watch herself in the mirror. Watching her begin the slow buildup to the peak of pleasure. And the quick glimpse she had of his swollen, fully-engorged cock told her exactly how aroused he was.

She let her knees fall even wider until she was nearly doing one of those crazy moves she'd learned in high school gym class, with her thighs almost touching the mattress. She watched her fingertips circle the opening of her vagina as if they were disconnected from her body, fire racing through her as if from an unknown source. Remembering what he'd asked her to do the other night, how aroused it made him, she dipped the tip of one finger inside, then daringly lifted it to her mouth and delicately licked it.

"Jesus," Zane breathed, his voice a low growl.

She let her gaze drop briefly to his hands, white-knuckled on the mirror, then lifted it to his face where the desire she saw nearly stole the breath from her. Holding his gaze, she repeated the action, dipping the finger, bringing it to her lips, letting the tip of her tongue peep out to lick her cream.

"Fingerfuck yourself," he commanded. "Play with your clit. Do it, Jamie. Let me see you pleasure yourself."

Shifting her gaze back to the mirror, she followed the path of her fingers sliding into her wet vagina until they disappeared to the knuckle. Her thumb rasped over her clit, setting up a rhythm that sped up her breathing. Her hands moving over that bare flesh mesmerized her, and the naked skin was more sensitive than she could have imagined.

As her fingers and thumb worked in choreographed cadence, the orgasm began low in her belly, gathering force, building, building. She wanted to throw her head back and give herself over to it, but she couldn't stop watching herself in the mirror.

When her climax grabbed her, she couldn't tear her eyes away from the reflexive movement of her hips. They hitched forward as her pussy sucked her fingers tightly inside. In a last, erotic movement, she raked a fingernail over her clit. Only then did she close her eyes and let the spasms take her fully, shaking her like a branch in the wind, every muscle in her body clenching and unclenching.

Zane's hand gripped her wrist and pulled her fingers from her pussy. In one swift motion, he bent forward, lifted her hips, and replaced her fingers with his tongue.

She couldn't breathe, all air trapped in her throat. Her brain was on fire as he pushed her into another orgasm, this one harder and more intense. She bucked against him, riding his tongue, a low, guttural sound that she couldn't believe was hers rolling up from her throat.

Everything fell away and there was nothing except Zane's wicked, wicked tongue inside her and the shudders that raced over her. Her vagina clasped around his tongue over and over again until she thought she would pass out.

It could have been a minute or an hour before he began to back off and bring her down, slowly, gently, lapping at her with softer and softer strokes. Finally, he lowered her hips to the bed, placed a warm, open-mouthed kiss on her bare mound, and scooted her up so she was solidly on the mattress. Kicking the stool aside he climbed up beside her, turned them both, and pulled her against him spoon fashion.

"Jamie, Jamie, Jamie," he murmured in her ear.

Her heart was trying to hammer its way out of her chest and her breath was coming in gasps, but Zane's big hand soothed and eased her. His lips trailed kisses along her temple and cheek and beneath her jaw. Eventually, her body began to ease from the high he'd taken her to. She laid her head against his chest, a liquid puddle drained of everything but the love for him that grew every time they were together.

His cock nudged against her buttocks and she realized that, once again, he'd taken care of her without thinking of himself. Even though she knew watching her was a complete turn-on for him, that he'd enjoyed the eroticism of the act, he was still hard as a spike and his balls had to ache.

"For a guy who says he wants to be in control and likes his sex rough, you're turning into quite the attentive teddy bear," she teased, her fingertips caressing the line of his jaw.

"Actually a grizzly," he joked. "But I'm stifling my growl until you get over your injuries."

Somehow the sex between them had gone from angry and vengeful to raunchy and rough to incredibly tender. She wasn't sure she could handle it, despite the fact that he'd told her he loved her. And she'd told him right back. No one had ever been tender with her, and it scared her. What if it all disappeared in a puff of smoke?

"I'm fine," she told him. "Headache's gone." *Well, almost.* "And it's hard to think about pain when you give me so much pleasure." She reached behind her for his cock and wrapped her small fingers around its thick width. "If you really want to make me feel good, then fuck me, Zane. Right now. That's what I want."

Zane's hand on her hip contracted slightly, and his breath hitched. "I promise I'll take it easy. Your head's still fragile."

"Just do it," she begged. "I have to feel you inside me." She lowered her eyes. "I have to wipe away yesterday's memories."

That awful, awful man on top of me, and his knife touching me, cutting me.

A tiny shudder skittered up her spine.

When Zane tilted her face up to his, she knew he saw what she was feeling in her eyes as blatantly as if she'd worn a sign.

"All right, darlin'." He kissed her, just a brush of lips against lips. Then one corner of his mouth kicked up. "Just remember. Kit's iPod will only block out so much noise."

"I'll be real quiet," she whispered, smiling back at him.

"Let's make this as easy on you as we can," he said in an equally quiet voice.

Rolling expertly onto his back, he grabbed a condom, which he deftly rolled in place, and then positioned her over him, his strong hands firmly on her waist to take her weight. He was careful to keep her thighs situated so there was nothing rubbing against the small bandages.

"Open yourself for me, darlin'," he told her. "Show me the way."

Obediently, she pulled aside the lips of her pussy, and he adjusted her until the head of his cock was perfectly aligned with her opening. He was so erect it took little effort to slowly glide her onto the rigid shaft and lower her until he was fully inside her. Her swollen lips hugged the fullness of his penis, and the thick head pressed against the mouth of her womb.

"Mmm." She closed her eyes, reveling in the feel of him inside her.

One of his hands moved, and in a moment, she felt his thumb dipping into her wetness and rubbing the sensitive tip of her clit, instantly spearing a response. Tiny shivers raced over her spine, and the muscles of her cunt quaked around him.

"That's it." His voice was low and warm, soothing and arousing at the same time. "Let me do it all, darlin'. This time you just relax and enjoy the ride."

He continued to stroke her with his thumb until she could focus on nothing but that one spot on her body and the waves of bliss rolling outward from it. The muscles of her cunt sucked at his thick length. Shudders continued to grip her as the heat inside her flared higher and her pulse throbbed and throbbed.

When she felt the first thrust upward, she grabbed his wrists to balance herself, holding on for dear life. He set a rhythm, not too slow, not too fast, using his hips to push up into her again and again and again. His rigid cock rubbed her inflamed tissues with each plunge, and that sinful thumb kept working its magic.

She kept her eyes closed, letting the electrifying feeling lance through her. Zane's breathing grew as ragged as her own, and the power of his thrusts increased. Her pussy clasped more tightly around him as if she could suck him deeper into her body. His hips thrust upward more powerfully and the swell of her orgasm grew.

"Now, Jamie," he hissed through gritted teeth. "Now, now, now."

He pounded into her, his hand still firm on her waist. The moment she felt the first gush of semen through the thin latex, she splintered, coming completely apart, tossed onto a plane of pleasure so great she wasn't sure she'd survive it. Soft grunts rumbled from his chest as he thrust again, short little jabs to carry her through the aftershocks.

Slowly, the tremors subsided and the muscles of her cunt stopped flexing around him. Her own breathing evened out as she filled her lungs with deep gasps of air. When she would have fallen forward onto his sweat-slickened chest he braced her and took her to the side again, careful of her breasts that still sported faint bruises from the attacker's hard fingers.

His breath was a warm current on her face as he kissed her eyelids, her nose, her chin. She didn't know whose heart was thudding harder, hers or his, or how to even separate the sound of the two. His kiss, when his mouth reached her lips, was so tender and gentle tears threatened to spill from her eyes.

"Hey, hey, hey." He lifted his head. "Are you okay? Did I hurt you?" He loosened his grip. "I'm squashing your poor, sore breasts, aren't I?"

"No." She swallowed hard and blinked the tears away. "I just..."

"Just what, darlin'?"

Jamie buried her head against his shoulder. "I never...I mean...this is so much more than I ever expected from you." She was afraid to look at him, afraid she was misunderstanding everything and he'd think her a fool. He'd said he loved her, but this was so much more than words. So much deeper.

His fingers touched her chin and tilted her face up to his. "Look at me, Jamie," he commanded.

She forced her eyes open to meet his blazing ones, emotions swirling in their darkness.

"Just because I like my sex rough and because I'm a hardass, doesn't mean I don't enjoy tenderness. I've just never had it in a relationship. With anyone. Or wanted it, before this." His hand caressed her cheek. "I...feel things with you I never expected to. Not just possession but a...a bonding. I want to be things with you that I've never been with anyone else."

"I love you," she said in a choked voice.

"I love you, too. More than I ever thought possible." He brushed his fingers across her cheek, then slowly eased himself from her body.

She was lying on her back when he returned from disposing of the condom. "I don't hear Kit banging on the ceiling so I guess we were quiet enough for her," she joked.

"I don't care who hears us." He slid into bed beside her and wrapped her up against him, being careful of her cuts. "Or who knows how I feel."

Jamie wanted to just sink into is warm hardness forever. Her hand smoothed the skin on his chest. "You sure you really want to go public with this? You could get a lot of flak from a lot of people. Especially at work."

He tensed briefly. "I do my job, and I do it damn well. No one can find a thing to complain about. And my men respect me." He rubbed her back, his hand drifting down to the curve of her ass. "Besides, I get the feeling everyone on my staff knows what's going on anyway. And everyone else can think what they want. As long as I do the job I was elected to do, they can't complain."

"I know you're checking into Grayson Ballou for me. He's a pretty powerful man who could make a lot of trouble for you."

He snuggled her head under his chin. "If he's dirty, I'd welcome the chance to take him on. I don't kiss anyone's ass." He chuckled. "Except maybe yours." He reached behind him and snapped off the lamp. "Go to sleep, darlin'. I'll keep you safe. Count on it."

Desiree Holt

Chapter Eighteen

Zane's cell phone buzzed as he was shaving at six in the morning. He grabbed it before it could wake Jamie. The readout was Roy's number.

"Did you even go to sleep last night?" he asked, wiping the last bit of lather from his face.

"I think so," was the comeback, "but I'm not sure. Three things. First of all—and I'm sorry I have to tell you this—but scuttlebutt around the county is that Danny Christopher did odd jobs for your mother. And some of them were very odd indeed."

Zane gripped the phone so hard he was afraid he'd crush it. "What kind of *odd jobs*?"

"We're still trying to pin that down, but she might have been using him at Grayson Ballou's direction. I'm sorry, Zane."

The worst of it was he could actually believe his mother would hire such a lowlife to threaten Jamie. Over the past few years, a lot of things she did had begun to bother him. He swallowed back the bile rising in his throat. "Find out what you can and let me know. What else?"

"Your friend Skip Conway left a message last night that he and his friends would be here around ten this morning. And number three, I think we should take a look at the entire Randall place in broad daylight."

Zane's stomach tightened. "Why? Did something else happen?"

"Not sure. One of the patrols thought he saw something last night, but by the time he got to the place, if there was anyone, they were gone."

"Did he have any idea what they might have been doing?" Zane asked. "Did they leave any kind of trace behind?"

"Nothing the guys could find. But someone, who doesn't want us to know, may be keeping an eye on the place. You want to meet me at the house, and we'll go over all the property?"

"Give me thirty minutes." He snapped the phone shut.

"Trouble?" Jamie was still burrowed under the covers, but she peered at him with one eye.

"Maybe. Probably." Zane yanked on his uniform slacks and shoved his arms into the sleeves of his shirt. "Has there been anything else *but* lately?"

She turned over so she could see him with both eyes, her forehead creased. "Not another body."

"No, thank god. At least I don't think so." He buttoned his shirt, then came to sit on the side of the bed, taking one of her hands in his. "How are you feeling? I didn't push you too hard last night, did I?"

"As a matter of fact, I think you were just what the doctor ordered." She reached beneath the covers to touch the nakedness of her cunt. "Oh, yeah. Home remedies are the best. Definitely."

"Good. Very good." He lifted her hand and kissed the knuckles. "I meant to pass something along to you last night, but somehow I got sidetracked."

Her smile was slow and seductive. "Imagine that."

"Witch. Listen, I got a new report on Frank's truck. It hurts my pride to admit it, but you were right all along. If you've got a large bottle of ketchup, I'll pour it all over the crow before I eat it."

"I was right? After all your macho chest beating," she teased. "I was right all the time?"

He nodded. "Yes, damn it. I owe you a big time apology, and I'm sorry I was such an asshole. Someone pushed him over that hill, just like you said. But you have to understand the circumstances. None of this other stuff had come up yet, and Frank was..."

"A drunken bum. I know, I know." She pushed herself up against the pillows. "But I just had a feeling something was off. Damn it all, anyway. He may have been the world's worst father and a useless human being, but he didn't deserve that."

"I know, darlin'." He caressed her cheek. "And I take full responsibility for missing it. Will you forgive me?"

Jamie pressed against the hand on her cheek. "I should make you squirm and really pay, but I think you're already suffering enough with this whole mess. Let's just find some answers here."

He hugged her against him, kissing her hair. Then he set her away from him and caught her gaze with his. "Okay, here's what we've got. We recovered some paint chips from the tail gate and send them to the state lab. They can analyze them and tell us what kind of vehicle they came from. We'll take it from there, although I'm not holding out too much hope." He brushed her hair back behind her ears. "This whole mess is getting more complex every day. Whoever's pulling the strings has got some brains and covers his tracks. Danny Christopher being the lone deviation."

"I know. What's with that, anyway?"

"Don't know yet, but we're working on it. Someone may have decided to go after you on his own."

I hope like hell it isn't my mother, and that I'm only imagining her involvement with Danny. What a load of shit that would be to dump on this.

She shivered. "I can't imagine what this is all about, unless someone wants the money that badly. But why keep trying to get me out of town?"

Zane stroked her naked body, pulling her

momentarily against his warmth. "We're going to find out, Jamie. I promise." He set her away from him. "Gotta go. I'll keep in touch when I can, but I don't want you or Kit going anywhere today. I have regular patrols coming by the house and if anything—I mean *anything*—seems off kilter, call me right away on my cell."

"Don't worry," she told him. "I'm not ready to go out and fight the world again yet."

His groin tightened. He reached between her thighs and stroked her naked folds, feeling the cream of her pussy coating his fingers.

"But I think you might be ready for something else." He groaned. "I wish I had more time right now."

"I do, too. Hot sex is a good cure for everything. Haven't you heard?"

He studied her face and saw something that had been missing up until now. Real fear. She'd been angry, a little scared, and hostile, but now her eyes were shadowed with terror. He had to tamp down the rage that bubbled up. He wanted to kill the people who'd put that look there.

He kissed her as if he never wanted to let her go, and in truth, he didn't. With one large hand, he cupped her breast, his thumb teasing a plump nipple. His tongue danced with hers as it ravaged her mouth, his blood heating and roaring through his veins. The nipple beaded against his touch, his cock threatened to burst from its confinement, and pleasure stabbed at him like lightening gone wild.

Holy shit! How can she do this to me so easily?

He wanted to throw her down on the bed, spread her legs wide, and fuck her until she couldn't remember her own name. It took all of his willpower to pull away and settle her back in bed.

"I'll check in with you every chance I get," he promised, fighting to control his breathing. "You and

Kit hang out and keep all the doors and windows locked."

"We will." She gave him an impish grin that temporarily wiped away the fear. "Go get 'em, Sheriff."

****

Roy Galvan and another deputy were sitting in a county SUV in the Randall driveway when Zane pulled in behind them. The deputy opened the passenger side door to climb into the back seat and Zane noticed the gym bag he carried with him.

"Are we exercising today, too?" Zane asked, taking the deputy's place in front.

"Leon is a camera whiz. He'll be taking photos. He also has a basic crime scene kit with him in the very lucky happenstance we find something."

"So where are we going?"

Roy backed out of the long driveway, but instead of turning onto the highway, he shifted into four-wheel drive and began a very bumpy journey across the scrubland of the Randall property.

The hundred or so acres looked either natural or unkempt, depending on who was asked. Tall prairie grass that had never seen a mower moved like feathery soldiers in the early morning breeze. Thick stands of mountain cedar, live oak, and sycamore made passage over the ground difficult, but Roy navigated it expertly. Anyone who lived in this part of Texas knew how to drive in this kind of territory.

"Are we just taking a tour of the property?" Zane asked after the first few minutes.

"Oh, ye of little faith," Roy said. "Hold on for one more minute."

Finally, they were at the back end of the property. Roy pulled into a narrow space, stopped the SUV, and got out, motioning for Zane to do the same. They were walking through a small copse of live oaks when Zane suddenly stopped, realizing what Roy wanted to show him.

Someone had very cleverly cut down enough trees, mostly mountain cedar, to leave space to drive a vehicle onto the property. There was actually room among the oaks for two or three large vehicles to park in scattered fashion.

Roy crouched down and pointed to the ground. "We haven't had rain in months, so nothing's been washed away. Look. You can still see tire marks that haven't been completely destroyed by the wind." He rose up and walked to the other spaces, pointing again. "I'd say at least two of the vehicles were vans."

"Illegals," Zane spat. "Coyote traffic."

Texas constantly battled the coyotes, people who for exorbitant fees smuggled men, women and children across the border from Mexico. Diablo County sat smack in the middle of the state, a good distribution point if the coyotes could get their cargo this far traveling the highways at night.

"That's my guess," Roy agreed. "Whoever's running this particular operation is getting them across the border then bringing them up here. But I don't think this is just a place to let them off. I think these people are being sold—either as slave labor or as part of the white slavery market. Either to private individuals or to brothels. And not just in this country."

"Jesus." Zane blew out a long breath and forcibly held onto his temper. People being bought and sold like so much cattle turned his stomach.

"One more thing." Roy led him into a narrow space between two oaks and crouched down again, pointing. "There's been blood shed here. Someone's been either killed or hurt badly. And not all that long ago."

He motioned to Leon, who opened his gym bag, took out a camera, and began taking pictures, taking great care where he stepped.

"Frank Randall had to be part of this," Zane said. "They couldn't use his property without his knowledge. And this is a perfect drop-off spot. Nobody ever paid attention to Frank, and there's nothing around back here for miles."

"My guess is he's been doing it for years. That's where he got the money to support himself and Jamie. Such as it was, anyway."

"And that's where the money came from that Jamie found."

Roy was the only one Zane had told about that, swearing him to secrecy until they knew more about what was going on. At the moment, the cash was locked up in the safe in Zane's office, signed in by both himself and Roy.

"Something must have gone wrong for them to kill Frank," Roy commented. "Even if he'd asked for more money, it couldn't have been enough to get him killed."

"You're right. It had to be something else. Something he either knew or discovered. But what?"

Roy shrugged. "Beats me. We need to go back to the office and take a good look at everything that's happened around here in the past six months. Something will jump out at us. I hope."

Zane took off his Stetson, ran his fingers through his hair, and stuck his hat back on his head. "How'd you happen to find this?"

"I had Jimmy Black Crow doing the hourly runs past here last night, just keeping his eye out for anyone around the house or anything unusual. He thought he spotted something in the trees here. Caught the moonlight hitting something. When he got here, whoever it was had left, but he got out his flashlight and took a look around. This is what he found."

"Someone was keeping an eye on the house."

"That would be my guess. Whoever it was beat feet when he saw Jimmy heading his way."

"Good work for Jimmy. I just hope he didn't step on anything important walking around here."

Roy shook his head. "He was real careful. You made sure to train everyone about preserving evidence, even when they don't know if that's what it is. He keeps a pair of mocs in his car, so he put them on before he got out."

"Smart kid," Zane grunted. "Remind me to tell him so." He paused, thoughts banging around in his head. "Here's another question for you. Frank Randall picked up enough odd jobs that no one questioned his ability to pay for things like groceries, and his utility bills can't have been all that high. But he had mortgage payments to make. Taxes to pay. How come no one ever thought it suspicious that he paid them all in cash."

"Maybe he opened a bank account," Roy suggested.

"And dumped huge amounts of unexplained cash into it? Without the bank asking questions?"

"So are you saying the bank is in on it, too? Christ, Zane. Dean Holman's practically Mr. Community. He's been president of everything from Kiwanis to the county playground committee. And he's run Holman Community Bank forever."

Zane was quiet for a moment. "While we're speculating, here's another nugget for you. Gray Ballou owns the majority of the stock in that bank."

"So now you're saying Ballou's involved, too? Wait a minute. Did you suspect the smuggling? And that Ballou was involved? Is that why those guys from ICE are showing up today?"

"Just covering all my bases. And my ass."

Roy looked at his watch. "Leon should be done here pretty quick, and we'll get you back to your car. You'll make your meeting in plenty of time."

The deputy snapped off a dozen more shots, then took plastic evidence bags, tweezers, and a felt tip pen from the bag and began gathering up the debris on the ground that had what they suspected was blood spattered on it. He sealed the bags, dated and initialed them, then had both Roy and Zane add their initials to his.

"Just adding extra weight to the chain of evidence," he told them.

Zane knew when the deputy returned to the office, he'd meticulously enter each item into the evidence log, then watch while it was locked up and another deputy signed the receipt. He'd do the same thing with the photos when they were developed, making extra copies for the sheriff. And he'd write a meticulously detailed report of what had been found today.

And Zane knew they'd need everything they could get their hands on if what he suspected was true. Something so horrific he couldn't even voice it to Roy Galvan, his second in command, until he was absolutely sure.

What with one thing and another, it was after nine o'clock before they were ready to leave the scene. Zane barely had time to get to his office, catch up on the overnight reports, and hold a quick morning briefing before the men from ICE arrived.

He stood to shake Skip Conroy's hand. "Thanks for coming. I hope you brought some goodies with you."

After introducing the two men with him, Skip reached into his briefcase and pulled out a folder, handing it to Zane. "That should cover everything you asked for."

Zane carefully examined each sheet of paper, making sure every detail was covered. When he looked up at Skip, the smile on his face had no humor in it. "Thanks. This should more than do it. I can't believe you got a federal judge to authorize taps on all of Ballou's phones."

"The next thing is to implement them," Skip reminded him. "That's what these two guys are for. It would help if we could set up the tap directly at the local service provider, but there are so many alternates these days that doesn't always work. And my guess is Ballou uses an Internet service, thinking it protects him from something just like this."

"So what do you do?"

Skip's smile was equally as humorless as Zane's. "Hack into his phone records just like the warrant says we can do, find the path to his provider, and lay on a digital trap. That way every call in or out to any of his phones will also come to us. Like I told you yesterday, we brought the van with all our comm stuff in it. Is there a place we can set up where people won't be too nosy? I assume you want this as quiet as we can keep it."

After the morning briefing, he'd called Jimmy Black Crow to compliment him on his discovery the night before. At the same time, he arranged with the eager young deputy to park the van at his house at the edge of town. Set in an enclave of adobe dog run houses inhabited by other Comanches, it offered the perfect location. Even if the vehicle raised questions, no one was going to ask them. And Jimmy, beside himself at being part of whatever was going on, would have succumbed to torture before giving away any information.

Zane knew some of the other people in the neighborhood. Despite his mother's disdain for what she referred to as 'the lowest class of our people,' he had felt a need to connect with them, and Jimmy had been a good conduit.

"We're trying to raise the image of Native Americans," Anita pointed out over and over. "Every ethnic group has its lower class. How will you ever get elected to a state office if you don't learn to avoid yours?"

"I'm not running for state office," Zane repeated just as many times. "You can take that off the table."

But it had become a running battle between the two of them, one that often made Zane think about leaving the area and her altogether. But his visits to Jimmy's house and his casual drop-ins to neighborhood events had given the sheriff a certain stature here. It wasn't just Jimmy who would keep these people silent. It was their respect for Zane Cameron.

"We pulled the LUDS from Ballou's home phone and each of his offices, too, as soon as we got the warrants," Skip added, handing him another folder. LUD was an acronym for Local Usage Detail and produced a record of every incoming and outgoing call to a certain number for whatever period was requested. "These cover the past two months. The most frequently called number belongs to a cell phone registered to a Manual Alvarado."

Zane twisted his lips in distaste. "Ballou's errand boy. He started out as a small time thug, and now he's graduated to a big time one, wearing thousand dollar suits and Ferragamo shoes."

"I requested Alvarado's LUDs, too," Skip said. "They should be feeding them to us shortly. But the increase in the number of phone calls in the past few days indicates something more than just business as usual."

"About the time Jamie returned," Zane realized.

"She's the one you told us about? The one whose property Ballou keeps trying to buy?"

Zane nodded. "But that's not all. Plus, I have a sharp young deputy, whose driveway you'll be parking in, who discovered something last night you'll want to know about."

He filled all three men in on the attack on Jamie

as well as what had been found on the Randall property.

"That attack doesn't fit in with Ballou's normal method of operation," he told them. "I can see Alvarado hacking up the two Mexicans to prevent identification. Especially if they'd botched the job he sent them to do. Neither Ballou nor Alvarado would have hired him to terrorize Jamie. He's got other methods."

Skip agreed. "It doesn't seem like the kind of thing a man in Ballou's position would sanction. Is it possible there's another player here? One that's getting impatient? If we can prove illegals are being smuggled over here and sold, one of the customers could be worried Jamie Randall will screw up the nice little thing they've all got going.

"The first thing we've got to do is prove there's actually an operation and who's behind it. I want to make sure we've handled our end properly if we're going to take on Grayson Ballou."

"Amen to that." Zane pushed himself away from the wall he'd been leaning on. "So let's get on with it."

****

Kit had already started the coffee when Jamie came downstairs, showered, freshly bandaged, and wearing a pair of Zane's boxers and an old Sheriff's Association T-shirt.

"I packed a suitcase for you," Kit told her, taking in her outfit. "Didn't Zane take it up to the room?"

"Yes. Thank you. But I needed something really loose and soft that wouldn't rub on my bandages."

"Oh, honey." She cast a critical eye over her friend. "How are you this morning?"

"Much better than yesterday," Jamie assured her.

Kit gave her a sly grin. "I hope the sheriff didn't rub on the bandages last night."

Jamie actually felt heat creep up her cheeks. "He took good care of me."

"I'll just bet he did," Kit laughed. "Too bad he didn't take such good care of the pantry situation here. I think the man lives on cold cereal and beer."

"He probably eats out a lot."

As they stared at the poorly stocked cupboard the doorbell rang. The two women looked at each other.

"I'll go," Kit said. "You get ready to hide."

"From who? Who would be stupid enough to attack me in the sheriff's house?"

"I'm not taking any chances. Who is it?" she called through the door.

"Deputy John Rinks, ma'am," came the earnest reply. "Here's my credentials."

Kit pulled the curtain away from the tiny window in the door to see an earnest young face and a badge wallet held up to the glass. "All right. Just a minute."

She waited while Jamie turned off the alarm, then opened the door but left the chain on. The deputy standing there was juggling three grocery bags. "Ma'am, Sheriff Cameron sent me to the store with a list because he didn't have time to go. He said his cupboard was a might bare."

Kit took the badge wallet and examined it again, then released the chain and swung the door wide. "How right he is. Come right in, Deputy Rinks."

"I can't believe Zane sent you grocery shopping for us," Jamie said, unloading the bags. "You must have more important things to do."

"It was my pleasure. The sheriff is a really good guy. His men would do just about anything for him." He grinned. "Even grocery shop."

A warm feeling of pride crept over Jamie. She'd suspected Zane had trained himself to be a top lawman and a good boss, but it was nice to hear it from one of his men.

She reset the alarm and went to help put the groceries away. Kit insisted on making breakfast, despite Jamie's protests that she felt fine, and they dawdled for a long time over the food, talking about anything and everything except the cloud over Jamie's head and the danger she was in.

"Once this is all resolved," Kit said, "and I'm assuming the good sheriff will take care of that, have you thought about what comes next?"

"What do you mean?" Jamie tore off a piece of toast and chewed on it slowly.

"Don't give me that, Jamie Randall. You know exactly what I mean. What happens with you and the hunk? And don't try to tell me there's nothing going on. I'd have to be deaf, blind, and stupid not to know what the situation is with you two. Especially after watching him with you at the hospital."

Jamie sighed. "Lordy, Kit, I just don't know. Staying in Amen doesn't seem nearly as bad to me as it once did. And I don't think I could walk away from Zane again. But then what? Do we even have a life here? I'm still that drunk Frank Randall's daughter, and Anita Cameron is going to do her best to make me the county pariah."

"I think those are things you need to let Zane worry about, honey. If you want to be together, the rest is just details to work out."

"You make it sound so easy."

"And you make it sound so difficult." She shrugged. "Who knows? Maybe Zane will actually want to leave here and get into law enforcement someplace else."

Kit insisted on cleaning up when they finished. "Tomorrow you can start pulling your weight."

Jamie stretched out on the wide leather couch with two throw pillows tucked under her head and flicked on the television. But within minutes she found herself dozing off.

Zane was walking through a cloud of fog again, naked, his eyes burning with lust. "I'll take care of you, Jamie. Don't you worry."

"I know." She reached out her arms to him. There didn't seem to be anything solid beneath her, but she didn't feel unbalanced.

He lay next to her, floating on air as she was, his mouth kissing her breasts where they'd been bruised. "I'd kill the bastard who did this if he was still alive," he ground out.

"Shh," she told him. "It's all right. I'm fine."

"I'll never let anyone hurt you again," he promised.

"Hold me," she urged, pulling him toward her.

He shifted to cradle her with one arm while the other hand drifted down between her thighs. "You're wet." He lifted his hand and rubbed his fingertips across her lips, painting them with her juices. "Share your taste with me." He bent and pressed his mouth to hers, licking her lips first with the tip of his tongue, then carrying the flavor into her mouth as his tongue swept inside.

Pleasure rippled through her, sending a fresh release of cream in her pussy and making her internal muscles clench in expectation.

"I'm going to fuck you," he said in a rough tone. "I love to feel my dick inside all that warm, wet heat. Feel you suck me inside you. Your pussy is so tight, darlin'. It just squeezes the life out of me. Does it feel as good to you?"

"Oh, yes," she breathed. "Fuck me, Zane. Now. Let me feel you inside of me."

"Not until I taste you first." He slipped his hands under her buttocks and lifted her to his mouth. The tip of his tongue swirled around her clit, sent shards of ecstasy through her. Her juices flooded his mouth, and he swallowed them enthusiastically. His tongue

probed her wet channel, pushing into it as far as he could then using the tip to reach those tiny sensitive places that sent off rockets in her body.

When he lifted his head, his mouth and cheeks were shiny with her cream. "You taste like the most delectable treat, Jamie. I could fuck you with my tongue all night, if I didn't want my cock in you so desperately."

"Yes, yes, yes," *she chanted.* "I want it, too. Now, Zane. Fuck me now."

He moved over her, his breathing uneven, his eyes fiery with need.

Wrapped in a sensual fog, she was shocked to look over his shoulder and see a black shadow move just beyond them.

"Get away from her," *a voice shouted.* "Right now."

The figure raised a hand with a gun, a sharp sound split the air, and Zane slumped forward.

"Zane!" *Jamie screamed.* "Someone help me. He's bleeding. Help me! Help me!"

"Jamie, wake up."

Someone was shaking her. Why didn't they help Zane? "He's bleeding," she screamed again.

"Come on, honey. Wake up. Jamie!" Hands shook her, and she opened her eyes to Zane's living room, Kit's scared face staring at her.

"What? What are you doing?" She pushed Kit away and raked her fingers through her hair.

"You were screaming the house down." Kit sat on the edge of the couch next to her. "That must have been some dream you were having. You scared the life out of me."

It all flashed across her brain, and she grabbed Kit's arm, squeezing her. "Someone's going to kill Zane. And it's because of me."

Kit brushed stray hair off Jamie's forehead. "Zane knows how to take care of himself, Jamie.

Nobody's going to kill him."

"No, you don't understand." Jamie shook her head in frustration. "This is the second time I've had the same dream. We're making love and someone kills him. Shoots him." Her heart rate speeded up as agitation consumed her.

"Honey, honey, honey," Kit soothed. "Zane is fine. *Will* be fine. He has too much going to let someone kill him."

"Where's my cell?" She looked wildly around. "I want to call him right now."

"Jamie, I think he's pretty busy right now."

"He said he'd check in, and I haven't heard from him. I think he's got a phone in the kitchen." She started to jump up from the couch.

"Stop." Kit put a restraining hand on her shoulder. "I'll get you my phone. It's right here."

Jamie's hands shook so badly she could hardly dial the number for Zane's cell. It took her three tries to get it right, but when she heard his voice she finally let out the breath she'd been holding. "You're all right."

"Of course I'm all right. Why?" His voice dropped. "Jamie, what's wrong? Has something happened? I've had patrols going by the house—"

"No, no one's been here except that cute deputy with the groceries. Thanks, by the way."

"Then tell me what's wrong. You sound rattled."

"You'll think I'm ridiculous." And she probably was. A dream was, after all, just that. A dream.

"Nothing's ridiculous. Tell me."

"Remember that dream I told you about? The one where you get shot?"

"Yup. Did you have another one?"

"Yes, I did." She swallowed. "In this one, whoever it is yells at you to get away from me, then shoots you in the back."

There was silence on Zane's end for a long

moment.

"See, I told you I'm being ridiculous."

"And I told you I believe in premonitions. Could you see who the figure was? Recognize the voice?"

"No." She rubbed her hand across her face. "It was just a shadow, and the voice sounded disguised. But, Zane?"

"Yes, darlin'?"

"Both times we were making love."

"Well, there you are." His tone softened, and she knew he was trying to reassure her. "You don't see me letting anyone into the bedroom with us, do you?"

"No. I just have this...awful feeling."

"I swear I'll be careful. And even if I can't make dinner, I'll stop by so you can see for yourself."

"Is something happening?" she asked quickly.

"Not yet, but we're working on it. I'll try to check in more often, okay? And I'll come by about six and bring Chinese."

"Okay." She turned so her back was to Kit. "Zane?"

"Yes, darlin'?"

"I love you."

"I love you, too, Jamie." His voice was low and deep and warm and sent shivers along her spine. "Nothing's going to separate us, you hear?"

"A-all right."

Kit took the phone back when she disconnected the call. "Feel better now?"

"A little. But I'm telling you, Kit. I have this terrible feeling in the pit of my stomach."

"Well, it's after twelve noon. I think we can allow ourselves a glass of wine. That ought to chase the bogeyman away."

Chapter Nineteen

"Are you aware the sheriff had men at our drop-off spot this morning?" Gray Ballou's voice was like sharp steel, slicing across the connection.

"Yes." Manny was sitting in his house in Copper Ridge. Tonight was the rendezvous, and they were in a world of trouble.

"That means we won't be able to use it tonight. Do you realize that, you idiot?"

Of course he realized it. He'd been stewing about it since he got away from the Randall property before the cop could tag him. He hadn't slept a wink, worrying about what they would do. What Gray would say.

He'd had such a nice little operation going. Smuggle a few illegals across the border and bring them up here. Sell them to the ranchers who wanted cheap labor. Everyone made some bucks and no one got caught. Then Grayson, for whom he did so many other things, got wind of it and decided to cut himself in. But the operation changed.

Now they were bringing mostly women over, selling them to customers who paid big bucks for them, individually or in groups, depending on what they were being used for. The littlest ones, eleven or twelve years old, brought the highest prices. Manny knew all about that. And the money. Oh, sweet Jesus, the money.

The money had affected Frank Randall, too. And others. People got too greedy. Manny would give a bundle to know where Frank's stash was. Jamie hadn't been on a spending spree. Even her furniture had been paid for by her friend. And damn her, she wouldn't go away. Wouldn't sell. Wouldn't leave town.

Now she and the damn sheriff were thicker than bees on honey. How the shit did that happen? He'd been assured Zane Cameron hated the white trash bitch and that she wouldn't be a problem. So much for taking other people's word.

He had enough stashed away now that he intended to make tonight's drop the last one. Then he'd disappear and Grayson Ballou could do whatever the hell he wanted to. He hadn't been able to buy the Randall land, so if he kept up the operation, he'd have to move it somewhere else.

And he'd have to find someone to cover for him as Manny did. It wouldn't do for the big Grayson Ballou to get his name dirtied. Not that Manny cared much. He just wanted to get the hell out of here.

Shit and damnation.

"Manny? Are you listening to me?" Gray's voice cut through his mental fog.

"I'm here."

"We still haven't found that money. If the sheriff's got it, there could be trouble."

"I haven't heard a thing," Manny told him. "And I'm keeping all my antennae out."

"You better get a few more. And we need a new place for tonight. Do you have one picked out?"

Manny sighed. There hadn't been a lot of choices. "I have some vacant land for sale halfway between Amen and Copper Ridge, off Eagle Pass Road. I can't get a buyer because there's a crazy Indian who lives a couple of miles away. The stories about him are enough to scare anyone off."

"I know the place. That's where Nathan Black Crow lives. You're right. There's no traffic around there at all."

"Everyone can come in from the back end of Eagle Pass. Almost all of the land is covered with trees of one kind or another, and there's a wide spot at one place for the vehicles to pull into. It will work for tonight."

"I know where it is. All right. I'll call my people. You get hold of yours. Tomorrow we need to have a long talk. And we need to do something about that Randall bitch."

"Not while she's holed up at the sheriff's house."

"I think I can handle that," Gray told him. "Let's just get by tonight. Then she'll be taken care of. Permanently."

Manny sat holding the phone for a long time after Gray hung up. Then he looked up the number for the airline he wanted. He'd go straight from the delivery to the airport and never even have to spit on this place again.

****

Skip Conway was on the horn to Zane the moment the conversation ended.

"I think we have a whole lot of big trouble," he told him and repeated what he and his men heard and recorded.

"Is the tape of the conversation enough to get the goods on Ballou?" Zane was in his office with the door closed, alone except for Roy. "I sure don't want him to skate."

"It would be nice if we could get him to the scene, but I don't think he gets his hands that dirty. In any event, I thought we could get together and plan a joint reception party for tonight. It's important for your guys to be in on this, unless there's someone you don't trust."

"No. I think that's a good idea."

Zane could hear murmured conversation, then Skip was back. "You aren't going to like this."

"Is there anything about this whole goatfuck *to*

like?"

"We triangulated his cell phone. He just made three calls, all of them giving out a new cell number and a brief message. And that gave us another thread to follow, which you won't be too happy to hear about."

"What do you mean? Who else did he call?"

The pause this time was a lot longer. When he finally answered, Skip's voice was as sympathetic as he could make it. "He called your mother, Zane. He called Anita."

"My mother?" Nausea crept up into his throat. "He could have called her about anything. She works for him."

"This was no work-related matter. He told her he'd given his buyers her number since he didn't trust his right now, and she was to coordinate everything with them for tonight."

Zane's gut clenched. He wanted to throw something. Hit someone. They'd never been close, to say the least, and they operated with completely different philosophies. From the time he was ten and his father died, they'd been like two strangers living in the same house. When she moved to Copper Ridge, it gave him a chance to put space between them.

Somewhere in the back of his mind, he'd always suspected his cool, remote mother had been more involved with Grayson Ballou outside her extremely high-paying job. But nothing like this had ever crossed his mind. Now he wondered just how far back it all went. If this was how she got her job so quickly. But he'd never expected her to be mixed up in something like this.

"What else?" he asked in a tight voice.

Skip repeated what he'd heard in reference to Jamie.

Zane tried to control the murderous rage

creeping over him. Forcing a control he didn't feel, he made his voice as even as possible. Being realistic about it, he would need help that he couldn't get exclusively from his own staff. It killed him to ask Skip what he wanted from him, but he had to divorce himself from this emotionally. Jamie came first.

"I guess I'll need to ask you for a favor," he told the man, his body vibrating with tension.

"Whatever you need, you know that. Can it wait until we get together?"

"Some of it. But someone will need to keep an eye on...my mother. I can't use any of my men. She knows them all. Including the ones at the Copper Ridge substation. Is there any way you can help 'em out here? We need to know where she goes and with who."

He wondered if Skip Conway could tell how much pain there was in his voice. His mother, damn it. He hoped whatever she was doing didn't splash over onto him.

"I already called San Antonio," Skip told him, "and there are other agents on the way, but they're a good two hours or more from here. Do you think she'll need watching before then?"

Zane thought for a minute, swallowing the bile rising in his throat. "No, my guess is she'll probably sit tight, at least for the moment. Can you get a tap on her land line and cell?"

"Just waiting for the warrant to be faxed to me." Silence for a moment. "I'm sorry about this, Zane. And also that Miss Randall seems to be in danger because of it."

"I'll take care of Jamie. Right now, I want to talk to my chief deputy."

"I'll call you when everyone gets here." Skip disconnected the call.

Zane looked at Roy, who was trying to make

himself invisible.

"You heard?" he asked.

"Only your end." He cleared his throat. "What's up with your mother?"

"More than I'd like. Have a seat. We have things to go over, things that go no further than the two of us right now. But first I have to make a phone call."

****

Jamie had managed to dig her cell phone out of her purse and was holding it when Zane called.

"Just checking in on my woman," he said with an attempt at lightness.

The possessiveness in his voice sent slashes of warmth through her body. "Your woman's just fine. You, too, right?"

"Safe and sound." There was a slight pause. "Listen, Jamie, there's going to be some stuff going on later tonight. I don't want you leaving the house. You *or* Kit. Okay?"

The warmth was replaced by slivers of ice. "This sounds dangerous. You'll be careful, right?"

He lowered his voice to the deep sound that made her pussy weep and her breasts tingle. "I promised, didn't I?"

"Just be sure you keep that promise."

"You've got the alarm set?"

"Yes. And all the doors and windows locked."

"Good." His voice sounded strained. "Jamie, it's very important that you don't go out for any reason or let *anyone* in. I mean *anyone.*"

Fear tickled at her nerves. "Zane, what's going on here? Has something else happened? Tell me the truth. Whatever it is, I can handle it."

Zane repeated what Skip had told him, that the tap on Ballou's phone had revealed to them that the man intended to deal with Jamie once and for all after tonight. "I'm just worried they may decide waiting until then is too long. Ballou may get antsy and decide to send someone after you today."

"I won't let anyone in the house. I wish we still had my father's gun." Zane had locked it up as evidence after the shooting at her house.

"Just stay away from doors and windows, and you should be fine. I'm going to have a patrol car take a run by once an hour, just to check on things."

"You go take care of business, lawman, and I won't have to worry."

But when she hung up the phone, she couldn't shake the feeling of dread that had gripped her since the last dream. And she had a distinct feeling Zane was still keeping something from her.

"Trouble?" Kit wandered in from the kitchen carrying a pitcher of iced tea and two glasses.

"Isn't that our middle name?" She repeated what Zane had told her. "Plus, I know there's something he's keeping back."

"Like what?" Kit filled the glasses and handed one to Jamie.

"I don't know. But I've got a weird feeling that just won't go away." She shivered as invisible fingers tickled her spine.

"Let's see if we can find a good romance movie on television, close the curtains, and hunker down on the couch. Our designated shopper included cookies with the groceries. I'll go get them. Nothing like cookies and a tearjerker to chase away the bogeymen."

****

They were all in Zane's conference room—Roy, his hand-picked deputies, Skip Conway and the rest of the ICE agents. Skip had replayed the recordings of the conversations for everyone and handed out printed transcriptions. A whiteboard hanging on the wall was covered with a diagram of the supposed smuggling operation, but everyone was sharply aware of the number of question marks where names should be.

Skip stood at the head of the table, shirt sleeves rolled up, his eyes like chips of marble. Zane had deferred to him to run the meeting.

"This has to be your show," he told the agent. "You've got the clout to make it work. If I try to arrest any of these people, they'll be out before the ink is dry on the booking slips."

The first thing they handed out was the basic lab reports Zane's staff had generated. The dried substance found at the site on the Randall property was indeed blood, and of more than one type. The techs had also managed to confirm the fact that more than one vehicle drove in and out of there, although the tracks were too faint for specific identification. But it was the blood that got everyone's attention.

Skip tacked an aerial map of the Randall property and the surrounding area on the wall next to the whiteboard. He'd drawn a circle around the place they examined that morning. Next to it was a shot of the Eagle Pass property described in the telephone conversation. The red circle there marked the new meeting place.

"We've forced the people running this operation to move the spot they've been using, so they had to find an alternate location," he told everyone. "The conversations we tapped indicate all the activity will take place about midnight. We have to assume they'll have eyes on the area somehow, so this will be dicey." He shuffled through some paper in front of him. "I've gotten permission to redirect a satellite so we'll have an eye in the sky at all times. The other thing we have to deal with is how to get our people in place without attracting attention." He glanced at Zane. "I think the sheriff can best address that."

"We'll have to leave all vehicles at least two miles away," he told them, ignoring the wincing looks he got from some of the men. "There are some hidden paths we can take, and some of it will mean belly-crawling. But if we wait until dark we can get in there without being seen."

He pointed to a spot on the second aerial shot.

"Jimmy Black Crow's grandfather lives here. Has for years. People have made up a lot of stories about him so no one bothers him. There's virtually no traffic around here at all. Manny Alvarado has a piece of land there he can't sell. That's probably why Ballou and his people think this spot was a good one to pick. I'll let Jimmy take it from here."

The young deputy stood up at the end of the table. "We can rendezvous at my grandfather's house. If we drive up after dark, lights out, we'll be okay. I'll lead you from there." He handed out sheets of paper. "These are directions to the house. The sheriff and Mr. Conway have set the rendezvous time for ten o'clock. We should allow an hour to get to the targeted spot without calling attention to ourselves. That gets us in place an hour before deadline."

"Plenty of time to set up and wait," Skip added.

"We're all good at that," one of his men joked, lightening the thick tension in the room.

Zane knew these were all experienced men. Jimmy Black Crow had the least experience but perhaps the most knowledge of what they'd be doing. In addition to the skills he'd learned from his grandfather, he'd had a tour of duty in Iraq before coming home to join the sheriff's department.

"One more thing." Zane broke in and told them about the bodies of the two young girls they'd found. "We're dealing with some real sickos here. I want them more than you can possibly imagine."

Everyone sitting at the table echoed his thoughts.

They spent the next hour going over everything

in great detail, making sure nothing was left to chance. Skip had left one of his men in the van at Jimmy's still monitoring the telephone taps. As the meeting was about to break up, Skip's cell phone rang.

"The van," he told Zane. "Everyone hold on for a minute." He listened carefully, murmured a few words and hung up. His gaze slid to Zane briefly then back to the men. "Ballou has...someone...contacting his buyers for him. I just received confirmation that everything's a go. Apparently tonight's delivery will include what they're calling 'special orders,' so there's more money than usual involved. That means they'll be more alert and probably more heavily armed. We'll go over this again when we meet at Nathan Black Crow's."

"Skip will handle the gear for his people," Zane said. "All of you on my staff will get your equipment when we rendezvous. That's all. Oh, and I know I don't need to tell anyone this, but not a word of this gets out. To anyone."

As soon as the men left the room, Zane turned to Skip. "I assume that was my mother you were referring to before."

Skip nodded. "We got the tap in place. From the nature of the conversations, she does this on a regular basis. I hate to say this, but I'm going to guess she gets a cut, too. I'm sorry about this."

Zane shoved his clenched fists in his pockets. "Not your problem. I should have seen it coming a long time ago."

"The hardest things to see are those in front of us, you know. Are you sure you don't want me to handle that? Keep it away from your office?"

"No, but thanks. I think I'd better do this one myself. I don't want anyone to think I shied away from it. Or looked the other way."

"All right. I've got someone sitting on her, so if

277

she starts to move, I'll let you know."

Zane nodded once. Memories were crashing in on him and none of them were pleasant.

****

Anita Cameron completed her last call, closed her cell phone, and tucked it into her pocket. How could that imbecile Manny have let things go to hell this way? Every decision he'd made had only given birth to another problem.

It's that bitch Jamie Randall's fault.

Everything had started to fall apart when Jamie came back to Amen. Why did she have to pick this place to lick her wounds? And just at this time? Anita had spent years building this life for herself after Mike Cameron's death, an event she still thought of as removing an obstacle to her future. He'd certainly been agreeable to everything in the beginning. Until he began to think of himself as more important than he was.

And the demands he made on her. What was he thinking, anyway? She'd married him to get away from the reservation and the nowhere life many Comanche who lived outside the res were relegated to. It had been hard work, turning herself into the person she was, getting Gray to see her in a different light. Establishing herself as a different person.

And Zane. God, she had such plans for him. Educated and a military hero, he had no place to go but up with Gray's help. She even, in her daydreams, saw him as the first Native American governor of the state. Certainly a congressman. She was sure she'd almost had him convinced until that whore showed up again. Now she was all he could think of.

Well, Anita had managed to get rid of Mike Cameron. She could get rid of Jamie Randall just as easily. After tonight, Gray would owe her big time. She'd remove the one obstacle to success, and Zane would be on his way up the power ladder.

She paused in the foyer to look at herself in the wall mirror, touching her perfectly styled hair, examining the minute lines at the corners of her eyes. Not bad for fifty-four. She could be of great value to Zane. And she'd choose a woman for him that would be a help rather than a hindrance.

Humming to herself, she headed for her bathroom to shower. She wanted to look good for her big act tonight.

****

Manny Alvarado poured himself a double shot of single malt scotch and tossed it down in one swallow. He shuddered as the liquor burned its way to his stomach. When the searing warmth had spread throughout his system, he poured another drink and carried it with him to his bathroom. He had plenty of time to shower and change before arriving at the rendezvous spot. For the coyotes, jeans and a T-shirt were too good, but for the representatives of the buyers, he needed a more elegant appearance. It would never do to let them think they were doing business with lower class.

He also had time for at least one more drink to calm his nerves. His conversations with Ballou today had grated on his nerves. He would love to point out to the man that he'd created this situation. He was the one who had the argument with Frank Randall and ordered Manny to get rid of him. He was the one who'd failed to find out where the old man had hidden the money. He was the one who made an issue out of buying the Randall property, calling attention to a situation that might have had other solutions.

Now it was up to Manny to pull their bacon out of the fire. Good old Manny.

Manny smiled to himself as he thought of the shock to Grayson Ballou when good old Manny up and disappeared.

As he stripped off his clothes, his cell phone rang. Looking at the Caller ID, he twisted his lips. Gray. Again. Sighing, he pressed the Talk button.

"What now?"

"I'm not sure that's the appropriate way to address a man who's helping you make a fortune," Gray spat out. "Especially since it's your stupidity that put us in the situation we find ourselves in."

Manny gripped the phone so hard he was afraid it would shatter in his hand. He only wished it was Grayson Ballou's neck.

"What do you want? Everything's set for tonight on your end, right?"

"I always take care of business. Just be sure you do the same. You have people arriving ahead of time to secure the area?"

"Yes." Manny gritted his teeth. "It cost more money, but I got a good team. They'll be in place an hour ahead of time."

"Are you sure that's enough in advance?"

"Damn it!" Manny exploded. "Will you let me do my job without second guessing me?"

"As long as you do it properly. No screw-ups tonight, Manny. This is the biggest payoff yet."

"Everything will be fine. Now let me get ready."

Manny snapped the phone shut and resisted the urge to throw it across the room. Instead, he punched in a familiar number.

"Tell me again you're all set for tonight," he said when the man he called answered.

****

Zane let himself into the house quietly. Before getting ready for tonight, he wanted five minutes to hold Jamie in his arms and kiss the life out of her. He headed toward the kitchen but stopped when he heard Kit's angry voice.

"You should have just hung up on the asshole,"

she was saying. "Or at least told him you weren't interested."

"The call startled me." Jamie's voice. Defensive. "Anyway, he was the last person I expected to hear from today. Or any other day, for that matter."

"So you get a call from your old boss telling you that the real story of what happened to you has been uncovered." Kit's voice. "All of a sudden the man who tossed you out with the garbage wants you to fly to Miami and talk about getting your old job back. Big fucking deal."

Every nerve in Zane's body went on high alert.

"But he also hinted the newspaper might repay some of my expenses from the law suit," Jamie went on.

"Yeah, right." Sarcasm dripped from Kit's words. "Like that asshole is really going to do anything to help you. He should have stood behind you from the beginning."

"All he wants to do is talk," Jamie protested. "That's all."

"Don't you think you should be running this past Zane first, before you commit to anything?"

"I haven't committed," Jamie denied. "Just..."

"Sounded like you were ready to pack and leave on the next plane."

"That's not true." Jamie was nearly shouting.

"Your first reaction, if you weren't going to tell him to go to hell, was to let him know you had someone in your life you needed to discuss this with."

"I just didn't know what to say to him," Jamie said, conflict evident in her tone. "I'm not sure he'll understand. It's a chance for me to vindicate myself. Make a lot of people grovel."

"That's the dumbest thing I've ever heard you say. Two hours ago you were so happy about your relationship with Zane. Now you're saying you'd just throw it over, run back to Miami, and do what? Regret it for the rest of your life?"

Pain sliced through Zane's heart, like a sharp knife. Just when he thought they'd finally gotten past all that old shit. When he was sure she trusted him. Trusted what they felt for each other. Yet apparently she was ready to dump him and this place all over again. So what did that say about everything between them? Was it all a lie?

"No, that's not it at all," Jamie said, her voice coming closer. "But what if I tell Miami no and Zane changes his mind about us? Doesn't want me after all?"

"What makes you think that would happen?" Zane didn't even recognize his own voice. He just stood rooted to the spot, staring at Jamie as she jerked, startled by his appearance.

"Zane?" Her hand shook and a splash of wine sloshed over the rim of her glass. "I-I didn't hear you come in."

"Obviously." He stared at her for a long moment, trying to read what was in her eyes. In her heart. "I thought we were well past that by this time. You told me you loved me. I said it back. Apparently the trust issue has yet to be put to bed."

"Zane..."

"Not now, Jamie. Somehow you managed to pick the worst possible time to drop this little bombshell."

He turned and headed for his bedroom. He didn't have time for this now. He had business to take care of.

Jamie was right on Zane's heels as he strode to his room, her stomach knotted, her heart pounding in a wild, staccato beat. What had she done? How stupid could she be?

She should never have mentioned the call from her boss to Kit before discussing it with Zane. Why did she even care about the damn job, anyway, except for what the apology did to her ego?

Shit, shit, shit!

She held herself in check as Zane changed clothes and did her best not to throw herself at him and beg him to stay. To forgive her. To tell her everything was all right. Would be all right. The sense of foreboding the dreams had brought still clung to her, and now she'd managed to drive a wedge between them.

She wet her suddenly dry lips and tried to make her voice as quiet as possible. "Promise me you'll be careful."

He gave her a tight grin. "I'm always careful. Except where you're concerned, I guess."

"Zane, the call just came in yesterday. I was looking for the right time to tell you about it, ask what you thought." She swallowed some of her wine, needing the liquid courage.

"You obviously found time to talk to Kit about it."

"I was just using her as a sounding board," she cried. "Honestly. I was so startled that everything had been cleared up and they'd offered me my job back."

"I'm shocked that you'd even consider it," he spat. "Especially after the way they treated you. But if that's what you really want, maybe we could have worked something out. I can work anywhere, you know. We could have figured out what to do. Together."

"You're right, you're right." She chugged the rest of the wine. "Can we just talk about it for a minute? Please? So when you leave here we aren't angry with each other?"

He stopped what he was doing and stared at her. "Now? You want to talk about it now when I have this whole thing tonight on my mind? When I shouldn't have to be thinking of anything else? I can't afford the distraction of anger, Jamie. I'll have to bury it until this is over."

She grabbed the shirt he was holding out of his hands and threw herself against him. "I love you, Zane. I do. I want you to believe that. I just…"

His hands gripped her arms as he set her aside. "I told you, we can't discuss this now. If everything goes all right tonight and you're still here when I get home, maybe we'll see what's what."

"Still here? Where else would I be?" She felt sick to her stomach. "Please be careful," she said again.

"Count on it. Anyway, I'm no novice at this."

"I know, I know."

When he pulled on the last of his clothes, her eyes widened at the transformation. Tonight he wasn't wearing his uniform, nor did he have on his jeans. Instead, his lean, muscular body was clothed in deerskin pants and shirt, with soft moccasins on his feet. His hair, released from the leather thong, was loose around his shoulder. He looked every bit the fierce warrior.

"Jesus," she breathed.

"I thought I'd give them something they weren't expecting." His eyes blazed into hers. "I guess I surprised you, too. I'm still the same half breed your father wanted to shoot, Jamie. That hasn't changed. What you see is what you get. Maybe that's what you're still running away from."

"I'm not running, Zane. I didn't…" She wanted to cry, and she had to swallow hard to talk past the lump in her throat. "You'll still be armed, right?"

He nodded at his gun lying on the table and lifted up the flap on a breast pocket to reveal his badge. "I'm not leaving *everything* at home. I'm cocked and loaded and ready for whatever happens."

"Thank god for that." She blinked hard at the tears burning her eyelids. *I won't cry. I won't.*

He gripped her shoulders, his eyes burning into

hers with fierce intensity. ""Do a lot of thinking while I'm gone, Jamie. A lot. Decide what it is you really want. Because this time whatever we decide, there's no changing your mind."

"I know. Oh, Zane."

"Later."

"I'll be waiting up. Worrying. You'd better call me the minute this is done, you hear?"

"We'll see."

He tucked his gun into his pants at the small of his back and strapped a wicked looking knife to the calf of his leg. Her heart tripped over itself as the beat stuttered, but she swallowed her fear and pasted a smile on her face.

"Be careful," she said one last time as he walked out of the room.

Jamie wrapped her arms around herself, trying to shut out the sudden cold, finally letting the tears roll down her cheeks.

Kit was suddenly beside her, enfolding her in her slim arms and making soothing sounds. "I don't know if I should tell you it will be all better or kick your ass."

"Ass kicking is probably the smartest thing." Jamie sniffed, rubbing her face with the heels of her hands. "God, sometimes I am so stupid I wonder if I even have a brain. What the hell was I doing, Kit? How could I even for one second think about throwing all this away? And now he's out doing something very dangerous. What if he..."

But she couldn't finish the sentence. She only knew she couldn't rest for a second until Zane walked back in the front door, safe and well. Could only pray that she hadn't screwed everything up yet again.

Chapter Twenty

They were all in Nathan Black Crow's living room, the ICE agents and Zane's deputies, checking weapons, night vision goggles, and communications gear.

"As soon as the pickup vehicles get there, we'll be ready to call in the license plates," Skip said. "But my guess is we'll only get the buyers if we can work a deal with the drivers or get either Manny or Ballou to crack."

"Manny would be a more likely target," Roy told him. "Gray will hide behind his expensive lawyers, but Manny will want to save his own skin."

Zane looked at his watch. "Right on time. All right. Listen up, everyone. Alvarado's men will be moving into place in about an hour. So we need to move out now."

"Jimmy, you ready to lead the way?" Skip asked. "Just tell us what to do."

Zane was used to creeping and crawling through foliage and trees, moving with no sound, brushing away the marks of his movement on the ground. Some of his men, also, had been on one of Jimmy Black Crows nighttime maneuvers before, but the federal agents were doing their best to swallow their groans and not make any noise. If it hadn't been so serious, Zane would have laughed.

By eleven o'clock, they were all in place, well-concealed and ready to rock. They all wore lip mics and ear buds, but communication was nonexistent at the moment. Skip had clicked his mic twice when he got the word the vans had left the airport. Now they could do nothing but wait.

A half-moon hung in the sky, obliterated now and then by dark, scudding clouds. Somewhere off in the distance coyotes wailed and a dog barked. Everyone startled when a group of white tail deer plunged through the bushes, loping through the trees, then settled back in place.

At last, the low beams of headlights cut through the night, moving toward the wide space in the trees from two directions.

"Remember," Skip whispered. "We wait until there's an actual exchange of merchandise before we move in. Just be ready."

A fourth vehicle, an SUV, pulled in next to one of the vans, and Manny Alvarado strode into the area. The drivers of the vans from the direction of Copper Ridge climbed out and opened the side doors of their vehicles, then stood waiting to load the new cargo.

Nausea rose in Zane's throat as the coyote and his friends roughly pulled the passengers from their vehicles. None of them could have been over thirteen, and in the dull lights of the vans, they looked terrified. Manny approached one group, looked it over, then grabbed the arm of a girl who didn't look to be more than eleven.

"I'll take this one," they heard him say. "Get the others loaded."

The moment the exchange had been completed, Zane, Skip and their men broke cover and descended on everyone. The element of surprise was so great and the force of the team so large the only damage was to the egos of the men involved in the white slave ring. They were caught unaware and didn't even have a chance to pull their guns. Not one shot was fired, for which everyone was grateful. There was a great deal of cursing in both English and Spanish, one man tried to kick the agent cuffing him, and Manny Alvarado was calling for an attorney and protesting his treatment. But the federal agents and deputies worked together like a well-oiled machine.

Skip had called the two agents and the deputy who remained behind at Nathan Black Crow's with the transport vehicles and to monitor the comm gear. By the time everyone was in restraints and the girls had been herded away from them, the vehicles arrived and the prisoners were loaded.

By two o'clock in the morning, the worst of it was over. The young girls had been taken to a safe shelter for the moment, and Skip and his men were on their way back to San Antonio with their handcuffed prisoners. It would be Skip's job to serve the arrest warrant on Grayson Ballou, but with all the phone records and Manny suddenly, as predicted, singing so loud and clear, no one thought there would be a problem proving their case.

"We'll be sorting it out for a long time," Skip told Zane. "But we won't have any loose ends here. Thanks for coming to me with this."

"Thank *you*. I'm happy to get this mess out of my county."

"You know," Skip said slowly, "the issue of your mother still has to be addressed. You sure you don't want to hand it over to me?"

Zane shook his head. "No. It's my responsibility. I'll take care of it. Thanks anyway. You still have your man sitting on her, right?"

"Just until tomorrow, though. Then I have to pull him. Unless you want to pick her up now?"

"Just give me until noon, okay? I need a couple of hours sleep before I tackle her."

"Okay. Call me when you're ready so I can let my guy know."

"Will do."

Zane watched all the vehicles pull away, then

went back to his office. He spent a few minutes with his men, thanking them all for a job well done and told them the reports could wait until morning. He was just getting ready to call Jamie when his phone rang. He looked at the Caller ID. Skip. He'd only just left. What could be wrong so soon?

"Zane?" Skip's voice was taut. "We have a problem."

****

The night seemed as long as a week to Jamie. She'd finally convinced Kit to open a bottle of wine, but even the mellow flavor didn't soothe her.

"Sit down," Kit finally ordered. "You're driving me nuts. These things take more than five minutes. You know that. We should have gone to bed."

"Oh, right," Jamie snorted. "Like I could sleep while this is happening. Anyway, it should be over now," Jamie protested, looking at her watch for the hundredth time. "He promised he'd call when it was done."

"Jamie, use your brain. They've got to sort out who does what with who and get the paperwork taken care of. When the feds are involved, it's even more complicated." She pointed to the big arm chair. "Sit. I'll get you another glass of wine."

Jamie had just found a comfortable spot in the chair when the doorbell rang. The two women looked at each other.

"It's two o'clock in the morning," Jamie said, her voice shaking. "This can't be good."

"Honey, if something was wrong, one of Zane's men would have called."

Jamie fisted her hands to keep them from trembling so much. "Unless it's *really* bad news. Then they deliver it in person."

The doorbell rang again, two loud, insistent rings.

"Let me see who it is." Kit set her glass down

and headed into the foyer. She flipped the switch for the porch light, peeked around the curtain at the door, and turned back to Jamie, stunned. "It's Anita Cameron."

"Now?" Jamie was just as shocked. "What the hell can she want at this hour?"

The bell rang one long, insistent tone, as if Anita had just left her thumb on it.

"I'd better let her in, or she's liable to wake up the neighborhood." Kit turned off the alarm, unlocked the door, and swung it open. "Mrs. Cameron, do you know what time it is? What's wrong?"

"I have to see Jamie," Anita said. "Right now. Let me in."

"What is it? Did something happen to Zane?" She poked her head out of the door. "Is anyone with you?"

"I'm alone, and I'm here to prevent something from happening to my son."

"Like what?"

"Do we have to conduct the conversation outside? I have to see Jamie."

"Come on, then."

As Kit turned to lead the way inside, Anita's hand came up, her fingers wrapped around a gun, which she swung hard at Kit's head. Seeing her friend crumple, Jamie leaped up, a scream frozen in her throat.

"What are you doing?" she asked when she could make her voice work.

"Come here, Jamie," Anita ordered. "Now." She pointed the gun at Kit's unconscious body. "Or I'll shoot your friend. Come on."

Her heart thudding against her ribs, Jamie walked toward the door on unsteady legs. "What's going on here?" At that moment, her cell phone rang.

"Don't answer that," Anita ordered. "Do not even

290

think about picking it up. I have big plans for my son, Jamie. Plans that don't include you. I told him to get rid of you, but he refuses to listen, so I guess I'll have to do it for him."

Jamie wasn't sure what she was hearing. "You're going to *kill* me?"

"That's the plan," Anita said calmly. "Then I'll marry Gray Ballou, and together we'll take Zane to the top of the political ladder."

"Anita, Gray Ballou is about to be arrested by federal agents. I don't think he'll be marrying anyone."

A brief look of uncertainty flashed across Anita's face. "Arrested? I don't understand."

She'll know sooner or later. Might as well be sooner.

"Tonight Zane and the federal authorities captured everyone involved in the operation he and Manny Alvarado have been running. Mr. Ballou is going to be a guest of the federal government for some time to come."

"You're lying." Anita's face twisted into an ugly expression. "You're nothing but a white trash whore and a liar. Now get over here, or your friend will be dead, too."

Jamie walked slowly toward the door, desperately turning over ideas in her mind. Somehow she had to get the gun away from this insane woman.

"Outside." Anita reached out and grabbed her arm, yanking her forward.

"Just how are you going to explain this to Zane? You think he'll just let me disappear and not ask any questions? What do you plan to do with my body? And what about Kit?"

"I'll take care of Zane. He'll be happy to be rid of you, once I make him see the light. And no one around here will wonder or care if your friend disappears."

"You're crazy if you think you can get away with this." Jamie tried to pull away from her. "Totally insane."

"Oh, really?" The smile on Anita Cameron's face was pure evil. "We'll just see who's crazy."

All Jamie could think of was the last, angry conversation she and Zane had. If she didn't live through this, that's the only memory he would have of her.

****

Zane disconnected the call from Skip and dialed Jamie's cell immediately. His stomach clenched, and he had to work to keep his hands from shaking.

"Come on, Jamie," he muttered. "Come on, come on. Answer."

The phone rang four times, then went to voice mail. Zane marched out of his office and found Roy Galvan sitting at one of the desks.

"Let's go," he said, grabbing the man by the arm.

"What's going on?" Roy had to run to keep up with him.

"Skip just called. The man he had watching my mother phoned to say she's on the move and most likely headed to my house."

"At this hour of the morning?" Roy threw himself into the passenger seat of Zane's Expedition and just barely managed to buckle himself in before the vehicle peeled out of the parking lot. "For what?"

"Nothing good, I promise you. And Jamie's not answering her cell."

"Maybe she's asleep."

"No. She was too wired to go to bed. Besides, she insisted she was going to wait up for me. And Kit's there. If Jamie can't answer, why doesn't she?"

They broke every speed record getting to his house. Thankfully the streets were fairly empty at this hour. When he turned onto his street, he nearly passed out at what he saw. His porch light was on, illuminating the walkway bright as day. His mother, perfectly dressed as always in silk slacks and blouse, was holding Jamie by the arm, pointing a gun at her head, and dragging her down the walk to a car.

What in god's name is going on?

Fear surged through him, along with the sharp realization that he loved Jamie Randall to distraction and he couldn't lose her. All the angry words from earlier faded away. All his resentment over the phone call Jamie received from her old boss. All the blows to his ego.

They still had a lot to settle, but they'd never be able to do it if she was dead. That wasn't the last thing he wanted to remember about her. He had to get her out of this.

Zane pulled to the curb and leaped from the SUV, forcing himself to walk calmly toward them. "Mother, what the hell is going on?"

****

Jamie's heart skipped at the sound of Zane's voice. Her first thought was, he was alive. Her second was, how the hell was he going to get her out of this? Anita's eyes had a wild look to them, and her fingers dug into Jamie's arm like steel claws.

"Get away, Zane." Anita's voice was sharp and edgy, with an obvious note of instability. "I'm taking care of things. Finally. Then you can move ahead with your life."

She's crazy. She's truly crazy. Oh, Zane, this is a no-win situation.

Zane kept walking slowly toward them. Jamie had noticed a car parked in front of the house next door and wondered who it was. One of Zane's deputies stood outside the Expedition they'd arrived in, his arm at his side, his hand holding his gun.

"Taking care of what? My life is just fine. There's nothing for you to do here." He reached out his hand as he continued to move slowly forward. "Give me the gun and let me take you home before you do something you'll regret."

"The only thing I'll regret is letting you make a mistake." Anita pressed the gun harder to Jamie's head. "I'm getting rid of this piece of white trash so she won't make a mess of your life."

Zane's eyes caught Jamie's, trying to send her a message.

I'll get you out of this. Stay cool. I'll take care of everything.

God, I hope so.

Her head was starting to pound again, and she gritted her teeth against a sudden wave of nausea.

Zane took another step closer, his eyes trying to catch his mother's, but her gaze was skittering everywhere. "You don't have to do this, Mother. I'll handle things."

His voice was still low and reassuring. Jamie didn't know where he found the will to keep it so steady. His gaze flick over her shoulder for a brief second, and she hoped Anita hadn't caught it. Someone was there. The man from the strange car? She held herself as still as possible, despite the gun barrel digging into her temple and the bruising grip on her arm.

"Go away, Zane. I should have done this when she first came home." There was no way to miss the vicious edge to the words. "Just leave. Gray will fix everything."

"Gray's not in a position to help you right now," Zane told her.

She tensed at that, her fingers digging even deeper into Jamie's arm. "This bitch says Gray's in trouble. Is that true? How is that possible?"

Jamie wasn't sure how much longer Zane could keep it going, as unstable as Anita was. Or how he'd answer her question. He was almost next to them now, still moving slowly. And where was the man behind them? Why didn't he hurry?

"Put the gun down, Mother, and we'll talk about Gray. There's no need for any of this. We can discuss this like reasonable people."

"Not as long as *she's* around."

Jamie sensed Anita's finger tighten on the trigger. Zane caught it, too, launching himself at the two women, knocking Jamie to the side as the gun went off. Zane grunted and slumped to the ground as the man in back of them grabbed Anita from behind.

"Zane!" Jamie screamed, scrambling over to him on her knees.

Oh, god, it's the dream coming true. Don't die, Zane. Please don't die. Please let me be able to tell you how much I love you.

"Help!" she yelled. "Someone help me."

Roy Galvan had come from the SUV on a dead run. He was turning Zane over and pulling up the deerskin shirt the man still wore. Jamie's eyes popped when she saw the Kevlar vest beneath it, the bullet lodged in the material. Roy unfastened the vest and pulled it away. A huge bruise was already forming just beneath Zane's rib cage, but there was no blood.

Jamie collapsed across his chest, unable to keep back the tears of relief.

"He's fine, Miss Randall," Roy Galvan reassured her. "Good thing he hadn't taken his vest off at the office. He'll have a hell of a sore spot, but that's all."

"*Damn* good thing," she agreed, unashamedly smothering his face with kisses.

A warm hand came up to rest on her back, and Zane's slightly ragged voice rumbled from his chest. "I told you I'd be all right, darlin'."

"Damn you!" She swatted at his shoulder, then leaned forward to hold him again.

"I'm sorry," he murmured. "I never expected her

to go after you."

"No, *I'm* the one who's sorry. Sorry you had to overhear that stupid conversation. Sorry I didn't just hang up on the call. Sorry I even for one second thought about leaving you. Oh, Zane." She rested her head on his chest. "I love you, and I'll stay as long as you want. Until you get tired of me."

"We'll talk about it later," he told her.

She swallowed hard, wondering just how that conversation would end up. Right now they were in the middle of a situation, and there were people around. Behind them Jamie could hear Anita cursing in three languages. She looked up to see the man who'd grabbed the woman, frog-marching her to his car, carefully avoiding the kicks she tried to aim at him even while her hands were cuffed behind her back.

"He's federal," Roy told her. "I called our office to send backup for him since the rest of the federal agents were already on their way to San Antonio." He raised his head as more headlights swept down the street. "And I'd say that's them now."

Jamie barely registered the activity of the next few minutes. She was vaguely aware that two deputies wrestled Anita into the back seat of their vehicle, still screaming epithets at the top of her lungs. She heard Roy speaking in low tones with them and the federal agent, then the two cars took off.

She tried to keep Zane flat on his back, but he insisted on sitting up.

"Man, that small gun sure packs a kick," he grunted, gently touching his bruised ribs.

"You should go to the hospital," Jamie insisted, trying to push him back down. She couldn't stop the tears that kept sliding down her face.

"I'm fine, Jamie." Zane looked over her shoulder. "Where's Kit? I didn't think she'd miss the excitement."

"Ohmigod. Kit. Oh, shit." She pushed herself up and ran toward the house, hollering, "She's hurt."

Kit was just sitting up on the floor of the foyer, holding her hands to her head. Her face was paper white and lined with pain. Before Jamie could get to her Roy lifted her in his arms and carried her to the couch.

"Anita conked her on the head with the gun," Jamie said. "Honey, are you okay? Let me get some ice." She raced into the kitchen, dumped ice cubes into a plastic bag, wrapped it in a dish towel, and hurried back to Kit. "Here. This is what they gave me at the hospital. Hold it to your head. It really helps."

"She should be checked out in the emergency room," Roy said.

"And you, too," Jamie insisted, looking at Zane who had slowly followed her into the house and was sitting gingerly in the big armchair.

More footsteps sounded on the porch, and Skip Conway let himself in. "Is everyone okay? I got here as fast as I could. Thank god I had my own car."

"I had two of my deputies take my mother to the city with your agent. I hope they get there in one piece. She was kicking up a storm."

Skip dropped down to the ottoman. "You don't know how sorry I am that she's involved with this. Or that we let her get to Miss Randall."

"You didn't know. How could you?"

"Still..."

Zane's face became a granite mask. "I have no illusions about my mother. We've never had what you'd call a warm relationship, and lately I've questioned a lot of her activities. Unfortunately, I think we'll also find out she was the one who hired Danny Christopher to hurt Jamie." He reached out to pull Jamie close to him.

297

"Jesus." Skip blew out a long breath. "Well, they'll call me from San Antonio as soon as she's processed and let me know what's happening. Meanwhile, you need to get those ribs checked out, and Jamie, your friend doesn't look any too good."

Zane was too tired and Kit too sick to protest, so Roy bundled everyone into his SUV and took them to the emergency room.

"This is getting to be a habit," Jamie said while they waited for the doctor. She was standing next to Zane, who sat on an examining table, holding his hand. "And not a good one."

"Tell me about it."

"Listen." She gripped his hand tightly, as if he might disappear if she let go. "I need to go be with Kit. I don't want to leave her alone. But I'll be back as soon as I can. And Zane? Please remember I love you."

When he didn't say a word, she dropped his hand and trudged out of the room.

Kit was next door, the doctor already checking her out. She reached out a hand for Jamie. "You sure know how to show your friends a good time."

Jamie snorted. "No kidding. How do you feel?"

"Like my head went through a cement mixer."

"I don't think she's got a concussion," the doctor said. "Just a big lump on her head. The cut doesn't even need stitches. But I've ordered a CAT scan anyway, and we'll keep her for twenty-four hours, just to be sure. Besides, she'll have a hell of a headache for a couple of days."

"Oh, good lord." Kit slid her glance to Jamie. "Are we keeping this place in business or something?"

"Just be a good girl and listen to the nice doctor," Jamie grinned. But she felt anything but humorous. Kit could have been killed tonight, a fact that kept smacking her in the face. As could Zane.

Zane!

Her head pinched at the thought of him. Would tonight be the last time they would ever be together?

She stayed with Kit until she'd been x-rayed and was finally taken up to a room. Zane had been diagnosed with nothing more than a bad bruise and released. The sun was up by the time they left the hospital and stumbled, fatigued, into the parking lot.

"I'll play chauffeur if you need to get back on the road to San Antonio," Roy told Skip.

"Thanks. I'll take you up on it. Zane, expect to hear from me sometime during the day. We did good work tonight."

Zane nodded. "The press will be all over us tomorrow, especially with my mother's arrest. When you take Ballou into custody, they'll have a feeding frenzy."

"If you can hold them off until afternoon, I'll fax you a copy of the statement we'll issue so we'll all be on the same page."

"No problem." He drew Jamie close and dropped a kiss onto her forehead. "Let's go home, darlin'. I think we've had all the excitement we need for one night."

****

She was so weary by the time they reached the house she could barely make it up the stairs. She wondered how Zane, with everything that had happened, hadn't passed out standing up. Still, there was no way she could go to sleep with so much unresolved between them.

In the bedroom he ignored her as he stripped and headed for the shower. Not knowing what else to do, she sat on the bench at the end of the bed, waiting and trying to figure out just what she was going to say.

Finally, when she'd chewed three nails down to the quick, he emerged with droplets of water clinging to his chest and a towel slung around his lean hips. His hair was loose around his shoulders, and he looked every inch the Comanche brave.

"Please can we talk?" she asked in a small voice.

"I'm tired, Jamie. Let's wait until morning."

"I can't," she cried. "I have to say this or I'll explode."

He stood in front of her, hands on his hips, eyes so black she couldn't see into their depths. "Okay. Go ahead. Talk."

"I made a huge mistake," she began. "I wasn't even thinking when I got the call from my old boss. All that popped into mind was that finally, finally my name would be cleared. Can you understand that?"

His eyes seemed to bore holes into her. "Of course I can understand that. Do you think I'm stupid? That's not what bothers me. It's the fact, first of all, that you even made a tentative commitment without talking to me first. I thought we were together, Jamie. On everything. This is something we could discuss like adults and come to a decision on together."

"I'm sorry." She was ready to throw herself at his feet. "You're absolutely right."

"But that wasn't the worst of it."

She looked up at him, frowning. "Then what?"

"When you said I might get tired of you." Anger stained his cheeks. "Want to end the relationship. Is that all you think of what's between us? Is there no trust after all? Or were you looking for a way out of a relationship with a half breed?"

"Jesus, Zane. No." Tears were running unheeded down her cheeks, and her heart felt as if it had stopped beating, the pain was so great. "I love you. Whoever you are. Can we just chalk it up to a moment of insanity?" She snuffled and wiped her cheeks with her palms. "I'd take back every word if I could."

He put his arms under her elbows and lifted her to her feet. His eyes held hers like magnets. "Look me straight in the face, Jamie, and tell me what you want."

"I want you," she said without hesitation. "I love you with all my heart, and if I never leave Amen again, it's okay as long as you're here. Please, believe me."

He was silent for so long she was almost afraid to hear what he had to say. At last he said, "I meant what I said when I told you I loved you. Did you mean it, too?"

"With all my heart," she told him, hope flickering for the first time.

More silence. She forced herself to wait patiently.

"Then come to bed. It's been a very long day. For everyone."

Jamie stripped off her clothes and slid under the covers next to his naked body before he could change his mind. She still wanted the details of what had happened tonight. But when they were finally in bed, her head nestled against Zane's shoulder, he ignored her questions and moved his hand from her arm to one of her breasts, drifting lazily over the nipple.

"Are you sure you aren't too tired or sore for this?" she asked. "You should get some well-deserved sleep."

"I won't sleep until I make love to you," he told her in a hoarse voice. "I thought my heart would stop when I saw my mother with a gun to your head. That's when I realized that no matter what, I wanted us to be together."

"I love you," she said again, pressing herself against him.

"I need to clean away the filth from tonight, too,"

he went on. "And lose myself in your body. I need to wipe the bad taste from my mouth with your sweet pussy juice and ease my heart by sliding my dick inside that tight little cunt. And I need to know we are well and truly bonded together. Don't deny me. I need you."

Her heart thumped at his words. He *needed* her. And not in a lustful way, although lust was a big part of it. He needed her to make him whole again. That was perhaps the greatest gift he could ever give her. Her fatigue fell away like a disappearing cloak and heat sizzled through her veins.

"Then let *me* take care of *you* for a change." She shoved her covers back, rose to her knees, and took his cock in her hand. "Just lie back and enjoy it."

His shaft rose thick and hard from the curls surrounding it and felt heavy in her hands. She bent forward and with her tongue lapped the darkened, flared head all around, using the tip to trace the crown, then probing gently into the slit. Zane jerked in her hands, and his breathing hitched.

She lifted her gaze to look at him. His eyes were closed, his arms straight at his sides, and his hands knotted into fists. Every muscle in his body seemed to draw tight and hard. When she licked the length of his shaft from root to tip, he jerked again, but his eyes remained closed, his mouth slightly open.

The slim fingers of one hand wrapped as far as they could around his cock at the root while her other hand cupped the heavy sac of his balls. The tips of her fingers played lightly over the fine hair on the surface, drawing another sharp breath from him. On impulse, she dropped her head lower and ran her tongue over the entire pleated surface of his testicles, lapping at it and nipping lightly at the underside.

Zane's big body tensed even more and his breathing became choppier, but he gave her free rein to explore him and use him. When her lips closed over the velvet head of his shaft, she began moving one hand slowly up and down, feeling the slip and slide of the soft skin over steel, the heat of his blood in the ropy veins that wound around it.

The tip of her tongue probed the slit of the head more deeply than before, mimicking what he did to her cunt with his own tongue. In and out, swirling around, then in and out again, drawing groans that shuddered through his body.

Her own arousal was growing rapidly. Where her cunt rested on the calves of her legs she felt the slickness of her pussy juices, so copious they were dripping from her. Shifting position without releasing her grip on either his cock or his balls, she straddled one hard, muscular thigh and rubbed her streaming cunt back and forth against his skin. At the same time, she moved the hand cupping his balls down to the cleft of his buttocks and probed with one fingertip at the tight opening to his ass.

"Jesus, Jamie," he exploded. "Keep that up and I'll lose all control."

"That's the idea," she told him, a wicked tone in her voice.

Reaching between her pussy and his thigh, she gathered some of her juices on her fingers, then rubbed them against his anus, softening the tense ring of muscle. She did it again, still rocking back and forth on his leg, the motion of her hand abrading her clit and sending spikes of pleasure throughout her body.

She inhaled a deep breath and let it out slowly. She was too aroused. This was for Zane, not her.

Rubbing her cream against his sensitive spot until she was sure it was well lubricated, she pressed the tip of one finger against the opening, forcing it slowly and gently inside. At first he tensed against it, but when she took his cock in her mouth again and began to jack him with her other hand, he stopped fighting her.

Jamie lifted herself from his thigh and knelt between his legs, lifting her mouth only enough to urge him to bend his legs. With his feet planted firmly on the mattress and his legs spread wide, she had greater access to that dark entrance to his body. And she began her rhythms in earnest.

Her hot mouth sucked the head of his cock, her tongue darting back and forth into the slit, while one hand increased the up and down motion on his shaft and her finger slid all the way into the dark tunnel of his rectum. As he moaned and his breathing grew choppier and choppier, she increased her pace more and more. She had never felt such power over a man, sucking and jacking him while she fingerfucked his ass. The pulse in her vagina throbbed, her inner muscles quivered, and her nipples ached.

She was so lost in what she was doing she almost missed the signs of his impending orgasm until he shouted hoarsely, "Now, Jamie. Now."

His magnificent body arched, she shoved her finger all the way into his ass and sucked hard on his dick as the first splashes of semen hit the roof of her mouth and ran down the back of her throat. Hollowing her cheeks to take him better, she sucked him dry, licking the head until she'd captured the last drop. Only then did she release him, listening to him drag air into his lungs, her hand on his chest to feel the galloping thunder of his heart.

Finally, when he was breathing easier and his heart rate had slowed, she left to attend to things in the bathroom. As much pleasure as he had given her, it thrilled her to be able to do this for him. When she returned to the bed, she was sure he'd be ready to sleep, and he was. Almost. One arm was out-flung to capture her, and his eyes were heavy-lidded with fatigue and sexual satisfaction.

"Where the hell did you learn that?" he asked, his voice slow and relaxed.

"I read about it in a book," she teased, snuggling against him. "Think you can sleep now?"

"In a minute." He raised his other hand, and she saw he'd taken the thick silver wand from the nightstand drawer. "I'm not in shape for much else, but I know you're horny and I won't let you go to sleep still aroused. Although," he said with a touch of humor, "it might not be a bad idea to keep you on edge."

"I'm fine," she insisted. "You need to rest."

"Oh, I will, darlin'. Believe me. In just a minute."

He rolled to his side and nudged her legs apart. There was no mistaking the cream clinging to the lips of her pussy or the darkening of her beaded nipples.

"Just close your eyes and go with it, Jamie. You need this, too."

Without preamble or foreplay, he slid the wand into her cunt and turned it on. The vibrations rocketed through her body like electrical charges, sizzling her nerves and kicking every pulse into throbbing action. When he pulled it out, she wanted to scream, especially when he placed the tip on her already raging clitoris and moved it back and forth in a steady motion.

She opened her eyes to see him watching her face, his own eyes dark with emotion.

"I know you're close," he said. "Let me watch you come."

Her hips jerked as he continued to torment her clit until finally she begged, "Now. Please now."

He thrust the wand back into her pussy and twisted the bottom to the highest setting, his eyes eating her up as she came apart next to him. The orgasm swept through her like the incoming tide, washing through every part of her body. Her inner muscles clenched around the vibrating wand, and she squeezed her thighs tightly around it, thrusting her hips in a fucking motion. Her hands went automatically to her nipples, pinching them hard, while Zane took her clit between the knuckles of two fingers and tugged on it as spasm after spasm griped her.

Then it was done, leaving her with an afterglow that suffused her body.

Zane slid the vibrator from her cunt and set it aside. Then he bent his head and took her mouth in a kiss full of so much emotion it brought tears to her eyes.

"*Now* it's time to sleep," he told her, turning her to spoon against him.

"And everything is okay with us?" she had to ask before she could close her eyes.

"We're fine, darlin'. If you want to go to Miami, we'll discuss it tomorrow. But we'll decide together. I love you, Jamie. That's all I know."

A sigh of relief escaped her. With his arm tight around her and one leg thrown over hers, her head tucked into his shoulder, she closed her eyes and fell into a soft blackness.

Chapter Twenty-One

The next week seemed endless to both Jamie and Zane.

The morning following the incident, over coffee, they got Miami out of the way first thing. Zane insisted she needed to confront her boss one last time, give interviews to whoever wanted them so her name could be completely cleared, then tell the asshole he could take his job and shove it.

"With pleasure," she grinned. "I can't believe I even considered going back to work for him for one tiny second."

"We all need vindication," he told her. "Our good name is all we really have. But we'll do this together, right?"

She grinned at him. "You bet." Then she sobered. "And thank you."

His answer was to lean forward and capture her mouth in a kiss that scorched her all the way to her toes.

Jamie brought Kit home from the hospital at noon, and after three days, Kit told her it was time for her to leave. They were sitting among the remnants of Sunday brunch, and Zane was in his den, making phone calls.

"I'd stay forever, sweetie," Kit said. "But you don't need me around here, stepping on your privacy, and you certainly don't need to spend your time waiting on me. I'll curl up in my hidey hole, and I'll be fine."

"I don't think you should be alone," Jamie protested.

Kit gave her a hug. "You can't be my caretaker, Jamie. The doctor said I'm fine, and the headache is gone. I wouldn't be going home if I didn't feel well enough, believe me. And you and the hunk don't need a houseguest right now."

They didn't say what they both were thinking. Kit could have stayed at Jamie's, but neither of them ever intended to set foot in that cursed place ever again.

"You know you're welcome to stay as long as you want." Zane had come into the room so quietly neither of them heard him. "I'm trusting your good sense that you wouldn't go haring off if you still didn't feel quite right."

"Believe me," she told him. "I can be a real baby. I'm fine, honestly. Besides, I think the excitement around here is getting to be too much for me. I need to get back to the quiet of New York." She winked.

"All right," Zane laughed. "When do you want to leave?"

"I'll call and see if I can get reservations tomorrow. That gives you the rest of the day to put up with me."

Over brunch Zane had given every bit of information about the killings, Frank Randall, and the white slave ring to both women, believing they deserved to know it all. He just barely managed to keep a lid on his anger when he got to the killings and the plot to get rid of Jamie. But by now everyone had been rounded up, arraigned, and remanded without bail.

"I think Grayson Ballou was the most shocked of anyone," he said. "When the feds showed up at his door with a search warrant and one for his arrest, he nearly had a stroke. He's keeping his high priced attorney plenty busy and screaming because the judge wouldn't set bail."

"What about the little girls?" Kit asked. "They

had to be frightened to death. What a terrible experience for them."

Zane's face sobered. "And then some. Right now we've got them in a good temporary shelter with some women who'll take excellent care of them until we sort this whole thing out. Skip said many of them were sold to the coyote for money."

"That's just disgusting," Kit said. "I can't imagine anyone selling their own flesh and blood."

"You'd be surprised what people do," Zane told her. "Anyway, the authorities won't return them to their parents, so another solution will have to be found."

"And everyone else is under lock and key?" Jamie asked.

"All of them. Manny Alvarado won't see the light of day for a long time. We learned from the coyotes he was siphoning off the youngest girls from each shipment for himself, using them for his perverted appetites and then killing them when he was finished. That's where the two bodies we found came from. We have the unpleasant task of combing the area for others."

"And everyone else?" Kit wanted to know.

"Guests of the federal government," Zane told her. "Most of them have taken a plea in exchange for a lighter sentence. At least we got the big guys, and that's what counts."

Many other things had come out in the process. Frank Randall had indeed been involved, letting Manny use his property in exchange for money. While he'd used alcohol to forget his part in a nasty situation, in the end he'd gotten too greedy and threatened to blow the whistle if they didn't come through. They nearly went crazy trying to find his stash after they got rid of him. Zane had turned the money over to Skip to be used as evidence.

But Zane had taken the biggest blows of all.

While his mother was ranting and raving, he'd learned that his father had also been involved in the traffic in illegals years ago, but his drinking made him unreliable. Manny and Gray had gotten rid of him, and Anita had stepped in to serve as the contact for each deal. Gray had paid her off with money under the table as well as her job and the house in Copper Ridge. He'd had no idea, however, that she expected him to marry her. It was probably the only laugh he had during the whole mess.

Anita's fingerprints were identified as among those on Danny Christopher's money, and she finally admitted hiring him to get rid of Jamie. She had visions of Zane as a rising political star and saw Jamie as a hindrance as well as a public relations nightmare. Zane was still wrestling with the fallout from his mother's actions and involvement.

The media had had a feeding frenzy. It wasn't often that one of the state's top businessmen and kingmakers and the mother of the county sheriff ended up in the headlines. They'd hounded Zane to death, and he'd stoically faced them all, sticking only to the public facts of the case and nothing else.

He had also refused to see his mother.

"I don't know what I'd say to her," he told Jamie. "She's like someone I don't even know. Besides, I might just kill her for what she tried to do to you."

He and Jamie had discussed what she wanted to do with her house and the property. She knew she wanted to sell it and next week would call a real estate agent to list it. She hadn't yet told Zane, but she wanted the money to be used for the little girls who'd been smuggled up from Mexico, to help them in some way to a better life.

Tonight Zane had come home from the office exhausted but satisfied at last that all the loose ends were wrapped up tightly.

"I feel like I've been swimming in a swamp filled

310

with muck and mire," he said, stripping off his clothes as he walked up the stairs. "Before anything else I need a long, hot shower."

"How about someone to share it with you?" Jamie teased, following him up the stairs.

He turned to her, his eyes suddenly alive with lust. "That's the best offer I've had in a long while. Come on."

It only took seconds for Jamie to pull off her clothes and toss them in the clothes hamper. Zane was already in the bathroom, adjusting the shower so the enclosure was already filled with a fine, hot mist.

Jamie stepped in next to him, and for a long moment, she stood with her arms wrapped around him, her head on his chest, letting the water wash away the last vestiges of the week from hell. She could hardly believe how much had changed since she'd slunk back to Amen in professional disgrace, hating every*one* and every*thing*. The revelation of the sick business one of the state's most admired men was conducting.

As the drops formed on their skin and slid off like liquid on glass, she felt renewed and reborn.

"I feel your mind burning," Zane teased, his big hand stroking her wet hair. "Thinking comes later. This is the time for feeling."

She looked up at him. "Oh? And what should I be feeling?"

"This." He pulled her arms from around him, took one of her hands, and wrapped her small fingers around his throbbing cock. "It needs attention. And this." He reached down between her legs and ran his fingers through the slickness of her slit. "Something else that needs attention."

"And exactly what should we be doing about it?"

"I know the first thing I plan to do." He lifted her by the waist and stood her on the seat built into a corner of the shower, spreading her legs wide. He took each of her hands and placed them on a wall for balance, then knelt on the tiles.

"Don't move," he told her. "Stay just like that. When we're finished today, you'll know who you belong to without any doubt at all. And who belongs to you."

Carefully spreading the lips of her cunt, he twirled his tongue around her clit, flicking the tip of it and sending sparks of pleasure shooting through her. She pressed her hands hard against the walls bracing her as Zane used his tongue to explore every inch of her sex. He lapped at her slit until she was shaking with need. She had to grit her teeth to keep from squeezing her thighs together or reaching out to grip his shoulders.

His teeth nipped at her clit, pushing her arousal even higher, as two fingers played tormentingly at her anus. When one finger pushed inside her back channel, she pushed against it, wanting more. The fingers of his other hand drifted lightly over the opening to her vagina without ever penetrating her, and the walls of her empty cunt clenched in desperate need.

Then, suddenly, he stopped.

Jamie stared at him. "What?"

His lopsided smile had the look of the devil. "Just wanted to get your attention. First we finish our shower."

She wanted to kill him. To beat at the solid wall of his chest. To scream at him. But she knew it would do her no good. He was a man with a plan and nothing was going to change his mind.

He lifted her back down to the shower floor and poured some of the shower gel into his hand. Rubbing it into a rich lather, he soaped her entire body, beginning at her neck and working his way down. Her cuts were nearly healed, and the bandages had been reduced to small, watertight strips. She barely felt any pain as his warm hands cupped her breasts, massaging the soap into them. His fingers pinched and tugged at her nipples until she was ready to scream. Every touch sent another electrical charge through her body.

One hand moved slowly through the valley between her breasts, down over her navel and abdomen to the mound of her sex. He added more gel to his hands, more thick lather, and rubbed it into the puffy flesh of her mound and the seams where it joined her thighs.

Apparently satisfied with his work so far, he sat cross-legged on the shower floor, nudged her legs apart, and proceeded to wash every inch of her cunt inside and out. The skin was ultra-sensitive since he'd shaved it, so every touch was magnified. His slick fingers lit hungry nerves as they reached far inside her, massaging the gel into her inner walls. Delicately, he pulled back the little fleshy hood that protected her clit and soaped every inch of that hot, greedy button. Grabbing a wash cloth from a hook, he then wiped away every trace of the soap, maneuvering the pebbled cloth inside her cunt and laving it in and out.

Jamie's legs were trembling, and she could hardly keep herself upright. But it appeared he wasn't done with her yet. Turning her around, he leaned her against the wall while he washed her shoulders and her back, massaging away the soreness of tension. He did the same with her ankles and calves, and the tender muscles of her thighs. Each time his knuckles brushed against the sensitive lips of her cunt, she wanted to push herself down on them, but Zane just laughed a wicked laugh.

When he spread the cheeks of her ass and proceeded to rub the lathered gel inside, she nearly lost it. His fingers moved in the motion of a very slow fuck, touching the nerve endings and heating her blood. Sensations cascaded over her while the pulse in her cunt throbbed stronger and stronger.

When he stood up and handed the gel to her, she wasn't sure she could make any of her muscles work properly.

"Now me," he grinned and dropped his arms to his sides.

Jamie teased him as much as he'd teased her, spreading lather over his flat nipples again and again and running her fingers over the hard muscles of his chest. She kneaded the rock-like muscles of his stomach, and when she reached his penis, she took her time sliding her soapy hands up and down its length. Her thumb played over the flared head, the pad of it opening the slit and pressing against it. His raged breathing told her he was as aroused as she was, but he wasn't giving an inch.

Not even when she nudged him to turn around, worked his back and waist, then plunged two soapy fingers into his backside. He jerked at the penetration, and a breath hissed through his teeth. She laughed low in her throat and kept up the slow, fucking motion he'd used with her.

Desperate, he jerked away from her and turned around.

"Enough. I don't want to come before we get to the good parts."

He washed his hair, rinsing it thoroughly under the spray, then shampooed hers, his fingers kneading the muscles of her scalp and chasing away any vestige of a headache that might be hiding there.

When they were completely rinsed off, he turned off the water and reached for two large bath sheets. He wrapped one around himself, then toweled Jamie dry and sat her on the vanity bench. Turning on the hair dryer lying on the counter, his fingers sifted lightly through the strands of her hair as he dried it, using a brush for the finishing touches. Then he took care of his own, leaving it loose on his shoulders.

He stood behind her, catching her gaze in the mirror. "Now we can get down to business."

Jamie was breathing through her mouth, panting, so aroused she thought her body would combust naturally. Zane had carried her to the bed, sat down on the edge, and stretched her face down across his lap. His warm hand caressed and stroked the cheeks of her ass. The sting of the first slap caught her off guard, but as soon as the lines of heat streaked to her pussy and thighs, she lifted her ass for another.

Zane chuckled low in his throat. "Like that, do you? I believe you might even get addicted to it. Maybe next week we'll go shopping and get a little flogger for you. Take things up a notch or two."

Just the thought of it had fresh cream soaking the lips of her pussy. When he separated the thighs and a slap landed on the lips of her cunt, she almost went straight up in the air. She knew his hand would come away soaked.

He spread the cheeks of her ass and used her juices to wet the cleft there, paying special attention to her anus. She lifted her head when his body twisted, and she saw him reach into the nightstand drawer and pull out a small shopping bag in hot pink.

"Is that where you get your toys?" she asked.

"Uh huh. I think I'll have to take you to San Antonio next week and introduce you to Annabelle."

She felt the cool slickness of gel as he rubbed it on her anus, then pressed two slicked fingers into her rear channel, making sure all the tissues were well lubricated. Then the plug, this one inflatable. God only knew when he'd had time to get it.

"You've been saving this," she said, trying to speak through her ragged breaths.

"Sure have. You have no idea how hot it makes me to see it disappearing through that tiny hole into your ass. I could come just from watching. Okay, darlin'. Take a deep breath and let it out slowly. I'm going to inflate this a little at a time."

She felt the burn and stretch of tissue and muscle as the plug increased in size. When he stopped squeezing the pump, she had the intense sensation of two cocks inside her ass instead of one fake one.

"Feeling full, darlin'?" he asked, his voice heavy with lust.

"Yes," she hissed and wriggled her butt.

Zane lifted from her his lap, turned her over, and placed her gently on the bed on her back. He stood over her, stroking his engorged cock, a tiny drop of fluid beading at the slit.

"Gorgeous," he murmured, licking his lips. "If only I could fuck you in every hole at the same time." He reached into the bag again and took out what looked like a butterfly, rubbed some gel on it and pinched it carefully onto her clit. "We'll wait for the nipple rings again until your bruises are completely healed. Maybe we'll get one of your nipples pierced and put a little gold ring there. And a matching one at your navel."

Her pussy fluttered at his words and she wished he'd get on with it. She was so desperate to come she wanted to scream.

"Cocked and loaded, right?" She barely recognized her voice as she tried to tease him into action, her eyes fastened on his engorged penis.

He removed a pair of fleece-lined handcuffs from the small shopping bag and fastened them to her wrists, then threaded the connecting chain through a spoke in the headboard. His eyes burned as they raked over her. "I like seeing you spread out and helpless like this. One of my favorite visions."

Next he bent her legs at the knees and spread her legs wide. His eyes were smoky as he rolled a condom into place.

"All right, darlin'," he breathed, his voice heavy with lust. "*Now* we're ready."

He moved between her thighs and pinched the butterfly. Immediately, it began to hum, vibrating on her clit and sending streaks of electricity to every nerve. As she writhed on the bed, turned on even more by her helplessness, Zane took his cock in one hand and slowly guided it into her drenched pussy, working it in and out. She hadn't thought he'd be able to penetrate her all the way with the plug in her ass, but Zane knew exactly how to work it, just how slow and easy to go until the tip of it touched her womb and his balls slapped against the cheeks of her still burning ass. She had never felt so full in her life, so stretched, so aroused.

Bracing his hands on either side of her, he moved in and out in a steady rhythm, increasing the pace with each thrust. Jamie felt a tight coil deep inside her begin to unwind. Her clit seemed to have a mind of its own, driving her need higher and higher and making the walls of her pussy clutch at Zane's cock, dragging across it with each stroke. The plug in her ass moved every time he thrust in and out of her, giving her the sensation of being fucked by two cocks simultaneously. If their previous lovemaking had taken her to places she'd never been before, this was even stronger. She wanted it and feared it at the same time.

She was swamped with such a feeling of eroticism it threatened to consume her. Every fiber of her body was poised for an orgasm that she feared would be so strong she couldn't stand it. Automatically, she struggled against it and tried to pull back, but Zane refused to let her.

"Go with it, darlin'," he panted, his face and chest covered with sweat, his eyes so dark they were almost black.

"Let me touch you," she begged. She loved the feeling of helplessness, but not as much as she wanted to touch him. Right now. "Please."

With his cock still seated deeply inside her, he reached up and flipped open the handcuffs. Her fingers wove through the silken strands of his hair, gripping his head. She wanted more of him, even though the pleasure was almost too intense to bear. She wrapped her legs around him, digging her heels into the small of his back to lift herself closer, take him deeper.

He increased the power of his strokes, not letting her pull away from the edge of ultimate pleasure. When the climax broke over her, she came completely apart, shaking with the strength of it, shuddering and convulsing as spasms ripped through her. She bathed Zane's latex-sheathed cock with copious amounts of cream as her gushing pussy clenched over and over.

She lost track of where she was, tossed into a whirling circle of exploding lights and swirling wind. She couldn't breathe with the powerful force gripping her, and each time she thought it slowed down, it would begin again, ripping through her body as if she had no ability to control it at all. It was pleasure beyond anything she ever imagined. Beyond anything they'd already shared. She wasn't even sure she could survive it.

At last, with one final thrust and a roll of his hips, Zane dropped forward, careful to catch himself on his forearms. Jamie shivered with one aftershock after another. Her heart was thundering against her ribs, pounding against the force of Zane's that threatened to break out of his chest. The only sounds in the room were their ragged breathing and the lazy swirl of the ceiling fan as it cooled their sweat-soaked bodies.

When his breathing was steady enough, Zane rolled to the side and off the bed. After carefully removing the plug and butterfly, he strode to the bathroom to take care of them and the condom.

She didn't even remember falling asleep, only waking up at sometime after midnight to see Zane propped on one elbow staring down at her. Her breath caught in her throat at the look on his face.

"I—is something wrong?"

He nodded. "Very wrong."

A stab of pain pierced her heart. Oh, god. Now what? Had he decided this was a mistake after all? Had he really not forgiven her?

"W-what's wrong? What is it?"

"Today is Saturday, or it will be when the sun comes up. We can't get a marriage license until Monday so I have to wait two more days to marry you." His voice took on a tentative note. "You *are* going to marry me, right?"

She swallowed the huge sigh of relief, rolled into him, and threw her arms around his neck. "The very first minute we can get it done."

"We haven't really talked about it specifically, you know. Maybe I got ahead of myself here. I guess I should have done the romantic thing with roses and champagne."

There was that rare note of uncertainty again. "No," she told him. "You're right on the money, as a matter of fact. Besides, I'm not a roses and champagne kind of girl."

"Things won't be all that easy, darlin'. All these people will be going to trial. We'll both have to testify. There's probably going to be a lot of fallout for a long time and more media coverage than either of us wants to think about. Plus, there's this little hang-up you have about Amen."

"I don't—"

He shook his head. "Let me finish. This is something I really did think about. I can't just pick up and leave until things settle down, but if you don't want to live here or you decide when we get to Miami that you want to go back to the city...well, I can always get a job in law enforcement somewhere."

She touched her fingers to his lips. "If this is where you want to stay, then I do, too. I'm done with Miami. I'll tell my story, and then I never want to see the place again."

"Good." He brushed his lips against her forehead.

"I'm through running, Zane. I told you that, and I want to make sure you believe me. What I found out there wasn't worth what I thought it was. I don't care where we are as long as we're together. I can even put up with this town for you. So yes, Zane Cameron, I will be honored to marry you. And to live with you here in Amen or wherever you want. Any time. Any place."

He bent his head to hers, his mouth like silk and satin against hers. Their kiss was so full of love and promise, tears gathered at the corners of her eyes. Zane fumbled in the drawer for another condom and, in seconds, slid into her already wet, welcoming cunt.

"*This* is where I want to be, Jamie Randall, soon to be Cameron. *This* is my favorite place. Right here, just like this. Inside you. I love you. Forever."

"I love you, too," she told him, clutching him harder as he drove home. "Forever."

About the author...

Desiree Holt has lived a life of excitement that brings the color to her writing. She was a summer fishing guide, a summer field hand where she was one of only three women working, a member of a beginning ski team that skied in competition (and no, no broken bones!). She spent several years in the music business representing every kind of artist from country singer to heavy metal rock bands. For several years she also ran her own public relations agency handling any client that interested her. She loves to tell the story of sending a singer up in a hot air balloon singing "Up, Up and Away in My Beautiful Balloon" and stopping traffic for four miles in every direction.

Before and between her two marriages she dated enough hunks to fill up two he-man calendars, one of whom taught her to shoot so beware, she's always armed. She's kept a fresh look at erotic romance by making sure the sensuality factor in her private life is always high. She's married to her own personal alpha hero who helps her with that.

Visit Desiree at www.desireeholt.com.

Do You Trust Me?

by

Desiree Holt

A cryptic message from her brother leaves Rina Devargas with a secret and no one to trust...

Carrying the fate of a nation in a locket next to her heart, Rina's life is turned upside down as her brother's partner, McCall, moves into her home under the guise of keeping her safe. Though she surrenders her body to his dark desires, someone betrayed John, and until McCall gives her a sign, Rina can't be certain that someone isn't him.

Assigned to protect her, Connor McCall must gain Rina's confidence the only way he knows how...

Having once shared a night of forbidden pleasure, McCall reawakens her submissive appetite for dominance. However, keeping his mind on the job and his hands off Rina proves difficult--remaining aloof from his feelings for her, even more so. He's been down that road and paid a handsome price for it—the life of a fellow agent.

With an assassination plot brewing and killers after Rina, will McCall gain her trust before it's too late? Or will their dangerous desires ultimately destroy them all?

Chapter One

Rina Devargas ran full out, arms pumping, lungs burning, every muscle in her body on fire. Her thick auburn curls had come loose from the gold clip at the nape of her neck and were tossing wildly about her face. The fabric of her slacks flapped against her leg where she'd ripped them running through a low hedge. She had no idea which direction to take, which building would be safe to hide behind. Too many open spaces. Too many street lights.

Behind her, she heard the slapping of leather on pavement as the man pursued her. He'd been waiting for her, watching for her to leave John's townhouse. As she'd slipped out the back door, sure she was safely away, he'd grabbed her, slamming her head into the brick wall. She wasn't certain, but she thought her nose might be broken. Blood had run down her face and onto her blouse. Only instant reaction and a well-placed knee to the groin had freed her from his grasp.

His shoes pounded on the pavement behind her, closing the gap with every second. Could she cut through a walkway between buildings? But what if it led to a dead end? Where was everyone, anyway, in this residential neighborhood of upscale town homes? Shouldn't someone at least be walking a dog?

Slap! Slap! Slap!

The echo of his footsteps sounded like rifle shots. Damn it, she had to find some place to hide quickly. Her car was back near John's place, so no hope of cutting back there. She tried to pick up the pace, but every step sent a jolt of pain through her head.

Turning a corner, she sprinted down the sidewalk, searching for a place with lights on. Maybe she could bang on someone's door, ask for help, if her appearance didn't scare them to death.

She stopped for one precious second to drag air into her lungs and froze when a muscular arm pulled her against a hard male body and a hand clamped over her mouth. Her heart actually stopped in mid-beat, and for a moment, she was sure she'd pass out.

"Don't scream," a voice whispered at her ear.

Rina's nose twitched as a familiar scent drifted in the air and the body pressing against her from behind had a remembered feel. She tried to turn her head to see her captor, struggling in his grasp.

God, surely not him. Not here. Not now.

The man pulled her into a nearly invisible tiny alcove where two buildings met, waiting until the running figure passed. Then he half carried her to a car that pulled up to the curb.

"You can let go of me," she mumbled against the fingers over her mouth.

"Not yet. And quit struggling. I'd hate to coldcock you," he growled. "But I will if I have to."

Opening the passenger door of the car, he shoved her inside. "Not a word," he cautioned as he changed places with the driver. He hit the accelerator, and they roared down the street. By the time they reached the bridge from Harbor Island to downtown Tampa, Rina had managed to slow her heart rate to somewhere between almost dead and hopefully alive.

She eyed the man next to her. Her nose hadn't let her down.

"Hello, McCall."

Of course it had to be him. The very last person in the world she wanted to see.

But he was paying no attention to her, speaking into a cell phone too softly for her to understand what he was saying. Blood dripped from her nose again, and she pulled up the tail of her blouse to blot it, the only thing she had since she'd lost her purse when the man attacked her.

McCall snapped the phone shut and dropped it on the seat beside him. "I should lock you up just on the grounds of stupidity." His voice was taut with tension. "What in the fucking hell were you doing at John's place tonight?"

Her hand went automatically to the locket around her neck "What were *you* doing there?"

"Uh uh. I get to ask the questions." He huffed a breath. "Have you lost your everlovin' mind?"

No matter what she said, it would turn out to be the wrong thing, so Rina just kept silent, blotting her nose and wishing she had a huge bottle of aspirin.

"Listen, you idiot," he went on. "You know the lengths we've gone to in order to keep your relationship with your brother a secret. In our line of work, families are prime hostage targets."

Rina knew that. When John had been accepted as a member of the ultra-secret anti-terrorist task force, every trace of their relationship had been buried. His boss had even gone so far as to acquire a phony birth certificate for her brother and a fake background. Any evidence that John Wilson, black ops operative, was her brother, John Devargas, ceased to exist. Except to Sully and the team.

"No comment?" he asked.

"Who-who was the man who attacked me?"

"Someone whose identity we'll never know now that you blundered into the middle of our stakeout."

She had never heard McCall quite so angry, but it couldn't be helped. The call from John had shocked her, coming out of the blue as it had. There was no way she could have refused his request, no matter what the rules were. Or what she made a mess of. "I left my rental car back there."

"Forget about it. I'll have someone pick it up."

"I, um, don't have my keys. I...that is...I lost my purse."

"Jesus Christ." McCall pounded the steering wheel. "Are you serious? You left your purse with all your identification where these people could get it?"

"What people?" *The ones John was afraid of? The ones who were after him? Had even maybe killed him?*

No. She pushed that thought out of her mind.

"What people?" she asked again, but McCall drove on in silence, his mouth set in a grim line.

Rina took a good look at him. His lean, muscular frame was dressed in the familiar all black, his thick black hair blending in with it. She remembered all too well the last time she had seen Connor McCall.

****

One year earlier

"I can't believe you were just in the neighborhood."

Rina stared at the lean, hard-faced man standing in her doorway. He was the last person she'd expected to see in San Antonio late on a Saturday afternoon. Or any other morning.

"Are you going to let me in, or should I stand here and give the neighbors something to gossip about?"

She stepped back and gestured him inside. He closed the door behind him, standing so close to her she could feel his body heat.

She shoved her hands in the pockets of her cutoffs. "So, what are you doing here anyway?"

"I have a letter for you from John. You know we can't just send it through the mail."

Her heart skipped a beat. "Is he okay? Nothing's wrong, is there?" She swallowed the fear that always rode just at the surface. She and John were both fully aware of the incredible danger in his job.

"No, he's fine. Just...off on a mission that will keep him out of touch for quite a while." He pulled an envelope from an inside pocket of his black windbreaker and handed it to her.

She nearly grabbed it from his hand and ripped it open. Then, realizing she didn't want to read it with McCall watching, she rushed to the kitchen.

"I don't suppose you've got a beer I could drink while I'm standing in the hallway?" he called after her.

Her cheeks heated. Where were her manners? "Sure. Come on in." She pulled a bottle from the fridge and twisted off the top. "Um, why don't you take it out on the patio? It's really nice out there this time of day."

He gave her a lopsided grin, a rare expression on his usually grim face. "I can take a hint. Let me know when you're through reading."

The letter was only two pages, but Rina read them over and over. John couldn't give her any details about his assignment, so he filled the pages with idle chatter and reminiscences. Since the death of their parents five years earlier, they'd made every effort to stay connected. In fact, it was their death in an explosion at the American University at Beirut that led to John's decision to join the task force.

Rina sat for a long time at her kitchen table, just holding the letter, squeezing back the tears at John's, "Love ya, Dusty," visualizing his face, and whispering a silent prayer for his safety. As she stood to carry it to her den and lock it away with the others, she realized she'd left McCall sitting outside

327

for more than an hour. His beer was surely long gone, but he'd sat patiently waiting for her to finish.

Sliding open the patio door, she stuck her head out. "Sorry. I didn't mean to take so long."

He unfolded himself from the lounge chair. "No problem. But I'll take another beer if you've got one."

"I have a couple of steaks in the freezer if you'd like to stay for dinner." *Now where did that come from? Invite McCall—the original granite man—for dinner?*

He stared at her, as stunned by the invitation as she was.

And suddenly she wanted him to stay, a connection to John she could hold onto a little longer. "Please."

He studied her as if wondering what trick she had up her sleeve. Finally, he nodded. "Okay. Thanks."

It was already well past six o'clock, so she took the steaks out and stuck them in the microwave to thaw, then began to gather ingredients for a salad. McCall sat at the kitchen table, drinking his beer and watching her with silver eyes that seemed to see right through her. He wasn't one for casual conversation so she worked in silence, acutely aware of his gaze on her.

As she went about her prep work, she wondered what on earth had possessed her to invite this man to dinner. He was the most antisocial person she'd ever met. She wasn't even sure he liked her. But he was a connection to John and somehow she felt she could touch her brother through him.

She'd lit the coals in the barbecue on the patio before starting the salad. As naturally as if they did this all the time, McCall grilled the steaks while she finished the dinner preparations. She didn't know if McCall was a wine person—she actually knew almost nothing about him except that he was the senior member of the team and the one John worked with the most—but she pulled a bottle of her favorite white from the fridge anyway.

Okay. We'll eat dinner. I'll pump him for information about John. He'll avoid all my questions, leave, and that will be that.

He answered her questions about John in short, terse sentences, but at least he could assure her he was alive and well. And maybe that was all she could hope for.

"Why do you use the name 'Rina'?" he asked in an abrupt tone. "Why not your full name? Sabrina."

She shrugged. "When I was a toddler I had trouble saying the whole name. All I could get out was Rina, so it stuck." She gave him a lopsided grin. "Shorter to sign in books, too."

Silence descended on the table again.

"So tell me about your family," she said finally, searching for a topic of conversation.

He shrugged. "Not much to tell."

"I don't even know where you live when you're not, um, working."

"D.C. But my folks have a place up north."

"Do you get to see them often?" *God, this is like pulling teeth.*

"Not as much as I'd like. My sister, either."

He had a sister? "Does she live up north, too?"

"Yes. She's a physical therapist at a hospital near there. She's living with my folks right now."

More silence. And somehow a certain tension that she couldn't identify had crept into the air. Whenever she looked up from her plate McCall's silver eyes were fixed on her. If the situation were different—if *he* was different—she would have said his gaze was devouring her. But she had no idea what was going on in his steel-trap mind.

For a brief, mad instant she wondered what it would be like going to bed with McCall.

Are you crazy? The man is an emotionless machine, and a member of your brother's team to boot.

She poured herself another glass of wine with a hand that trembled slightly. McCall picked up on it and narrowed his eyes, but she managed to lift her glass and sip the liquid without spilling it.

Get a grip, Rina.

At last, the meal was over and McCall helped her clear the table. She poured the last of the wine into their glasses.

"Thank you for dinner," he said in a formal tone.

"You're welcome."

McCall put his wine glass down on the counter, and without warning, reached for her, brushing his lips against hers. Just a brief contact, but it seared her down to her toes. Her bones felt as if they were melting, and she could have sworn the ground shifted beneath her feet.

Move, her inner voice commanded, but not one of her muscles would obey.

He traced the seam of her lips with his tongue, an artist's stroke painting the surface. A tiny sound whispered from her mouth. As if it were a signal he was waiting for, he captured her in a kiss so hot it burned her lips. His hands cupped her face, holding her in place while he fed on her, his tongue pressing inside and tasting the texture of her flesh.

She gripped his wrists but not to pull them away. She couldn't have broken the kiss if someone paid her to.

Time stood still while he devoured every corner of her mouth, his fingers lean and hot against her cheeks. When he lifted his head, his silver eyes had darkened to almost black.

Rina felt dazed and weak.

He studied her face, his breathing uneven. "Two choices. Either tell me to leave or tell me where your bedroom is."

She had trouble getting the words out. "Upstairs. Last door on the right."

He kept his eyes riveted to hers, something unidentifiable lurking in them. "I won't hurt you."

Her breath caught in her throat. "I didn't think you would."

"All right, then."

He lifted her, as if she were weightless, and took the stairs two at a time. Inside her bedroom, he set her feet carefully on the floor and drowned her in another of his kisses. With his mouth still fused to hers, he backed her up to the bed, sliding his hands under her T-shirt and cupping her breasts.

Rina thought she might faint, his touch was so arousing. Her panties were soaked enough just from the kisses that she was afraid the evidence of her arousal would slide down her thighs. She was hardly aware of him lifting the T-shirt over her head, unclasping her bra, and tossing both to the side.

"Jesus." His long fingers plucked at her nipples, teasing them into diamond-hard points.

When he lowered his mouth to take one nipple between his lips, she nearly fell backwards. The wet heat of his mouth made her nipples throb. He moaned softly against her flesh, the sound reverberating through her body.

"I think we have too many clothes on." His voice was heavy with desire. He made quick work of her shorts and thong, guiding her onto the bed before stripping off his own clothing. He reached down and snapped on the bedside lamp.

Rina's eyes widened as she took in the lean, fit body with its matte of dark hair curling on his chest. It arrowed over a flat abdomen to his groin, forming a nest around the most impressive erection she'd ever seen in her life. The flat head of his cock was a deep purple and ropy veins pulsed beneath the skin.

The sac of his testicles rested against his thighs, heavy and tempting.

He lay down beside her, pulling her into another hot kiss, one hand caressing her breasts, gliding over the slope of her flesh, rasping at her already swollen nipples. When he moved his mouth to bite gently on one of them, her insides convulsed.

One arm slid beneath her, arching her back to give him better access to her breasts while the other hand traced feathery patterns over her belly and down to her mound. When one finger parted her labia and stroked the already-slick flesh, she whimpered and lifted herself into his touch.

He was like a tiger unleashed. Feral and hungry. He touched her everywhere and with a need so great it shocked her. His skin was hot, burning her, and her own hunger rose to meet his.

With one last, brief thought for her lack of sanity, she fell into the maelstrom his touch created. Her pulse throbbed in her everywhere. A lightning storm couldn't have generated more power.

His mouth nibbled, sucked, his tongue licking a trail over her feverish skin from nipples to cunt. He was a master of torment. If she'd been able to think at all, she'd have wondered how this grim, silent man had become such an accomplished lover.

Her nipples felt as if they were bathed in liquid heat, each nip of his teeth sending jolts directly to her womb. His fingers parted the lips of her sex, tracing a line from end to end as he focused on her breasts. When he slid two fingers into her waiting heat, the tips curled to search for her sweet spot. His thumb pressed on her bundled nerves, massaging with a steady stroke.

"God, you feel good," he breathed. "You are so wet it feels like heaven. I'll bet it tastes even better."

Shifting, he knelt between her legs and, with his hands cupping her ass, lifted her to his mouth. The moment his lips closed on her, she spasmed, her inner walls fluttering. He held her in a firm grip as he teased and tormented her until she felt as if flames were licking at her. His tongue glided in and out, scraping over every inch of her wet channel.

He was voracious, eating at her like a starving man. When her first orgasm rolled over her and she poured into his mouth, he lapped greedily at her juices. When the spasms slowed, he began again, lapping at her, stroking her with his tongue, driving her up the erotic spiral of hunger until she had no control of her own body. Again she convulsed, hips jerking in his grasp, the walls of her sex grabbing at his tongue as she shook uncontrollably.

And still he worked her relentlessly. When the third orgasm overtook her, she shattered completely, every muscle in her body clenching, the flesh of her pussy quivering. Splinters of her consciousness tumbled through the air, and colors flashed behind her closed eyelids.

Finally, he lowered her hips to the bed.

Exhausted, she lay back on the pillows. Surely now he would give her a moment to rest.

But rest wasn't in McCall's vocabulary. Moving up, he straddled her so his swollen shaft bobbed at her lips.

"Take me," he whispered in a hoarse voice. "Let me feel your lips on me. Come on, Rina. Suck me with that hot, sweet mouth. Just thinking about it is driving me crazy."

Automatically, she opened her mouth. Taking his shaft in one hand, he guided himself past her teeth until he was pressing on her tongue. She began to drag on him with her lips and swirl her tongue around the velvet flesh covering solid steel. Her fingers wrapped around him to give herself better leverage. His testicles pressed against her chin as she pulled and sucked, his taste a heady flavor.

"Stop." Abruptly, he jerked away.

"What..."

"I'm so ready, and I don't want to come in your mouth. Not this time."

He shifted off her and, with practiced ease, flipped her over to her stomach, tugging her up to her knees. His fingers slipped into her, gathering her moisture and painting it on the tight ring of her rear opening.

She shivered. "McCall?"

"I don't have a condom with me so we have to improvise. You'll like this. I promise. Trust me, Rina."

He began working first one, then two fingers into her rectum, preparing her, one hand on her belly, holding her up tight to him. She tensed at his first invasion, muscles clenching to shut him out.

"You've never done this, have you?"

She shook her head.

"Take a deep breath," he told her and pressed the head of his cock against her puckered opening.

At first it burned, his penis so big and thick it stretched her unbearably. But then, with a tiny pop, he was past the entrance and moving steadily to fill her. The burn turned from painful to delicious as hot and cold chased through her system, igniting nerves she didn't even know she had, setting the pulse in her womb to throbbing with a deep, insistent beat. Whatever functioning brain cells she might have had left disappeared as he pushed her onto a plane of arousal beyond anything she'd ever felt before.

"Breathe," he told her again.

Then he was all the way in, pumping his cock in a steady rhythm, the thick length rasping the sensitive skin inside the dark tunnel along the way. His balls slapped against the backs of her thighs, his arm like steel supported her, his hand spread across her belly to hold her to him tightly. She fisted her hands in a pillow and breathed through her mouth as he increased the pace of his strokes. Harder, faster, he filled and retreated, filled and retreated. Up and up the spiral she went again, every muscle quivering, every nerve firing.

His body tightened and clenched, his fingers pressed harder into her belly. When she felt the first splash of his cum, she climaxed, rockets exploding through her and hurtling her into space. The orgasm wracked her body, shaking her even more than the last one. McCall's body pressed into hers as he rode out his own convulsions.

Exhausted and spent, sore everywhere, she simply collapsed. He lay atop her, still shuddering. Sweat slicked their skin, and their hearts beat like kettle drums. She would have easily fallen asleep that way, his cock still impaled in her ass, but he withdrew from her slowly and turned her over.

"Shower," he murmured.

She shook her head, trying to burrow back into the pillows.

McCall made a sound suspiciously like a chuckle, then simply rose from the bed and gathered her up in his arms. In her shower, he bathed her as one might wash a baby, gently, his fingers probing all the right places, washing away the remnants of the most explosive sex she had ever experienced in her life. When he was satisfied they were both clean, he dried them off with her big towels, carried her back to the bed, and tucked her under the covers. She thought he bent and kissed her, but it could have been her imagination.

She slept dreamlessly and woke feeling pleasantly sore. Her hand stretched out, seeking human flesh, the memories of last night springing to life in her mind, but the space next to her in bed was empty.

McCall was gone.

To purchase *Do You Trust Me?* and other erotic titles, please visit our on-line bookstore at www.thewilderroses.com.

CPSIA information can be obtained at www.ICGtesting.com
Printed in the USA
BVOW011831020413

317103BV00009B/100/P

9 781601 547125